Kind Heart

Jenna discerned that it was not her father who held her—such a thing was impossible, her father had departed this life two years ago. Who gave her such a loving embrace? Wiping her tears away with a determined fierceness, Jenna pushed herself away from the man who had held her for over five minutes. She looked up into the inquiring eyes, burning down on her.

"Oh!" she cried, after a deep indrawn breath. "Your Majesty! I... did not know... it was you." Other words did not come, she was speechless. Embarrassment flooded her and she remembered that she should curtsy. Bowing her head, she sank into a low curtsy.

"You thought I was someone else?" he asked, his deep voice issuing a sarcastic tone to cover the pain he felt at her reaction, "You thought I was Kind Heart?"

Pulling herself to her full height, Jenna looked up into his face, saying, "As a matter of fact, Your Majesty, I did think you were Kind Heart... your leather vest is the same... as his... as his... was..."

"Where is he then?" he interrupted, demanding, "Why is he not here to comfort you?"

What They Are Saying About
Kind Heart

Written in the style that is uniquely Carolyn Ann Aish, KIND HEART is an exciting medieval mix of intrigue, romance, subterfuge, and secret identities. The reader is swiftly pulled deep into this fast-paced adventure as those who move in royal circles strive to fulfill their desires and destinies, often with little regard to those who get in the way.

David L. Repsher, editor
Scribes Valley Publishing Company
Knoxville TN
scribesvalley.com

Kind Heart

Carolyn Ann Aish

A Wings ePress, Inc.
Inspirational Romance Novel

Wings ePress, Inc.

Edited by: Leslie Hodges
Copy Edited by: Elizabeth Struble
Senior Editor: Lorraine Stephens
Executive Editor: Lorraine Stephens
Cover Artist: Chrissie Poe

All rights reserved

Wings ePress Books
http://www.wingsepress.com

Copyright © 2003 by Carolyn Ann Aish
ISBN 1-59088-841-3

Published In the United States Of America

Wings ePress Inc.
3000 N. Rock Road
Newton, KS 67114

Dedication

To those fans who have grown from childhood into adults. May you all enjoy KIND HEART as much, or more, and read it as many times...

Prologue

Shrouded in mist, the Royal Palace seemed far away, as if it were encircled with disintegrating threads of giant cobweb. Yellow candle flames bravely struggled to bring substitute sunlight inside the arched windows.

Orange flares spaced evenly along the wide, spike-topped wall intensified deep shadows of the night. Guards beneath flares seemed as lifeless as the wall itself, not even as animated as the flickering flames.

Closer and closer came the sound of hoofbeats, slowing to a trot, now walking. Closer. The horses halted a distance from the gates. Guards nearest the back gate of the Royal Palace heard two horses breathing heavily. One horse stamped impatiently then snorted. No one moved. Nothing out of the ordinary was happening—yet.

A youth released a small boy from the saddle front, gently lowering him to stand on his boot-clad feet on the frosty cobblestones. The boy walked boldly to a guard who stood to attention at the gate.

"Open the gate. Take me to King Cyranius!" Prince Edward's boyish voice trembled with uncertainty as he voiced these commands. His shrill tone disappeared quickly into the yawning midnight.

The two closest guards did not move nor did they look down at the child. However, several pairs of eyes traveled now, in interest, to the large black stallion from which the boy had dismounted, then across to the other magnificent animal upon which sat a well-dressed nobleman, wearing a feather-plumed gentleman's hat.

"Please. I've been rescued..." Prince Edward stepped closer, looking up at the guard. Backing away, he sidestepped across to the other, peering up at the clay-like face. His tired eyes lit with recognition and he stepped closer, saying, eagerly, "Take me to King Cyranius. My brother." Prince Edward looked back at his rescuers. He called, "Captain Frayne will not look at me..." his voice was questioning—what should he do next?

Captain Frayne started at the sound of his name. He stared down at the boy, wondering if such a thing were possible. The child wore the prince's clothes and he looked like Prince Edward— travel-stained, dirty-faced, his hair tousled—was this possible?

"You... are... Prince Edward?" the other guard asked, his voice disbelieving, his eyes also confirming the answer as they took in the boy's resemblance to the prince. Calls came from other guards, "The prince? Is it the prince?"

The captain stepped toward the horses, shouting, "You two, identify yourselves!"

"Show them your ring, Boy!" the larger rider called. With a swift pull of the reins, he turned his horse, making it rise to pivot on strong back legs. The other horse did not turn. The young rider sought assurance that the boy would be accepted for whom he really was.

"He *is* Prince Edward. Take him to the king!" the younger rider called and copying the other, urged the horse around as guards hurried from their posts.

"Halt! I command! Halt! In the name of King Cyranius, halt!" Captain Frayne shouted as he ran towards the disappearing horses. Darkness swallowed both animals and riders and the hoofbeats diminished into the night, fading quickly as they left the city perimeter.

"Who are they?" a guard spoke to his comrades, not expecting anyone to answer.

The young voice of the prince sounded out again, "That was Kind Heart and his son... it was Kind Heart's son who rescued me from those evil men."

One

An argument raged in the throne room. Three barons disputed loudly among themselves. Consumed in their heated debate, they forgot where they were.

King Cyranius raised his dark eyebrows very slightly, his eyes locking with those of his Royal Adjudicator. With a prompt that was imperceptible to most, the Adjudicator signaled the Royal Orders Controller who nodded at the herald to strike the large brass gong with the huge clanger held at the ready.

"B-O-N-G-G-G-G-G-g-g-g-g-g-g-g -g -g-g—"

The sound reverberated ominously around the throne room causing the three barons to fall to their knees before the king.

"Yes! His Majesty should have your heads! You dare to argue in front of your king? You dishonor the throne. It's a capital offence!" the Royal Orders Controller denounced when the echoes had faded. He himself knelt with his face turned toward the throne.

The three men bowed their faces to the cold floor, as was expected. King Cyranius had the right to end their lives for this transgression, known as 'Contempt of the Throne.' The deep silence caused dread to rise, choking the minds of the guilty trio.

Young Prince Edward, seated on a footstool to the left of his brother's throne, smirked broadly at the three grown men who groveled on the floor. He was here to learn and had certainly seen his brother's eyebrows twitch and the chain-response of the king's officials.

"Rise all," King Cyranius commanded. The men stood, waiting, their heads bowed.

"You've come to us complaining about this lady, Jennifer Gifford, whom almost a year ago, we believe, and justly, we repeat, justly, inherited her father's extensive lands. As the lady is sole heiress, she may run the estates as she wishes so long as the taxes are paid and she does not break our laws. There's been no breach of law from the Gifford domain for decades.

"You're all suffering from a chronic case of covetousness, or simply greed." The king waited until all three barons looked up at him.

"Yes, greed," he said severely before surrendering to his personal presuppositions. "However, we cannot but fail to agree that a woman, in sole charge of the largest domain in Cyran, is a recipe containing the rudimentary ingredient for disorder and disaster." The king paused, his eyes roving across the three.

Baron Sidney was the most handsome baron, impeccably dressed in the latest fashion and well manicured. *Perhaps a little short of stature for a baron, but nevertheless very much a nobleman,* the king mused.

Baron Zerka is the tallest but he's not been furnished with many facial rewards. He certainly does not decorate what he has to the best advantage, the king thought. Zerka's dark brown, ill-trimmed hair was plastered to his small head. A thin moustache was longer on one side than the other. He wore a very heavy earring in one ear, causing the lobe to hang down, giving him an overall lopsided appearance. One eye had a squint, making it smaller than the other, but the king was not so unkindly as to criticize nature's misfortunes.

Some things cannot be remedied, he reminded himself.

Baron Ferrah was the oldest baron of the three. Short, stocky and fat, he obviously enjoyed both eating and drinking to the bursting point—his clothes were so full that the seams suffered nervous breakdowns all over his irregular form.

Some people wish not to make remedies, but rather to further their obesity and complicate their attributes...

The king turned to the prince. "Prince Edward. We invite you, on our behalf, to offer advice to our kingdom's three most ambitious barons." The king spoke his brother's name with love, but the rest of the sentence was well groomed with cynicism toward the three.

The prince stood and the barons, as one, bowed to him. They waited, red-faced, wondering that the king would ask a nine-year-old boy to give advice on an adult matter.

In the stillness of the great chamber, Prince Edward's youthful voice sounded out, clear and precise, "Greed, like hunger, can be satisfied if the supply is constant." The prince then asked, "Is any of Your Graces unmarried?" His question surprised everyone, including King Cyranius. The King frowned at the men, awaiting their answers. The expression on His Majesty's face warned the men that this child's question was his own.

"Yes, Your Majesty," Baron Zerka replied, "I'm unmarried."

"No, Your Majesty," Baron Sidney replied.

"No, Your Majesty," Baron Ferrah said, bowing again.

Red-faced, the barons felt like children in the nursery standing before a juvenile nanny.

All eyes were upon the prince, who enlightened everyone by proclaiming, "Baron Zerka, who must be well old enough to have a wife, shall gain the Lady Jennifer's hand in marriage. Then all three will have equal shares in her land. However, the land shall be divided into four. As each of you has a castle, Lady Jennifer's castle and the corner of land adjoining the king's land shall belong to the king. We need a castle south of the mountains from which to maintain law and order in the southern domains. When Lady Jennifer and Baron Zerka are married, the remaining land shall be divided into four."

No one dared laugh, least of all the king.

Very seriously, the older brother asked, "Tell us, Prince Edward, why should Baron Sidney and Baron Ferrah, each with a wife and both with satisfactory estates, share in Lady Jennifer's land?"

Prince Edward almost shrugged, but remembered in time that his brother had censored him twice before for making what the king labeled, 'that peasant-like gesture.'

"Baron Zerka won't need the whole estate, one quarter should be enough, and all three barons should be rewarded for bringing their contest to the right place—to the throne. How much better than taking matters into one's own hands and causing war, domain against domain with unnecessary bloodshed." he raised his eyebrows, copying his brother's mannerism, and waited.

King Cyranius began his conclusion for this case, making his brother's words his own, "To delay, and hopefully preclude, the previous-mentioned disorder and disaster, our Royal Command is that Baron Zerka be united in wedlock with Lady Jennifer. When the marriage certificate is in hand, her estates will be divided into four," he paused, allowing the scribe time to record his words. "Gifford Castle and its surrounding estate will belong to Prince Edward."

The king spoke to the barons, saying, "Perhaps the gaining of one quarter of the Gifford Domain will give you good reason to work together for the furtherance and continuance of peace in our kingdom. Your lands will all join each other rather than bordering the said lady's.

"You will report progress to us in this matter, Baron Zerka. Your king and Prince Edward shall be invited to your wedding and to view the prince's castle at the same time. You're dismissed." He performed a theatrical wave using the back of his hand. The gong sounded, declaring that the adjudication session was over for the day.

Bowing to almost touch the white marble floor, the barons left the throne room. All three smirked broadly and their minds seethed with schemes for the future—what they would do with so much more land. Then, frowning, Baron Zerka wondered how he would manage seeking Lady Jennifer's hand. Every time he had approached the said lady, he had felt like a field mouse challenging a lioness in protection of her cubs and den. He shuddered, then, recalling her youth and beauty of face, he smirked again.

As soon as the doors closed, the prince stepped close to the throne. "I'm looking forward to meeting that lady, Cy. She must be an ogre. You should have seen Zerka's face. He didn't look like he wanted marriage. Only the land."

King Cyranius had seen Zerka's face. It had fallen, at least one side had, when he heard Prince Edward's advice. But then the king had perceived what his brother had missed. It was the gleam in Zerka's eyes when he heard the words, "Royal Command." King Cyranius was sure Zerka would use these words in requesting Lady Jennifer's hand in marriage. The king knew Zerka would use the Royal Command to his own advantage. Royal Commands were not to be ignored! The king's words would be Zerka's weapons—his sword, his mace, and also his shield.

"How old is the lady?" Edward asked.

"I've no idea," King Cyranius said, wondering himself.

"She must be an ogre," the prince repeated.

"Very likely," the king agreed, remembering their mother. "A woman standing in a place of leadership is most dangerous..."

The prince sighed. He wished he had seen and known their mother. He had heard from rumors and gossip that she was 'an awesome creature.' But every painting of her had been destroyed when Cyranius V came to the throne. Like his brother, Edward's views of the 'fairer sex,' were tainted by true reports of their mother's domineering administration of cold-blooded cruelty.

He sighed again and said, "Thank you for the castle, Cy."

"Edward, if you are to learn from today there are two things: one is the meaning of not counting your chickens before they hatch. Can you explain the analogy?"

Prince Edward's face wrinkled a little, showing he was deep in thought. Then he replied, "The castle is the chickens and the barons are the eggs..." To the prince's disconcert his brother laughed loudly, joined by all in the great chamber. When the laughter subsided, Prince Edward's scowl softened as he tried to redeem himself by adding, "If Lady Jennifer won't marry Baron Zerka, then we won't have a castle, but we'll have egg—on our faces," he said, causing the laughter to resume. This time, the king did not laugh. He had seen the hurt on his brother's face.

In a small voice, the prince said, "Until we hold the title deed, we can't claim the castle is ours. What other lesson need I learn today?"

"You're nine years and nine months old today, my brother. You're to be king one day. It's my wish that you're considered an adult from now on. You're no longer a child, and we shall have another throne placed here, today, on my right...

"Being an adult gives you many privileges that far outweigh the restraints," the king said in his kindliest voice. "From now on, Edward, you need not wait until I ask your advice, you may give it without being requested. Of course, you will think deeply before you speak to be certain your words are the wisest advice or suggestion, words that I myself might say. And my brother, wait until others have completed their speech, never interrupt."

"You should still use your signal to me, brother, perhaps a little less conspicuously? The slight lift of your left forefinger to caution me?" Prince Edward smiled as he spoke, "I promise to heed it and beg you to use it so that I shall not cause contempt for the throne by too much familiarity."

"You show great wisdom for your age, brother," the king said, affectionately. "Only a very wise person chooses to be accountable, and indeed, it's good to be accountable." Before Prince Edward could speak again a figure dressed in rich military attire was announced into the throne room.

"Major Frayne!" called the herald.

The major, having snatched his plumed helmet from his head as he strode toward the throne, bowed low waiting for the king to speak first.

"You have news?" King Cyranius asked, his mind racing to recall any particularly pressing military matter.

"Yes, Your Majesty. Today, we had reports that the man known as Kind Heart, has been at work again. He rode across the southern border into our kingdom, bringing back the group of eleven children who were stolen last week. You remember the report of raiders? And you said, Your Majesty, there was nothing we could do about it unless we invite war."

"Kind Heart," whispered Prince Edward, his blue eyes aglow. He remembered his brother's words that he may speak without being invited. Biting his bottom lip, the prince began assembling his ideas about Kind Heart.

"Where are the children now?" the king asked.

"Kind Heart left them at the gates of the Southern Casern, District thirty-five, before riding off toward the north. The children told the captain there that Kind Heart said the soldiers would escort them to their respective homes, but Kind Heart also warned that if the kingdom does not want a repeat raid, the military must have a stronger presence in the southern villages."

"Just the two? Kind Heart and his son? Just two conducted this rescue?" the king asked, wondering how such a daring recovery was possible, and successful. Eleven children, stolen no doubt, to be sold as slaves.

"Pardon the correction, Your Majesty, but again it was just one—and he was alone."

"One? The younger or the elder?"

"The suggestion is, Your Majesty, that it was the younger one, somewhat grown—he was tall but thinner than the Kind Heart of years gone by. This was the first time in three years that there has been such a close encounter with him by the military. He wore the hat with the purple plume... and it's reported that this time he wore a mask."

"A mask? How exciting! He's come back again!" Prince Edward exclaimed excitedly in the short pause. "We thought he had given up riding around as Kind Heart. Oh, Cy, could you put out that reward notice again? Could we not try to find him?"

Major Frayne frowned at the prince. He was not used to having the lad speak out like this. Using the king's shortened name—no one dared such a thing! Ignoring him, he spoke to the king, "As in past years, Your Majesty, Kind Heart works for the good of our kingdom. He does not break the law, other than the wearing of the mask and his continued passive refusal to identify himself."

"He's breaking the laws of other kingdoms. Kind Heart is wanted in Aponia for interrupting the wedding between King Maslen and Princess Anastasia. Her stepfather is still at a loss to know where she went and where she's living."

"King Maslen has increased the reward for the capture of Kind Heart. He wants him alive," Major Frayne said.

"He's a man we must identify, Frayne," the king said, frowning. "Not that we would hand him over to Aponia, the marriage was an appalling idea. King Maslen should seek an heir in one of his loyal knights.

"But we don't want bandits from Aponia on our soil hunting down a ghost! For the sake of kingdom security, we need to know who he is, whom it is we deal with. We need to negotiate with him to keep him on our side. More so, if the son has taken over his father's identity. Or perhaps it's someone else this time? Who else works with him? He can't work entirely alone!

"Kind Heart must allow his king to know his true title, or he is king himself and therefore commits treason. We will not condone private conspirators, secret agents, in our country even if they do not rob or kill, but do the opposite, restoring, doing good..." he paused, wondering, as did others, if his last sentence made sense.

The king, however, decided to continue in the quest to discover the identity of the elusive Kind Heart. His fervent desire to discover Kind Heart's identity caused him sleepless nights, especially after his brother's return from ransom-demanding kidnappers. Prince Edward had arrived home before the deadline for presentation of the ransom. Although it was now three years ago, the drama of it all was remembered as if it had happened yesterday.

The prince's return had been seen as a miracle, a heart-wrenching godsend! Instead of a corpse, his brother, alive and well had been returned. How had Kind Heart, who had for twenty years previous, done deeds of wondrous kindness and rescue? How had he achieved what no other could do? No one could give an answer other than to suggest that Kind Heart was not flesh and blood, but a super-natural being, perhaps even an angel.

King Cyranius' thoughts returned to his promise to his father, to love and protect his younger brother. How he loved Edward, but it was Kind Heart who had protected him, Kind Heart whom had rescued and saved the prince.

Over the years of Kind Heart's amazing exploits there had been few clues and only for five or six years had he taken a companion, perhaps his son, along with him as helper, now proven to be successor or—survivor?

The king resolved again to do all within his power to discover Kind Heart's identity.

"Post the request for information and inform every soldier there will be promotion and further reward if any are instrumental in bringing us this Kind Heart—unharmed of course. And tell them it is my command to leave his mask on. We alone, in this throne room, will learn Kind Heart's real name." The king paused, deep in thought.

"Brother, the postings of the past have never found Kind Heart, so why don't we do something different like posting a command to Kind Heart himself? If he's a just and honest man, won't he give himself into our hands? Especially if we tell him in the letter that he'll be welcomed in our palace even if he wears his mask. And we should mention again that the king wishes to reward him for his many deeds of kindness and for my rescue. You offered them great honor and large rewards, but they did not come. No one came..."

Deep silence followed the prince's suggestion.

King Cyranius turned toward the scribes, saying, "Yes. A command, a letter, duplicated of course, posted in every district on every notice board—sent to every baron, to Kind Heart, from King Cyranius. But not a word about any reward for Kind Heart himself. We shall have men of all kinds, not the kind heart ones, all with masks if we suggest a reward. No. Write that Kind Heart shall receive a pardon if he comes alone to the palace and reveals himself to the king and prince alone. Write that he is in danger of committing treason if he will not reveal himself to his king." Turning to his brother, the king added, "Even after three years, Edward, you'll remember his face."

"Oh, yes, Cy. It was the kindest face I've ever seen. And his eyes—in the sunlight they were the soft purple of the iris in our garden. Then in the shadow they were blue. I could never forget his face, it truly was kind. Even his father had a kind face, though much older."

Both the king and the major had heard these words many times previously.

"Inform the military of the offered reward and promotion," the king repeated. "Someone, somewhere, will know something! Send young

Captain Derrick to the Southern Casern to question the rescued children. Perhaps we'll learn if the Kind Heart who rescued them is the same as he who rescued our prince."

"Yes. Ask them the color of Kind Heart's eyes. They must have seen them," the prince added.

"Bring us your report as soon as possible. Take a brigade to the place where Kind Heart was last seen. Search the woods there and bring us a report on the area—whose land it is and where the paths and roads lead." King Cyranius then concluded, "Of course, if you bring Kind Heart himself you'll be rewarded, Major. Remember, don't allow him to be harmed and have no one, including yourself, look on his face."

Bowing deeply, once to the king, then to the prince, Major Frayne backed himself ten paces from the throne before turning to stride from the great chamber.

Two

The young Lady Gifford stared in dismay at the overdressed, overjeweled man who stood before her in the reception hall of her castle.

Baron Zerka smiled thinly on one side of his face, but his lip soon turned downward at the sound of the lovely lady's refusal.

"No, Your Grace, Baron Zerka. And don't take my answer as being... entirely... personal. I've no intentions of marrying... not anyone, ever. Apart from your gaining Gifford Domain and its castle, there'd be little else for you in such a union." Jenna's tone held no trace of hostility, but her mind seethed with many sarcastic sentences she wished to hurl at the pompous, high-strung baron.

"It's not just for me, Lady, that I ask..."

"Then who else?"

"Well, yes for me, but your land... it'll be shared by the landowners bordering your estates..."

Jenna stared at Zerka as though she believed he had lost his senses. "I will never marry, and..."

"But one needs heirs. Who? What..."

"I intend to adopt an heir, Baron, but that's my affair, not yours. Good day." She turned to the tall man employed as overseer. "See the baron out, Tory."

Zerka was not finished. He hurled the golden spear.

"You refuse me, Lady Jennifer. But you cannot refuse the king!" To his surprise, she did not look wounded at all.

Jenna frowned and said as though puzzled, "The king has not requested my hand, Baron, what then should I refuse?"

"Ah... no. But it's His Majesty's Royal Command. King Cyranius himself said it is his Royal Command, that I gain your hand..." He smiled thinly as Jenna stepped backwards as though pricked by a sword point. At last he had made a strike.

"Royal Command? You spoke to the king about this? He gave you a Royal Command? I cannot believe such a preposterous thing! Let me see it. Where is it?" she asked, stepping closer, glaring at him so deeply that he cringed. It was not at her anger, but at the extraordinary pain he felt from the lights in the glare of her large, deep-set eyes.

She's so beautiful, he dared to appreciate, *I wish she didn't have her hair so hidden... like a matron...I don't even know what her hair looks like, what color it is... and her black dress! Black! Why she persists to wear such a morbid color... she'd look much better in red...* Zerka realized she had asked a question. Breathing heavily, he was confused now in this battle of words.

"Where? What do you mean... where? How can His Majesty's Royal Command be here?"

"If the king truly gave a Royal Command, then I must see it. Where is the scroll with His Majesty's Royal Seal? Did he not put it in writing? He does not just speak words into the air! We all know he has several scribes. How can I know it is His Majesty's command if I cannot see it?"

"I heard it," the baron said lamely.

Jenna expelled a frustrated sigh. She dared not verbalize her thoughts—*again we have it that women must be so ignorant, they just obey the word of any man who puffs his thoughts into the sky.*

With well-practiced effort, Jenna kept her voice even and soft, "If His Majesty commands a rightful landowner of his kingdom to marry, then he must write it down so that it may be seen. Or I shall not believe it! Please leave me, Zerka, and don't return. I'll not marry you. I don't believe our king would command such a thing!" When Zerka stood staring, his mouth moving as though to speak, Jenna repeated, "Good day, Baron." She did not wait for him to depart, but swept past him, toward the door.

"Wait... Lady Jennifer; I wish to consult you on another matter... the letter we barons have to circulate... the one that came last eve... about that masked man, Kind Heart... I saw him," he realized she had disappeared through the door and had not stopped to allow him to 'consult' with her. He continued, speaking louder into the empty doorway, "He rode across my estate, and several villagers saw him. I hope the king doesn't think it... he is me. I ride well, but never, no never, would I wear a mask... no. Rode into the woods, on our border, he did. I wondered if he came out of the woods on to your estate? Did you see him, or did any of your people see him?" He stared around the reception chamber, his face reddening at the amusement upon the young servants' faces. He had been talking to himself. Turning, he strode out into the foyer.

Taking his hat, cloak, and gloves from the doorman, Zerka said, "Tell Lady Jennifer that I will return when I have the command in writing from the king. Yes, that is what the others will tell me to do." He drew a deep breath and muttered, "Now I have to face them... Ferrah I can tolerate, but Sidney will be furious about her refusal."

Jenna swept into the large castle office. She was noticeably angry, which was an uncommon occurrence. The servants stood, staring at the heightened color in her cheeks, awaiting her commands. Never had their mistress lost her self-control, and they wondered if this was a first.

"Write for me, Polonius, a letter... to His Majesty, King Cyranius." She continued speaking as the scribe affixed a fresh scroll to the writing board and took up a quill, "Zerka, or I should call him 'Smirka', visited here, requesting that I marry him. If I had agreed, my land would be divided— it will include Sidney and Ferrah of course. How intolerable. I suppose I'd be allowed at least to keep my castle." She laughed, but it was not a happy laugh. "Perhaps Zerka would live in his castle—while I live here?" This she asked without hope in her voice. Jenna paced stiffly across the room to stare out the arched window.

"He had the nerve to suggest that King Cyranius has issued a Royal Command that I marry him—Zerka! How could such a thing be? Is it possible?"

Polonius, now dipping the quill, replied, "The gaining of your estates, Lady, is an obsession to those three. But to imagine they have the king's support? It could be possible, Lady. It's known that the king has a peculiar hatred for women, especially those whom providence has given any authority. His mother ruled while she lived, and she was extremely dictatorial, very intemperate. Only after the birth of Prince Edward, when Queen Georgiana died, did the fourth King Cyranius rule at all. Then, he only had four years, God rest his soul. He was softer, perhaps more human, than his son, King Cyranius the fifth. And now, unless he marries, there won't be a Cyranius the sixth but an Edward the first. I pray young Edward isn't such a hater of women."

Jenna frowned. Polonius was getting old; repeating himself; telling her things everyone knew. She asked, "The question is, should I write this letter to King Cyranius?"

"My first advice, Lady, is to leave things be. You're right in saying the command must be in writing. But if it's put in writing and is a Royal Command, what will you do then? Marry Baron Zerka? You'll be compelled to do so."

"What I was going to do... was to write to the king and hopefully preempt Zerka's obtaining the written command. If I petition the king for the right to adopt an heir, a male heir, and state that I wish not to marry, then hopefully he won't issue his fateful command! The king himself has made it known that he won't marry, yet he would force it upon me. I couldn't tolerate Zerka, of all males! He... he would turn me into a twisted, lopsided person!" Catching the twinkle in Polonius's eyes, she pulled one side of her mouth into a smile. Together they laughed.

Polonius may repeat himself, she thought, *but he has good advice to offer, his reasonable opposition serves to confirm my own thoughts.*

"You're right, Lady, as usual. We'll write the letter to the king. It may help that you wish to adopt an heir. Shall I write that you, like your esteemed king, are not disposed to marriage... to anyone?"

"Yes, but make his part, an innuendo, not a statement," Jenna said, turning as the door opened. A woman-servant hurried in, her face red. She was flustered.

"Come, m'lady, please come, it's Lady Judith... downstairs... she's collapsed."

Jenna called over her shoulder as she hurried ahead of the servant, "Word the letter to the king for me, Polonius. Let me see it as soon as possible so it can be dispatched before sunset. I want it in the king's hands by morning."

Jenna spoke as she hurried along the passage, "What happened? How long has Lady Judith been here?"

"She just arrived... must have walked the last bit, her horse is lame they say—the lady's been beaten again. I sent for our doctor."

Jenna flew toward the central staircase, her heart in her mouth. Judith... her very dear friend, Judith. How much more could one small body endure?

They met on the stairs. Tory carried the unconscious figure in his arms, followed by the castle doctor. Without a word, Jenna turned back and hurried to open the door leading to one of the guest chambers.

Morning turned to afternoon, but Jenna would not leave Judith's bedside. Servants came and went, messengers brought scrolls, others offered verbal reports. Polonius presented his completed letter. Jenna read it, signed and sealed it and sent it on its way. She read two letters sent by King Cyranius:

To: Kind Heart

Having crossed borders recently, secretively and without Royal Permission, you are in dire danger of committing treason against the throne. All the good you have done is at risk of being nullified by your continued error in lack of identity. However, if you will reveal yourself to King Cyranius at the Royal Palace, you shall be pardoned and may be of great future service to the Kingdom.

Cyranius,V, King of Cyran.

The letter was signed and had been sealed with the Royal Seal of His Majesty.

The second letter, addressed to the baron of each district, asked for information leading to the capture of the masked Kind Heart. If captured, Kind Heart was to be taken, unharmed, to the king. No one was to remove his mask—this was a Royal Command. The baron who assisted in Kind Heart's arrest would be greatly rewarded.

"Royal Commands are said to be irrevocable," Jenna said to herself. She leaned forward to catch the faint sound of Judith's breathing. "Please God, don't let her die. And please God, give me wisdom to be able to help her." A thought came to her mind and at first she discounted its validity. But it returned and persisted in its urgency. *Kind Heart would not allow Judith to suffer such beatings. Perhaps if Kind Heart goes to the king, he could petition for her. But will the king listen? Will the king accept a request from Kind Heart, in lieu of the reward that was promised three years ago? There's no offer of reward in this letter. Perhaps the king no longer wishes to reward Kind Heart...*

Jenna pondered on the problems as she worried over the fate of her dearest friend. The doctor paced in and out, feeling Judith's brow, hemming and hawing, and Jenna knew from past experience he would tell her nothing. *I'm just another tiresome woman to Doctor Breck,* she reminded herself. *He treated me like a child while Father was alive and now he treats me like a servant-woman, or a piece of furniture. At least I don't get sick, I'd hate that...* Jenna stared again at Judith's pale face. Both eyes were black, one check swollen.

Taking up the large volume of the Psalms of David, Jenna began to read aloud. She read nonstop for over an hour. Judith had not moved, and now the last remnants of light in the large bedchamber had fled.

Judith, dear Judith. Your friendship has made me so rich... I cannot imagine life without you. Please, Dear God, don't let Judith die...

Servants lit enough candles in the candelabra to lend light to all corners of the large guest chamber.

A rap on the door preceded its being opened.

Tory hurried to Jenna's side, speaking as softly as his deep voice allowed, "Baron Sidney is at the gate asking after his wife. Shall we give him entry? He's in an antagonistic mood..."

Jenna stood, her thoughts racing. "I'll come down. Doctor Breck, please accompany me."

Baron Sidney, with a score of his soldiers, waited, mounted, outside the gate. As soon as the drawbridge fell and the portcullis was raised, the riders entered the castle grounds. The baron dismounted to face Jenna. "My wife is here, I believe?" he asked, his voice hoarse. It was obvious he did not know for sure.

"Yes," Jenna replied.

"Yes?" he said, staring around the small garden area. "Then where, may I ask, is she? Why did she not come out to greet me?"

"You know why, Baron Sidney," Jenna said, feeling her anger rise for the second time this day.

"All I know is that she disappeared... took a horse and rode... right out of the castle! Early this morning. They say she rode... all the way here..."

"It is a wonder she could," Jenna said quietly, "The horse went lame and she had to walk the last distance. But she cannot walk now."

"What? What happened to her? Did she have an accident?"

Jenna knew better than to accuse the baron. She had learned that to argue with a man, any man, was a dangerous thing to do. She turned to Doctor Breck. "Your wife has been badly beaten, Your Grace," the doctor said, his voice low as if he wanted only Sidney to hear.

"What? Was she attacked while riding here? Was the horse truly lame, or injured by thugs?" he spoke loudly. Turning to the captain of his soldiers, he said, "We'll have to bring those who attacked Lady Sidney, to justice..."

"It wasn't like that, Your Grace," the doctor said, again keeping his voice low, "Lady Sidney was caned... with a cane. Some other blunt instrument was used on her back and face."

Sidney stepped so close to the doctor that their noses almost touched. Very softly, the baron said, "It may have been that she was beaten with a strong switch from the woods..."

"Or the handle of a riding whip, Your Grace," the doctor added, not moving an inch. He whispered, "One just like yours, Your Grace."

Sidney, his face crimson, turned to Jenna, "I'll borrow one of your carriages, Lady Jennifer, and I'll take my wife home."

"Your wife is seriously ill... dangerously so," the doctor contradicted.

"I'll take her home—and our own doctor will care for her," Sidney said firmly.

"If you move her from the chamber where she lies, Your Grace, she will die," the doctor said. He waited, but Sidney did not speak. At last he was shocked into speechlessness.

"Come and see her," Jenna finally said, feeling both grateful to Doctor Breck and disturbed that Judith was so ill the doctor was championing her. Turning to the captain she added, "The baron will enter my castle alone." She did not speak her mind, that Sidney's soldiers were most unwelcome. This was the first time any of Sidney's personal army had been inside her castle gate.

Baron Sidney stared down at his unconscious wife. He was silent for several minutes, his eyes affixed to her face. "You say that... that... she will die? Can... can I not take her home?"

"No, Your Grace," Doctor Breck said.

"Perhaps you could send for your own doctor, Sidney. He'll verify Doctor Breck's opinion," Jenna suggested.

Sidney started. He had not realized Jenna was in the room. "Yes, yes. Do that. Send for Doctor Thorn," Sidney said without looking around him. He sat on the stool by the bedside and lifted his wife's small hand into his own. Jenna could not believe her eyes—as Sidney gently kissed Judith's small smooth hand, tears slid down his cheeks.

Three

Jenna stared at the scroll upon which was written the Royal Command of Cyranius V, King of Cyran. She found it difficult to comprehend. To be commanded to wed! Not only that, but to marry Baron Zerka! She read the footnote:

Your letter is acknowledged and the contents noted as expressed in the above Royal Command.

The words of the command passed before her eyes again, as her mind raced wildly to formulate a way of escape.

Royal Command of Cyranius V, King of Cyran; To Lady Jennifer Gifford of Gifford Castle and Domain; For prosperity and future harmony in Cyran, you are hereby commanded to receive suit from Baron Zerka for your hand in marriage. Upon signing the wedding certificate, you shall, together with Baron Zerka, own both his castle and estates, together with one quarter of the Gifford Domain. Your land shall be divided into four; the castle shall belong to Prince Edward, heir to the throne of Cyran. Gifford Castle shall retain its name, in memory of Baron Gifford and his honorable contribution to the kingdom. Northern land and that surrounding Gifford Castle, shall be included into the King's land, but shall retain the number twenty on the map. If no heirs are born from your union with Baron Zerka, your request to adopt an heir shall be granted.

"He's spelled my name wrong, Polonius," Jenna said, passing the scroll to the scribe. "It's one thing to constantly mispronounce it; but the man... the king... did not bother to check what my name really is. The rest is so unsatisfactory that I could scream!" She paced across to the window and stared out at the gray of the day.

"Others call you Lady Jennifer and you don't correct them, Lady," Polonius dared to say. "But I agree, this is written by the king. He, of all people, should get it right. But the fact that your name is Jennava and not Jennifer will only gain you a slight reprieve, perhaps a few days," Polonius said. "But you are most certainly permitted to ignore the command until the king summons you."

"Summons me?"

"He will, no doubt, hear from Zerka if you refuse again and the king will summon you to answer him on the matter. You'll have to stand before your king."

"Or... perhaps it's legal to send a proxy?" Jenna asked hopefully, knowing that this was what she wanted to do.

"Yes," Polonius answered, "but if King Cyranius won't accept your excuses or reasons, he'll issue another command with your name on it, spelt correctly."

"There has to be another way," Jenna said, pondering. She decided to visit Judith's bedside to see if her friend's condition had improved.

Baron Sidney had sat beside his wife for over two days now, refusing to move. His own doctor, Thorn, had confirmed Doctor Breck's judgment that the lady should not be moved. Jenna hoped improvement would come soon. Sidney's presence in her castle made her feel uneasy.

"Excuse me, Lady, but I must speak with you," a young lad said to Jenna as soon as she stepped into the passage. He looked around fearfully, adding, "Alone."

Jenna stepped out onto the long northern balcony, one of two balconies in her castle. The sun battled in vain to disperse the dark rain clouds, but succeeded only in delaying precipitation. Jenna drew her cloak around her slim form.

"Kevin? How long have you been here?"

"Yes, milady, I've just come from Baron Sidney's castle. I exchanged with Gavin but we're both keeping out of sight anyway—as long as the Baron is here. 'Twould be rather bad if he saw me and remembered he has one like me..." Taking a deep breath, Kevin said, "It's Brother Patrick... he's why Lady Judith was beaten."

Jenna frowned. "Patrick? What has Patrick to do with Lady Judith's beating?"

"It be said they were having a... a... affair..."

"That's ridiculous!"

"It wasn't ridiculous to them at Mayern Castle," Kevin said, his voice trembling, "And Brother Emil says I must tell you that you have to call for Kind Heart. He has it all set up. You have to tell Kind Heart that he's arranged passage in and out of Mayern, but no one else could carry it off, and several soldiers will help Kind Heart, but they can't do it on their own. It be better that Kind Heart who hasn't got no one to answer to, should make the rescue."

"Rescue Brother Patrick? But where is he?"

Kevin shuddered and tears slipped down his thin face, "In the torture chamber, 'neath the dungeons," he said sadly, "he'll die if he stays another night, and it seems like they want him to die, too."

"I... I, yes, I can contact Kind Heart. Promise me, Kevin, this is no plot to capture Kind Heart, is it?"

"Cross me heart and swear to die," quoted Kevin, making the appropriate gestures with his hands and arms.

Jenna felt sure that Kevin told the truth as he knew it. "Tell me all Kind Heart needs to know—who to meet at Mayern, when and where."

~ * ~

It was damp underfoot, for which Kind Heart was thankful—hounds would have difficulty in detecting a distinctive scent. The barking and howling of Sidney's watchdogs merged with the howling of the wind. Kind Heart shivered in both apprehension and from the excitement of this venture. Rarely before had Kind Heart been involved with so great a number of 'aiders and abettors' within 'enemy territory'.

Kind Heart adjusted the leather mask, making it more secure. It was a great relief to realize that the numerous dogs had ceased barking. Kind Heart had a fear of dogs trained to be vicious. It was also known that such animals were incensed to greater ferociousness by masquerade, and Kind Heart knew the mask would provoke the guard dogs.

As Kevin had promised, two hours after midnight a rope snaked itself down over the wall originating from a southern crenel of the castle itself. Kind Heart climbed it easily and gained the rampart. After quick investigation in the opposite direction, Kind Heart found a suitable place to fix the end of one of the two long rope coils carried up the wall. Hauling on this rope carefully brought up the strong cane chair the intruder had brought especially for Brother Patrick. With nimble fingers Kind Heart tied the chair out of sight, over the wall. This chair was Kind Heart's undeclared method of rescuing the prisoner from the castle.

Kevin had said that a cart would be waiting in the courtyard and two sympathetic soldiers would open the gates for the escapers. Kind Heart felt sure that if a capture were to be made, it would be in this courtyard where the largest number of soldiers could be deployed. It was well known that Kind Heart was an expert with the sword and the staff and could fend off a large number of contenders. Never had Kind Heart killed a man but many had been wounded, rendered helpless, to protect and rescue the oppressed.

Following the boy's directions, Kind Heart hurried to the southern tower door.

One by one each supporter, each soldier, each servant whom Kevin had named stepped forward from his preplanned place to show the way. Kind Heart took great care to scrutinize every arch, every door, every aperture, by which to escape if the situation turned sour.

Again, the intruder wondered if the whole drama were not a scheme to capture the masked 'rebel', Kind Heart. How opportune it would be, when the king himself had offered rewards to the barons. But several things rang true about this scenario—Lady Judith so ill, having been beaten, being the main one. Sidney was away from his castle—how could he be involved?

With loud, ominous complaints, bolts and bars crashed unlocked and the door to the torture chamber opened. The smoky atmosphere in the passage increased. Kind Heart ignored Sidney's two soldiers, now in a favorable position to attempt a capture, and stepped into the dreaded chamber. This was the first time the young Kind Heart had been in such a place. A torture chamber!

Two prostrate figures lay on the stone floor—the dungeon-keeper and the torture-master. Stepping nimbly, with sword outstretched as before, Kind Heart drew closer and closer expecting the men to leap up and make their preplanned capture. The men did not move—Kind Heart could scarcely perceive that they breathed.

They've been drugged! Kind heart's arteries throbbed in relief, the men looked as though they had drunk too much. This being almost impossible for such men, the only other eventuality was that they had been deliberately rendered unconscious.

A low, despairing moan caused Kind Heart to spin lightly on boot-clad feet. Sidney's soldiers still stood by the doorway, staring at the leather-clad figure with the ridiculous feather plumed hat. They were overawed at this close encounter with the famed and feared Kind Heart.

"Patrick? Brother Patrick!" Kind Heart's feet flew to the chained prisoner who moaned. Beaten and bloodied, Brother Patrick rested on one foot, the only space upon the stone floor free of sharp spikes. The wall was a mass of glittering, razor-sharp spikes. There was nowhere for Patrick to lean or rest without piercing his bruised skin.

Sheathing the sword, Kind Heart hurried back to the thick wooden table near the dungeon-keeper. Upending food-plates and rough tin goblets, Kind Heart snatched up the solid wooden tray. Taking it to Patrick, it served as a cover over the spikes so that Patrick could stand on both feet. Kind Heart gently placed the man's bruised feet on the tray.

One by one, the pins slid from the shackles around Patrick's wrists. Kind Heart felt heartened that the shackles did not need a key and was encouraged to know that Patrick still had some strength and will left in him.

"Try to walk," the rescuer urged.

Patrick attempted to cooperate, but his legs and feet would not obey. "Sorry... I'm... so sorry... I... can't."

The soldiers at the door parted, allowing a robed figure to enter the chamber. Kind Heart's eyes strained in the smoky atmosphere. This was what had been expected. But here in the torture chamber? They were going to attempt their capture here?

"Here, let me help," the kindly voice seemed to come from heaven itself. It was Brother Emil.

Together they supported Patrick, moving out the door, flanked by the watching soldiers who did not follow. Kind Heart wondered what story they were going to concoct about this 'break-in' and 'rescue'. How simple it had been—so far. Along the passage toward the stone steps, then, up, up, up—one by one, it was very slow and tedious.

"The cart's in the courtyard and the men await to open the gate for you," Brother Emil said, confirming Kevin's words.

Patrick's body began to quiver and quake, then the man moaned loudly, collapsing into unconsciousness.

"I'll carry him and lead the way if you'll watch our backs," Emil said, collecting the man into his strong arms.

Ignoring these words, Kind Heart unsheathed the sword, saying, "We'll not go left here, we'll go right. Do as I say, Brother Emil. It'll be much easier this way—you can tell Baron Sidney that you were forced, at sword-point." When the monk did not move Kind Heart pressed the sword-tip into the clothes on his large back.

"This is not supposed to be a trap, Brother Emil, and I'm making sure that it's not. Kevin does not believe it to be so, but what do you think? Walk as you answer."

The monk stepped in the direction Kind Heart indicated, saying, "I... I... I hope not. But I have not been as sure as the lad. He believes everyone speaks the truth but when I heard that Lady Sidra was involved, I..."

"Lady Sidra? Sidney's stepmother? I didn't know she was here. How long has she been here? Keep walking, Brother, faster please and take the next right turn."

The monk did not answer, for deep in the castle a shout sounded out, followed by many more. "Hurry," breathed Kind Heart. "I'll not leave Brother Patrick here to be further tortured or questioned. You must exert yourself to go faster." With sword in one hand, and the other threaded through Brother Emil's arm, Kind Heart urged the man into a run.

Choosing the narrow spiral step-case up to the south tower, Kind Heart was retracing earlier footsteps in reverse. Men's voices, calling instructions, became clearer as they gained the rampart. The dreaded dogs barked and howled. Shouted commands were incomprehensible as they were too distant, but Kind Heart knew that the trap had been set in the courtyard where the cart was waiting. But the 'bait' was now missing and the trap empty!

The cane chair was as it had been left. Kind Heart drew it around to the stone walk. "Sit Brother Patrick in the chair," Kind Heart said, thankful for light from the moon at first-quarter.

Kind Heart's fingers trembled as they worked to strap the unconscious monk into the chair. Wrists to the supports, neck to the tall back, waist, chest... the shouting rose with the barking of the dogs. Kind Heart fixed the two ropes together, lowering the chair carefully down the stone wall, playing out the thick rope with care. "Go, Brother Emil. Make haste to the western tower and complete your escape." Kind Heart did not need to repeat this directive. Emil's feet moved faster than ever and the monk disappeared into the deep shadows. The dogs were released from their leashes and the barking became frantic as the animals mounted the stone steps. Heavy boots joined the chorus as soldiers followed the dogs up the steps.

Kind Heart emitted a shrill whistle, followed by another. With expert movements, the leather-clad figure rappelled to the waiting horses.

Dogs and men arrived on the rampart above. Confusion caused the men and dogs to run aimlessly from crenel to crenel, seeking the prey.

Time was lost positioning the cane chair upon the second horse, but Kind Heart was pleased that the rope had not yet been discovered. The chair was finally secured so that the back of it lay down on the horse's back. Patrick half sat, half lay on the horse. "Halt! Who goes below there? Name yourself!"

"Get down there!" The rope flickered and snaked and Kind Heart guessed that someone was now descending.

Mounting the large brown horse, Kind Heart fixed the two reins together. Trotting, cantering, galloping. In spite of the trap prepared, Kind Heart had again done the impossible—rescued an innocent person, and escaped.

How many more times? Kind Heart asked, *How many more times will I be free to help the oppressed? But then, that was a very comfortable rescue... I struck no one and am uninjured myself.*

Four

King Cyranius frowned, whilst one of his secretaries read aloud the letter from Kind Heart. It had been presented at a border post in District eighteen, east of Zerka District, and couriered to the king with great haste.

"King Cyranius V, King of Cyran; Your letter is noted. It is with deep regret that I read the word 'treason' in your letter, Your Majesty. Never have I worked against the King or Kingdom of Cyran. The intent of Kind Heart has been to help the oppressed and to rescue those who are unjustly treated or wrongfully imprisoned. I am unable to reveal myself or my identity, Your Majesty, and will therefore endeavor to discontinue behaving as Kind Heart. You shall, therefore, no longer hear of my exploits. My prayer is that you shall take better care of the kingdom and its precious people, including the children, for without them we have no future. I beg Your Majesty's forgiveness for disappointing you. Signed, Kind Heart."

"Yes, we are greatly disappointed," Prince Edward declared. "I feel angry with him! How dare he accuse us."

King Cyranius said, "It's more than an accusation, brother! It's defiance! We'll not allow any subject in our kingdom to defy us! We'll smoke him out yet." Turning to his brother, he asked, "Perhaps we can word another parlance, brother?"

"I say, give him enough rope and he will hang himself," the prince said, glibly.

"Yes," the king agreed.

~ * ~

Just hours after reading the letter from Kind Heart, the news came that Kind Heart himself had illegally entered Baron Sidney's castle and a prisoner had been stolen from the dungeon.

The letter was from a confidant of Major Frayne, a spy.

"It was a prisoner, Sire, who was receiving just punishment for his crime and the man Kind Heart, whom we'd hoped to capture, made his escape taking the prisoner with him. It's said he bewitched the guards and enchanted the dogs. He leaped right over the castle wall with Brother Patrick in his arms! All by himself! No one helped him. Disappeared into thin air! There was not a trace of either of them, anywhere."

"Kind Heart broke his word!" Prince Edward said.

"Yes, indeed," agreed the king, "He promised there would be no more exploits and here we have one!"

"He did say 'endeavor'," one of the king's counselors interjected. The royal brothers glared at him as if he were a malodorous mouse.

"This is consuming us!" the prince declared, unable to keep his thoughts to himself, "We have to find Kind Heart!"

"Yes, indeed," agreed the king, also engrossed in solving the mystery.

Another report arrived, sent by a recently employed informer, engaged by the king, living in Mayern Castle:

I have discovered, Your Majesty, that Lady Gifford of Gifford Castle is involved with Kind Heart. To what extent I do not know, but I've learned that a servant boy from Mayern Castle has an identical twin at Gifford Castle. They exchange places often and report to Lady Gifford. It was one of these twins who went to Gifford Castle to ask Lady Jennifer to send Kind Heart to rescue the prisoner. I have this from the lips of Brother Emil himself. He trusts me and I don't want to cause him to be suspicious of me as I hope to learn more to report to you...

The report went on to explain how Kind Heart had used the chair for the rescue and that horses had been waiting beneath, a large brown stallion and a black horse.

The king was scornfully pleased to hear that the lady was involved in some way, the 'ogre' who would soon wed the unfortunate Zerka.

Perhaps she was the accomplice for whom he was searching? Kind Heart used horses and helpers. The circle seemed to be growing smaller.

King Cyranius, discussing the matter with his counselors, including Prince Edward, decided that Kind Heart must have his base in or near the Gifford-Zerka area of the kingdom.

"This is where we should concentrate our efforts to capture the elusive young man.

"Send a Royal Command addressing Baron Zerka and the Lady of Gifford Castle. The messengers shall deliver the commands one hour after sunrise tomorrow, and wait on both Baron Zerka and Lady Jennifer for their immediate replies. They shall be told to stop what they are doing and reply within an hour, or they shall be brought before me."

When the scribes were ready, the king dictated:

"To Baron Zerka and Lady Gifford:

Due to defiance against the Crown by the man known as Kind Heart refusing to identify himself, we command that a Declaration of Loyalty be sent by you, written by your own hand, avowing that you have no knowledge of the man Kind Heart, his whereabouts, his activities, or his identity. This Declaration shall be given into the hands of the Royal

Messenger who shall wait upon you, with his escort, until you have given it into his hands. Do not delay, for the smallest delay will be counted as insubordination. The degree of the insubordination will determine the degree of judgment upon you."

The king signed and sealed the scrolls and they were given into the hands of two Royal Couriers who left the royal stables, each escorted by a quad of guards.

"In his exploits over the last few years, Kind Heart has been seen with three different horses—a brown stallion, a black gelding and a large silver-gray horse with a white mane and tail," the king said. "After the Declarations have left the two said castles, we want soldiers to search all the stables in the area, in particular in the Zerka District and the Gifford District. Such magnificent horses will easily be identified—they must be stabled somewhere! We should have thought of this before."

"We should have them bring those twins," Prince Edward suggested, his eyes sparkling. "The boys will tell us more about Kind Heart." He longed to meet someone who knew Kind Heart, or better still, Kind Heart in person.

"Yes," the king agreed, "have them brought to us and treat them kindly, but guard them diligently. Commission two squadrons to apprehend them for us simultaneously... dispatch one to Mayern and one to Gifford. They must wait until the declarations leave the castles. We shall have a meeting with Kind Heart yet. One way or another, we shall!

"Do you think the barons will lie?" Edward asked, his voice betraying the excitement he felt.

"Zerka will be most eager to vindicate himself—yes, he could lie," the king said, his mind sorting all he knew about the baron, "but if he's truly genuine in his declaration of having no knowledge of Kind Heart, I believe he'll visit us. He'll be so eager to please us, he'll appear here as fast as his horse can bring him."

"And Lady Jennifer?"

"We shall see," the king said.

"Perhaps we shall all meet the old ogre soon," Prince Edward said, causing the counselors to smile.

~ * ~

Baron Zerka awaited Lady Jennava in Gifford Castle reception hall. Because he threatened to remain overnight if she would not see him today, Jenna decided to do as Polonius recommended and speak with him.

Zerka stood as Jenna was announced to the hall by the young herald. "Lady Jennava." As protocol demanded he bowed, expecting her to curtsy. She did not but stood before him, her beautiful face as unreadable as a doll's.

"I'll not stand upon ceremony, Lady Jennifer. We both know you have the king's Royal Command. And that latest command, mine came an hour ago… I replied instantly, of course, but the only sure way to combat the threat of this Kind Heart fellow damaging our reputation with the king is to have our lands joined in the way he, that is, the king, commands. I want to set the date for our wedding… two weeks from today. I'll meet you in your chapel on the hour of…"

"No!" Jenna could keep silent no longer. She wished she could use the excuse that her closest friend was seriously ill, lying upstairs and that Baron Sidney had invaded her home, increasing his unwelcome intrusion with his small 'court' and an expanding company of unwelcome soldiers. Plus the problem of her having to hide Brother Patrick and gain a doctor's care and help for him in a secretive manner—but these things were immaterial to Zerka. Then the latest command from the king. It arrived half an hour previous, and the courier had warned that if she did not reply before the hour was up, she herself would be taken to face the king. Jenna's thoughts swam as she tried to shake off her weariness of mind.

I must get rid of this bothersome bug, she told herself. *I have to write a reply to the king. He is very clever… he's forcing me into a corner…*

"The king spelled my name incorrectly in the Royal Command," she said, feeling it to be a cowardly excuse. Polonius had advised her to use this explanation to gain a few more days reprieve. A few days—yes, she needed time—but there was no time to reply to the king's last command. The Royal Messenger awaited in a small reception chamber, with his four soldiers, all partaking of refreshments, no doubt keeping close watch on the hourglass they had positioned in the center of the room—it would be half empty.

Or perhaps it's still half full. I have half an hour to decide what to write... how to answer the king. Perhaps I should just go and see him... no, to write will give me time to prepare myself... Jenna had to make a conscious effort to pull herself back to Zerka and his demand.

"The Royal Command is void if the king cannot spell my name correctly," she asserted.

"Then I'll ride myself and have it rectified," Zerka said, wanting also to declare personally to the king that he was not aligned with Kind Heart in any shape or form. "And... and I'll return with the Royal Command myself." He wished she would tell him what part of her name had been misspelled. "It'll be in the Royal Records," he muttered, adding as he bowed, "We *shall* be married, Lady Jennifer, we shall be married." Baron Ferrah's face flashed across Zerka's mind as he said this. Ferrah had been angry, very angry, at the delay. He had built a model of the land he would gain and was positioning workers' villages upon it.

Baron Zerka rode from Gifford Castle muttering, "Now I have to ride to see King Cyranius. What an impossible woman! But what a woman! She's so very irksome," he told himself, smiling thinly. "Very irksome. I'll need a very heavy hand to bring her into line and keep her there!"

~ * ~

Jenna reentered her office and saw both Polonius and Tory were deep in deliberations. King Cyranius's letter, with two official royal scrolls on the desk between them. At her entrance, they stood, their faces grave.

"I do not pray often, Polonius, Tory; but this is one occasion that I need to commit myself into the hands of the Almighty." So saying, Jenna moved across to the elaborate window seat fixture and knelt with her face turned to the window. Her mind flashed to a story her father had told her when she was just a small girl. *Daniel... he knelt three times a day; not just when he was in trouble, he did it every day. When things were well and there seemed no need to pray, Daniel prayed to God, he knew God.*

Jenna shook off the feeling that almost overwhelmed her, of being so alone and needing Divine strength. She tried to form words to pray aloud. *I don't have the right to pray to God, I don't even know him.*

"I cannot pray, Polonius. I feel too troubled," she said, turning and rising from her knees, "Pray for us, please."

Bowing his head, Polonius said, simply, "God, help us."

Tory agreed, adding, "Yes, God, please take time to lend us assistance..." and he continued supplicating for some minutes, closing with, "...according to the Divine Will of Our Father, Who Art in Heaven..." and together, they repeated The Lord's Prayer.

"Amen," Jenna said, trying to rid herself of the feeling that God would not hear her parroted words.

Seating herself at the desk by which the two men now stood, Jenna took the quill in her slender hand. Drawing a deep breath, she wrote her reply on the parchment bearing the Gifford Coat of Arms.

Both Polonius and Tory nodded seriously in agreement when she gave the document to them to read.

"I don't wish our loyal staff and servants to be forewarned," she said, and her lips trembled slightly before she gained self-control to continue, "but I may have to go into exile... leave the Kingdom of Cyran. You two, of course, will be welcome to come with me and continue in my service, and it will have to be made known that any others who wish to come..." Jenna paused as her mind raced over the ramifications of leaving her home, "and... when... if... we have to leave, it will likely be with great haste..."

The men nodded seriously.

Having sealed the Declaration, Jenna said, "Take it to the king's messenger, Tory." Turning to Polonius as she rolled together the two scrolls on the desk, she urged, "Place these in a small locked chest. I'll need to take them when I am summoned to stand before King Cyranius.

~ * ~

Later that morning, Judith's health showed improvement. The doctor had been persistently dabbing oil containing arnica on her bruises. The swellings had gone down and the bruises were fading. With Baron Sidney's help, the doctor had coaxed Judith to drink fruit juice with a tincture of arnica and healing herbs in it. Every few drops she swallowed were of benefit, the doctor told the attentive husband. Jenna could only look on, feeling resentful towards Sidney, yet thankful Judith was making progress. Judith had spoken to her husband, just a few words, but she had spoken.

Having checked on Brother Patrick who was being cared for by trusted servants who also used the arnica treatment and herbs, Jenna decided to snatch an hour's sleep. Before she reached her bedchamber, Kevin flew to her side.

"What's wrong?" she asked. He breathed deeply and looked terrified.

"It's Gavin!"

"What... what has happened?"

"I... I don't know... it... it feels like... like... I feel like I'm... he's... being smothered. I have to go and find him."

The sound of boots marching into the marble hall beneath came to Jenna's ears. A voice called a command, but the words were indistinguishable.

Jenna frowned. Kevin and Gavin always sensed when the other was in danger. Could it be possible that someone had discovered their duplicity?

Taking his hand, she pulled him around with her. "Come," she said, "You must hide... promise me you'll keep silent and I promise you, Kevin, that I'll find out what's happened with Gavin."

Having hidden Kevin in a secret cavity along the corridor, Jenna hurried back toward the top of the central staircase. Captain Derrick met her, face to face, followed by four soldiers. She knew by their uniforms that they had come from the capital.

"Lady Jennifer?" he asked, his voice rising, questioning, unsure. She wore black, but her face looked very young, too young to be the landowner, the lady of the castle.

When she did not speak, but stood as though frozen, he said, "I'm Captain Derrick and it's in the name of King Cyranius that we ask you to deliver into our hands the twin boys Gavin and Kevin, for questioning." He tendered the scroll containing the king's written command.

"Questioning? By whom?" she asked.

"It's a Royal Command, Madam and it's not for you to question us, but obey. Read the king's scroll."

After watching Jenna obey the captain asked, "Do you know where the boys are, or shall we begin by summoning every servant into your great hall?"

"I... yes, I'll request that our guard have the gong sounded to assemble everyone into the great hall," Jenna said and added, "We have one boy here, Captain Derrick, his name is Kevin."

"Then sound the gong," Captain Derrick urged, pleased that she cooperated. "We'll wait in the great hall."

Jenna nodded to the young Gifford castle guard who had followed the king's soldier's up the stairs.

While the gong clanged, once, twice, three times, the summons for all within hearing to meet in the great hall, Jenna paced back to her office. Polonius and Tory waited at the open door. She gave them the king's scroll.

"You have two obvious choices, Lady—to take Kevin into hiding or to surrender him to the king."

"You cannot surpass this progression of summons and commands, Lady Jennava," Tory said, his voice filled with sympathy.

"I know," she replied, "I just fear that the momentum of the pursuit is gathering all in its path. Those I sought to protect are becoming victims of the king's ghost hunt.

"I promised Kevin I'd discover what happened to his brother. They need to be together. Please watch the stairs for me while I fetch Kevin. I must speak with him before he's taken from here."

Drawing Kevin out into the corridor, Jenna said, "Your brother will likely be on the way to the king's palace. They want you too, Kevin. I don't believe they'll harm you in any way but will ask you some questions. I want you to promise, Kevin, that you'll answer truthfully on all matters concerning both you and Gavin."

"Even... about Kind Heart—and you?" Kevin asked.

"Yes," she replied, "you must answer the king's questions with the truth... as you know the truth, and remind Gavin to do likewise, Kevin, do you promise?"

"Yes, Lady Jennava."

"If it be the king, or another at the royal palace who questions you, you must tell the truth, all of it."

Jenna descended the central stairs to walk between king's soldiers waiting at the bottom. Kevin followed her and together they entered the great hall.

Walking to Captain Derrick, she said, "I would like to introduce you to Kevin, Captain, and I ask that you take care of him—he means a lot to us here at Gifford Castle. Perhaps, Captain, you may also announce to King Cyranius that I shall wait upon him tomorrow morning, early."

Five

Zerka arrived at the royal palace, having ridden without resting. At the announcement that Zerka was waiting in his reception room, King Cyranius decided, at first, not to see him for a while. Having read Zerka's melodramatic Declaration of Loyalty, both the king and the prince felt an encounter with the groveling baron to be a waste of time.

However, all pressing matters for the day had been dealt with, other than awaiting news from the captains who had gone to apprehend the twins from Mayern and Gifford Castles.

"You may announce Baron Zerka," King Cyranius said.

As expected, the baron entered the throne room bowing and stammering the words he had written in his declaration. Then came the news that the king had not expected.

"Lady Jennifer still refuses me, Your Majesty," he said.

The king did not speak; he knew Zerka had more to say.

"She claims, Your Majesty, that her name is incorrectly written on the Royal Command."

Turning to the scribes, the king ordered, "Bring me a copy of the command..."

"I have a copy here, Your M... M... Majesty," Zerka said, taking a step back at the heightened tone of the king's voice. Turning, Zerka nodded to his own secretary who had followed him into the throne room. The scroll was given to the king's chief scribe, who in turn took it to the hands of the king.

"Lady Jennifer Gifford," the king read, frowning, "J-e-n-n-i-f-e-r-G-i-f-f-o-r-d," he spelled, then said, "is that not how Jennifer Gifford is spelt?"

"Yes, Your Majesty," Zerka answered. Shaking his head so that his one long earring and lobe swung like the pendulum on a clock, but out of time, he said, "She's so very irksome, Your Majesty. I believe she's stalling us."

Speaking to the chief scribe, the king said, "Fetch the Record Book of Noblemen, and we'll discover how this irksome lady's name was spelt in the record of her birth."

The record book was brought and opened at the pages containing the register of the Twentieth District of Cyran, with the Gifford family tree. A scribe gave it to the king.

"This is very interesting indeed," the king said, standing and taking the book down to the large, ornately carved podium around which the scribes stood. Setting the book above the ledge upon the sloped platform, the king turned the page.

Zerka took a step toward the king, but a guard moved toward him, in warning. When Zerka stepped backward, the guard also stepped back into his place.

Prince Edward hurried to his brother's side, asking, "What is it?"

King Cyranius flicked his left forefinger so slightly that no one but the prince noticed. Prince Edward moved back to sit on his seat at the right of the king's throne.

The king was silent for a minute, then said, "It is Lady Jennava Charlotte Gifford—J-e-n-n-a-v-a, not Jennifer... and she has a second name, Charlotte. But it's this fact that concerns us... the lady has a brother, five years her elder, Charles Richard Gifford. There's no record of his death, only his birth. Where is Charles Gifford? Why does *he* not rule his castle? The recorded date of death of Lady Elizabeth Gifford was almost twenty years ago, after the birth of her daughter, Jennava. Lord Gifford died of an illness, two years ago. Why is the son not mentioned, other than his birth, twenty-five years ago? Should there not be a Notice of Installation as Baron of Gifford? There's a Notice of Installation here, dated almost two years ago, for the installation of Jennava Charlotte Gifford. What happened to Charles Richard Gifford?"

No one spoke.

The king returned to his throne. "Baron Zerka, what do *you* know of Charles Richard Gifford?"

"N-n-nothing, Your Majesty. I've never heard of such a person. There's only been Lord Gifford and his daughter, Jennifer... Jen - Jen - Jenna - Jenna-ver."

"Have the matter checked thoroughly," King Cyranius said to his scribes. Turning to the Captain in Charge of Throne Room Orders, he commanded, "Arrange a company to ride to Gifford Castle to confiscate all record books. Have them bring back the secretary or chief scribe and find the oldest servant-man in the castle—take a carriage for these men. Check before you leave Gifford if there's a tomb or grave for Charles Gifford. Find out if he lies with his parents or somewhere else."

No one spoke while the king's employees moved off to carry out his commands.

"It's most unusual," Prince Edward said, then was quiet at his brother's signal.

"If Lady Jennava Gifford has not sent a Declaration of Loyalty, then she will be at this moment being escorted to us here. One way or another, we shall meet her."

King Cyranius addressed Zerka, saying, "There'll be no wedding until this matter is fully investigated. Return to your district, Baron, and await our further instructions."

Zerka opened his mouth to protest and state that he would remain in the capital but he decided he should not argue with the king. Bowing, he left the chamber.

~ * ~

The courier bearing Lady Jennava's Declaration of Loyalty entered the throne room. As instructed, he took the scroll to the throne and placed it in the hands of the king.

After reading the Declaration, the king was silent. Beckoning the King's Herald, he said, "Read it for us."

The herald's voice boomed out in the silence of the great chamber: "To King Cyranius, King of the Kingdom of Cyran: I, Jennava Charlotte Gifford, Lady of Gifford Castle, do write in my own hand, affirming my loyalty to the Crown, the King and the Kingdom of Cyran. I am unable to avow no knowledge of Kind Heart, or the whereabouts, activities, or identity. Signed Lady Jennava Gifford."

"That means she *has* knowledge?" Prince Edward asked, "Lady Jen-Jenna-va—she knows Kind Heart? She knows his whereabouts and who he is? We shall certainly have to meet her..."

"Bring her to us!" the king said grimly. "In the name of the king, have Major Frayne bring her here!"

A fore-rider entered the throne room, snatching his helmet off as he bowed.

"We have both servant-boys, Gavin and Kevin, they'll be here within the hour, Sire. Gavin was taken from Sidney Castle, and Kevin from Gifford."

"Yes!" Prince Edward said softly.

"We shall adjourn until they arrive," the king said.

They walked from his throne room amidst the bowing court. Prince Edward walked behind, but hurried to his brother's side as soon as they were through the doors.

"I have a choice idea... it's simply amazing," the prince said, "I can scarce keep it to myself... please, Cy, may we discuss it?"

Six

Gavin arrived at the king's palace, twenty minutes before his brother. He was ushered to a chamber in the servant's quarters where he was commanded to wash and partake of a drink of water.

Escorted along the wide marble corridors, Gavin trembled at the spacious majesty of the palace.

The room into which he was thrust was of such large proportions he could not take it in right away. Three men, all richly garbed, sat at a desk behind which stood two palace guards. A young pageboy in elaborate clothes stood near the table, by the wall. Gavin felt self-conscious of his plain brown tunic and bare feet.

Bowing nervously, Gavin tried to calm himself. His heart pounded loudly in his chest and he found it difficult to gain his breath.

"Your name?" the older man at the desk asked.

"Gavin, Sir, it's Gavin."

The scratch of the quill was the only sound in the room.

"Your address?"

"Mayern Castle, Sir."

"Your position there?"

"I'm a servant-boy, Sir."

"What are your duties, Gavin?"

"I carry well-water to all facilities, Sir, including the pitchers in the bedchambers."

"And you carry messages, Gavin, don't you?" the king asked.

Gavin looked at this younger man who sat in the middle of the two scribes. Never before had Gavin seen such a man. It was as if this character dominated the whole room.

"Yes—Sir," he answered.

"You take messages to Gifford Castle and you sometimes exchange places with your twin brother, Kevin, don't you?"

There was a silence after the king's question, then Gavin lifted his chin, looked the man in the eye and answered, saying, "Yes, Sir."

"Do you understand what the punishment for an informant might be, Kevin?"

"I... I've seen Lord Sidney's torture chambers, Sir."

"You have, have you?" the king said, altogether surprised at the lad's forthright truthfulness. "And how would you feel if you were imprisoned in such a place?"

Gavin did not reply, but bowed his head.

"Kind Heart would no doubt rescue you," the king said with sarcasm in his voice. The raising of Gavin's head and the thrust of his chin was answer enough.

"Tell us what you know about Kind Heart," the king commanded.

"I... I'm not sure, Sir, whether or not I should answer you."

"And if it were the king who questioned you?" King Cyranius asked cynically, expecting the lad to speak against the throne.

"Oh, I'm sure I should have to tell all I know," Gavin replied, "Yes, I'd tell the king."

The king was quiet then. He wondered at himself having agreed with his brother's idea to meet these boys in a less threatening place than that of the throne room, not as king and prince, but in an informal manner.

"Your brother, Kevin, will be arriving in a short while," the king told Gavin, "and if you keep silence whilst we question him, you may stay in the chamber here. Do you understand?"

"I'll be quiet, Sir," Gavin said. A guard took him to the far end of the room where he stood between two others.

~ * ~

When Kevin entered the chamber, Captain Derrick followed. The latter was motioned to remain in silence until the questioning was finished.

Both the young prince and the king felt they were reliving the previous encounter. Except this time, Kevin spoke of being employed at Gifford and not Mayern. Kevin reacted the same way as his brother, with the same mannerisms and giving the same answers.

Then, as before, the king asked, "Do you know what the punishment for an informant would be, Gavin?"

"I... I... Lady Jenna would not allow us to be punished, Sir."

"It is she who employs you to inform, is it not?"

"Yes, Sir, but no, Sir, it's not exactly true."

"Who then employs you, besides Lady Jennava?"

"Lady Jenna... Jennava does not want us to inform, Sir... but she has to catch us both together before she can stop us. We don't let her see us... together..."

"And how do you suppose she'll feel toward you, to know that you're telling us all about it?"

"She made me promise to tell the truth, Sir, to whomever questioned me."

"When did she say that?"

"Before I was brought here, Sir."

The king frowned, then asked, "Tell us what you know about the man, Kind Heart... or did Lady Jennava command you not to speak of him."

"Oh, no, Sir. She told me to tell you the truth and she asked that I tell Gavin, too, to answer with the truth. I promised her... we would tell the truth."

"You did, did you?" the king asked, feeling perplexed.

"Tell us all you know about the man Kind Heart," he commanded.

"Where do I begin, Sir?" Kevin asked earnestly.

Prince Edward's eyes widened. He longed to join the questioning, but had promised to be quiet. As though his brother knew his yearning, the king's left forefinger moved slightly. The prince leaned back on the wall, still eager, awaiting his brother's first question.

"How and where did you first meet Kind Heart, Kevin?"

"We... that is, Gavin and I, met the first Kind Heart when he rescued us from... from a slave cart, up in District four—we were being taken to Aponia. Kind Heart rescued all the children and took us back home with him. Our village had been destroyed and our parents were killed."

Sitting straighter in his chair, the king asked, "Where is Kind Heart's home, Kevin?"

"District twenty, Sir... in Gifford Castle."

"And do you know who it was that rescued you from the slavers—the real person behind the mask?"

"He didn't wear a mask, Sir, and we do know who he was."

The king leaned forward, clasping his hands, asking, "Who was he?"

"Lord Gifford, Sir."

The king frowned then asked, "How long ago was that, Kevin?"

Pausing to calculate, Kevin answered, "About six years ago, Sir, when we were about five years old."

"You're speaking of Lord Frances Charles Gifford, Lady Jennava's father?"

"Yes Sir."

The king sat back, his mind racing with this new information. How simple it all seemed now. His eyes flickered over to where Edward stood and he saw the delight on his brother's face.

"Tell me, Kevin, do either Gavin or you know who acts out the part of Kind Heart now, today?"

"I... we... we're not sure, Sir."

"Who do you suppose it may be then?" the king urged, his voice kind as though he spoke to his own brother.

Prince Edward started, feeling surprised. The king's tone had changed. Perhaps it was that he was hearing what he wanted to know.

"Perhaps Lady Jenna has a brother," Kevin said.

"You're not sure?"

"No, Sir, we're not sure."

"What makes you suggest, then, that she has a brother?"

"A few rumors, Sir, suggested that there was a brother a few years older than her, and Sir, even though he wears a mask, we think she looks like him... that is, a little, perhaps the eyes, Sir. Kind Heart has purple-blue eyes, Sir."

"And Lady Jennava has these eyes?"

"More blue perhaps Sir, but yes, but hers are larger..."

Lifting his head, the king called, "Bring Gavin here to stand before us."

The twins exchanged mixed glances as they stood close together before King Cyranius.

"Do you have anything to add to what your brother has told us, Gavin?" he asked.

"Only that what he has said is the truth, Sir, and..."

"Yes?"

"Lady Jenna will be pleased you brought us here, Sir."

"Pleased?"

"Yes Sir."

"Why would it please Lady Jennava?"

"Oh, Sir, she's been trying to catch us together for years." He smiled and turned to his brother, saying, "You don't think so, do you?"

"Yes, she could have," Kevin answered.

"Pardon? What question did you answer, Kevin?" the king demanded, annoyed at this illegal exchange, yet wondering that they seemed to know what the other thought. At least their tongues were loosened and they had relaxed now. Edward's idea was of use, after all.

"Lady Jenna told us, many years ago that she would not allow us to carry on informing—it was her father's idea, you see, Sir," Gavin said.

"But we don't do it for Lady Jenna, we do it for Kind Heart—we owe him our lives," Kevin continued, "he was there as well, the younger one, when we were rescued."

"And we think, perhaps, she could have arranged for us to be brought to the king," Gavin said.

"Lady Jenna? Jennava?" the king asked, "How could she arrange this?"

"She's a very clever lady," Kevin said.

"Yes, she said one day that she would catch us out and she has, I suppose."

The king smiled briefly, then said, "We'll have Lady Jenna-va here soon, Kevin and Gavin—she shall be brought to the king tonight."

"She shall?" Kevin asked, a pleased look crossing his face.

"Shall we see the king, too?" Gavin asked.

"Yes," the king said agreeably, "you shall." Turning to a guard, he said, "Take our young guests to a chamber to dine—my brother may join them and ask as many questions as he pleases with other selected company as well." Speaking to Edward, he said, "When you've finished, Edward, tell them about us, won't you."

The young prince was delighted to be allowed to go with the boys. Even though there were four guards watching and listening, he asked questions until he could think of no more.

The twins told him about the rescue of poor Brother Patrick. Their voices lowered when they spoke of the 'affair' that Lady Judith and Brother Patrick were rumored to be conducting and that neither boy believed it was possible. Edward listened, enthralled, asking questions about the exciting escape from Mayern Castle.

He then listened to the boys' adventures and how they kept out of Lady Jenna's path.

"She's like a bat... she flits here and there and everywhere," Kevin said, rising and diving about the room to illustrate his metaphor.

"She goes riding with Kind Heart every morning," Gavin said, "she rides very well, too."

"And Lady Jenna is coming soon," the prince said, "We're looking forward to meeting her," he said.

"You'll meet her, Edward?" Gavin asked.

"I hope so," the prince replied, standing, "my brother is the king—you were questioned by him and I'm going to be there when they bring the ogre in. I'll tell you all about it."

The twins' mouths dropped open simultaneously. Standing together, they bowed as the prince left them.

Seven

"The king will send for me," Jenna said to Polonius and Tory, "but I'm not waiting for his escort. I'm in great need of a ride, as are the horses and after been cooped up, I need to feel the wind on my face, catch some sleep and be there at sunup."

"And Kind Heart?" Polonius asked.

"Kind Heart cannot reveal the identity, not until the time is up," she said. "In one way, I shall be pleased when it is all over."

"You shall?" Tory asked.

"Yes," she said firmly, "I shall."

"As for you, faithful servants of my father and to me, I expect the king shall send for you, too."

"For us?" Tory asked.

"It's my advice for you both to be ready..."

"And the chest?" asked Polonius.

"I'll take it with me."

"But, perhaps we'll be there before you, Lady, if we're summoned tonight..."

"Then you must tell King Cyranius that I'll come in the morning, early. Otherwise, you shall say very little until after Kind Heart has finished it forever."

"You see it coming to that, Lady Jennava?" Tory asked.

"Yes, when the time is up Kind Heart will not ride again," she avowed.

"I'll be pleased," Polonius said, "You know I've never agreed..."

"Then you shall, with King Cyranius, have the final victory, Polonius," Jenna flashed these words. She turned on her heel, causing the black underskirts of her lace dress to rustle. She felt too tired to listen to repetitive banter. "One more thing," she said, turning back, "If you are forced into a corner, it is my command that you tell the king the truth... tell him Kind Heart's identity if you have to... he will not believe you, but you must not lie on my behalf nor must you suffer in any way."

The men bowed as she left the chamber.

"She cannot mean that we break *our* vow," Polonius said.

"If she will not break the vow, then we dare not," Tory agreed.

Jenna hurried into her bedchamber, instructing her personal maid as to what she wanted packed in the small bag she would carry with her.

"Judith," she breathed this name. Hurrying to the guest-chamber where Judith lay, she was not surprised to know that Lord Sidney was making arrangements for a carriage to transport his wife back home, against the doctor's wishes. But Judith was much improved, anyone could see this...

"Dear Judith," she said as she sat and took the slim cool hand in her own.

Judith's eyes flickered open.

"Jenna... oh Jenna, how glad I'm to be here with you. Stay with me... please stay with me..." Judith's eyes closed but her hand held Jenna's tightly. "I feel I walk in a dark place... a valley..."

"The Lord is my shepherd..." Jenna quoted, squeezing Judith's hand. Judith's face softened into a smile.

Jenna waited until her friend slept again, then carefully wriggled her hand free. She longed to stay but knew that to delay much longer could mean that she would have to stand before the king this night, and Jenna did not want to do that—it would ruin her lone ride and destroy her freedom. Kissing Judith's forehead, she left the chamber.

Almost running now, Jenna carried her small leather bag to the lower chambers of the castle. She unlocked a door using the key she kept on a belt at her slim waist. Breathing a sigh of relief, Jenna locked the door behind her and leaned upon it. She wondered if she could take time to nap now but thought better of it. The woods could soon be teeming with the king's men and it would be much harder to gain access to the path she wished to ride.

Traversing the secret passages of Gifford Castle in darkness was second nature to Jenna. She had played down here since she could walk and it was home ground.

Arriving at a small door beneath the castle wall, Jenna entered the chamber. This was where her father had donned his costume—the place of transformation into Kind Heart. With meticulous care, Jenna dressed in clothes belonging to her, clothes that also belonged to her clandestine character, Kind Heart.

Her long auburn hair was, as usual, plaited and coiled about her head and she pulled on the thick wig of shining dark-brown curls. Over this she pinned the hat with the bright purple plume. Peering in the small round mirror, she saw two large eyes looking back at her, glimmering with purple lights seeming to match the feather.

A few deft strokes of makeup to blacken her eyebrows and the addition of the dark brown moustache, the mask, and the transformation was complete.

Whistling a slow tune, she moved along the dark snake-like tunnel, forcing herself to stride as she had practiced and not to take the smaller feminine steps of Lady Jennava.

Exiting into a small cave-like stable, Jenna called to the groom, "Garth, are you here?" She spoke in a much louder tone than usual.

"Yes, Sir."

"I'm taking Cloud and Oak, Garth. Put a sidesaddle on Cloud, and I'll saddle Oak."

"Lady Jenna goin' to meet with you, Sir?"

"Lady Jenna will ride Cloud, but later, Garth."

"When might I expect y' to return, Sir?"

Jenna smiled, Garth always asked this question and Kind Heart's answer had been the same from her father's lips, "When the Good Lord sees fit to bring me home safely, Garth." She added, "It'll be a day or two, Garth."

"I'll take a walk then, Sir, and visit me brother in the village."

"Take Midnight with you Garth, and have his shoes checked at the farriers."

With the leather bag strapped to the back of Cloud's saddle, Jenna led the two horses out of the concealment of the cave-entrance and into the thick woods.

Checking that Cloud's saddle was safely attached, Jenna fixed the reins to the front of it so that they could not drag or catch on a twig. Mounting Oak, she commanded Cloud to follow. Picking her way through the dense trees, Jenna led the way, moving in a direction she often took.

Soon they galloped free, over open meadows, heading toward the mountain ranges. Hopefully, by sundown, she would be clear of the ranges and riding down the other side toward her destination—a small hut used only by Kind Heart. The path chosen was a shortcut not used by other riders because it was too treacherous. But it trimmed hours off the journey around the mountains. Jenna knew this time would be better spent gaining needed sleep.

~ * ~

Long before sunrise, Jenna washed in a cold mountain stream and changed her garb, leaving Kind Heart's costume in a trunk hidden in the small hut where she had slept.

Dressing herself in a black riding habit with her hair hidden under a black wimple complete with hat and veil, Jenna rode on Cloud, keeping him at a walk through the wooded areas and away from the two villages between the mountain range and the palace. A half-moon lent light to the sleeping countryside.

The sun had just risen when Jenna viewed the palace from a hill on the southern side. Her eyes took in everything around the huge building—the walls, the towers and turrets, the guards.

She called softly into the trees, "Stay Oak, boy. Listen in case I must whistle for you, but stay out of sight and away from trouble."

~ * ~

As Jenna steered Cloud toward the main gates, a small company rode towards her and she knew she had been seen.

Horsemen surrounded her and she rode in the midst of them the rest of the way to the royal palace. No one asked her name, there was no need. This was the lady who had been reported as missing from her castle home last night.

Both Polonius and Tory had been transported to the palace and had told the king, "We apologize, Sire, but we cannot speak of Lady Jennava, or of Kind Heart. Lady Jennava has papers about the matter and said she will wait upon His Majesty in the morning, early."

King Cyranius had ordered that a watch be kept for the lady. It was expected she would arrive in a carriage but when it was reported that a lady in black, on a silver horse with a white mane and tail, rode in from the south hills, the king knew she had kept her word. That she had come from the south and not the east meant that she had taken the much longer route south, around the range. King Cyranius supposed this was so his soldiers would not apprehend the irksome lady. She must have ridden most of the night.

The fact that she had no escort with her had not been reported to the king, but as he watched her ride into the outer courtyard, he wondered. The riders accompanying her all wore the uniforms of his guard.

Prince Edward joined him on the balcony. "Where is she, Cy? Have I missed her?"

"If you watch, she'll ride through the southern arch on her way to our stables."

The prince drew a breath in wonder as the lady came in view. The stark blackness of her habit and cloak looked incredible against the flowing white mane and tail of the magnificent horse.

"What a horse!" he said, then spoke aloud the king's thoughts about the lady, "How well she holds herself."

They waited, then Jenna appeared, surrounded by the king's guards. Her cloak trailed behind her on the ground, causing the king's servant, walking behind carrying her black leather bag on one shoulder, to keep well back.

"She's all in black," Edward said, his voice filled with awe. "It's true, she wears black. Like a bat all right!"

Turning to an attendant, the king said, "We'll see Lady Jennava right away. Have Polonius and Tory wait on us as well."

"What about Kevin and Gavin, would it not be wise for them to be present?" Edward asked.

"Why would it be wise?" the king queried.

"I should think it would in-intimidate the lady," the prince said, "she'd know that we have them on our side then," he said.

"You think they're on our side?"

"Yes... they said she is an old bat!" he exaggerated.

"Perhaps they should come then," he said, smiling at his young brother's excitement. "I'm glad you think they're on our side."

"They'd be good to have around our palace," Prince Edward said, "Imagine how we could use them..."

"Don't get ideas... they could be used against us, too, just as they were, against Baron Sidney."

"Lady Jenna used them to protect her friend, Judith... but I'm not sure that Sidney's wife should have been protected, not if she was unfaithful. I don't know what to believe about her... Lady Judith Sidney, that is."

The king had heard about Edward's discussion with the twins, from Edward himself as well as from questioning an attendant who had been present. He frowned. The improprieties of life were all around and he would never have enough arms, or shields, to prevent his brother from learning about them sooner than necessary.

They neared the king's door leading to the throne room and the two fell silent.

The king's herald announced, "Lady Jennava Charlotte Gifford, Lady of Gifford Castle."

Jenna entered the throne room of which her father had spoken. It was more magnificent than she had imagined. As she walked, taking small, feminine steps, she surveyed the chamber, appreciating the work and substance that had been invested in the painted ceiling below which was a wide, gold-embellished frieze.

Jenna knew instinctively that the oval pattern inlaid in the marble, about ten feet in front of the dais, was her boundary while in this royal chamber. Stepping to the center of the oval, she curtsied low. The full skirts of her riding habit flared out on the floor around her.

In spite of his presuppositions, Prince Edward was reminded of the gracefulness of a black swan.

"Rise," the king commanded.

As she rose to stand before the throne, the prince wished he could see her eyes, but they were hidden behind the veil of her hat. The veil covered her face to the top of her lips.

A guard followed Jenna, carrying the small chest she had declared had to accompany her. On opening the chest, two scrolls had been viewed but not read, and the lady had been permitted to have the chest presented to the king.

"You have papers to present, Lady Jennava?" the king asked.

"Yes, Your Majesty," she answered, her voice soft and very feminine.

The chief scribe walked to the guard and took the chest from him. Moving up the steps of the dais, he placed the chest in the king's hands.

Everyone waited while the king read the two scrolls.

Jenna glanced along the rows of people who stood both sides of the throne room. She saw Polonius and Tory on one side, flanked by guards and Gavin and Kevin on the other, also flanked by guards. Raising her eyebrows at the twins, she smiled.

Prince Edward stared at the lady's smiling lips. He wondered why she smiled, and why it seemed such a nice smile. Her rose-pink lips were perfectly formed and the young prince felt a strange feeling inside him. Had he seen such a smile before? Perhaps it had been the smile of his mother? But he had been too young to know, hadn't he? If only this lady would smile at him as she smiled at the twins, he wished.

Looking across at his brother, the young prince frowned. Others would not notice any change in the king's face, but to Edward, his brother's eyes looked at the papers as if they could not believe the words. King Cyranius held them, one in each hand, reading them a second time.

"The court will leave the throne room," the king announced, surprising all who knew him. This was unprecedented! Never before had the court been commanded to leave in the middle of a session—the king always conducted rare or very private royal matters in another chamber.

Reluctantly, the members of the court made their obeisance to the king and left the great chamber.

The king, the prince, the guards, the scribes, the king's herald, Polonius, Tory, and the twins with Lady Jennava, were the only ones left in the massive chamber.

"Read them aloud for us," the king said to his herald.

Taking the scrolls in his large hands, the big man read the first, "To my dear friend and confidante, Lord Frances Charles Gifford, dated this year, the last of the tenth century, nine hundred and ninety-nine, written by the hand of King Cyranius IV, king of Cyran.

"Having been faithfully served by the said Lord Gifford, I grant him and his heir, Freedom of the Realm.

"It's signed by the hand of King Cyranius IV, father of King Cyranius V, and bears the royal seal."

He shuffled to the second scroll and read, "To our loyal, faithful servant who calls himself Kind Heart, dated this year, the fifth of the new millennium, one thousand and four.

"Kind Heart's deeds of courage are too numerous to list, the lives he has rescued too many to name. Among them, my own. We therefore grant Freedom of the Realm, to him and those who hereafter ride in the cause of right using his name to four generations, including his chosen successor. Those who know Kind Heart's identity and who assist him in his exploits shall have their confidentiality protected by the crown. This scroll shall be presented to my heirs if and when the need arises.

"It's signed by the hand of King Cyranius IV, father of King Cyranius V, and bears the royal seal."

Silence reigned for several minutes.

Prince Edward could keep his question no longer, "Tell us, brother, please, what is Freedom of the Realm?"

The king's face took on a perplexed look.

"Explain it for Prince Edward, Sir Tamsin," he asked, looking to his chief scribe.

"Freedom of the Realm, it is what its title states. The recipient of this rare honor is free to do in this kingdom as he—or in the case of Lady Jennava, if she is heiress of Lord Frances Charles Gifford—she pleases," the scribe said.

Frowning, Prince Edward exclaimed, "But that would mean they could break any law or do anything?"

"The recipient is considered of such noble character that he... she... would continue in his... her... loyalty and law-abiding activities," the scribe explained. "The character of the person and his abilities and activities are such that the king would never doubt that he would do only good in the kingdom. The Freedom of the Realm is the ultimate trust that the king may bestow on a human he knows would serve him until death if need be."

The prince tried to think of something to say that would make sense. *I'll be stuck with this too,* he told himself, *but I don't mind... Kind Heart is wonderful!* "Then Kind Heart did not break any law by entering Lord Sidney's Castle?" he asked, "Or... or... by defying us... or defying the king?"

"Kind Heart is unable to break the law," the scribe said.

Silence lasted a full minute.

"Lady Jennava," the king finally addressed his subject, "Pray tell us, your father, Lord Frances Charles Gifford—he was Kind Heart?" As soon as the question was out of his mouth, the king wondered if he had the right to question this lady. If Freedom of the Realm was hers, then she was his equal!

"Yes, Your Majesty," she answered, surprising him. So far, Lady Jennava had been very cordial. She did not appear to be at all tired, but held herself still and erect, in spite of such a long ride. And he had deliberately not allowed her time to refresh herself or change.

The king decided to ask another question, "Your brother... Charles Richard Gifford, he is Kind Heart, now?"

Prince Edward held his breath.

"I'm avowed not to answer as to Kind Heart's identity, Your Majesty. Should it not be for Kind Heart to reveal that to you, Sire?"

The king stared down at the slim lady dressed in black. He felt he was on the chessboard in the position of having his opponent cry 'check mate!' Or was it yet just 'check?'

"We need time to consider our position in the light of these scrolls," he said dourly. "In the meantime, Lady Jennava, we wish you to remain here in our palace."

"Sire, do you mean to say I'm under house arrest?"

"Until I determine who it is that the Freedom of the Realm belongs to, Lady Jennava. Yes, if you put it that way, you're under house arrest." He indicated Polonius and Tory with a wave of his hand and the twins, saying, "All of you, from Gifford Castle are included in the restriction to remain here."

Rising, the king strode from his throne. Jenna curtsied low and bowed her head, waiting until the sound of his footsteps faded, before she rose.

Prince Edward followed his brother but did not speak until they entered their private sitting room.

"Should you really do that, Cy? Place her under house arrest? Why?"

"Lady Jenna, Jennava, is neither Lord Frances Charles, nor Kind Heart. She may not even be her father's legal heir, certainly not if her brother still lives. I find her irksome indeed!"

The scribes entered the chamber and King Cyranius said, "There's much we don't understand about Lady Jennava and her brother and Kind Heart. Bring me the documents that were confiscated from Gifford and have a search made of my father's personal papers to ascertain whether he kept a copy of these statements of Freedom of the Realm. How do we know that these scrolls are not clever copies?"

"How indeed?" Prince Edward agreed. "If they're real, our father would have made copies, I agree, brother. We always make copies of everything, don't we?"

Eight

Jenna conceded she would endeavor to enjoy her 'house arrest' and seek to gain as much sleep as she could. Respite from people, with their dilemmas and dramas would be a treat. With both Polonius and Tory here in the capital, there would be no one at her castle to take the messages that would arrive, including those for Kind Heart. Perhaps the messages would be conveyed to the palace? She had not thought of such a dilemma and had made no arrangements. Perhaps her captain of guards, Captain Duff, would assume responsibility. She hoped so.

Having been escorted to a lavish guest apartment by guards who remained outside the door, Jenna requested the bath to be filled and that a woman-servant attend her. She had expected this luxury to be hers when she had arrived, not to be escorted immediately to the king.

The one gown she had brought with her was of deep blue silk, a dress she had never worn. *Now is a good time to come out of mourning,* she had told herself. *It's been two years but I still miss Father so very much.*

A sense of strange guilt flooded her as she realized that her previous disquieting grief had faded. *Time does help heal.*

After the bath, Jenna dressed in the nightgown she had brought and went to bed to sleep.

The maids took the exquisite blue dress to be pressed. Details circulated about the beautiful young Lady Jennava with the porcelain-like skin and amazing flame-gold hair.

It had been a long time since Jenna had divulged herself in such uninterrupted, peaceful sleep, even at night.

The dull sound of the outer door clicking open roused her and she opened her eyes. Whispered voices came to her ears and she discerned women speaking—or was it a child whispering or a maid? Realizing where she was and that guards stood outside the outer door, Jenna rolled on her back and sank, once again, into deep sleep.

Prince Edward crept through the archway from the sitting room into the bedchamber and closer to the bed. *This is most irksome,* he told himself, *I wanted to talk with her but they say she sleeps.* He inched closer to the bed, feeling peeved that the lace curtains were pulled all the way around the four posts. Stepping to the corner, he peered through a long, thin gap. His mouth dropped open—she was so beautiful in her white lace dress, like a sleeping princess. Auburn hair splayed out like a vibrant sun on the thin white pillow, its lights glimmering with healthy luster. He stared and stared, unable to take his eyes off of her. Then she moved, and the prince stepped away reluctantly, but unwilling that she would wake and find him there.

When Jenna woke again, she lay listening to birds twittering in the thick vines outside the open palace windows. Afternoon shadows were lengthening, and Jenna realized it was later than she had expected.

A voice came from the other side of the room, "We did not wish to awaken you, Lady, but to leave you as long as possible. King Cyranius and Prince Edward have invited you to dine with the court in the great dining hall. There's less than an hour before they begin."

Sitting up, Jenna saw two women standing close to the wall, watching her. *I must have slept deeply, no one ever enters my bedchamber at home without my knowing.* Perhaps... but I did sense someone came and went...

Swinging her feet over the side of her bed, she realized why she had not heard footfalls—the floor was carpeted.

The women stared as if dazzled, not at the beauty of Jenna's exquisite lace nightgown, but at Jenna. Never before had they seen a lady with such radiant loveliness. Then they gasped at her words to them.

"Convey my apologies to the king. I'm not here to dine with him, but to receive his verdict."

"But, Lady, you can't say no to the king... or the prince."

"No one says no to them!" The servant-women were in agreement on this—had they not permitted the prince's entry to the lady's room, though it was most improper?

"Then it shall be a first," Jenna asserted, "I partake of my meals in solitude. Have a tray brought here to the sitting room. I prefer uncooked vegetables, fruit and perhaps a little fish."

The women, both harrumphing loudly, strode from the room to seek higher advice. They returned with two women servants, both begging Jenna to change her mind. She refused them.

A senior servant-woman entered the chamber, again requesting that Lady Jennava dress and come down to the dining hall. "No one is prepared to tell the king that his guest refuses him, Lady Jennava," she said.

Jenna did not speak her thoughts. *Guest? I'm not a guest, I'm a prisoner.* "Let no one put themselves out to tell King Cyranius—he'll soon see I'm not there and will dine without me." *To be sure, I can't understand all the fuss!*

Pulling the matching lace over-gown over her nightdress, Jenna said, "Leave me now, I wish to be left in peace." The women left the chamber. Brushing the tangles from her long hair, she felt deliciously relaxed and at ease.

Having partaken of a second goblet of the cool water from the pitcher on the sideboard, Jenna curled herself on the window seat, looking out at the beautiful hills to the south. *Oak is out there somewhere... I hope he's safe and enjoying his freedom.* She closed her eyes, imagining the magnificent brown gelding cropping sweet grass in a clearing in the forest. The last hours of sunlight would filter through green leaves to dance on the sparkling brook where Oak would drink.

I'm hungry, she told herself, *very hungry, I haven't eaten anything since early this morning and it was just those berries I collected near the hut.*

The outer door was flung open and an arrogant young captain strode through the curtained archway into the sitting room. Self-controlled though he was, he was unable to prevent his eyes from widening in wonder when he beheld the king's reportedly irksome guest. Light from the setting sun inflamed her incredible hair and just a flicker of his eyes over her expensive lace night attire caused his pulse to race. What a breathtakingly beautiful young woman.

Bowing low, he tried to recall what he had come to say. Romance danced in his moonlit mind. Closing his eyes, he struggled to remember why he was there. Then he recalled the concern on the woman-servants' faces, their frustration. He'd come to order the irksome lady to get her irksome person down to the dining hall!

Keeping his eyes on the floor, he stammered, "Lady... Jennava, the king will be in the dining hall... he... will be waiting... for you... it's not acceptable... you must come..."

Startled and unnerved that a man of the military should enter her chamber unannounced, Jenna wondered if she should not just comply. She wanted this man out of her space! Perhaps the king would come next? How unpleasant that would be! She must go to him, then. How bothersome!

With her eyes upon the women who had followed the captain into the room, she said, "Leave me, and I shall comply then. I'll dress as quickly as I can."

"I'll wait to escort you, Lady Jennava," he bowed and looked at her again. She was still there, not an illusion, a dream, or a specter in his imagination. He stared, unable to move as she uncurled herself and slipped from the window seat, gliding like a swan across to the archway that led to the bedroom. He swayed forward, longing to follow her.

Prattling their appreciation to him, the women brought his feet back to the floor. Two matronly servants followed Jenna, pulling the curtain closed across the arch. Their reproachful eyes on his red face spoke a score of words.

Forcing himself upright, the captain stepped out into the corridor. He stood there, longing to see her again.

"Captain Ross, are you all right?" one of the guards asked.

The captain did not reply but stood opposite the door facing it, waiting, his eyes fixed upon it. Puffing out his broad chest, he felt deep pride. *One word from me and she did as I said. I'm more overpowering than I realized.*

Nine

Escorted by Captain Ross, Jenna entered the dining hall only two minutes late. Used to quick costume changes, Jenna had dressed herself in record time rapidly twisting her hair into a coil and pinning it to sit at the nape of her neck.

"Her hair looks much nicer when it's all loose," Prince Edward whispered to his brother. King Cyranius frowned deeply, giving Edward a questioning glance, wondering when the lad had seen Lady Jennava's hair 'all loose'. Did his disappearance this afternoon have anything to do with his claim now?

Jenna curtsied low to the king and prince who sat together at one end of the massive table. When Jenna arrived at the place allocated to her between two middle-aged women of the court, everyone, as one, sat. Waiters carried in trays of food.

Surveying the table, Jenna was not surprised at its length, only its width. If she wished to reach for something in the middle of the table, she would have to stand. Then she realized she would not have to do that, for from the walls of the dining hall stepped out an army of footmen, one for each guest, to serve them. The table became a hive of industry as each waiter sought to please, and a hum ensued as directions were given by each assignee.

The selection of food was amazing and Jenna found among it all she desired—fresh lettuce, radishes, young carrots, sprouts, button mushrooms, with platters of mixed salads. Filling her plate with a variety of raw vegetables, Jenna waved away the various spicy dressings offered her.

"She's eating all the things that are still alive," the prince whispered to his brother, "and she's not accepting any flavors to hide the taste of those... raw things."

Feeling quite safe he would not be heard above the hum, the king said, "You must look to your own plate, Edward."

"At least it's not going to run away," the prince muttered as he stabbed at a piece of well-done venison steak. He felt peeved that his brother had not allowed the lady to sit by him. Chewing fiercely, he glared along the row of people to where she sat, looking so very beautiful in the forget-me-not blue dress that matched her eyes. She had devoured her huge helping of salad and had directed her waiter to spoon fish out of its lemon sauce onto her plate.

The prince ate little; he was too busy watching Lady Jenna. She selected fresh fruit chunks with grapes and wedges of lemon that were meant for garnishing.

"She's eating the live decorations, now," he hissed toward Cyranius, not taking his eyes off her. Again, Edward wished she sat beside him so that he could watch her more closely and perhaps speak with her.

A ring Lady Jenna wore on the middle finger of her right hand, a chunky gold ring with a large oval ruby set into it flashed a three-year-old memory into the prince's eyes. He had seen this same ring before! It had been on the littlest finger of the older Kind Heart man. The prince stopped chewing.

Jenna glanced along the table and caught the stunned look on the young prince's face. Even from this distance, she saw that he stared at her hand, then his eyes looked into hers. A blink of her eyes to the ring and back to the prince, told her what the boy remembered.

How could I have forgotten to remove Father's ring? she chided herself. Keeping her eyes fastened to Prince Edward's, she placed her fork down and dropped both hands into her lap. When her hands returned to the table, the ring had disappeared.

Prince Edward turned to look at his brother, wondering if Cyranius had seen what had happened. The king was also looking along the table to where Lady Jenna sat. Edward chewed furiously, knowing he must not speak until his mouth was empty.

Wondering whom else may have seen her ring, Jenna glanced along the row of guests but all were busy with their own food selections. A number glanced her way but most eyes, if directed anywhere, were turned toward the king.

Standing against the wall, behind the prince and the king, was a row of palace guards. Jenna recognized Captain Ross and Captain Derrick. Their captain's sashes made them distinctive. Both young men stared at her, their eyes fixed.

Jenna's eyes moved to the prince, then to the king. The royal pair watched her and she dropped her eyes back to the fruit on her plate. *I must not feel intimidated, I'm allowed my father's ring. But what a faux pas... Prince Edward may remember it was father's ring—the prince has one very similar, more gold with a smaller ruby... I remember how he commented about Father's when we rescued him. How could I have forgotten?*

"She has Kind Heart's ring," Edward whispered as his brother leaned towards him.

"It was Kind Heart's?" the king asked. He remembered his brother telling him about Kind Heart's large ruby ring.

"Yes. See... it's like mine, only mine has a smaller ruby." He extended his right hand to display his ring.

Looking back at Lady Jenna, Prince Edward saw her drop her hands into her lap again. She lifted the large cloth serviette from her lap to pat the corner of her lip. The prince again wondered if the ring would roll off on the floor. He wished and hoped it would. He doubted that the lady would dive under the table to rescue her ring and he would command that a footman find it and bring it to him.

King Cyranius could only imagine Jenna's illusion—with her left hand she dabbed her mouth and with the other, concealed by the large square serviette, she dropped the ring down into the front of her gown into her cleavage.

A messenger stepped to the king's side, bearing a golden tray upon which sat two sealed scrolls. After breaking the seals and reading the scrolls, the king rose from his chair. Everyone at the table rose to their feet and the king, followed by the prince, left the dining hall. Other men, as if on cue, followed the path of their king.

The court settled back to the table and conversations sprang up, the hum growing louder. The lady on Jenna's left introduced her husband who sat on her other side, "Sir Edgar, my husband, King Cyranius's third scribe... I expect he'll be called upon if the king has messages needing replies. The communications must be important. He, that is, the king, does not allow trivial matters to interrupt our meals."

Within a minute, Sir Edgar was summoned.

The matron the other side introduced her husband, "Sir Ruben, adviser to King Cyranius, my dear, this is Lady Jenna about whom you've advised our king."

"I'm pleased to meet you," Jenna said congenially, nodding past the small lady to the even smaller gray-haired man. His reply was a return nod.

"How many advisers does our king have?" Jenna asked.

"Seven, the perfect number," Sir Ruben's wife answered.

The other lady asked, "You're out of mourning now, Lady Gifford?"

"Yes."

"You govern Gifford Castle and the estate? It must be an awe-inspiring task, is it not? To do the overseeing usually performed by a man?"

As politely and simply as she could, Jenna answered the questions, giving affirmatives to all. She was questioned, but knew it was only polite chitchat. They already knew all about her. Their strained conversation made her wonder if they had been told not to discuss Kind Heart who was obviously the gossip of the table—she could hear the name repeatedly whispered.

Before she could verbalize a question those at the far end of the table stood and, like a wave, everyone followed.

Prince Edward returned to the dining hall, no doubt, Jenna thought, to finish his meal. She had noticed that he had eaten very little. Again, everyone stood.

The prince circumnavigated the table, coming to a standstill beside Jenna's chair.

"Lady Jenna, we'd like your presence with us," he said.

Jenna had no choice but to place her hand on Prince Edward's extended arm and allow him to direct the way to the exit from the dining hall.

"Actually, I wish to speak with you myself," Prince Edward said when they were in the wide corridor, "while my brother is awaiting the arrival of a witness, I shall become better acquainted with you, Lady Jenna... Jennava." Turning, he spoke to two pageboys who followed, "Have them let us know when the visitor arrives to see us. We'll be in the Orange Room."

The way the prince spoke, Jenna felt certain that the so-called 'witness' was someone she knew.

Directed to the Orange Room, Jenna was pleasantly surprised to find that it was a huge indoor-outdoor chamber with a small grove of orange trees in the center. A gorgeous aroma lingered in the air, the scent of orange blossom.

Situated to face the northwest, the chamber was lit by retiring crimson flames from the setting sun.

"Wait outside," Prince Edward said to the one pageboy who had remained.

The prince himself pushed the door closed with a resounding bang. Sitting on a low, backless sofa, he indicated with a wave of his small hand that Jenna be seated beside him. Glancing around the chamber a little nervously now, Jenna knew that the prince was out of order. But how could she, a mere female in his eyes, question his own protocol? She did not wish to make the boy angry with her, maybe she could win him to be, even a little, on her side. Drawing a breath, she mentally worded her protest. Her father had told her to be straightforward, tell the truth, or to be silent.

"Sit," he commanded.

"Excuse me, Prince Edward, but I should not do that."

"Why not?" he asked, irritated, "All right, then stand. I wish only to question you, not to eat you."

If he had not looked so serious, Jenna would have laughed aloud.

"Does... your brother... the king... know that we are here, alone, together?"

"What has it got to do with him? He has matters to take care of and I can't speak of them. He's very busy."

"I... if I may speak woman to man, Your Highness?"

The prince puffed his chest out and Jenna knew she had at last said something to please him.

"Speak then."

"Your Highness, we should not be unchaperoned."

"But... you're old enough to be my mother..."

"Excuse me for contradicting you, Your Highness, but I'm not old enough nor am I your sister."

Standing, the prince said, "Then what shall we do, Lady Jenna? I wish to talk with you privately about Kind Heart and we're wasting our time arguing about the right and wrong of what I have already purposed to do."

"Perhaps, Your Highness, you'd be so good as to show me your home here, and we'll talk as we walk."

"That's a choice idea, Lady Jenna," he said. Striding to the door and throwing it open, he extended his arm.

She placed her arm on his, and together they walked into the corridor. The sound of boots marching preceded the arrival of Captain Ross, two palace guards and a messenger.

Bowing, the captain said, "Your Highness, the king has asked us to report the location of our guest, Lady Jennava, and to keep him informed."

Speaking to the messenger, the prince said, "Tell King Cyranius that Prince Edward is escorting Lady Jennava on a tour of our palace. We'll move clockwise, having begun at the Orange Room.

The prince smiled at Jenna and she felt his appreciation.

The lad now comprehended that it would not be acceptable for the king to hear that the lady and the prince were alone in the Orange Room, even if he still believed she was old enough to be his mother. She was almost twice his age and very tall too, even if she wore flat-soled slippers unlike those high heeled things other women of fashion wore on their feet.

Peeved to know that Captain Ross and the two guards would be following Lady Jennava at the king's orders, the prince said, "It's an unwelcome intrusion, Captain, you must stay at an unobtrusive distance." While Jenna smiled at the prince's words, the captain's face was sour.

Jenna's fascination with the palace grew as she toured the huge edifice. She had not before been particularly interested in viewing this building, but to know that the prince had grown up here, had run up and down all the stairs, and had loved all of its chambers and corridors, made the palace seem a friendly, more homey place. She wondered if the older royal person had enjoyed his childhood as much as his brother.

The prince told how Cyranius had played 'hide and seek' with him, how he had enjoyed romping in this awesome place as far back as he could remember.

The prince's commentary included many childhood escapades.

"Cy always made it very exciting," the prince said, his questions forgotten.

"When I was a boy and felt weary of the court, I hid here..." he said, opening a panel in the wall of the lower gallery.

Smiling to think of this boy saying, 'when I was a boy,' Jenna picked up her skirts as she stepped up a staircase. The prince glowed to see her smile—how beautiful she looked when she smiled.

Edward revisited his happy earlier childhood and realized for the first time in his life that it was a thing of the past now. No longer did Cyranius go running down corridors, chasing him—life was so much more serious now they were both much older. The lad grew silent.

The prince announced that they were going to view the Long Gallery where the royal art collection was housed.

Never before had Jenna seen such a variety of paintings, ornaments and exquisite pieces of furniture. Along a wide hall rooms with no doors opened into each other, changing colors, carpets and furnishings. As the prince named each different section of the Long Gallery, Jenna delighted herself in examining the valuable coordinated displays of armory and weaponry throughout the centuries that matched paintings of battles, horsemen, castles and army encampments. Paintings of previous kings of Cyran adorned the walls of the royal gallery.

"This is the music chamber," the prince said, and asked, "Which instruments do you play?"

"I'm not musical," she said, "at least I don't think so. I never had the opportunity. Do you play?"

"Yes, and I'll play the national laud on this very new instrument. It's called a harpsichord," he said. Seating himself, he played the piece set on the music stand, perfectly in time.

Jenna noticed a messenger arrive while the prince played. The man spoke to Captain Ross.

Swiveling around on the stool, the prince looked at Jenna, expecting praise for his faultless playing.

"Pardon us, Your Highness, but King Cyranius requests that Lady Jennava go to the Throne Room."

"Oh bother, we haven't even had time to talk yet," the prince said, realizing he had not questioned her about Kind Heart, "bother."

Ten

The Throne Room was brilliantly lit with the lights of hundreds of candles burning in three large chandeliers.

The prince was announced as soon as they arrived, and Jenna found herself summoned immediately after he had entered the room. At first it seemed a repeat of her first encounter in this chamber, then Jenna recognized a man, over at one side, standing between two guards. It was Kind Heart's groom, Garth.

Jenna's heart raced for a few beats and she wondered that the king would allow his meal to be interrupted just because he had discovered someone closely linked to Kind Heart. *Unearthing Kind Heart's identity is obviously a priority to the king,* she mused.

The king's deep voice sounded out in the great throne room, "Lady Jennava, we have summoned you here because we have some grave matters reported to us, matters of concern to yourself and matters purporting to kingdom security." The king spoke to his chief scribe saying, "Allow Lady Jennava to read the scroll from the man who calls himself 'Knight Red' from Aponia."

Prince Edward sat forward in his huge chair, watching the lady's face. He knew the contents of this communication but in the adventure of being with the lady and, also knowing this news was not his to reveal, he had pushed this 'grave matter' from his mind. The Prince now wondered if the lovely lady would disgrace herself and throw a fit or faint.

Jenna took the scroll from the scribe and quickly read the scribbled words,

To the King of Cyran:
We have commandeered the castle located in the district of Gifford. All servants and personnel in the castle are our prisoners. When you deliver into our hands the man known as Kind Heart, we shall return the castle.

A scrawl at the bottom was distinguishable as being 'Knight Red, Aponia.'

Passing the scroll back to the scribe, Jenna looked up at the king, waiting.

"You've nothing to say, Lady Jennava?"

"I'm sure, Your Majesty, you and your army are well able to take care of a few bandits who illegally enter our kingdom and play the tyrant."

Turning to Prince Edward, the king demanded in an accusing tone, "What did you tell Lady Jennava about this matter, Edward?"

"He told me nothing," Jenna snapped, inwardly chiding herself for not realizing he would think this. Her outward calm was no mirror for her racing thoughts, but she did not want to share these with the king. With effort, she softened her voice, saying sweetly, "Prince Edward revealed little other than the interesting places he used to hide while Your Majesty was playing with him."

"Well, Lady Jennava, you speak correctly, we are well able to take care of the matter of Gifford Castle. We've ordered a section of our army to prepare to leave here tonight, and tomorrow they'll set siege on the castle—"

"We have?" Edward asked excitedly.

"That won't help those loyal Cyraniun subjects who are trapped inside the castle—Knight Red's prisoners," Jenna said.

"Perhaps Kind Heart will rescue them?" the king said, his voice filled with sarcasm. "This brings us to another matter. We have Groom Garth here who was discovered in Gifford Village, near Gifford Castle, at the farrier's place, with a certain black stallion we believe belongs to the man, Kind Heart. The military, under our orders brought Garth and the horse here. Garth admits to being employed as groom for Kind Heart's horses. He also says, Lady Jennava, that Kind Heart left the stables in the woods near Gifford, with two horses. One of which, you rode here to the capital. Kind Heart rode the other, Garth said. He also told us that you and the man Kind Heart, are very closely aligned." He waited and when Jenna was silent, he asked, "Is this true?"

"Yes."

"Garth here says that Kind Heart is not your brother. Your brother went to live in Rosenberg when he was ten. Garth has confirmed the record that states Sir Charles Richard Gifford inherited a castle belonging to his maternal grandfather. We're having this matter checked, but perhaps you yourself could confirm whether this is true or not?"

"My brother lives in Rosenberg," Jenna said.

"And your father trained someone else to perform as Kind Heart?"

"Yes," Jenna replied, "He trained someone else."

"This man, Kind Heart, and you, Lady Jennava, are intimate friends?" When Jenna did not reply, he said, "To quote Garth... you are lovers?"

Jenna's eyebrows rose and she looked across at Garth. His head was bowed toward the floor. She struggled to prevent the smile that rose from such an idea. Poor simple Garth. He adored her, almost worshipped her and Kind Heart was a thorn in his flesh. Garth knew that Kind Heart would go into the secret room at the end of the tunnel, and that Lady Jennava emerged. When Lady Jennava entered the room first, it was often Kind Heart who exited. She bowed her head to hide her rebel smile. Garth had been perfect for the task, as groom he never suspected the truth and did not have the intelligence to discern that the two were one.

King Cyranius is tainted against women... he'll never believe I'm Kind Heart—not unless he removed the wig and moustache himself... and may the sky fall before that happens, she thought.

"Gavin told me that Lady Jennava goes riding with Kind Heart every morning," Prince Edward said.

These words increased Jenna's confidence that these royals would never guess her duplicity.

The king glanced at his brother, wondering if he should not pursue this matter at another time.

"Are you and Kind Heart... lovers?" the prince asked, having ignored his brother's signal to be silent.

Jenna, keeping her head bowed, decided not to answer.

The silence seemed to echo from the throne room walls sending back a 'guilty' verdict. Murmurs rippled through the court but still the lady did not speak. Prince Edward opened his mouth to speak but thought better of it, and closed it again. The quietness became embarrassing and the king knew he had to break the impasse. He felt deep annoyance.

"We take it then, Lady Jennava, that your silence is verification," the king said, waiting. But the lady did not look up nor speak. The king's face mirrored his great displeasure.

"This brings us to the third matter concerning you, Lady Jennava. An urgent communication from Lord Sidney arrived, petitioning us on your behalf... with a message also for you... take the scroll to the lady, Sir Tamsin."

The chief scribe gave the roll to Jenna and she read:

It is with grave concern that I interrupt you at the Royal Palace, Lady Jennava, but my wife's pleadings have left me no choice. Since arriving home, Judith's state of health has declined. Doctors at Mayern do not believe my wife will recover. However, I feel that if you could come, there may be hope. Without your visit, I fear her soon demise.

Jenna looked up at the king, who said, "On a separate scroll, Lord Sidney petitioned the throne for your leave to go to Mayern to be with Lady Judith."

"I must go," Jenna said.

"We believe it could be a trap, engineered by Knight Red," the king said.

"This is Lord Sidney's hand, Your Majesty, I doubt he had time to confer with those who sequestered the castle before he sent this. I must believe it. I must go."

"We'll not allow you to leave here, Lady Jennava." In the brilliant light of his throne room, King Cyranius saw her pale face turn pink and he knew she disagreed. At last he had been able to read her reaction.

"You don't understand, Your Majesty. Lady Judith... and I... I promised I would be there for her when... if... we are... the closest of friends..."

"Closer than Kind Heart?" he asked, his voice deeply sarcastic.

Jenna felt a nerve snap and she retaliated with the truth, "No one could be closer to me than Kind Heart!"

The silence that followed her condemning statement accompanied eyes connecting with others to share misconceived enlightenment.

"Perhaps Lady Jenna could ride with the army that is going to Gifford," the prince suggested, knowing that the lady was greatly displeased. He wanted to see her smile again. In his child-mind he had no comprehension of the fantasies flying free in the overripe minds of the adults surrounding him.

"Lady Jenna—Jennava—will remain here!" the king said firmly. "For her own safety. Since she has the closest of liaisons with this man, Kind Heart, what do you suppose Knight Red would demand if he were to capture her as well?"

Jenna drew a deep breath, wanting time and space to consider her options—certainly not to be another minute in this throne room with this insufferable king! *He speaks about me as if I am an absentee—somewhere in another kingdom, or out on the moon.*

"He'd have us both, Your Majesty," Jenna said, "Kind Heart would be locked in a cage and taken off to King Maslen. Then all Your Majesty's problems with Kind Heart would be solved."

The king glared at Jenna. She dared to mock him. What an irksome woman indeed!

Jenna curtsied and said, "If I may take your leave, Your Majesty, I'd prefer solitude in the quarters you've so kindly allocated me."

Frowning, the king could not believe she was dismissing herself from him—he the king and she a mere subject, a woman at that! A foreign sense of temper rose within him, a feeling that made him want to provoke her. He needed to show her that he was in charge. He did not want to force her to stay here though, she obviously was not impressed with her king one dot. What more was there left to say about Kind Heart? Did he not understand it all? Yes, only too well. It *would* be better for her to be removed from his royal presence.

"Escort Lady Jennava to her quarters, Captain Ross and double the guard at her door."

~ * ~

Jenna paced back and forth in her small sitting room, to the window and back to the door. Four servant-women in the chamber stared at her in disdain.

"I will retire and I shall be left alone," Jenna said firmly, wishing there were a door, not just a curtain between the sitting room and the bedchamber. "I shall undress myself if you please. I do not wish to be disturbed."

The women did not please, but complied and, murmuring their disapproval, stayed in the sitting room.

Snuffing out the candles in the chamber, Jenna opened the window shutters, admitting misted light from the moon. Dressing in the black riding habit, Jenna pulled the hat firmly over her hair. Rolling her blue gown and night attire, she placed it with the leather bag as well as a fleece mat from the floor into the bed, arranging the cover so it appeared someone lay under it.

With care, she pulled the lace curtain closed all the way around the bed.

Climbing out the large window and over the sill, Jenna supported herself by holding on to the vines, which thickened as she descended. The reluctant moon obliged and hid behind a cloud.

Within minutes, Jenna was over the first palace wall anprecariously balancing on the second.

"Hey!" a guard called as the moon, now bold, revealed the black figure. "Halt! In the name of the king! Halt!"

But Jenna was on the other side of the wall, losing herself in the close-knit alleyways of the capital city. Knowing that if she were sighted the northern exit would be where she would be expected to attempt an escape, Jenna wove back through the city to the southern wall. Distant cries and hoofbeats gave her confidence that a search was being mounted in the area she had been seen.

Soon she was running across a field and into the woods. Skirting the edge of the woods, she began climbing the steep hills towards the range.

Looking back, she saw that the palace was bright—lights had been lit and shown from every window. It was breathtaking, looking at the palace, a mass of towers and turrets, balconies and windows. What a beautiful building!

Torch lights moved atop the towers and along corridors, traveling in different directions... she wondered that they searched for her so intensively. She turned back to the task of climbing to a place where it would be safe to whistle Oak to come. Not yet. If mounted guards were sent this way... she must not allow them to catch her now.

I'll rescue the prisoners at Gifford and I'll take care of Knight Red... then I must visit Judith... please Dear God, don't let me arrive too late...

Jenna literally ran down the other side of the hill, knowing she was out of view from the palace. Climbing the other side, up, up, she paused when she knew she would be able to see the palace again. The lights within it seemed stronger than ever. She wondered what the king would be thinking of her. *Does it matter what he thinks?* she asked herself. But deep inside her, in a place she never before knew she had, a feeling welled up, a feeling of sorrow that he believed her to be a lady who had a secret lover.

Turning, she gave a long, low whistle, resuming the climb up the long grassy slope toward the forest. A second whistle was answered with a distant glad whinny. Oak was there and he was safe and well.

Soon the horse stood by her side, trembling with the excitement of her presence, her kind touch. She mounted his bare back and he turned, knowing the way to go... home.

~ * ~

Finding the military discussion in the throne room tedious, Prince Edward had requested leave of his brother and had followed the path of Lady Jennava. Arriving outside her quarters, the prince paced back and forth in the corridor, mustering the courage to enter. He longed to have his many questions about Kind Heart answered.

How many horses did Kind Heart own and ride?

How did Kind Heart manage to travel about the country so fast... it had been reported that he had been at different ends of the kingdom all in the same day.

Would she show him Kind Heart's ring?

Had Kind Heart given her the ring because they were lovers?

Was it the same Kind Heart who had rescued him... and the one who was Lady Jenna's friend... her lover?

Would Lady Jenna arrange for him to meet Kind Heart?

Captain Ross stood opposite the heavy oak door. Two guards stood at attention on both sides of the heavy oak door.

The captain scowled. The confrontation in the throne room had revealed that the beautiful lady was spoken for.

"I wish to speak with Lady Jenna... open the door for me," the prince commanded.

Prince Edward stepped into the sitting room and stared at the four servant-women, all looking back at him.

"Lady Jennava has retired and does not want anyone to disturb her."

"She must have just gone in there!" the prince declared. "I wish to speak with her. Tell her to come out into the sitting room where we will be chaperoned by you all."

With a smug look on her face, the eldest woman entered the bedchamber. She returned for a candle and went back to order the lady to rise.

After calling several times, the servant-woman pulled back the curtains, then the bedclothes. She gasped loudly at the sight of a black leather bag that appeared in the dimness to be an animal, a dog or perhaps a large black cat. A cry followed her gasp.

"She's gone! But, where? Hurry! Help! Help find her!"

Prince Edward followed three servant-women into the bedchamber. He rushed to the window, staring down at the telltale vines.

"She wouldn't climb... all the way... down... there... would she?" he asked, his voice strained, then answered, "yes, she would... she was too willing to return to her chamber... fetch Captain Ross, have him search this room and sound the alarm. Perhaps she climbed to a lower level, we must search the palace for her. Cy will be furious!"

Captain Ross ordered that the candles in the bedchamber be lit and a more thorough search made. He stared out the window, down the thick vines, wondering if he himself would dare to climb all the way down—certainly not a delicate lady like her... never!

Eleven

Jenna, now dressed as Kind Heart, dismounted Oak in a small glen that they both knew very well.

"Stay. Hide, Oak, stay," she cautioned him, after rubbing him down. He nuzzled his nose against her chin, and she slapped her palm on his neck several times, knowing he liked her to do this as a parting gesture.

With great stealth, Jenna crept through the woods to the stables, wondering again if Garth had told the king's men of this place. She crept around a tree, watching and waiting. All was still and quiet. An owl hooted and the crickets continued singing.

Not a thing was out of place as Jenna made her way back along the snake tunnel into Kind Heart's room where she strapped specially made deerskin soles beneath her boots. Unlocking the door, she then relocked it before closing a concealing wall.

Entering a rarely used corridor, Jenna moved to the far end where she opened the wall, climbed to a small landing and closed the wall. She climbed down a narrow ladder and again opened and closed a secret handle-less portal. A long, wide corridor lay ahead and Jenna walked to the end.

Pressing at a different place in the wall, Jenna carefully descended, down, down, right down into the heart of her castle. She walked with care—it was more than a year since she had come this way and it had only been to make sure that the spiral step-way could be traversed safely.

Running her fingers along the wall at a dead-end, Jenna felt for a knob in a crevice in the stonework. Pressing the knob brought the results Jenna expected—she opened the secret portal into the dungeon. This large prison-chamber had been unused for over fifty years. She wondered if the man Knight Red had opened it and imprisoned her loyal staff here? She prayed he had—to perform rescues elsewhere in the castle would be more difficult.

The odor and noise bombarding her senses was answer enough. Children sobbed inconsolably—cries, sighs and voices, the lazy clinking of chains, all was gloom and doom. Dim light from a flare at the other end of the one chamber revealed a myriad of faces, bodies and limbs, all having been forced down into this miserable place of hopelessness.

Moving stealthily, Jenna wove through those who lay sleeping on the stone floor to the other end of the dungeon, to the light. No one stirred to challenge the newcomer.

High above the torchlight was the only exit from this dungeon—a large, round wooden trapdoor locked into the stone ceiling. Jenna felt relief that it was closed. The only way in from above was to lower a long wooden ladder and climb down. The trapdoor was so far removed from the prisoners beneath, that guards were not needed.

Near the torchlight was a figure Jenna recognized. He sat, unchained, his head between his knees. It was Doctor Breck and she wondered if he slept. Touching his shoulder, she placed her forefinger on his lips. Looking up and seeing the black-clad figure, the doctor clambered to his feet. His mouth dropped open and after looking up his eyes moved in concern around at the walls of the dungeon before turning back to stare in amazement at her and Jenna felt vulnerable. Doctor Breck had been the castle doctor for more than her lifetime. Although she had never been sick, he had lived in the same castle as she all her life. Never before had she been so close to him in the role of Kind Heart.

Choosing the husky tone she used for Kind Heart, Jenna said, "There's a way out, to safety, Doctor Breck. We must wake all the adults, tell them not to speak and when I've freed them, we'll have the strongest choose a sleeping child each to carry... the passage is narrow and they must take care."

One by one and joined by those they shook, the menfolk awoke, standing to stare in wonder at Kind Heart, hoping they were not dreaming.

Setting a small bag of tools on the rough stone floor near the torchlight, Jenna chose a strong chisel-like instrument and a small hammer. Working as fast as she could, she began freeing the men who wore chains. The large links were rusty and cracked open with little effort.

Over sixty Gifford castle guards were chained around the perimeter of the large stone chamber. Their uniforms and boots had been removed and they wore only their cotton under-tunics. Two had been beaten so badly they could not be roused.

"How many are with Knight Red?" Jenna asked the man she recognized as Captain Duff, her own Controller of Castle Security. She longed to question him as to how the castle had been captured, if any lives had been lost, where were his children, and his wife? But knew that she must keep to the relevant facts if they were to complete the escape and regain the castle.

"He had about twenty... he took us by surprise... they herded the women and children together and threatened to kill them all... we surrendered." He shook the shackles off his hands, and stretched his arms. Still shaking his hands, he asked, "There is a way out?"

"Yes, when all are ready, I'll show you—"

"Why not leave the women and children here? Us men can go up and deal with them... there are more of us than there are of them."

"We won't leave anyone down here, but in the safety of a secret tunnel," Jenna said, speaking in a gruff tone, "We'll lock new prisoners down here... Knight Red and his cohorts," She worked as she talked, cracking another shackle apart. Some shackles did not have locks, but pins that could be removed easily. Others needed a key to release them, and these were the ones Jenna tackled with the chisel and hammer.

"Here, I can do that now," Captain Duff said, "My hands have lost their numbness and belong to me again."

Jenna gave the tools into his eager hands and strode over to direct the women and older children to the opening in the far corner. Repeatedly she heard the name, Kind Heart, whispered. Some of the children reached out to touch her as she passed.

Speaking to Doctor Breck, Jenna gave instructions, "It's very steep, about a hundred steps. We'll place a woman or man between each child who can climb... Doctor Breck, you should go first. The passage at the top widens and ends at a wall where you must wait, sit and rest.

"You, Sir," she spoke to a large man she knew to be the chief groom of the castle stables, "you should stay at the rear. Everyone must remain quiet, sit and rest. It'll be very dark, but I promise you all in less than an hour we'll come for you and, by then, the castle will be yours again."

A silence stole over the adults as they began moving out through the aperture and up the steep steps. Men and women carried the smaller, sleeping children.

Many Gifford guards had been spread-eagled against the wall with ill-fitting shackles and chains that were too short. These took the most time to release but soon all the guards who had been chained were free and regaining use of limbs that had lost feeling.

Tying the tools back into the kit, Jenna fixed it to the belt at her hip again. She spoke to Captain Duff, "There's another passage out of here, Sir. The castle shall soon be yours again."

Striding to the corner from where the groom had just disappeared, Jenna said, "Bring the torch." She reached down to the knob in the crack. With a grinding sound, the wall turned back to become a closed corner again.

Taking the stave with its burning light to another corner, Jenna said, "Follow Captain Duff in single file. When you come to the end of the passage, Captain, there's a door. Enter the chamber. It'll be dark but you'll find flint and cressets to light. When you view the chamber, you'll all know what to do."

Reaching down, Jenna twisted a knob similar to the other, except this one had to be turned until she had felt it click seven times. The designer had not intended prisoners to escape from this dungeon, but it had been designed for him, if such an incarceration ever happened. This was the first time Jenna had used the mechanisms for an escape.

The men filed past the slim black-clad figure with the plumed hat. Several clasped her hand and arm in the military way of a silent pledge of loyalty and commitment.

When there were just a few men left, Jenna said, "Bring the two unconscious men, we'll place them out of harm's way... through this wall. You can return for them later."

Once the aperture was closed and Jenna had checked that the two men lay in safe positions on the stone floor, she extinguished the torch and began her ascent.

Captain Duff turned the handle with great caution. He half expected this door to be locked. It was like a crazy dream, Kind Heart turning up in that impossible dungeon, it was like magic! All hope had been abandoned, there was no way out. The captain had been so low he had even prayed... then help had come.

Feeling around in the chamber, Captain Duff's heart almost skipped a beat. He felt racks... and in the racks were sword sheathes, dozens of them... and in the sheathes his fingers felt the hilts of swords. This was a weapons' chamber, one he had never been in previously. His mind raced. *How does Kind Heart know of this cache? How does he know the secrets of the tunnels of Gifford Castle?*

Gasps of surprise and glee came from the other guards as they too comprehended the weapons' stash. One man found the flint kits and cressets.

When Jenna stepped up into the chamber, the room was alight. The sixty guards barely had standing room but all were busy, choosing their weapons—swords, daggers, bows, arrows and quivers, arming themselves.

Moving to a shelf near the exit portal, Jenna selected a metal staff with a blunt mallet-like ball on each end. She held it upright, like a soldier would his spear.

Captain Duff, his weapons in place, stood waiting for his subordinates to complete their selections. Then, raising both hands above his head, he said, "Three silent cheers for Kind Heart!"

All hands raised, the men silently acknowledging their rescuer as the Captain counted to three.

"If there are twenty brigands, Captain, then I say we assign each one of the enemy to three of us," Jenna said, "And I say we take them all, alive, and we chain them with new chains in the lower dungeon, where you were imprisoned."

"Right," Captain Duff agreed, then commanded, "We'll honor Kind Heart's wish... no bloodshed. Get them down, alive. Form trios... perhaps Knight Red and his men will still be in the great hall, as they gloated to us, feasting..." his voice turned to bitterness, "they kept some of the women folk there to cook and serve their food, and..."

"Millie? Your wife?" Jenna could not prevent herself asking, "and... I did not see your children, Captain."

"The children are safe, Sir... the children went, yesterday, to visit friends in Zerka District. But Millie... she's upstairs somewhere..." He frowned at the interruption and the change in his thinking. Kind Heart had asked the question about his wife as if he knew her... with concern for his children. The Captain found it off-putting. Who was this young man? He had a soft voice, not a man's, but a teenager's. Captain Duff had never before spoken with Kind Heart.

Jenna recognized the distraction she had initiated and bit her lip. She had previously warned herself not to do that because it was the sort of thing woman did—men forgot all else when a battle was at hand. She had damaged Kind Heart's disguise, she felt sure of this. She spoke gruffly, "Let's move out and regain the castle. I'll enter the great hall first. I'd like to meet Knight Red. He wants me alive, I hear."

As the captain had supposed, Knight Red and four of his closest cohorts were in the great hall. They had finished eating, but were still drinking while pouring over a sheaf of maps of the Kingdom of Cyran. The rest of the brigands were out on the walls and at the gate, on guard. Jenna supposed that the womenfolk were in the kitchens, and felt glad they were not here to be used as human shields.

The doors to the great hall were wide open, two Gifford guards lying on the stone floor, stabbed through their chests, used now as door-props. Anger surged in Jenna's veins and mingled with feminine sorrow. They *had* killed in her castle. One young guard lay in a pool of blood, his eyes wide open. She knew his name to be Jonathan. He had been married but a month. Jenna swallowed, averting her eyes, not wanting to think of spilt blood, it made her feel sick.

Noiselessly, Kind Heart entered the chamber. Captain Duff and a dozen guards, looking strange with their weapons fixed over their under-tunics, followed. Their bare feet silent on the stone floor, they formed a half-circle behind her.

"Knight Red? You wanted to meet me?"

As one, the four grasped their swords from the table in front. Swinging around, their swords extended, the men called the name together, "Kind Heart!"

Knight Red, performing a well-practiced evasive movement, leapt up on the tabletop. The four men beneath extended their swords to form a barrier in protection of their leader. Before any one else could move, Kind Heart, using the strange metal staff, vaulted over the barricade, exercising a complicated head-over-heels movement. She landed upright on the tabletop, causing the four to twist upwards in amazement, lifting their swords. Swinging both herself and the staff, Jenna bashed the hilt end of the sword, forcing it from Knight Red's hand. It flew harmlessly across to clatter against the wall on the other side of the hall.

Gritting her teeth, Jenna calculated the strength of her attack. She did not want to kill these men, but render them helpless. Swinging the staff, she butted two men on the sides of their heads, then one the back of his neck. Swinging it at Knight Red to smash the dagger he had ready to hurl at her, then the fourth man—first the dagger from his left hand, the sword from his right, then butting Knight Red under his chin as she swung the staff upward and side-kicking at the fourth man's jaw as he clambered up on the table. He fell backwards, lying unconscious and Jenna wondered if he had cracked his head on the stone floor. Knight Red somersaulted to the floor, collecting a sword from one of his unconscious accomplices.

"Come down here and fight like a man!" Knight Red challenged pointing the sword, first at her, then at the floor. The Gifford guards stopped their advance to allow Kind Heart to give the expected answer.

Throwing the staff to Captain Duff who deftly caught it, Jenna drew her sword and somersaulted to the floor where she stood facing Knight Red.

The knight stood, about eight inches taller than her height, including her thick high-heeled boots. He was more than six and a half feet tall and Jenna calculated that he was taller than King Cyranius. In this split-second, she cautioned herself not to think about the king but to keep her mind on this evil man who thrust his sword at her.

Knight Red was broad-shouldered, and unlike the king, large bellied. He sported a bright red beard and huge bulbous nose. Jenna estimated him to be in his early thirties.

"Ha! You're no more than a boy!" he said, his voice happy. He stepped closer.

Jenna did not flinch, but thought, *If only you knew... I'm not much more than a girl!* She smiled grimly and reminded herself of the maneuver she must make. Her father had taught her to anticipate her opponent's moves—she would be swift, decisive and sudden. But wait... let him attack... twice, she would twice duck, then sidestep... but be alert... he may surprise her yet...

Jenna ducked the sudden slash of his sword, powerful enough to sever her head from her neck. She then jumped the slash he made at her feet, knowing she was moving by instinct. She waited. His movements had been unpredictable. Swinging her sword, she was playing for time. He slashed at her and the moment was there... twisting the sword and pivoting herself in a full circle, she caught his weapon with such force that it flew from his hand. Jenna held her sword-point at his Adams apple.

"Don't move a muscle!" she warned.

Red Knight looked stunned and asked, as others before him had, "How... did... you do... that?"

Lifting her free hand, yet keeping the sword at the man's throat, Jenna gestured to Captain Duff. As if in a daze, the captain placed the staff in her hand.

"Take my sword," she said.

With his own extended at the felon's face he obeyed, a sword gripped in each hand. Moving to the back of the large man, Jenna sent a well-calculated blow to the back of his head. He did not move at first, so she repeated the blow. He slumped over slowly, face down to the floor.

"Bind him and take him below, put him in chains," Jenna said fiercely. From all she had heard of this man, he could yet rise up and challenge them.

Returning her sword into its sheath, she spoke to Captain Duff, "Make sure you capture all the others, I'll go down and release those below. The king's men will be here in around an hour, to set siege. Take the red flag down and put the Gifford flag up, that way Major Frayne will know that you have control again."

"Yes Sir!" Captain Duff said, saluting, feeling he would wake up from a dream and find himself still chained in the dungeon. *What a swordsman! He's like magic! And Knight Red is right... he's not much more than a boy.*

Twelve

King Cyranius summoned Polonius and Tory, demanding, "Where would Lady Jennava go? Back to Gifford?"

"Perhaps, Sire, but she'll more likely go to Mayern... Lady Judith and her were very close, like sisters."

"But she has no horse... she'll not attempt to walk that far, surely?"

Both Polonius and Tory stared at their king. He looked back at them, asking, "You don't think...? How could he...?"

"Kind Heart?" Prince Edward asked, naming the name in his brother's mind. "Did Kind Heart help Lady Jenna escape? Yes, Kind Heart would have a horse and Kind Heart would ride with her to Gifford. Perhaps he'll kill Knight Red, then he'll take her to Mayern..." Prince Edward saw his brother's left forefinger rise, and now it waved from side to side.

The atmosphere was barbed with anger, emanating from the king.

"It's my command, Sir Tory, Sir Polonius, that you tell us, now, who it is we deal with in this man, Kind Heart! Tell us, do you know his identity, his name?"

"Yes, Sire," Polonius said, bowing his head.

"Yes, Your Majesty," Tory agreed, then added, "But we cannot say, Sire."

"He can enter our palace and take a lady from our custody and you have the audacity to say 'we cannot say?' I command that you tell me!"

Both Tory and Polonius stared at each other and shook their heads—the king would never believe that Kind Heart was Lady Jennava, they both knew that.

"What then?" the king demanded, "You defy the crown and choose to commit treason?"

"I speak for both of us, Sire... we do not defy you, Sire... we rest upon the fact that your own father gave both Lady Jennava and Kind Heart 'Freedom of the Realm,' Sire, and we swore a blood-oath the previous Kind Heart, before he died... therefore we plead with you that you await young Kind Heart's own timing to reveal... the identity... to you."

"You believe he will reveal himself?"

"Kind Heart will, Sire, we're both sure Kind Heart will."

"What makes you so sure?" the king asked, feeling perplexed. He had the power to command these men to be whipped, to be forced to tell Kind Heart's identity. Part of him wanted to use the king's power and the other part wanted to be patient... and the 'Freedom of the realm'... that was another matter, very perplexing...

"We know Kind Heart, you see, Sire," Tory said, "Kind Heart has a longing not to continue as Kind Heart... the role has become a burden, a great burden."

King Cyranius stared in anger at the two men. They knew Kind Heart's thoughts, it seemed, and they protected him. Perhaps it was that they defended Lady Jennava as well... yes, the two were closely linked, that was obvious. A feeling that the king did not recognize rose deep within him. It was jealousy and in that moment he vowed to himself that he would not rest until he had a close encounter with Kind Heart and learned exactly who the man was.

The young prince's voice broke into his thoughts. "You should ride to Gifford Castle and bring Lady Jennava back here, brother. She has no right defying us and going off with Kind Heart!" He bowed his head, saying, "I know it's against the crown's security that we both go, so I suggest you make haste."

"We cannot both go," the king agreed, his mind made up. "Sir Lowell has returned from his vacation. He will come with me. If we leave now, we will not be far behind the siege company, in fact we may catch them if we hurry." He did not mean the siege company, it was the lady he was thinking about.

Thirteen

Dawn had not broken when Jenna, wearing a black cloak over a black dress, rode to the forest edge, just north of Mayern Castle.

"I'm sorry, Boy, but I'm going to leave you tethered. Let's see if we can find some edible leaves." So saying, she dismounted and led Oak into a thicket where she tied him securely. Hoofbeats sounded out and Jenna moved further into the thicket. The large company passed.

"Just be quiet, Boy, or I'll have to walk home, and that won't make me feel too happy. I hope I won't be long... but I really have no idea, do I? If Judith is well, I'll come soon... but..." she left the whispered sentence hanging.

~ * ~

Low gray clouds choked the rising daylight and as Jenna swung the three-pronged hook on the end of the rope upward to the battlements, she felt glad for the tardiness of the sunlight. Weariness caused her to breathe harder as she climbed the wall, and she warned herself not to lose her grip on the rope. With care, she peered over the top of the parapet. A guard headed her way and she lowered herself down the wall again, waiting for his heavy footfalls to pass.

Having concealed the rope, her cloak and riding gloves in a previously used hiding place, a crevice beneath a step, Jenna cautiously descended into the castle. It was not until she was in the wing where Judith's bedroom was located, that she was seen and recognized.

"Lady Jennifer is here," a servant announced to Baron Sidney as he sat at his wife's bedside. The man stood, turning to look at the open door, but his eyes held little hope or welcome—he believed she was too late.

Jenna entered the bedchamber wanting to see one person only, her dear friend, Judith.

Sidney did not speak but stepped aside, leaving the bedside chair vacant.

Judith's eyes were closed. Her face was so white that she appeared as one dead. But Jenna heard the sound of her labored breathing. The atmosphere of the bedchamber swam with an odor Jenna remembered. How long ago was it? She felt transported back to another bedside, that of her father's. Aromatic oil burned in the room, but another smell mingled with it, the odor of death. Jenna suddenly heard her own heart beating loudly in her ears. Her eyes misted over.

"She sleeps at last," Sidney whispered, "we gave up hope that you would come..."

"Where are the physicians?" Jenna asked.

"There's nothing... more... they can do... she... they said... she'll not wake again... I said I wanted to be a alone with her... until..."

"How did this happen?" Jenna asked, "If she was well enough to journey home when she left Gifford Castle?"

Sidney did not answer. He bowed his head.

Jenna sat closer to the bed. Taking Judith's hand in her own, she leaned closer to her friend's ear, saying, "Judith, it's Jenna, I'm here."

"They... the doctors... said she'll not speak again..."

Judith's eyes flickered and Jenna called again, "Judith, dear Judith, it's Jenna... I'm here..."

Without opening her eyes, Judith spoke, her voice a whisper, "I knew you'd come... I knew God would answer my prayer..."

Jenna squeezed Judith's hand a little, wishing she could impart health to the wasted body lying before her. Anger rose within her to think of Sidney, the abusive husband who had so beaten his wife she had not recovered...

As if she read Jenna's thoughts, Judith spoke again, "Don't blame Sidney, it was not his fault... Jenna."

Jenna tightened her lips.

Judith's eyes opened and they filled with tears, "Sidney did not beat me... he could never beat me."

"Judith, don't speak of it!" Sidney said, stepping closer.

"I... want... to speak... with Jenna... alone," Judith said, her voice barely a whisper.

"No, I won't leave you..."

"Please... Sidney... please..." Judith begged.

Standing, Jenna spoke to two women-servants, "Leave us," she commanded. Turning to Sidney, she said, "You heard your wife, she wants to be alone with me,"

"I'm not leaving her!" he said.

"Not even... as a last wish?" Jenna did not say it, but the thought went out, *How could you not grant her last wish to speak with me alone?*

"Jenna," Judith said.

"Yes, dear," Jenna replied, sitting close to her.

"It's all right. Sidney knows... it was Sidra."

"Sidra?" Jenna repeated the name, not comprehending. What did Sidra, the stepmother, have to do with anything?

"Sidra... beat me. She... she made up the... story... about Patrick and I..."

Jenna heard Sidney groan. Turning, she asked, "Is this true?"

Sidney did not answer, but hung his head.

"Sidney... knew all along... it was his stepmother... but... he let... everyone think... it was he. Sidra... she's so... powerful..."

A silence followed, then Judith spoke again, "Sidra... it was she... her men... put Patrick in the dungeon."

Judith's eyes closed and Jenna leaned closer, wondering if she had stopped breathing. She had.

"Judith, dear Judith," Jenna said, thinking... *she's dying, dear Judith... she's dying... she can't die...* Jenna's eyes filled with tears.

Then with a rasping indrawn breath, Judith began breathing again. Her eyes opened.

"Jenna... Sidra... she... wants... you..."

"Wants me?" Jenna repeated.

"She... Sidra... wants to capture you... she believes... you will... bring Kind Heart... to her if she captures... you."

"Don't worry," Jenna said, squeezing her hand.

"Promise me, Jenna... promise me... you will... give up... give up... Kind Heart..."

"Yes... yes... you know I want to..." Jenna said, conscious of Sidney's presence still in the bedchamber.

"I... I... want... you..."

"Yes?"

"I... I want you... to come, too..."

Jenna did not speak, her emotions threatened to overwhelm her.

"You have to promise to come, too..."

"Yes," Jenna whispered, "I promise."

"But... you can't come... if you don't know the way..."

"I'll come," Jenna said, "God will not exclude me, Judith, dear. God is loving and good."

"But... but... it's not... what you do... if... anyone could get to heaven... because they are kind... and good... it would... be you, Jenna... but it's not good deeds... no, please... but faith... you must have... faith..."

"Dear Judith, don't distress yourself," Jenna said. Tears ran down her cheeks and more filled her eyes, blinding her. She had not cried like this, not since her father had been buried.

Judith's strength seemed to rally as she said, "God gives eternal life as a gift, Jenna, you must receive His gift..."

"I do, Judith, I do."

"No, Jenna, you haven't, that's why I don't want to leave you... I have to be sure... that you... will come, too." Judith grasped both Jenna's hands and pulled herself forward. Sitting upright, she stared into Jenna's eyes, saying, "Don't cry, dearest, don't cry." She pulled Jenna's face on to her thin shoulder, surrounding her with trembling arms, saying, "I have always loved you, Jenna, you have been the dearest sister to me, the closest friend. Promise me... Jenna... that you'll not rest until you know for sure that you'll come to Heaven, too. Promise!"

Jenna felt so overcome with sorrow that she could not answer.

"Promise me, say it!"

"Dearest, don't distress yourself," Sidney said, stepping close to the bed, placing his arm around her shoulders, supporting her. His cheeks were also wet with tears.

"Hush," Judith said, her voice soft and her breath heavy, "We've settled our lives, Sidney, now it's Jenna's turn. I... I can't make you promise me, Jenna, but I'll die in sorrow if I die believing I'll never see you again..." releasing herself, she slid her hands down Jenna's arms. Still clutching Jenna's hands, she gave herself to Sidney's strength. He eased her back to lie on the waiting pillows.

Jenna spoke, urging, "You must fight this, Judith... you must not die..."

"It is not for us to choose," Sidney said, his voice flat.

"I... should not still... be here..." Judith said, "But I had to wait... to see you... to be sure... nothing matters... this life is nothing... only that we choose... heaven... forever..."

"I believe I am... I will... go to heaven..." Jenna said. Knowing this was not the answer Judith needed, Jenna added, "I'll search the matter out, dear Judith, I'll not rest until I feel sure in my soul that I'll follow you..."

"You promise?" Judith asked with a faint lilt in her voice, "you promise you'll seek until you find?"

"I'll seek until I find," Jenna promised.

"To life eternal?" Judith asked, closing her eyes and releasing her grip on Jenna's hand.

"To life eternal." Jenna repeated, her eyes spilling tears again.

Sidney leaned closer. Judith's breathing ceased again and it was a full minute before it resumed.

Jenna moved to the end of the bed. Kneeling, she began praying that God in His great love and mercy would spare Judith's life. *While there is life, there is hope,* she reminded herself. But deep inside her, she felt grief-stricken. Judith was dying.

Judith continued stack breathing for over an hour. Sidney pulled a chair close to the bed, taking his wife's hand, sobbing into the bedcover.

Rising, Jenna helped herself to a drink of water from the sideboard. She could hear Judith's breathing, though more even now, it tore into the silence like an ominous countdown to eternity.

"You're... you're... leaving?" Sidney asked.

"I... I'll be in your chapel... if Judith asks for me again." Jenna replied. She could not tell him that she had to leave that chamber—it was too real a reminder of her father's parting—the helpless, hopeless feeling seeped through her emotions, threatening to overcome her. She had rescued countless victims as Kind Heart, but she was unable to rescue the ones she loved most from the clutches of death.

Jenna did not remember the walk to the chapel, but she was conscious of arriving there. Colors filtered through the stained glass circlet in the huge dome above, and Jenna felt comforted as she blindly read verses of Scripture engraved in the pillars all around the chapel.

"The Lord is my Shepherd, I shall not want..."

"Though I walk through the valley of the shadow of death, I will fear no evil..."

The circular room seemed to swirl, and Jenna knew that she had allowed herself to go too long without eating or sleeping. It was warm in the room, too warm. Taking a small velvet bag from the tie at her waist, she pulled out a long thin vial. Removing the stopper, Jenna dabbed the oil mixture on her temples. Lavender and rosemary oils mixed with others, revived her. The aroma scented the warm air.

Jenna sank to kneel, conscious that others also prayed in this beautiful chamber. Scarcely had she prayed, when her head leaned forward on the wooden pew and she slept. A faint shuffle brought her back to lucidity and guilt flooded her as she realized she had, indeed, slept.

Dear God, she prayed silently, *If it would help Judith, please let her know that I shall do as I promised. I shall give up Kind Heart. I shall seek Your Will for my life and in seeking I pray that You will help me find eternal life... if it is a gift, a simple gift, then show me, God, how I may have this gift for myself.*

Fourteen

King Cyranius and his escort of fifty horsemen selected fresh horses from the Gifford Castle stables. The king was eager to arrive at Mayern Castle—he hoped to encounter Kind Heart as well as Lady Jennava.

His thoughts raced with his galloping horse, sorting over all he had seen and heard at Gifford Castle. He was yet still amazed. Met by messengers sent back from the siege company, King Cyranius had received the news that Kind Heart had entered the castle, freed the prisoners and had incarcerated Knight Red and all his cohorts, save one. One escapee had been detected after Kind Heart had left—a man had been seen descending the outer wall of the west tower and had escaped into the woods. The siege company had been commissioned to search for him.

The king wondered about the man, Kind Heart. By all accounts, he was invincible, what an extraordinary warrior! Like the Kind Heart of old, he had ordered that none be killed, that they be taken as prisoners. King Cyranius had to make a decision, what to do with Knight Red? The man was an illegal entrant into Cyran—he had killed, he had taken hostages, made threats. It would have been simpler if Kind Heart had killed them all but now, the king knew, he would have to send Knight Red back to King Maslen with the warning, never to return. The cohorts would have to be returned as well, for to keep them would invite unwelcome war with Aponia.

~ * ~

Jenna's feet trod a repeated path, from the chapel to Judith's bedside, then back again. She felt unable to stay in Judith's bedchamber but having left, was drawn back, praying that some improvement in Judith's condition would greet her.

Sidney did not move from his wife's side.

On Jenna's fifth entry to the chamber, Sidney spoke, his voice little more than a whisper. "I've received forgiveness from Judith but I also need your forgiveness, Lady Jennifer... or rather, Jennava... I've erred greatly and now reap the harvest of my mistakes." He waited and when Jenna did not speak, he continued, "I should never have allowed my stepmother, Sidra, to be alone with Judith... I didn't realize... not at first... then I didn't want to believe... she... Sidra... beat me when I was younger... though she wasn't much older, she's always intimidated me... I've finally realized her power over me... and I've forbidden her, ever, to return here... but it's too late..." he bowed his head to hide his tears. "It's too late... and I'm sorry, so sorry." Hiding his head in the bedcover, he sobbed as Jenna had never before heard a man sob.

Judith lay, her eyes shut, her breathing erratic. Weariness combined with a wave of depression, and Jenna knew she must do something to regain her own equilibrium. Perhaps she could also do something for Judith.

Jenna moved downstairs to the pantry where she asked the hovering servants for access to their herb garden and dried herb collection. Selecting a combination of fresh and dried herbs, a little garlic and parsley, she brushed the servants aside. Having washed and chopped the fresh herbs, she prepared a jug of liquid, mixing the herbs and the crushed garlic with hot water, adding cold water to cool it, then straining the juice. Taking a flask of mead, she combined the two liquids in a large jug.

A mug full of this pungent elixir revived Jenna greatly. It was as though she could feel strength seeping back into her veins. The remainder filled a flask and a mug. Taking a tray and a spoon, she commanded a servant to carry her preparation upstairs.

"Drink it, Sidney, it gives strength and courage."

"What is it?"

"Herbs... and mead..."

When he did not drink, but stared at her, then at the mug, she said, "Don't worry, Sidney, it's not poisoned... see..." With that, she drank from the mug. "It'll keep me awake and full of energy for twenty hours or more." she refilled the mug from the flask and held it toward him, saying, "It's my cup of water, given in His Name. It won't give me eternal life but I've always believed that revenge is a lost cause. To hate is an utter waste of time. I'd much rather feed an enemy than be responsible for him starving..."

Sidney frowned, his face blank.

"All right, if you must really have me say it, I forgive you. Sidra is a villain, treacherous, untrustworthy and she's always intimidated you."

Taking the mug in both hands, he downed its contents, then gasped and shook his head. "Garlic! It's got garlic..."

"And parsley... and other herbs... they all work together... tell me, Sidney, where is Sidra heading?"

"She rode out early this morning with her henchmen, to find you... to do mischief, I feel sure," he stood as he spoke, and reached for the flask the servant held, saying, "We should give some of that to Judith... I feel... more alive..."

"I was hoping you would say that," Jenna said, adding, "It will give Judith strength and help her, she may talk to you... here, let me, I have a spoon, I made this same drink for my father."

To both Sidney and Jenna's disappointment, Judith refused to take more of the herb drink after just a few drops. She closed her lips and clenched her teeth, causing the liquid to run down her chin.

Jenna abandoned the impossible task and left the flask and spoon with Sidney while she trekked to the chapel to seek solace again. The drink had energized her and she decided to walk the circuit of the castle corridors before returning to Judith.

Sidney met Jenna outside the bedchamber door. His face was white and he leaned upon the wall. His mouth opened but no words came at first. Then he said, "She... talked to me... then... she wanted the window open... and then... she... went. She's... gone... Judith's gone..."

Entering the bedchamber, Jenna felt her heart pounding in her head. Judith's face was radiant, she smiled, her eyes wide open. At first glance, Jenna felt incredible happiness—Judith was healed, she was well. Color had returned to her cheeks but she was unmoving, breathless, dead. Her blue eyes stared out the open window. Running to the window, Jenna looked out at the blue sky—not a cloud now, not a tear marred the fathomless aura. The sun, right overhead proclaimed it was noon.

Turning back, Jenna saw the fixed smile, the blueness of Judith's beautiful big eyes. Shaking her head, Jenna moved back to the bed. "No," she murmured, "no."

Judith was dead.

"No!" Jenna said, much louder, "You can't die! You're smiling!" She shook her head, backing to the door, saying, "No one should be happy to die! No!"

Jenna was blind to the doctor who entered the room. She did not see the hovering servants, lined up along the wide corridor where several castle officials stood, their backs to Jenna, all looking toward the staircase, waiting...

Sidney had moved further along the corridor, wringing his hands, looking confused. The announcement had just been voiced to him, that the king had arrived in the castle and was ascending the central stairs, with an escort of his guards, to confront Lady Jennava.

"No!" Jenna cried as she gathered up her skirts, running along the corridor in the opposite direction, ascending the stairs to the parapet, hoping without hope, to look upward into the blue sky and see Judith's soul as she ascended to heaven. "No!"

Sidney bowed to King Cyranius as he trod on the top step and turned to walk along the corridor. The king heard Jenna's cry and like many others, thought it was because of his arrival.

"Sire..." Sidney said, his face whiter than white..."Sire... my wife... she... she... she..."

"Lady Judith is ill, Baron, I trust she is on the improve?"

"She... she..." he could not say it again.

The doctor, having closed Judith's eyes and covered her with the bedcover, came back along the corridor.

"Lady Judith is dead," he announced.

"Please, accept my condolences," the king said, as was expected. He felt at a loss, he had never met the baroness, Lady Judith. But he had not come to meet her.

"Where is Lady Jennava?" the king asked.

Heads along the corridor turned, and fingers pointed toward the step-way at the far end.

~ * ~

"Judith!" Jenna called into the sky. "Judith." She closed her eyes and memories washed over her like a wave. Judith with her golden-blond hair, a mass of curls—they had been friends since they were three years old.

Like Jenna, Judith had lived with her father who was landlord over two thousand acres of land between the Gifford and Mayern Districts. She had been brought up in a Grand-House with servants and a governess. As they grew older, the two girls had shared their lessons with tutors employed by Jenna's father. The two had been inseparable. When Judith was not staying at the castle with Jenna, Jenna was staying at the Grand House with Judith. That was, until Jenna was ten years old—then Jenna's father began the rigorous training of his daughter to become Kind Heart. The girls had to meet in secret. This had lasted for three years, then Judith's father had died. Sidney married Judith and thus the land was joined to his district.

Even with the amazing exploits that she shared with her father, Jenna still managed to see Judith. Many times, in the middle of the night, they climbed together to this very parapet to discuss their heart-secrets.

I have no one now, Jenna told herself, looking out into the blue, giving her weight to the hard ledge of the crenellation. *I thought I'd have a friend, all my life... oh God... you've taken her from me... but she was so good, so trusting, so kind... how can I go on?* Tears dripped to the dry stone ledge. *She should have told me about Sidra... I should have guessed... Sidney did love Judith, he just could not stand up to his stepmother... I'd like to cane Sidra... I could hate her, but no, Father says hate is a waste of time... dear Father... he expected so much of me, but he loved me. I want him here now to hold me, I need him to hold me. Father, dear Father...*

Jenna's thoughts were in the past when the king, standing only a few feet from her, called her name.

"Lady Jennava."

She did not hear him, the wind had snatched his words away.

Judith was dead! How could it be true? Jenna laid her head in her arms upon the ledge and wept dismal tears. She gave herself to her grief, and her shoulders heaved with heart-wrenching sobs.

King Cyranius waved Captain Ross with his guard-escort back. Stepping closer, he waited, unsure now. Minutes passed, and still the lovely lady wept.

Jenna felt a hand touch her shoulder. Unable to think, she pushed herself away from the ledge, turning to see who had come to her but her tears blinded her. It was not Sidney, this man was much taller. Suddenly, the height and build of the man in front of her was counterpart to her father, and Jenna felt herself divided between the past and present.

"She's dead. Judith is dead," she said brokenly, turning to face him. Somehow, her father had returned to give her the comfort she so needed.

His strong arms wrapped around her and she closed her eyes, leaning her head into his chest, feeling comforted by a familiar smell, his leather riding vest.

Never before had the king been in such a situation. He could feel her grief, he enveloped it and it mourned on him in the trembling of her body against his. Resting his chin on her head, he held her tighter, longing to be able to soothe away her sorrow.

She wept quietly now, and he was unable to speak to shatter the comfort he knew she received as her trembling began to diminish.

Jenna discerned that it was not her father who held her—such a thing was impossible, her father had departed this life two years ago. Who gave her such a loving embrace? Wiping her tears away with a determined fierceness, Jenna pushed herself away from the man who had held her for over five minutes. She looked up into the inquiring eyes, burning down on her.

"Oh!" she cried, after a deep indrawn breath. "Your Majesty! I... did not know... it was you." Other words did not come, she was speechless. Embarrassment flooded her and she remembered that she should curtsy. Bowing her head, she sank into a low curtsy.

"You thought I was someone else?" he asked, his deep voice issuing a sarcastic tone to cover the pain he felt at her reaction, "You thought I was Kind Heart?"

Pulling herself to her full height, Jenna looked up into his face, saying, "As a matter of fact, Your Majesty, I did think you were Kind Heart... your leather vest is the same... as his... as his... was..."

"Where is he then?" he interrupted, demanding, "Why is he not here to comfort you?"

As though stung, Jenna backed away from him. She longed to be anywhere but close to this man! Her eyes took in the king's escort of guards. The handsome Captain Ross stood just a few feet behind and Jenna realized he had seen their king comforting her and they had all heard his questions.

How could she tell them the truth? He despised her, she was sure of this. He thought she loved a man named Kind Heart. Was there nothing she could do about it? Nothing she could say?

"Do you love him?" King Cyranius asked.

"Love... him? Who?" she felt disoriented.

"Kind Heart?"

"Kind Heart?" she remembered her father and her eyes expressed love for him, then they clouded. Her father was dead and she had inherited his role, Kind Heart. Her father was dead. Judith was dead. Why was she still alive? How could she bear life without them? And the king, he hated her for her liaison with Kind Heart, she felt sure. She could survive with a little love but she would rather die than be hated.

"You love Kind Heart," the king said with finality. "I shall command that it be arranged for you to marry this man, Kind Heart. He will do what is right. Does not Kind Heart stand for right? If he loves you, and you love him..."

"No!" Jenna said fiercely, "You don't understand. I hate Kind Heart. I wish Kind Heart were truly dead! Kind Heart should have died with my father!"

Jenna's hand flew to cover her lips and she wondered how she could say such things. To speak ones mind was an offence her father had often warned against committing.

"You're tired, Lady Jennava, you must have traveled all night and today you've lost your friend... perhaps you should go to your chamber and rest... come, I'll escort you there..."

Her eyes locked for a brief second with the king's and she discerned both pain and kindness in their depths.

"I... I have no chamber here. I am... I have never been welcome in Baron Sidney's castle... I cannot rest here, I'll go home..." Her eyes flickered quickly around the parapet, the crenellations, the walkway, the battlements.

Jenna had met Judith here many times. Often Judith had been followed here, but before Jenna's presence had been discovered, Jenna had made her escape. Gathering her skirt in one hand, Jenna turned and pulled herself up into the crenellation with the other.

"Lady Jennava! What are you doing? Come down! Please... come down..." King Cyranius reached his hands out toward her, but did not move. He knew they were at the castle's highest point and as his heart raced within his chest, he was afraid that if he rushed at her, she would topple over the edge. The color drained from his face.

In that instant, King Cyranius knew that he cared for this irksome lady in a way he had never cared for any woman. He willed her to live, *Let her live*, he prayed urgently. It was as though his heart stopped with the dread of the thought of her falling to smash upon the ground beneath the castle. A feeling of anguish, such as he had never known, swamped him.

Captain Ross and the guards also stared in horror at the lady. She calmly turned before dropping, disappearing over the edge. The men gasped as one, in horror, then all held their breaths. None moved for some seconds, they waited to hear the dreaded 'thud,' as she landed on the ground. Not a sound came to their pounding ears.

Copying King Cyranius as he hauled himself up into the wide gap, Captain Ross stared down, down, down the side of the shear drop to the gravel road.

"No! I can't see her! She's gone!" the king cried. He felt ill. His head swam—he hated death, and disliked heights.

"She's gone! She's not on the road! But... she can't just disappear—look, there's a ledge there, not far down," Captain Ross said, his eyes scanning from the top, searching for footholds. Turning around, he slowly copied the lady's actions and holding on to the ledge, he lowered himself over, sliding his boots downward until he felt a crevasse in which to place the toe of his boot. Inch by inch, he lowered himself until he reached a concealed sill. Leaning out with his face pointing upwards, he called, "She must have entered this portal here, Sire."

"Then go on in and see if you can find her and we'll follow... we'll come down... down the steps..."

Fifteen

The staff servicing Gifford Castle was not unduly surprised when Lady Jennava turned up, late afternoon inside the castle, demanding that a hot bath be prepared and food brought since this was a repeat of other occasions.

While waiting Jenna asked an older, lesser servant to request that the Controller of Castle Security, Captain Duff, come to her office to meet with her. It was protocol to inform him that she had returned home. Also, she wished to inquire as to the well being of the two guards wounded by Knight Red and his men. Her castle seemed to have an overabundance of king's guards, in place of her own castle guard. The old servant confirmed Jenna's own thoughts; the king had taken over Gifford Castle.

"Captain Duff be gone off to be with his wife and children. Y' see milady, the king has been here and he gave your captain leave and others who had been thrown in the lower dungeon. One of the king's captain's in command here... and others of the king's orficials have been put in y'orfice... what with Sir Polonius and Sir Tory still bein' in the cap'tal, y' know, like at the king's palace. Still, king's orders they say an' y' see, a lot of dispatches has arrived, all sorts of letters an' scrolls, an' they be busy takin' care of the communeecashins milady..."

Jenna had seen the king's flag flying on the topmost tower of her castle and she knew that King Cyranius had not only been here, he had commanded his own captains to manage the security of the castle.

"In that case, I'll be unwelcome in my office. Therefore, perhaps by the time I've bathed and dined, I'll not have too long a wait before the king attends us here..."

"Oh, but the king is gone, m'lady, he went to Mayern..." the old servant's voice trailed off when he realized that it was Lady Jennava that the king had gone to find.

"Never mind, Maurice, he'll return soon. I'm sure of that!" Jenna could not understand why she felt such dread at the thought of being close to the king again.

~ * ~

King Cyranius left Mayern less than half an hour after Jenna had disappeared. He had commanded that the castle be searched, and when she was not found, he decided she knew a way of leaving the castle, undetected, and had, as she said, returned home. How she left the castle was a mystery, as was the place she had left her horse.

"Perhaps," Captain Ross suggested, "Kind Heart was waiting for her. He's been in and out of this castle before..."

"Yes, but can you imagine Lady Jennava climbing all the way down the wall?" King Cyranius was in a mood that he could not understand— one half of him was anxious as to the lady's safety, and the other half felt furious with her.

"It's hard to imagine, Sire, but she did climb from a great height at the palace," the Captain replied, adding, "Perhaps Kind Heart was waiting to guide her feet to the portal ledge just down from the parapet. I can't imagine she did it alone. Then, she just disappeared."

The king did not speak. The matter was exasperating and he felt deeply angered that he, the king, had ridden all the way to Mayern to speak with Lady Jennava and Kind Heart and they had both made a fool of him. The look on Captain Ross's face did not suggest anger toward Lady Jennava, but a definite expression of marvel. King Cyranius's anger increased and he felt less kindly toward Lady Jennava, perceiving that one of his closest captains, a friend from childhood, was untowardly enamored with the insubordinate lady.

As he rode back to Gifford Castle with his escort, the king decided he would not allow Lady Jennava to slip through his fingers again. It would not be easy, for she was in her home territory and Kind Heart obviously knew all the secrets of Gifford castle. He cogitated on how he might keep Lady Jennava in check. *Words,* he told himself. *Words on paper... I shall have a document written and we shall see if Lady Jennava will not submit to it. The pen is stronger than Kind Heart's will.*

~ * ~

Having bathed and dined, Jenna decided to seek entry to her office. Three men worked there, discussing the communications received, placing them in order of priority for the king.

When Jenna was announced to the office, they ceased their talk and script to stare at her.

"If there are communications I need to receive..." Jenna began, feeling like an intruder. This was her office.

The eldest man spoke, "We've been commissioned by King Cyranius to organize the communications for his perusal..."

"There's nothing for you to do," a younger man said, while the third man added,

"We have it well under control."

"Then I take your leave, gentlemen," Jenna said, adding, "If I may ask one question. Are Knight Red and his companions... still residents in the lower dungeon here?"

The three men looked from one to the other, then the eldest answered, "No, Lady Jennava, Knight Red... he was... transported... early this morning... elsewhere."

"Elsewhere?" Jenna asked, feeling both surprised and dismayed, "Where?" When the man did not reply right away, Jenna asked, "Is it a secret?"

"No, Lady Jennava," the man replied, "King Cyranius sent him and his men, with an escort, back to Aponia."

"Was Knight Red and his men, in chains?" Jenna asked.

"Yes, they were transported in two carts..."

"How many of the king's men rode in the escort?"

"Forty."

"Forty of the king's men for twenty bandits?" Jenna questioned, then added, "I pray that they reach the border with no outside interference..."

"You think Knight Red has other... men waiting... that perhaps he could... return here?" the man asked, his voice trembling from nervousness.

"Not here," Jenna replied, "but I feel sure he'll make trouble... elsewhere... perhaps Mayern... but then, you three should be the first to receive his new demands, and you're all brave enough to deal with that." She managed to keep her tone light, eliminating expression of her inner sarcasm.

The three men stared at her, then at each other.

"The king's soldiers will see that they cross the border into Aponia," one of the younger men said, "on our part, we support the king's decision. He'll not invite war with Aponia... you must know, Lady Jennava, Knight Red was here with King Maslen's blessing... to capture and take Kind Heart to Aponia... to answer... charges..."

Bowing her head but slightly, Jenna spoke before exiting, saying, "If the king wishes to speak with me, I shall be in the library."

~ * ~

Lady Sidra reined her horse to a halt when she saw that it was as she had perceived. Knight Red was ahead with his men chained in two carts, escorted by forty of the king's men.

Speaking decisively to her male counterpart, James, she knew she had his support to make a rescue attack.

The place ahead was perfect and Sidra barked orders to her men to divide into two, overtake the company from the sides, then ambush. Reining her horse back, she guided him off the road and up an embankment from where she could watch the action in safety.

~ * ~

The guards at the gate of Gifford Castle gave the king the news he expected—Lady Gifford was in residence and she had been there for over an hour. He questioned his guards about her arrival.

"No, Your Majesty, she did not ride through the gate and her horse is not in the stables."

King Cyranius spoke to Captain Ross, saying, "Organize this company and the siege company to surround the castle and form a watch of the wall, from all points. If either Kind Heart or Lady Jennava, comes or goes from the castle, we need to know at which point the exit or entrance was made. Have the men search the woods for horses."

~ * ~

Captain Ross, with two guards, entered the library to check if Lady Jennava was actually there. Leaving the guards outside the door, he returned to the king to report her whereabouts. That she was where she had announced would be a surprise, he knew.

~ * ~

King Cyranius entered the library with Sir Lowell, Captain Ross and a scribe following.

Jenna was seated at a reading table near the window, not reading the Bible open in front of her but watching the king's men out of the window. She could see them keeping within view of each other around the outer perimeter of the castle and others, searching the woods, while yet others were setting up camp. Having seen the king's arrival, Jenna wondered at his delay in seeking her out for himself. She now felt impatient to have the interview over, to have the king take his guards and leave her castle. She hoped he would return to his palace and send both Polonius and Tory back to Gifford. *If only things were as before. I hope the king will recognize my status as owning Freedom of the Realm, surely he'll understand the importance of keeping his father's bequest to my father and me.*

"King Cyranius, King of Cyran," a guard at the door announced. "Sir Lowell, Commander of Kingdom Security and Captain Ross, Second Captain of the King's Army."

King Cyranius entered the library, and Jenna stood to curtsy.

The king sat in the chair Jenna had vacated and his eyes fell upon the open Bible on the desk. Folding his arms, he looked up at her with a forbidding set to his face.

Sir Lowell spoke on the king's behalf, "Lady Jennava, we have two matters to discuss with you. The first is the matter of your father's... more personal... records. We believe there's another office in this castle—one in which these records are held. We have a team of selected men waiting downstairs, to take every book off of the shelves here in the library so we may discover any secret portals, or, Lady Jennava, you may choose to cooperate and save us time and prevent any damage to the books."

Jenna hesitated—she did not want to open Kind Heart's office. This was one of the last places she wanted King Cyranius to discover. How could she have been so unprepared? Her mind ran over the contents of the office—how much would the king discover from the diaries therein? Both her father and herself had been meticulous in their writings that they did not divulge Kind Heart's identity, but all records—every quest, every escapade, the location, the names, if known, of the rescued victims were in the diaries. Jenna looked at the king, and her eyes linked with his. She could not endure the disapproval she read in their depths and she bowed her head. The king was determined to pursue Kind Heart to the end. How could she fight this overpowering king tide? One by one, he was tearing down each secret in order to ensnare Kind Heart.

Jenna knew that she would have to sacrifice the office secrets and the safe in order to conceal the more crucial secret exit from this library. The office had an exit to the wall, but the other exit linked with the main secret passages in the castle. If every book were pulled out from its place, the secrets could well be discovered.

"Well, Madam?" Sir Lowell demanded.

Jenna kept her head bowed, deliberately stalling. If she appeared at all eager, they may guess that the library held another much more important secret.

"Madam?" the commander persisted.

"I am *not* a madam!" Jenna said severely, keeping her head bowed. That they believed her to be one, was obvious, but she felt their false presuppositions hard to tolerate.

"Shall I bring the men up, Sir?" Captain Ross asked.

"No," Jenna interjected, "I'd prefer not to have books or the shelves damaged... many of the books are very old, some are fragile..." she again paused, intentionally.

In a low voice, she told them what they wanted to know, "There is an office off the library here and you're right, Sir Lowell, my father's records are within. Another secret cavity contains a safe for the family jewels, I believe. We've not opened the latter for some years."

"You do not wear the Gifford coronet... or the tiara?" the king asked. Barons often wore their golden coronets, and baronesses delighted in their jeweled tiaras with matching necklaces and earrings.

"I have never had the occasion," Jenna said, then speaking while turning away from them, she continued, "I'll show you the office... it would be most difficult to open it without the right key... the wall would have to be demolished... and I'd hate that." She strode across to the open door. Closing it, Jenna twisted the ornate door handle around, unscrewing it. "That locks the outer door, gentlemen," she informed them, "short of battering it down, no one can enter now."

Shadowed closely by the three men, Jenna moved to the far corner where she removed two large volumes from the shelf. Using both hands, Jenna unscrewed the doorhandle shaft, opening it to reveal a key-like instrument attached to the inside of the shaft. She fitted the key into the matching groove in the wall behind her. A series of clicks sounded out and the men stepped back as one. The whole wall of bookshelves swiveled around to reveal a room.

The four stepped into the large office and Jenna hurried to the large desk intending to light one of the large oil lamps. However, before she could do so, a large hand clamped over hers.

Sir Lowell reached out with his other hand and felt the lamp. It was cold. He strode around the desk to the open book and felt the other. "I thought so, it's still very warm and someone has been here very recently." Taking the flint from Jenna's hand, he lit the two lamps.

The king has chosen well in Sir Lowell, Commander of Kingdom Security, Jenna thought, *He's as sharp as a sword tip, sharper and he misses nothing, his mind's eyes are constantly seeking for things unseen by others.*

The open inkwell, the open diary and the abandoned quill, all spoke the same message. Someone had left in a hurry.

"Kind Heart, of course," the king spoke for all. While he strode around the book-lined chamber, Sir Lowell sat at the desk and moved the lamp closer to the open book.

"There'll be another exit from here..." turning, the king looked at Jenna.

"Yes, of course," she said at the same time running her mind over the words she had just written in the diary. She moved to the place of the exit. Removing a book, she plied the key and opened the wall. "You may need a light," she said.

"Where does it lead to?" the king asked.

"To the outer wall."

"Is it far?"

"No, Your Majesty, quite close, about a dozen steps away."

"Then we shall take a look... perhaps you'd like to lead the way?"

Jenna did not answer, but stepped into the narrow passage. Captain Ross followed, holding the lamp high to send light ahead.

The passage ended at a stone wall. Using both hands, Jenna pressed appropriate places and a small section swung open. The wind was sucked forcefully into the passage and the lamp was extinguished. Jenna bent to step out on to a ledge built on the outer wall of the castle.

Captain Ross stepped out beside her, followed by the king. There was room for just the three.

"This ledge is concealed from below," Jenna explained. "I use that rope ladder, behind us, to climb to the ground.

King Cyranius peered over the low wall at the edge of the ledge. Stepping back, he leaned on the castle wall. "You... you climb... a rope ladder... all the way down there?"

"My father told me that a fear of heights is only because you concentrate your eyes on the ground, Your Majesty, if you treat the present place as being equal to the ground and do not focus downward, then there's no danger of dizziness," Jenna said, speaking in a congenial tone of voice.

"That's what I do," Captain Ross said, agreeably. To him, Jenna was a wonder. His eyes shone as he stared at her.

King Cyranius saw admiration written all over his captain's face and he frowned. "I shall try to remember that, next time I need to escape," he said, sarcastically. Still looking at his bemused captain, he added, "As for me, I like my feet planted firmly on the floor." Turning, he entered the passage again.

"It's astounding, Your Majesty!" Sir Lowell said, standing as the king reentered Kind Heart's office. "All his exploits... the past three years... but how he travels so far and so fast... his horses must be outstanding." He waited for Jenna to follow Captain Ross into the office, then said, "This latest diary is written by your hand, Lady Jennava. Kind Heart dictates to you and you are his scribe... he returns here after his travels... this is his headquarters is it not?"

Though Sir Lowell asked a question, Jenna knew he needed no answer. She bowed her head, feeling that if anyone guessed her identity, it would be this detective-like man. *Although he does not look like one, he has the mind of a ferret,* she thought, *and the eyes of an eagle.*

Sir Lowell stood, asking, "How did you and Kind Heart know we were coming? The outer library door was not locked when we arrived?" As he spoke, the soft sound of a high-pitched 'ding-ding-ding' rang out loudly. The men's eyes all turned upward to the sound.

Jenna pointed up at the small gong, nestled among the books on the highest bookshelf. It was connected to the wall. "There's your answer, Sir Lowell. One person has just stepped on the first three steps ascending the one narrow step-way leading to the corridor along which is this library. I heard nine rings and knew that three people were coming. I had plenty of time in which to extinguish the lamp, exit from this chamber, replace the books and return the door handle to the outer door... then to seat myself to be somewhat composed when you entered. She bowed her head, hoping that Sir Lowell would not go out on the ledge. The door to the passage was still open. If he saw that the ladder was up, he would be asking how and when she managed to go out there as well to raise the ladder, and he would know that Kind Heart had not exited that way.

But Sir Lowell and the king, together, read from the diary upon the desk. They were silent as they read, the king turning the pages, first of all backwards, then flicking the large volume closed and opening it to begin at the front.

"This diary was started when the younger Kind Heart began his exploits... with Lady Jennava's father, Lord Frances Charles Gifford. There's a mass of reading here..." the king said, looking at Jenna, "You have been very helpful Lady Jennava, for which we are grateful. Perhaps you could save us time and tell us what we need to know..." he paused and Sir Lowell took up the question.

"Where has Kind Heart gone and what is his name?"

A heavy knock, though muffled, sounded out on the library door.

"Your visitor has arrived at the door," Jenna said, thankful to have this interruption. How many times would she have to reaffirm the vow her father had forced her to take? "Shall I replace the handle and open the door?"

"Yes," the king replied, "but leave this office open—we shall have all the books examined and the relevant ones transported to the capital."

Followed by the guards, a messenger stepped into the library, saying, "I was sent from the office with a communication, addressed to 'Kind Heart-care of Lady Gifford,' it's marked 'urgent rescue—life or death'..."

"I'll take it," Captain Ross said, "return to your duty," then to the guards, "stand guard." Closing the door, he carried the sealed scroll to Sir Lowell who broke the seal.

Jenna entwined her fingers together, feeling indignant and frustrated. These men seemed determined to take over her life! She would fight it until the end.

Puzzlement flooded Sir Lowell's face. "It has a few words and numbers, it must be some kind of code," he said, passing the scroll to King Cyranius who was now seated at the table, engrossed in the last diary written by Jenna's father. He turned pages, seeking for the entry concerning Prince Edward's kidnapping and rescue.

"Sire?"

King Cyranius took the scroll and glanced at it. Scarcely looking up, he tendered it to Jenna, commanding, "Read it for us, Lady Jennava."

Jenna read the scroll to herself.

"I meant aloud!" the king snapped. He had found the entry for which he was looking.

"A small child has fallen down a dry well shaft... the well is narrow, very and a man cannot fit... down it..." Jenna's eyes flickered across to the opening leading to the outer wall. How providential that she had not closed the exit. "It's a task for Kind Heart..." she began.

"You must not," Sir Lowell said, stepping to her, grasping hold of her arm to prevent her making a dash for the exit. Before he realized what was happening, he found himself crashing forward, falling to the floor. With an imperceptible movement, she had unbalanced him.

Captain Ross extended both arms, preparing to catch her as he rushed to follow her sudden flight. Before he could utter a word, she was gone and the narrow exit closed noiselessly in his face.

King Cyranius rushed to the wall. "We need the key, but it's in the outer door... the doorhandle... she... how did we let her get away like that?"

Captain Ross, feeling foolish and confused, shook his head, while Sir Lowell rubbed his sore shoulder. The latter had no idea how he had landed on the floor, somehow he had tripped. He glanced back at the stone floor by the desk. What had he tripped on?

"Shall we pursue her? Sire?" Captain Ross asked, "If she informs Kind Heart, then perhaps we'll find them both at that well."

"But what well? Where is it?" he asked, "She took the scroll with her..."

"She... she has to get through the cordon, Sire," the captain said lamely. He had no doubt that she would. "I'll go... and see what I can discover... which way she went..."

Sixteen

Kind Heart arrived at the site of the well in Sweetwoods Village, just inside the District of Zerka. Captain Duff, who had written the message, waited at the edge of the well. Millie stood, stony-faced, as if in a trance. An ancient little man, Millie's uncle, sat on the ground with his head in his hands. Small children hovered around but were kept back by their fearful mothers. Jenna recognized a small boy and a toddler as being Captain Duff's sons, Aaron and David. Villagers stood brooding, now silent, staring in awe at the newcomer.

The captain's voice trembled as he said, "It's our Jenny... she had been crying, but she's stopped... not a sound now... what can we do? It's been over two hours... I can't fit in the hole, or I'd have climbed down and we can't dig around it for fear of burying her..."

Having peered down the small hole between the half-rotten boards across it and called to the child without a reply, Jenna strode back to Oak, removing her hat and gloves and lifted a thick coil of rope off the back of the saddle. Sitting as close as she dared to the hole, she knotted the rope around her ankles, one by one, to allow them some freedom of movement.

"Lower me down the shaft... take care to listen when I call stop and I'll pull Jenny up. Take heart, Captain, there is a draught of cool air rising from the shaft... unless she's badly injured, she should be safe."

"It is a long way down Sir," Millie's voice spoke in Jenna's ear, "Her cries were faint. You might need extra rope."

Another length of rope was added to the first and a villager went to fetch more.

Jenna bent her head into the hole, pulling herself downward. She wondered if her shoulders would fit through the opening. If it got any narrower, she could get stuck. Reaching with her hands ahead, she doubled over at her waist. The shaft had widened.

As Jenna was lowered headfirst down the well, down, down, down, her mind flew back seven years to the birth of her namesake, Millie and Duff's eldest child. The girl had been born just after she had begun riding with her father as Kind Heart. A new Jennava had been born and a new Kind Heart had been launched.

The lowering of the rope ceased, and a voice, now muffled, shouted, "We're adding more rope, call out when you get there."

Although Jenna was very robust, she could feel the pressure of blood pounding loudly in her ears. Down, down, down. She feared the child's condition, falling this far. But in her experience, she had found that children survived under fearful conditions where an adult would perish.

"Jenny... Jenny... wake up," she called. She felt the girl's hair, her head was slumped on the cold clay floor of the well. Feeling around in the cold air that fanned her face, Jenna could not feel any of the sides of the base of this well. She wondered if water had once entered from wherever the draught was now blowing.

The girl woke and began flailing her arms in the air, swinging at Jenna in a dangerous manner.

"Ahhh!" the girl screamed. Then, "Who... who are you?"

"They call me Kind Heart..."

"I knew... I prayed... you'd come!" her trembling voice had a slight lilt in it.

"Are you hurt?"

"My... my feet... I landed on them... I think it is broke... my knee, it bent... I can't stand up... I'm going to be here forever... I prayed and prayed, but God can't hear me down here..." she began to sob.

"Hush, darling, your mommie and dadda are up there, Jenny, waiting to take you home. Lift your hands and let me grasp your wrists, Jenny.

"I can't. I can't get up."

"You don't have to Jenny, dear, just let me take your arms and I'll hold you." Jenna wrapped her hands around the girl's thin forearms as she lifted them upwards.

"Pull us up!" she shouted, hoping they would hear. "Pull us up!"

The rope had been extended to its limit and Jenna knew that they were deep in the earth.

Up... up... up, they were hauled, the young girl crying out, repeatedly, "I can't! I'm going to fall! I can't hold on anymore."

"I've got *you*, Jenny, you don't need to hold, just relax," Jenna called. Taking a deep breath, she exerted all her concentration to maintain the tiring grip on the girl's arms. She would not think of the depth of the well, how far above the bottom they were now—she must hold on, and never let go.

Men pulled on the rope until they hauled Jenna's feet up and out of the shaft. Taking her feet and legs, they dragged her across the splintered boards. Gravel grazed along her leather mask and down her left cheek and chin. A spear-shaped piece of wood dug deep into Jenna's neck but her cry of pain was lost in the exuberant cheers and applause as men took hold of Jenny's hands and pulled her to safety.

Young Jennava was hugged and kissed and cried over, while the girl complained loudly, "My legs are broke!"

Tugging the spear-like splinter from her neck, Jenna felt a warm wetness flow into her hand. She pressed the small puncture in her neck, realizing this was the first time she had been injured. Pain stabbed up her neck and into her jaw, and she sat with her head bowed, pressing the wound fiercely, feeling her heart throbbing beneath her fingers.

"Are you hurt... Sir?" Captain Duff's voice was filled with concern. Drawing his dagger, he cut the knotted rope from around Jenna's riding boots. Crouching closer to the motionless figure, he urged, "Let me look... Sir..."

"No. I'll be all right!" she said in a determined voice, waving him away. She stood up with her back to the spectators who now craned to see Kind Heart. Dizziness swamped her and she realized she had become upright too fast. The earth seemed to revolve all around her and Jenna felt foreign feeling, faintness, engulfing her. Captain Duff supported her, helping her to remain on her feet and not fall forward.

"It's all that upside-downess," he said, "and you're bleeding, Sir, let me look."

"Help me to my horse, I must go," Jenna urged. She did not want to see blood, never did she want to see blood. It made her feel faint, the thought of it. As well as sharing the role of Kind Heart with her father, Jenna shared his phobia, the sight of blood. As long as she did not have to look at it she would be all right. She closed her eyes not wanting to see what she knew was on her hands and running down her leather vest.

Captain Duff sensed Kind Heart's weakness and pried her fingers away from her neck, unaware that within him, he wondered at her hands, though bloodstained, being so small, so slim. He pushed her head back. Descending sunlight fell on Kind Heart's mask. The graze on her lower cheek bled but the other wound, a deep puncture, ran with blood. Using his large thumb, he pressed the incision fiercely, holding her head with his other hand, drawing it against his strong shoulder in a vice-like grip.

The villagers' attention went back to Nancy, the old midwife who examined Jenny's legs, declaring that one was twisted at the knee. She gave instructions to a boy to fetch wooden splints and a bandage.

Jenna closed her eyes and her head spun in an alarming manner. She felt herself go limp and blank.

"That's right... just let it be for a few minutes and it'll stem," Captain Duff kept his grip on Kind Heart's neck, wondering at the same time if he should urge Kind Heart to lie down. He thought better of it. Kind Heart was believed to be invincible.

Jenna heard a volley of voices, all inquiring about Kind Heart, but she kept her eyes closed waiting for Captain Duff to finish with the pressure he administered. At the same time, she determined to make the captain swear secrecy regarding the injury. *I hope I can hide it, or questions will be asked... a link could be made.* Then she wondered, *Does it matter? One way or another, the king is going to find me out... perhaps it'll be this injury.*

When the captain finally proclaimed that bleeding had ceased, Jenna said gruffly, "Tell no one about that, Captain Duff."

"About what?" he asked, and smiled.

"And... tell your family, and the villagers... keep the rescue secret."

His eyes met hers. He stared at her glistening, dark-brown hair, obviously a wig, at the thick moustache, the mask, then he asked, "What rescue?"

He walked with her to the side of her horse.

"Have the well filled in, tonight, right away, with gravel," Jenna said, pulling on her hat, then her gloves. She did not leap into the saddle as usual, but accepted his leg-up. Yet a little unsteady, she urged Oak into a canter.

Jenna stabled Oak, washed the blood from her hands and changed back into the black gown. Opening a box in Kind Heart's chamber at the end of the secret passage, she drew out a flask that her father had told her was to be used only when she sustained a wound that bled. All the huts had similar medicine boxes in them.

In the light of the lamp she had lit, she read, 'Drink a mouthful and rest an hour. Take another mouthful, repeat four times.' She smoothed an arnica-based paste on her cheek and neck, all the time wondering at the potion—it was over three years old, what if it were too old to do any good? She needed to find the recipe to make fresh, she told herself. Drawing a deep breath, Jenna removed the stopper and drank a large mouthful from the flask. It was very bitter and sour. She waited, but the pain did not diminish. *I don't feel very brave right now,* she told herself. *I won't want to go on another quest, at least, not for a few days.*

Arriving in her bedchamber, Jenna closed the panel and wished she could, indeed, lie down for an hour. Hurrying into her dressing-room, she snatched up a large black silk scarf and draped it around her shoulders and neck, linking it so that the folds rose up to cover her mouth and cheek.

~ * ~

The king heard three dings, followed by three more, then another three. Still in Kind Heart's office with Sir Lowell, he was reading a diary, completely absorbed by the dramatic adventures contained in the volume.

Captain Ross reentered the office, followed by Jenna.

King Cyranius got to his feet, staring at her as if he did not know her. He wondered how long it had been—it did not seem more than an hour or two... but he had been so engrossed, time had lost its meaning.

"What is the hour?" he asked.

"Sunset is about half an hour away," Captain Ross said.

The three stared at Jenna as she announced simply, "I'm back. You had another matter, Your Majesty... you said there were two matters... we've seen to one, you're here in my father's office..."

"Kind Heart's office," the king corrected. "He's an exceptional young man. I'd most certainly like to have a close encounter with Kind Heart. These records reinforce that we have much to thank him for..." he looked at the commander.

Sir Lowell took the prompt, "Yes, there's another matter we wish to inform you of, Lady Jennava... but we were interrupted in a most rude and unacceptable manner. We trust it won't be repeated. The other matter should indeed take care of it... I should speak of it now, Sire?" Receiving the king's affirmation in the form of a nod, Sir Lowell stepped backwards from the desk where he had been writing on a scroll. His voice took on the tone of an orator.

"Lady Jennava Charlotte Gifford, according to the laws of Cyran, you're yet a minor female, unmarried. You therefore require a guardian until you are of age, which for a female to be a landowner in your own right, is twenty-five years old. We have, on your behalf, written to your brother in the kingdom of Rosenberg, requesting that he receive you into his care until you are of age," the man paused then continued, "If, however, you marry, according to our laws, your husband will be your custodian. Until this matter is settled, either with your brother, or with a suitable husband, you shall be a ward of the crown."

Three pairs of eyes bored into her and Jenna felt crushed. She was most unprepared to receive such a dictate. She swayed on her feet, but not one of the men moved to support her.

Jenna grasped the one hope left to her, "What is to be done... about the Freedom of the Realm?" she then added as if by afterthought and speaking through clenched teeth because her jaw throbbed, "Your Majesty."

Sir Lowell spoke, and Jenna knew they had discussed this answer. It was a repeat, and expansion of that given back in the throne room, "Until we have ascertained whom it is that owns the legacy, it shall not be yours, Lady Jennava. Never was it offered to a woman. It belonged to your father, the Lord of Gifford, and, or, Kind Heart. The honor cannot be yours.

"You should introduce Kind Heart to us. Obviously you know where he is at all times... have you not just returned from delivering that scroll so he can make a rescue?"

If only you knew, Jenna thought, stepping forward to press the fingers of both hands on the desk to gain needed support. She struggled to hold back tears. The silence deepened and she bowed her head. A tear slipped down her cheek, followed by another. She could not ascertain if it were the pain from her throbbing wound or her loss that brought the tears.

"Tears, Madam?" the commander asked, unkindly.

"Why should I not shed a tear?" Jenna replied, looking at the face above his large frame. "I have lost my closest friend today, which is the worst loss, but I have also lost my home." They did not speak, and Jenna lifted the black scarf to blot her tears and said, "My brother has already made it clear he does not want me."

"When did he tell you that?" the king asked.

"He was present at my father's funeral," Jenna replied.

"It's difficult to believe a brother not wanting his sister. He does not want you?" the king persisted.

"No... Charles does not want anything to do with me."

After a short silence Captain Ross asked, "Because... because of Kind Heart?" he did not add the thoughts of all three men. *Who would want a sister who had an unholy alliance with an itinerant do-gooder?*

"It's not as you believe," Jenna began, then added, "but it *is* because of the character, Kind Heart, in that you are right. Charles wants nothing to do with Kind Heart. He would not take the role and when he inherited our mother's, brother's estate in Rosenberg, it was a way out for him. But... but Kind Heart and me... it's not as you believe but it's not the right time for me to explain—like Polonius and Tory, I'm under an oath... and even if I could tell you... you would find yourselves unable to believe... it," Jenna looked at the men's faces, one by one, all staring at her. They perceived she was speaking under great duress.

The king's frown was the most difficult she had to bear. With her eyes on his, she said, "I do not blame you, any of you, for your false assumptions. It... most of it... is my own fault."

Captain Ross felt sorry for Lady Jennava, something was different about her—perhaps she had been crying before coming here?

Sir Lowell frowned, feeling no sympathy for the lady who appeared to be distressed. One cheek looked a little swollen, beneath her left eye. He wondered at her wearing the scarf pulled up so high around her neck. It was a warm day. He sensed a medicinal odor in the room, and wondered if she had a sore throat and had rubbed some salve on her neck.

No one spoke for some seconds, then the king tried to close the short meeting by saying, "You look tired, Lady Jennava. We'll dine at sunset, then we'll all retire early. We'll leave at first light for the capital."

Leaning, now, palms down on the desk, Jenna frowned and said, "For myself, Your Majesty, yes, I'm very tired. I shall retire immediately. But tomorrow, I shall remain here at Gifford until Lady Judith's funeral, which I shall attend."

"Perhaps you did not listen, Lady Jennava," Sir Lowell said, "You are a ward of the crown and, as a ward of the crown, you do as you're told."

"Who then, who is my guardian?" Jenna asked, feeling fearful. She knew she would hate the answer.

"The king and his counselors, including myself, are responsible for you," the commander replied. "As I have successfully brought up four daughters and seen them satisfactorily married, you will be directly accountable to me and my wife who is at present in the capital."

"I have then, indeed, lost much today," Jenna said, now unable to keep the disdain from her voice, "Most of all, I have lost my freedom."

"If it's freedom to do as you please, to come and go and to allow this... this... that man, Kind Heart, to command your time and your life, then indeed, Madam, you have lost your freedom!" the commander retorted, then added, "For your own safety, you shall not leave this castle again until the morning when you shall ride with the king's escort. You shall attend dinner this evening in your great hall, as I understand you rarely do, then you shall remain in your bedchamber all night. Are we understood, Lady Jennava?"

"I understand your command, Sir Lowell," Jenna replied. Her tone left the men wondering if she would still dare to disobey.

Jenna found herself shadowed by two guards when she left the library. She pondered on perhaps exiting by means of a secret passage, of leaving the castle and never returning, but where could she go? To one of the little cottages, hidden deep in the forest? How long could she stay there? Loneliness was a thing Jenna hated. She enjoyed a little solitude, but not more than a day, at the most, two.

But to ride to the palace tomorrow morning? The long way around? To forfeit Judith's funeral? True, it would not be convened for at least a week but how could she not make her last farewell?

Seventeen

Jenna ate very little of the sumptuous meal convened for the king, in her castle. She felt extremely frustrated. It was one thing to obey her father when he was alive but to find herself, almost three years after his death deemed a minor under the command of a man whom she considered hated her, was a different matter altogether.

My father loved me, she reminded herself. *Love I can live with, but hate, it's soul-destroying. He hates me. I see it in his eyes. He disapproves of everything about me, everything I do. He's completely unendurable!*

To Jenna's surprise, after the meal a band of entertainers was announced. Entertainment? At Gifford? This was unheard of here. She longed only to lie down and rest.

In spite of the pain in her neck and her continued melancholy, Jenna enjoyed the clowns and particularly the jester's routine. There were jugglers also, and musicians. Their exhibition was carried out on nimble, well-trained feet, and Jenna was intrigued by the swiftness of the jester's movements. The clowns staged a sword-fight using similar progressions of movements to those her father had taught her, and the jester, with a well-practiced, elaborate routine, felled them all. He came close to where Jenna sat and bowed to her before bowing to the king. She clapped enthusiastically with everyone else after this concluding act.

The potion is working and my pain has lessened, she told herself, feeling better.

The king stood abruptly, and the hall became a wave of people standing, curtsying and bowing. Jenna realized how weary she was—she looked forward to a good night's sleep in her own bed.

It's been a while, she thought, watching as the king made his exit. *I'll appreciate my feather mattress tonight...*

"I'll escort you to your quarters, Lady Jennava," Captain Ross said.

I'm sure you will, Jenna said to herself. Captain Ross had been staring at her all evening. It was now obvious to Jenna that the captain was behaving as though captivated by her. Such open affection in a man's eyes was foreign to Jenna. A pair of guards joined the captain, forming the escort.

As her foot touched the bottom step to ascend the central staircase, the main door to the castle flew open and a young courier, still wearing his complete riding gear, hurried across the flagstones of the open foyer, followed by a guard. The messenger carried no scroll or pouch. Rounding the great pillars, he called, "The king! I must see the king! Where is the king?"

Jenna stepped back to the base of the staircase, watching as the man was directed upwards. He rushed past her.

"Stay close to Lady Jennava, and when she's safely in her quarters, stand guard outside the door," Captain Ross commanded then hastened up the stairs after the messenger. A verbal message of great importance was being delivered to the king and the captain wanted to be present.

Jenna had ascended only five steps when a young voice sounded out from the foyer below, "Lady! Lady Jennava! I came home to see you. Dadda and Mommie came with me." It was young Jenny.

The guards looked at each other, raising their eyebrows. They had no orders that denied the lady greeting some visitors.

Jenna stepped between the guards and down the stairs. Captain Duff, still dressed in his casual clothes, carried his daughter. She had one leg heavily bandaged to above her knee, and the other foot bandaged to the ankle.

"I broke my leg," Jenny informed her. The girl's face was flushed and she smiled.

"Remember, Jenny, don't talk about our secret," Captain Duff whispered.

The girl's younger brother, Aaron, lifted his arms for a hug from Jennava. He whispered in her ear, "She fell down a well and Kind Heart rescued her... we saw him, but Dadda says not to talk of it."

"I want to tell Lady," Jenny said, indignantly, watching enviously as Jenna caressed the hair of the toddler, David, half asleep in his mother's arms.

"Here, let me carry you to the upper sitting room, Jenny," Jenna said, taking the small girl in her arms. "We can talk privately there." She wondered that Jenny was so bright, so talkative.

"I wanted so bad to come home," Jenny chatted as her namesake carried her to the chamber, followed by the rest of the family and trailed by the two guards.

"Shut the door behind us, Duffy," Jenna said, using the familiar name her father had affectionately given his loyal captain.

Jenna sat on the long cushion-covered window seat, still holding the excited girl who began describing her adventure in detail.

Millie took her tiny son to a low sofa in the corner. Sitting down, she began nursing him. Aaron snuggled up, near Jenna, closing his eyes. Captain Duff dragged a footstool closer and sat on it. He looked weary. Struggling to make himself comfortable, he turned and pulled a fleece mat closer and planked himself down on it, stretching himself as if he would have slept.

"I surprised myself and felled asleep down the well, then when I woke, Kind Heart rescued me."

"How bad is your leg? Is it really broken?" Jenna asked, her eyes on the captain's face. She saw that he closed his eyes. Jenna relaxed.

"I can't walk on it at all. Dadda said it's sprained somehow. That's like being broke, isn't it?"

"Jenny twisted it badly," Duff said, his eyes still closed, "Nancy said it was a bad twist. She gave her some medicine for the pain... that's why she's a bit giggly."

"We're so grateful, Lady, that you managed to get Kind Heart to come so quickly," Millie's soft voice purred into the conversation. "We're so thankful. We just wanted to get back here..."

"He said not to speak of it," the captain said, his voice sleepy, "but we knew you would want to know. And Jenny wanted to come home. I wanted to know how Kind Heart fares. He... he sustained a wound. It was a slow journey home..." He opened his eyes, asking, "Did he get back? Have you seen him? Do you know how he is?"

"Kind Heart?" Jenna asked, then added, "Kind Heart arrived home safely... resting now..."

"I came to see you," Jenny said, hugging her again. Jenna winced, the girl was hurting her neck.

Captain Duff, having heard what he wanted to hear, let his neck muscles relax and closed his eyes. and Jenna wondered if he slept. It was something she liked to do too, snatch a few minutes sleep and awake feeling refreshed. She wished she could sleep now, but Jenny chatted on and on nonstop.

Jenny looked up at Jenna's closed eyes and said, "I'd like t' sleep too, like Dadda, but somehow I'se wide awake!"

"I should let you lie back on the cushions here," Jenna said, lifting her carefully off her knee, "and when your dadda awakes, I'll take you to your room.

"No, I'd rather stay with you!" Jenny cried, her voice strangely shrill. She clung to Jenna's neck.

"There, there, it's all right," Jenna said soothingly as the girl hid her face in the silk scarf.

"It was dark, in the well... I thought I wouldn't see you again... or Dadda... or anyone..."

The slippery scarf entangled in Jenny's arms. The silk slid off Jenna's shoulders. Jenny, using both hands, wrenched the scarf away, dropping it behind Jenna.

"Oh," she said, her voice shrill, "You did get a bruise! How did you get it?"

Jenna twisted around, reaching for the scarf.

"How did you get it, Lady?" Jenny asked, again, her voice fearful as her little eyes saw the raw wound, "it looks like you got stuck with a dagga—"

"It's just a graze." Jenna said, her eyes flicking across to see if the captain still slept.

Duff stared up at Jenna, frozen, unable even to blink.

A sense of vulnerability flooded Jenna's veins. *This is what it will feel like, to have people realize the truth. I will be forever hated... misunderstood...*

Captain Duff sat upright, wide awake, open-mouthed, staring at her. The puncture, under her jawbone, in her neck, was red and angry, swollen with deepening blackness haloing it. His eyes moved upwards to Jenna's cheek, also bruised, grazed. The side of her face was noticeably swollen. He closed his eyes, bowed his head and shook it, opened his eyes, stared at her again.

Jenna snatched up the scarf. Her eyes again met with the captain's.

He gaped at her wound, the bruises. Closing his eyes, he sought to recall which side of Kind Heart's face had been injured. Disbelief changed into enlightenment, then amazement, again disbelief. His face paled, then reddened. He stood and turned away from her, pacing across the floor, his head bowed.

Turning, Captain Duff's mind teemed with a myriad of images of Kind Heart—Kind Heart's father, Lord Gifford, Lady Jennava. Quests, messages, rescues.

Striding back, the captain knelt in front of Jenna as if to take his daughter into his arms. Instead, he took Jenna's hand in his own and turned it over as if searching for blood. But it was the smallness of the hand he sought to compare. Like a flash of light, he realized this was the same hand.

"Tell no one of this, Captain Duff," Jenna whispered.

"What?" Jenny asked, her voice now a little sleepy. "What don't we tell?"

"What don't we tell," he repeated softly, lifting his daughter into his arms. "Lady Jennava is tired, we shall all retire to our quarters. Perhaps we shall see you at breakfast, Lady?" he turned, and called, his voice trembling, "Millie... you... you're... not asleep, are you? Millie..."

Turning back, he watched Jenna replace the scarf around her neck. "You should have some compound put on that... that... graze, Lady," he said softly

"I've put something on it, Duffy... it feels better than when... it happened... I'll put more on it... and yes, I'll see you at breakfast. It'll be early. After that, the king is leaving for the palace and I—"

The solemn sound of the outer castle warning bell interrupted Jenna's words—clang-clang-clang-clang-clang, summoning the military to amass in the castle courtyard. The off-duty sentries in the village and surrounding cottages would come from as far away as the bell could be heard.

Jenna's eyes met the captain's—they both wondered what calamity triggered the need to amass the military.

"I must go, Lady..." he began.

The door flew open and a messenger entered.

"King Cyranius summons you into his presence, Lady Jennava."

"Where is he?" she asked.

"In the sanctum, Lady," he said, following her as she exited the chamber, "it's most serious, Lady Jennava, it is."

Eighteen

Jenna was announced into her office to find it alive with men in uniforms. The guard called her name a second time and the room grew quiet. Eyes turned to look at her and men stepped aside as she drew closer to the king who sat at her desk. She curtsied, waiting. King Cyranius did not look at Jenna, nor speak. A deeply perplexed frown creased his handsome brow. Bowing his head, he stared at the floor.

Sir Lowell spoke and Jenna noticed his voice had an entirely different note in it. Instead of arrogant disdain for her, he was notably respectful.

"We request that you fetch... or find... Kind Heart and give him a message, please, Lady Jennava." He tendered a scroll, holding it as if he half expected her to refuse. "It is of grave importance. You're free to leave the castle and take the message to Kind Heart. After that, we request that you return here and report to me, to remain in safety of the castle."

Jenna wondered if this were a trick, a trap set to capture Kind Heart. Taking the scroll in her hand, she looked at the king and curtsied.

Sir Lowell again spoke, "Tell Kind Heart that the king will be riding from Gifford district within the hour... if Kind Heart wishes to consult with King Cyranius, or if he needs assistance, the king and his army shall be amassing outside the palace as soon as the steeds can carry us there... hopefully before sunrise."

Jenna saw that every eye was on her. Turning, she left the office. A feeling of emptiness, of aloneness, swamped her. Something was wrong, dreadfully wrong. The king needed Kind Heart. But why? Jenna hurried to her quarters, conscious that no guards, no one, followed her. Quickly checking that her quarters were uninhabited, Jenna locked the door and hurriedly broke the seal, opening the scroll near the bright lamp on the small writing desk in her sitting room. The message read:

Kind Heart,

We received communication from Knight Red that he escaped his escort, rode to the capital and has seized the palace. Prince Edward is hostage in the palace. Knight Red demands an exchange—Prince Edward for you. If you are able to rescue Prince Edward, we shall forever be grateful.

Cyranius V, King of Cyran.

"Prince Edward," Jenna breathed the name, recalling his bright personality, his humor and intelligence, his liking of her. Was he now a prisoner of Knight Red?

Jenna wondered that the king had not offered some kind of reward or bribe but then she realized that the king was far too astute to do such a thing. Kind Heart already owned the Freedom of the Realm, what more could the king give? And Kind Heart was known for his ability to right wrongs and to rescue the innocent. Closing her eyes, and wanting only to rest, Jenna also wished she could postpone this difficult quest for at least a week.

Crossing to open a secret cupboard panel in the wall, Jenna poured herself a mug full of a similar energy blend to the one she had made at Mayern. She drank the contents.

A fist hammered at the outer door of Jenna's quarters and the handle was tried.

"Lady Jennava! Lady Jennava!"

Recognizing the voice as belonging to Captain Duff, Jenna hurried to unlock the door.

Now dressed in his uniform, the captain stepped into the room, closing the door soundly behind him.

"I heard that Knight Red has the prince... at the palace—it's unbelievable! They said that Lady Jennava has been requested to take a message to Kind Heart about the crisis. May I be of help to you, Lady?" he asked.

"Yes," Jenna said eagerly, thinking, *I'm not feeling up to this, any help will be beneficial.* "Fetch a horse... one from the Baronial Stables, either Thunder or Moon, and bring two coils of rope. Meet me at West Crossing as quickly as you can, Duffy. You must ride alone."

"West Crossing, Lady?" Duff's question was doubtful. One did not ride west, to go north.

"Kind Heart will be waiting near West Crossing for you, so make haste," Jenna replied, "You must ride out the Gifford Road ahead of the king's company."

Saluting, he hurried from the chamber, reminding himself that a captain did not question his commander. But how could she possibly be waiting for him at West Crossing? She was still here!

Jenna hurried from her bedchamber running all the way through the confines of the secret passages to Kind Heart's secret chamber and changing quickly into Kind Heart's riding gear. Gathering up her dress, she selected some small but useful equipment, pushing it all into a leather bag that she would strap to Oak's saddle.

The stables in the woods were unusually silent. Jenna remembered that Garth was still in the capital. She saddled Oak. Before leading him from the cave, she realized that she had not prayed as was part of her commission as Kind Heart. Kneeling to pray she sensed her deep need, both physically and spiritually, for help beyond human resources. Also, had she not promised Judith that she would seek God until she found Him?

Please, God, help me to find You, and to know You in the same way that Judith knew you... she knows You now... she's with You now... God please help me... Unbidden tears flowed down her cheeks.

Oak snorted impatiently and stamped his feet, interrupting Jenna's respite. Leading him from the cave, out through the dense thicket, Jenna mounted and gave him his head to canter along the narrow woodlands paths, guiding him ever west, cutting through forest around which Captain Duff would ride. Light from the moon lent silver to the trees, illuminating the circuit she knew so well.

Jenna had but a short wait for her captain. She saw him coming in the distance, taking the west turn from the Gifford Road towards the crossroads. One road went north, the other south, then just a hundred yards down the road, West Crossing split the road into two more—one pointing south, the other to Zerka District.

The captain reined his horse near the milestone at the crossing. Jenna urged Oak to join him. He rode Moon, and the two horses greeted each other excitedly. Reaching over, Jenna petted the side of Moon's face and he nuzzled her hand with his nose.

"Give Moon his head, Captain, I'll be out in front—just make sure you hold on well. There are a few tricky patches, especially on the mountainside. Turning, she pointed north, right into the moonlight. We go up over there."

Captain Duff stared at the dark wooded mountain range ahead, his mouth dropping open.

"It's really quite straightforward," Jenna said lightly, "especially after the crossing above the waterfall on Lesser Mountain.

"Good boy," Jenna spoke to Moon, then she whistled softly and said, "Follow Oak, follow."

Jenna arrived at Kind Heart's cottage on the north slopes of the mountain range, just before midnight. Leaving Oak to graze, she hurried inside and lit a lamp, set a fire in the fireplace and lit it. Fetching cool water in the urn, she laid the tiny table for two. Going to a cupboard, she opened a metal chest and placed some of the contents on two plates at the table.

When the captain arrived, it was to find a hot herb drink waiting, together with some strange leathery biscuits. Jenna, having soaked her portion was already eating.

"My father taught me to take adequate sustenance before embarking on a quest that commands physical and mental skills. Eat them, Captain, you'll receive both sustenance and strength."

"What are they?" he asked.

"A mixture of fruit and fungi, pounded to a leather and dried in the sun. The herb drink will give you energy to keep you going all through the night."

While the reluctant captain ate and drank, Jenna outlined her plan to rescue the prince.

"Don't try to be a hero, Captain, the one thing we need to keep in mind, is that we're here to secure the safety of the prince. After we have rescued Edward, I'm sure Knight Red will want to leave the country as fast as he can. We just need to remove his negotiating power."

Nineteen

Irregular night silence and nighttime sounds portrayed that the capital city slept, unaware of the drama enacted inside the palace. Jenna slithered down the trunk of an ancient tree having left Captain Duff perched high in its branches.

While climbing the southern palace wall, she reasoned that Knight Red had sworn the occupants of the palace to secrecy, threatening the prince's safety if city residents were informed. *If the city had known,* Jenna thought, *few would have slept and a large crowd would have congregated. Knight Red must have silenced the guards and replaced them with his own men.*

Jenna laid the wire over the wall between the spikes.

Clinging precariously to the edge of the wall, Jenna waited while guards sauntered past beneath her. Peering down at their retreating figures, she saw that the men wore the uniforms of the king's guard. *By their swagger... they do not march in time... they're Knight Red's men,* Jenna thought, then, *or, this could be a trap, set by the king... but his coconspirator would not expect Kind Heart to be here yet. He would not believe Lady Jennava could have delivered the message so rapidly... I must watch that I don't walk into a snare... but I cannot conceive that Cyranius would use his brother as bait... no, but Knight Red is possible of such a diabolical tactic as finding a way to enter the palace and holding the prince hostage... he would have known the king was in Gifford...*

Lowering herself over the wall then dropping to the ground, Jenna waited patiently as a large dark cloud moved lazily toward the bright three-quarter moon. Listening and watching, she stayed, frozen in the dark shadows as a guard strutted around the far corner of the palace. Wearing no uniform, but well decorated with weapons, the ornamentations of which glinted in the moonlight, this man's stance was barbarian. His appearance gave Jenna the answer—strangers, indeed, were here at the king's palace.

Drawing a deep breath of summery night air, Jenna waited as the man walked the length of the southwest wing of the palace. He paused in a crook beneath the round wall of a tower. Deep voices carried to Jenna, men asking if 'all was well,' affirming that it was. One man emerged, continuing his orbit. He disappeared into another nook, and Jenna wondered how far his circuit would take him.

Darkness intensified and Jenna, releasing strong wire from the coil she carried, hurried across the short distance between the sentry wall and the palace itself.

Climbing the very vines she had once descended, Jenna was as noiseless as a hunting cat. The window at the top was open and the bedchamber in darkness. Drawing the wire tight now, she climbed above the window and fixed the wire firmly around the thickest vines, crimping it with a small tool. Feeling her way to the bed, Jenna found it empty. The sitting room was in darkness and Jenna cautiously opened the outer door, just a slit. The corridor was lit by the lone flare of a torch, shining brightly in its stand, three doors ahead. Soft murmurs of voices drifted to Jenna. Four men slouched on the carpet, playing a game with dice and cards. Two others stood to attention outside the door, their granite-like faces lit by the flare. Again, Jenna perceived, these men were not king's guards, but were mercenaries. She wondered if they were Knight Red's men—they were better dressed than she remembered his men.

Closing the door, Jenna hurried back to the outer window. She climbed around the vines, then along the outer wall, carefully counting the windows. Each guest apartment had three.

The ninth window, like the others, was open and Jenna climbed inside the room. Whoever slept here was indeed important if six men had been commissioned to guard the door. The palace was vast and Jenna felt sure that unless Knight Red had somehow solicited help, his twenty men would be stretched to their limits. It seemed too simple that the prince was in this guest chamber, too easy, and Jenna felt every nerve in her body tingle, on guard.

Moving soundlessly across to the bed, Jenna knew that someone slept here—the breathing was heavy, almost a snore. It could not be the prince. Kneeling down, Jenna deftly swung her backpack to the floor. Removing her gloves, she pushed them into a pocket. Reaching into another pocket, her fingers drew out strips of strong fabric.

Jenna slipped behind the net curtains of the four-poster bed, wishing she had a light. Patting the bed with a feather-touch, she knew someone small slept there. Scarcely touching the form, she moved to the face. It was a child, and Jenna felt sure it was the prince. He stirred a little at the light touch of her hand on his cheeks, but did not wake.

Who sleeps on the other side of the bed? she wondered as she crawled around. She felt a flask on the floor, such as a man would carry for his liquor. *It must be Knight Red. The breathing is heavy, he's been drinking, it could well be Knight Red, or else someone he trusts enough to have sleep with Prince Edward...*

Jenna's fingertips sensed that the feet in the bed were those of an adult and she moved to the head. With swift, decisive movements, she gagged the person's mouth, threw back the quilt and bound the two hands. To Jenna's surprise, she heard the rattle of chain-links. One hand bore a shackle. This adult was chained to the junior person in the bed. It was a woman's dress that she felt as she hurriedly knotted the ankles together. A woman. The female captive began to contort and writhe in the bed. Protesting grunts were silenced as Jenna pressed on her throat, with a gruff warning, "Not another sound!"

"Who's there?" a trembling boyish voice came to Jenna's ears, and she heard his in-drawn breath. Believing he was about to yell or scream, Jenna dived across her captive, reaching for Prince Edward's mouth to prevent him uttering another sound.

Slowly Jenna loosened her hold, asking, "To whom are you chained?"

"Lady... Lady Sidra," the prince said, then asked, "Are... are you... Kind Heart?"

"Yes. I'm going to remove the chain, then we'll leave..." Jenna felt for the small pair of pliers in her pack. Within seconds, she forced the links apart and, although he still wore a shackle on his wrist, the prince was free. Like Lady Sidra, Edward was fully clothed.

"I'm sure you can climb, Your Highness?" Jenna asked. Not waiting for an answer, she pulled a harness from her bag, saying, "I'm going to strap you to me, and I'll support you."

Prince Edward found his voice again, saying, "We'll have to hurry. Knight Red ordered the guards to check on us twice hourly. I must have fallen asleep, so I don't know when they came last..."

Jenna fed her hands into her leather gloves and secured the backpack fixing the harness on her back as well.

"Let's go..." barely had the words escaped her mouth than Jenna heard the outer door being unlocked. "Go."

The prince followed Jenna, but they had just climbed out over the ledge when the flare of a torch lit up the bedchamber. The guard swore, and a shout sounded out loudly. The flare poked out the window, and Jenna saw a man's face staring out at them as she guided the prince along the perilous ledge.

"Get out there, after them!" a man's voice called, and one man climbed out the window, slowly following their flight. Shouted suggestions made Jenna realize that they would go to the other rooms to try and prevent the escape.

"Call Knight Red!"

"Get men on the ground, they'll climb down when they reach the vine!"

Prince Edward forced every muscle in his body to move as fast as Kind Heart urged. Soon he felt strong vines under his hands and feet. But instead of climbing down, Kind Heart guided him upward.

"Climb up further," Jenna hissed, pulling on his hand. After a slight hesitation, the prince obeyed.

"Keep still and quiet, they're in the bedchamber below us."

Above the window now, they clung to the vines, watching as men's heads appeared, looking downward.

"They've gone! They must've reached the ground!" one man called.

Jenna held her breath, expecting them to look up toward them.

"Get down there with the others!" another shouted.

A woman's voice joined them, screaming, "Get going you fools! The prince must not get away!" It was Sidra.

Jenna tugged firmly on the wire, once, twice, three times. It rose higher, until completely taut. Jenna knew that Captain Duff had not slackened in his watch. With care, she fixed a round wheel over the wire, carefully securing the metal clip so that the wire was enclosed.

Her mind flicked momentarily to the last time she had used this wheel for a rescue. Her father had been at the other end. It had been a long time since she'd had someone to work with who knew her as Kind Heart.

"Put your hands right through the straps, and hold tightly to the straps at my shoulders," Jenna instructed, gripping the wheel's hand-piece. "Don't look down and don't let go!"

Knight Red's men, together with a dozen of Lady Sidra's small army, arrived beneath the vine to hear the sound of a strange whirr above them. As the descending moon glanced out between the clouds, a strange figure was seen to fly overhead—Kind Heart, bearing the smaller form of the one they knew was Prince Edward.

The men stood, open mouthed, staring upwards, turning as the apparition flew out over the palace wall, disappearing into a row of ancient trees.

"He flies"

"Kind Heart can fly!"

A shrill voice screamed loudly from the window between the vines, "You fools! He does not fly, he has a rope! Look! Follow him! Climb up there and follow him! If he can do it, why can't you?" The answer came with a snap as the wire was cut by Kind Heart's hand.

Jenna felt pleased that she had estimated the height of the guest-room windows so accurately, that the flight had gone without a hitch.

You cannot afford the smallest mistake when life is at risk, she recalled her father's warning.

"You did it! You did it!" Prince Edward said excitedly, clinging now to a branch, and looking back, over the top of the wall to his palace home.

"You did it!" the captain agreed.

"*We* did it!" Jenna corrected, adding softly, "We couldn't have done it without you, Captain."

An ominous voice sounded out in the predawn air, "Get out there and find them! Don't let them escape!" It was Knight Red.

"They're up in the trees over the south wall!" another man shouted.

"Are you going to fight them?" Prince Edward asked.

"Not this time," Jenna said. "Hold on to me as before, Your Highness. You must leave before they arrive."

Jenna let down a length of rope and slid to the ground, followed by Duff who quickly mounted Moon. "Please get on the horse, Prince Edward," she urged.

"I'll ride with you, Kind Heart," he said defiantly.

"Not this time," she said, lifting him bodily off the ground and handing him to the captain who moved forward to give the prince space to ride tandem behind him.

"Another time?" he asked eagerly.

"We'll see," she said, as she mounted Oak.

She watched the captain urge Moon to walk between the trees and out of sight. Turning Oak, she guided him closer to the wall, waiting.

"Look, there he is! Kind Heart!" a deep voice called. Jenna saw the leader of the pack, holding a flare, pointing a crossbow at her. Lifting her feather-plumed hat from her head, she waved it, waiting for them to move a little closer.

Urging her horse into a canter, she rode towards them but behind the trees, out of the range of the bow, around the last tree and towards the outer city street. Now galloping Oak, she hoped the ruse would work and Knight Red would follow her. She would lead him east, then south, before turning back towards the west.

Very soon, Jenna perceived that no one rode in pursuit. She turned off the main road to gallop across well-known meadows through a wooded area and back to the city's south side.

~ * ~

The captain and the prince dismounted at the preplanned place near a small wood, high on the closest southern hillside where Jenna had left a pack of food and basic supplies.

"Lie down, Your Highness, rest," the captain urged, spreading a thick rug on the ground.

"Is Kind Heart coming?" Prince Edward asked.

"Kind Heart will join us soon," Duff said, his eyes turned towards the palace and his ears ready to hear hoofbeats.

"It looks as if they are having a party in our palace," the prince said. It seemed every light had been lit, light glowed from most portals of the central building.

"Ah... Kind Heart... here comes Kind Heart," the captain said with a glad note in his voice.

As Jenna reined in Oak and dismounted, the prince stood, pointing and staring down at his home. His mouth fell open, but words did not come.

Turning, Jenna's eyes followed the path of Prince Edward's pointed finger.

"They... they've set fire to the palace," Captain Duff said, his voice disbelieving. Flames darted hungry fingers from windows and balconies. An explosion of flames within the palace sent larger flames spewing out the higher windows. The fire grew in intensity, spreading rapidly.

"The trees..." Jenna said, looking across to the ancient belt of trees, now a blaze of orange flames, fanned by the wind blowing from the west. She felt shocked to her very core. The prince was safe, but not the residents of the palace.

"I did not imagine Knight Red would do such a thing... I should have suspected such a deed. Stay here, Captain... stay with the Prince," Jenna said, "Don't move from here until I return myself or send someone for you."

"Where... where... are you going?" Prince Edward asked, his voice trembling.

"I must see if anyone is trapped in the palace... and fire could catch on thatched roofs. I must warn people to move out of danger... help them... the children..." she pulled her horse around, repeating, "Stay here, Captain Duff, and keep Prince Edward safe!"

Twenty

A foreign orange glow pulsated in the northern sky, flickering brighter, and yet brighter. Above it, an enormous black cloud billowed, moving lazily east.

"What can it be?" Major Frayne asked.

"I've no idea," King Cyranius replied, puzzled, and alarmed, "I can't imagine... we should be able to see when we gain the next rise." He urged his horse into a gallop.

Having gained the crest, the king stared in horror, pulling his horse to a halt as he tried to comprehend the scene before his eyes. The capital city was ablaze. To the left of the city, a pall of black smoke rose from the palace, illuminated by flames from the city itself. The city was so bright, it seemed an orange sun illuminated it. Yet the sun had not risen. King Cyranius blinked away threatening tears, knowing he was too late. Half the city was burnt out and the other half impossible to save.

"Edward! We must find Edward... and... my people... their children..." Fear and dread rose in his throat as he spurred his horse into a gallop. Before a mile had passed beneath his horse's hooves, he discerned that the road ahead teemed with people, fleeing the city. A quarter-mile ahead of the evacuees, rode a company of palace guards.

They met head on, yet a mile from the city gates, and quickly learned the awful news.

"Kind Heart rescued Prince Edward, and the burning of the palace and the city was Knight Red's reprisal."

"Where is Prince Edward?" the king asked.

"Kind Heart took him to a safe place, he said."

"The palace? How bad is it?"

"Knight Red poured oil into every chamber, Sire, on every floor, beneath every tower, apart from the brick structure, the marble pillars, and the shell, it's burnt out."

Another guard spoke, trying to offer consolation, "Kind Heart said that it can be redecorated and refurnished. He said that the stairs, the walls and the structure are sound but the fire has destroyed all wooden fixtures, the furniture and the furnishings. To quote Kind Heart, Sire, we must thank God that no lives have been lost. Kind Heart released scores of guards trapped in the south towers of the palace. Knight Red had intended to capture Kind Heart when he came to rescue them, but Kind Heart made the rescue first and the joint company sent both Knight Red and Lady Sidra, and their cohorts all on their way... he—"

"Lady Sidra? She was there?"

"She was part of it all, Sire. It was Lady Sidra who attacked the company escorting Knight Red... it was her idea to ride to the capital and seize the prince while you yourself were away, Sire. It was Sidra who came into the palace with a phantom message from you, Sire. Prince Edward came for the message, and she grabbed hold of him. Her men produced crossbows and there was no other course to take than to protect the prince's life, to do as they demanded."

The other guard spoke, "We are hoping, Sire, that you'll commission a company to ride out and see if there were any survivors of the original fracas, when Sidra released Knight Red. Our brothers were in the company, Sire, and some of them were left on the cart in the chains worn by Knight Red's men. We asked Kind Heart to send men out there, but he said they had to stay until the people in the city were all safe... and he wanted the refugees to have protection in case the bandits returned but now, everyone should be out of the city, so...”

“See to it, Major Frayne,” the king agreed, “and take enough men to make sure that Sidra and the knight are riding in the right direction. We don’t want them to return to Cyran again!”

The king stared at the devastation ahead. *If they could do this... in one night...*

“Send me word as to which direction Knight Red and Sidra are riding.”

The leading evacuees drew closer.

“Is everyone leaving the city?” the king asked, wondering where they could all go. He had no home now, either.

“Kind Heart suggested that we stay together and that we go to Gifford District. He said that the court could reside in Gifford castle and the city people would be welcomed into the village. We’re to send word to Gifford to have food and water sent out to meet the travelers, Sire, and he said he’ll have tents brought in from Zerka and Mayern to house the military.”

King Cyranius was speechless. So much had happened, so much decided, and he was powerless to stop this tidal wave, the abandonment of his city.

~ * ~

The sun was rising over the eastern hills to be greeted by a mixture of dark clouds and smoke, when Jenna, riding Oak, led Cloud up the hill towards the small woods where she had left Captain Duff and Prince Edward. Moon, cropping grass, looked up at the sound of her approach.

Prince Edward was deeply asleep, oblivious to her presence.

The captain strode to her side, as if to assist her to dismount.

“I’m not stopping, Duffy, I’m going home... there’s so much to do... I must send food back for the evacuees, the last have just left the city for the twelve-hour walk and they’ll have to rest on the way. I’ll send carts for the children and the aged, but it will take me three hours to ride home.”

"Three hours? You can't do it in three hours!" he exclaimed, doubting, "it took us longer than that."

"We came the longer way over Lesser Mountain," Jenna said, "There's a shorter way over Tulip Mountain."

"Over... over Tulip?" he asked, aghast. "You ride over... that?" looking up, he saw that the peaks were covered, swirling with dark clouds. "Your horse is too tired, Lady..."

"You're right, Duffy, Oak is too tired." She drew Oak close to Moon and climbed across on to the latter's back.

"Not bareback!" he exclaimed, "Let me put the saddle back on him..."

"Less weight..." she looked down at the prince, asleep on the rug, his back to them both. Pulling off her mask, then her hat, she said, "Wake the prince and give these to him. Take him down to the city gates—his brother will soon be there, waiting. I told a guard that I would send Prince Edward to the gates. They'll all be traveling to Gifford, Duffy, but make sure you take them the long way around." She smiled with him, then added, "Take the provisions with you, the king will be in need of some sustenance, there's little that's edible left in the city."

With a wave, she turned Moon and rode up into the woods.

Twenty-one

Icy rain fell on Mount Tulip and Moon slithered and slid on the treacherous schist as Jenna flicked the reins to encourage him to continue with the ascent through the narrow pass. Even at this height, sleet was uncommon for this time of year. During the winter, Jenna would never have attempted this traverse—for three months the mountain was covered with snow. In winter, even the journey over Lesser Mountain was treacherous.

Dismounting, Jenna braced herself against the angry elements and led Moon across the razorback path. The rain drenched her face and ran down her neck, soaking the silk scarf she had tucked in to hide her injury. She wished she had kept Kind Heart's hat, it would have given her some protection now. How could she have forgotten how changeable the weather could be on the higher mountain? Jenna hoped the refugees would not suffer such a downpour.

The journey took Jenna almost four hours and when, beneath the mountain clouds, she caught sight of her castle bathed in sunshine, she felt great relief. She shivered, not from being so wet, but from the fierce fever that possessed her.

The cave-stable was silent and Jenna entered Kind Heart's room feeling faint from fatigue. Swiftly pulling off the wet boots, she also threw down the leather trousers, the vest then the under-vest. Lined and padded, it disguised her femininity and was also a body shield and it could repel a sharp arrow. The wig was sodden and she was wet to the skin. She removed her lace-edged chemise, then dressed in the last dress she had left in the room, a black gown with a full skirt, suitable for riding. She paused only to drink from a flask to quench her burning thirst.

I long to rest but I cannot, she urged herself. *I must order the food and carts to be sent. I told the king's men I'd take care of this ... the children will need food... it's a long walk...*

Mounting Moon, Jenna rode through the woods and around the front of her castle to the gates. As lady of the castle, she commanded immediate attention from the few guards who had remained, and very soon carts were being loaded with barrels of water and food supplies.

"The king and his court will be traveling on the road south to Gifford here, and they'll need these supplies as quickly as we can have them conveyed there," Jenna said. She drew in a deep breath, feeling dizzy, ill.

"We need guards to escort the carts... and we must close the castle gates here... Knight Red could ride here yet..."

"Lady Jennava, they said you were here," Millie rushed upon her in the castle courtyard. "Do you know anything about Duff? He's been gone all night and I don't know where he went."

"He went with Kind Heart, Millie, and he'll be with the king when they return," Jenna answered, feeling breathless.

"Lady... you're not well..." Millie said in concern. She lifted her palm to feel Jenna's brow, "you have a fever!"

"I'll... I'll... be all right, if I can rest..." Jenna said. She longed to lie down on her own bed. The stone walls seemed to rotate, and it was as if the mountain cloud descended upon her, stealing her strength away. Jenna struggled helplessly against her weakness.

"Lady Jennava! When did you return?" the commander hurried down the steps to the courtyard, "How long have you been here?" His eyes took in the carts and the supplies being loaded. "What's going on here? What are you doing?"

"Sir Lowell!" Jenna stared at him, trying to remember why he was still here. Should he not have gone to the capital with the king? She felt lightheaded, confused, "I... the king... the palace, it... burnt... Knight Red... everyone is coming here..."

Jenna could fight her fever no longer. Closing her eyes, she succumbed to the blackness that enveloped her.

Castle staff, loading food supplies on to the carts, stopped in surprise. Lady Jennava was being supported by Sir Lowell and Duff's wife, Millie. No one could recall the lady ever being ill. A tall footman strode over and gathered Jenna into his arms.

"She done fainted," he said, his voice filled with amazement. "Don't just stand here, Millie, fetch Doctor Breck. I'll take her to her bedchamber." Looking at Sir Lowell, he said, "Go ahead, Sir, tell someone to open the doors for us."

Twenty-two

The instant they arrived at Gifford Castle, King Cyranius and Prince Edward were given the news, "Lady Jennava is very ill. Doctor Breck says that she has been struck in her neck with a poisoned arrow and she suffers a dangerous fever. She may not recover..."

"We must go to her," Prince Edward said, determined. Although extremely weary from having ridden the magnificent white horse nonstop from the capital to the castle, he yearned to see her again and was most grieved that she was ill.

"Who fired the arrow?" the king asked quietly, moving closer to the guard who had voiced the bad news.

"No one is saying, Sire, but I think... when the lady was distressed with her fever, she revealed something..."

"We'll both go to her," the king said, stroking his horse's nose before striding around to his brother's side. He wondered if Kind Heart knew about his ladylove's injury. That Kind Heart had rescued the horses from the burning royal stables, was yet another reason to be grateful to the courageous rescuer, the king thought. *I'm indebted to them both... if*

Lady Jennava had been unable to take the message to Kind Heart, I cannot begin to imagine where Edward and I would be now... at best, waiting upon Knight Red's designs. But... now she's wounded... ill... He would not admit to himself or anyone else, that he wanted to see her. Perhaps the guard had exaggerated and she was not so ill... how could she possibly have been hit in the neck by an arrow? A poisoned one at that? Who would do such a thing?

To the king's surprise, Sir Lowell sat by the bedside, cradling her small hand within his large one.

Millie and Doctor Breck attended Lady Jennava who lay, pale and still. Her neck was swathed in a bandage holding fast a poultice that Doctor Breck had applied to draw out poison from the wound and to bring about healing.

Millie curtsied low and the doctor bowed. Sir Lowell stood, also bowing.

"Who did this?" the king demanded.

The doctor shook his head. Millie was speechless, she had never before been so close to the king.

"We should speak about it alone, Sire," Sir Lowell said, then asked, "My wife... Edris... do you know, Sire... is she safe? The palace? Was it truly... burned?"

"The inner palace was destroyed and will have to be rebuilt," the king began, and his brother spoke at the same time, his voice flat, "Lady Edris was rescued by Kind Heart. We were all rescued by Kind Heart." The lad's eyes were upon Jenna. He thought she looked very ill.

The king spoke again, "Lady Edris has been very brave. She is accompanying some young children and their mothers in a score or so carriages that were removed from the grand-houses before they caught fire." While he spoke, his eyes remained on the lady's face—she lay so still that she seemed as one who was dead. He could not distinguish whether or not she breathed.

"What... what... is your... prognosis... Doctor?"

"The fever has diminished, Your Majesty, but if she does not regain consciousness enough to partake of some liquid and nourishing food, then there's no hope."

"No... hope?" the prince asked, his eyes wide, "do you mean... she will die?"

"I'm afraid so, Your Highness," Doctor Breck affirmed, "she's not deeply unconscious, but seems to be more in a state of lassitude... as if suffering exhaustion. We... Sir Lowell and I... we've been trying to wake her, but I'm of the opinion that she does not wish to be awakened. Lady Jennava has always been very strong, both in mind and body." Turning to the commander, the doctor said, "You should tell His Majesty, Sir Lowell."

"Tell us... what?" the king demanded.

"I need to walk," the commander said, his eyes passing a message to the king that he did not wish to converse here, in this chamber. "Perhaps Prince Edward would take my place... Lady Jennava seems comforted by having her hand held." Prince Edward needed no second urging. Sitting down, he lifted the lady's hand to rest between his two, surprised to feel it was quite warm. She looked so pale, he had expected her to be cold.

~ * ~

"While Lady Jennava was ill with her fever, she repeatedly said that Kind Heart was to blame—it is Kind Heart's fault that she was wounded. She said that Kind Heart was not careful enough... of course, Sire, I pressed her about the matter and she did not take kindly to it. She did not want to speak about it, but with my persistent questioning, she said that Kind Heart's failure to think ahead had caused the injury." Sir Lowell told the king, "I didn't think it to be a good idea that the prince hear such words against his hero."

"Did she say that Kind Heart actually fired the arrow?" King Cyranius asked, feeling puzzled.

"No... and she said it was not an arrow, but a spear of wood—to me, the same thing, but again, I have to admit that she was a little delirious at the time... she spoke about her father and Kind Heart, as if they were harsh task-masters in her life, she seemed bitter toward them both."

"She has spoken against Kind Heart before," the king said, "it was after Lady Judith died. To speak frankly, I was confused. It is as though

161

Kind Heart torments Lady Jennava. How could he save so many lives, but treat his lady with such callousness? She spoke of hating him. Is it that she dislikes his exploits, that she is afraid for him, that he will be harmed? It's very puzzling. I can't imagine Kind Heart wounding her in any way. It seems impossible."

"When she recovers, we'll ask her about it," Sir Lowell said. Although neither man said it, they both thought *if... if she recovers...*

"Then... when she recovers, wait until she's stronger before you question her again," the king commanded, adding, "Perhaps Kind Heart will come? Someone will tell him she's ill...? Keep a guard at her door, and keep me informed."

Jenna woke, feeling very thirsty. Her eyes focused on the handsome profile of the young prince who stared out the bedroom window.

Refugees from the city had been arriving for over an hour now.

Looking across the room, Jenna saw Millie, seated in a chair, nursing her youngest child. The old servant-woman who had brought the child to her, stared in wonder as Jenna pulled herself to sit upright, asking "Fetch me a drink, please Irma."

"Ahhh! But you're awake!" Irma hurried to the bedside, then bustled back to the sideboard, reaching for the jug of fruit juice and filling a goblet.

"Lady Jenna!" the prince's face broke into a wide smile. He had thought she would never wake. He watched as she took the goblet in her hands and thirstily downed the contents.

"Take David back to Nanny, Irma, and fetch Doctor Breck," Millie said. Looking at Jenna, she added, "He went down there when the carriages arrived. He wants you to have some soup if you can sustain it..."

"Perhaps I'll dress and go down and get it myself... I feel as if I have slept for a week." Pushing back the bedcover, she swung her legs over the side of the bed and attempted to stand. A deluge of dizziness swamped her, and she sat back on the bed.

"Lady, please... lie down, you're not fit to be up and about, not yet." Millie rushed to support Jenna.

"I'll go for Doctor Breck," Prince Edward said, alarmed. The lady had been near death, and now she wanted to rise and dress.

~ * ~

Doctor Breck was pleased with Jenna's progress—she consumed an amazing amount of the nourishing soup he had ordered to be kept ready for her. Then she slept. After ten hours, the doctor grew concerned again, the lady still slept! It was two hours more before she woke.

For three more days, Jenna slept the sleep of the dead, awoke to partake of the meals ordered for her by Doctor Breck, then again she slept. Color returned to her face and Jenna felt herself growing stronger. She longed to be up, out of bed, but Doctor Breck disallowed it.

~ * ~

Jenna stretched her arms and sat up in the bed, looking eagerly at the tray containing scrambled eggs and crusty bread-rolls, with a platter of every fruit imaginable beside it. *This is real food, I'm tired of all that soup.*

"What a pity," Millie said as she pushed the shutters wider, "Not a cloud in the sky... not a tear to fall from heaven..."

"Why would you want it to rain today, Millie?"

"Oh, it's all right, but, the blue sky matches her eyes."

"Whose eyes?" Jenna asked, then, before Millie replied, she knew whose eyes had been so very blue.

"Lady Judith, it's her farewell today. Pity, Lady, I know how much you would wish to be there. The service will start in just over an hour, then she'll be buried."

Jenna's heart raced. So it was today, this morning. She did not speak, but began to eat from the tray. She needed to take her fill; it would sustain her for the ride to Mayern.

Millie left the bedchamber with the tray, and Jenna, now alone, quickly dressed herself in a black riding habit and donned a hat with a concealing face-veil. Within minutes, she opened the secret panel, closed it and was hurrying along through the secret passages to the cave-stable where she remembered leaving Oak. *I don't remember if I left a food bag for Oak... I was so weary... I still feel tired, as if my strength has been drained away.*

A dull chipping, hammering sound came to Jenna's ears—someone was working just beyond the stone wall at the end of the passage. She knew she would have to backtrack and work her way around to the cave-stable through a different exit. She thought of Garth, he must have returned with the refugees from the city. *He will have shown the king and his men to the cave-stable, and they're determined to find the passage. It will take them a long while... but they'll likely gain an entrance...*

Jenna's fears were well founded. She crept into the cave-stable to hear men's voices mingling with the demolition noise. *King Cyranius has wasted no time in getting his men on the trail of Kind Heart,* Jenna thought. *But I'm not going to miss out on my final good bye to Judith. After that, well, after that nothing else really matters.*

Knowing that it would be difficult, if not impossible, to secure her own horse, Oak, Jenna decided that any one of the king's horses would do. She hoped the king's men had ridden around to the cave-stable and when she looked out, she saw that she had hoped rightly. Tethered in the glade, were a dozen horses, all on long leads. Not a guard was in sight. All the men were inside, working on entering the hidden passage, hoping to discover one of the most vital secrets belonging to Kind Heart.

Jenna ignored the pile of saddles abandoned on a tree stump, and mounted a horse, pleased that no one had been left on guard. Not a soul appeared to watch her ride off bareback, through the woods, towards the west before turning south, then east, completing a circuit around the back of Gifford Castle, keeping herself concealed from the guards on the battlements.

Dizziness flooded Jenna for the first mile and she kept the horse to a canter, then as she felt strength increasing in her trembling hands, the open road appeared and Jenna urged the horse into a gallop.

After five miles on the dusty road, Jenna took to the woods again, taking a shortcut from Gifford district and into Mayern, avoiding the small villages along the way.

Twenty-three

Jenna arrived at the baronial cemetery on the hillside a little east of Mayern Castle. She tethered the horse just inside the woods and painstakingly gathered a large bunch of giant blue forget-me-nots.

Wondering how long she would have to wait, Jenna carefully lifted her black skirt with her free hand and cautiously descended the steep hillside. Walking around the ornate iron fence, she opened the gate and sat on a carved wooden seat. She could see the massive headstone of Judith's parents' grave. Sidney had insisted that Judith's father be buried here, then Judith's mother's remains were transferred from the family cemetery to lie alongside him. Jenna had been present with Judith at the interment.

Sidney's ancestors, including his father, were buried in this cemetery. Jenna sat, remembering. Sidra had been heart-broken at the funeral. Her heartbreak had lasted for a week. When she learned that Sidney had inherited everything, she had begun her wandering, returning to Mayern Castle only for short periods of time. *Sidra has always hated me,* Jenna told herself, *and she hates Kind Heart even more... Sidra lives only for herself...*

A freshly dug grave solemnly yawned its earthy mouth, exhaling an earthy odor with not a soul other than Jenna to wait for its resident to arrive. Everyone else was at the castle chapel.

The sun still shone in a brilliant sea of blue, with not a cloud to offer the hope of sympathetic tears from the heavens. *How well Millie knows me,* Jenna thought, *she knows that I feel comforted if it rains at a funeral.*

The sound of singing came to Jenna's ears, and she knew the procession was moving from the castle chapel to Judith's final rest. It was the Twenty-third Psalm that sounded out, "The Lord is my Shepherd." The hymn grew louder and louder. Hundreds had come for this sad occasion.

At first, Jenna thought of nothing other than her dear friend, Judith, lying in the polished coffin carried by six matched pallbearers, Sidney's footmen, dressed in black. But as she stepped behind Sidney himself who walked alone she looked quickly around, feeling relieved that Sidra had not been such a hypocrite as to come today.

Brother Emil read comforting Scriptures, and the coffin was lowered into the grave.

Baron Sidney stood close to the open grave, he did not move and the minutes passed slowly. His shoulders heaved and he swayed. Jenna wondered if he would faint. She herself felt strangely tired—this moment hovered like the edge of eternity trying to enter back into time. Jenna remembered her vow: *I'll search the matter out, dear Judith, I will not rest until I feel sure in my soul that I will follow you to life eternal. I'll seek until I find.*

Jenna's eyes blurred and tears slipped down her cheeks. She brushed them with her black-gloved fingers and they melted into the silky fabric.

How lonely Sidney seemed, standing there. Women sobbed loudly but strangely, no more tears came to Jenna's eyes. *I feel I'm not wholly here,* she mused, feeling detached. *Perhaps it's my illness, but my wound is healed. Maybe I overdid myself and used too much stamina in rescuing the prince, then exhausting myself during the fire... after that, I rode home, over that cruel mountain, and it rained... I've never felt so drained... but I feel much better, just strangely apart from it all... like, it's not really happening ...*

Sidney cast a handful of soil into the grave, then stepped back. The six pallbearers took up spades and began to fill the grave. Before they had finished, Sidney turned away. He shot a brief, stricken stare towards Jenna, his eyes taking in the blue bouquet, but not recognizing her, he bowed his head and moved away.

Jenna placed her flowers on the soil mound and others moved forward to cover the grave with floral tributes.

Sidney had almost reached the road where footmen waited with his carriage, when a voice whispered urgently into Jenna's ear, "Lady Jennava Gifford, come with me, walk across to the gate and continue walking up. Come now, don't resist, or there'll be more graves to dig today! Knight Red has his arrow aimed at Sidney and others at the womenfolk. Move now, or they'll shoot! Come! Hurry! Lady Jennava!"

Jenna did not look at her companion, but stared up at the hillside above, where she had left her horse. Her blood pulsed much quicker through her veins. Knight Red stood beyond the cemetery fence, halfway up the hill, a loaded longbow in his hands. Some forty men stood in a semi-circle, above and around the perimeter of the cemetery. Most men pointed arrows loaded into longbows, those closer held crossbows ready to fire. If all these men released their arrows, then reloaded, the death toll would be great.

Knight Red is commander of this spectacle, she told herself. *I have to get to him, I have to stop him, or there'll be much bloodshed. Sidra's men must have joined with his, perhaps she's there... waiting... yes, there are horses up on the tree line. They'll have the horse I rode here. They're taking me so that Kind Heart will give in to their demands... they shall have us, both.*

Before the mourners could comprehend what was happening, Jenna, with one of the pallbearers gripping her arm, walked around the grave, and in the opposite direction to the crowd.

He quickened his step, urging her on, and Jenna heard cries of terror sounding out now. People in the crowd had seen the marksmen. She walked faster, not looking back, but kept her eyes on Knight Red, up the hill, with his hand up, waiting to bring it down if she did not obey her captor.

Many mourners hurried to crouch behind headstones, whilst others ran in the same direction Sidney had gone.

One of Knight Red's men was there, at the gate, holding it open, keeping his crossbow pointed at the diminishing assembly.

Sidney heard cries of terror coming from behind him, and he turned to look down at the chaotic scene. People surged out of the cemetery running towards him. His eyes moved beyond the gate on the other side of the cemetery where he saw the black-clad lady, a man drawing her along, his fingers gripping her wrist. She was now on the field-grass, moving up the steep slope. His eyes, scanning the slope, took in the extent of the stratagem.

Sidney had never seen Knight Red in person but he knew by the red hair and beard and the size of the man that this was the loathsome warrior from Aponia.

As one frozen, he watched the lady climb the hill. It could not be possible, could it? Lady Jennava was reported to be ill, seriously ill. He had sent a message to Gifford Castle, giving the time for the service in his chapel, stating that it would be followed by the interment, and a message had been sent back that Lady Jennava was too ill to attend.

"Quick, ride to the castle and have the bell tolled, tell my guards to ride here." Sidney watched his footmen run to carry out his command.

Mourners, having reached the roadside, turned to watch. A murmur rose as hoofbeats grew louder, horses were arriving, causing a cloud of dust to rise.

Knight Red's men began to ascend the hill, behind Jenna, turning to watch if anyone followed. They had orders to fire only if Lady Jennava refused to come or if others tried to prevent her.

Captain Ross, followed by a small group of king's men, dismounted their horses and pushed their way through the crowd, past Sidney's carriage and to the front of the gathering.

"Lady Jennava?" the captain asked, knowing he needed not to speak her name. The conclusion was obvious, he was too late and he had too few men. Lady Jennava was a prisoner of the dreaded Knight Red. He had come to check if she had indeed ridden here for Lady Judith's interment, but like the doctor and the king, he did not believe she could sustain the ride. He watched now as the lady climbed the hill, the black-clad footman assisting her, pulling her up behind him. Could it be her? Would she not be too weak to climb that hill?

"Where is Kind Heart?" the captain asked, his eyes examining the arena, hoping for a way out, but it was impossible.

"I haven't seen him," Sidney said hoarsely, adding, "If I'd dreamed it was Lady Jennava, I would not have left her at the grave... I cannot believe it is her... perhaps it is someone else?"

Captain Ross did not answer. The lady had arrived just below the savage assassin.

Knight Red reached his left hand down toward Jenna, still holding his loaded bow in his right hand. The footman stood beside Knight Red now, his fingers still around Jenna's wrist.

In a flash from the past, Jenna remembered one of her father's quotes: *He who hesitates is lost.*

It's now! she told herself. Taking a firm hold of Knight Red's large thumb, locking her fingers around it, Jenna pulled with all her might, throwing herself backwards as forcefully as she was able. Taken unaware, Knight Red and the footman lost balance and fell forward.

The footman released Jenna's wrist in shock, diving head first down the hill, somersaulting head over heels.

As Jenna fell backwards, Knight Red slammed against her, the bow and arrow folding beneath his right arm.

The point of the bow tore through into the veil of her hat, flinging it from her head.

Rotating sideways, they rolled over and over, down the hill. Jenna clutched Knight Red's wide leather belt, tucking her head in against his broad chest. She felt his arm grasp her around her neck, then slacken. They rolled faster and faster.

The speed diminished, and Jenna knew they were approaching the base of the hill. Not many feet away would be the iron fence. As Knight Red rolled over top of her, she released her grip on his belt.

The footman smashed, face first, into the iron fence, breaking his neck.

Knight Red rolled over, his back against the fence.

Slowly collecting herself up and shaking her hair from her eyes, Jenna heard the whistle of an arrow—it missed her head by a hair's breath. She saw the color of blood—it was on her arms, her black gloves and dress were soaked.

Knight Red lay with the arrow he had carried embedded deep in the side of his chest. His eyes were open, and Jenna knew he was dead.

An arrow struck its target, and agonizing pain tore into Jenna's thigh. She turned to see a furious group of Knight Red's men shooting arrows at her. The man closest released his crossbow bolt, but it flew wide.

Jenna backed toward the gate but she stumbled, the searing pain in her thigh threatening to bring her down. She could not bear the pain. Arrows fell to ground, all around her. Some ricocheted off the iron of the fence and the gate. An arrowhead pinged off the gate, gouging her forearm.

Sidney, Captain Ross, and the king's men, having rushed down to the cemetery level, took cover behind the headstones and brick surrounds closest to the fence. Arrows fell all around them. They feared the lady would not survive the deluge.

Sinking to the ground, near the gate, Jenna covered her face, praying, *Please God, don't let an arrow hit my face... who'll mourn me? Please God, I don't want to die, not yet. Help me to live, that I might have time to seek You. I promise, if You let me live, I'll keep the vow I made to Judith. I'll not rest until I search the matter out, I'll not rest until I feel sure in my soul that I will follow Judith... to life eternal... I'll seek until I find.*

The arrows stopped falling for a few seconds, and Jenna pulled herself up to stand, turning to look up the hill to see if the men had gone. Men with long bows had used all the arrows in their quivers, but those with bolts left were patiently reloading their crossbows. One man, his face distorted in fury, was not far from her. He stepped closer, the crossbow pointed at her. Jenna braced herself, expecting the bolt to hit her in the heart. She knew she could not run and stood her ground, hoping he would not shoot an unarmed woman.

A bolt tore into Jenna's shoulder. Other bolts fell all around her, two entering Knight Red's chest, other's finding resting places in the footman's body.

A woman's voice screamed ominously across the small valley. "Retreat you fools! Retreat!" The sound echoed across the cemetery and Knight Red's men retreated up the hill to the woods to their horses. Sidney's soldiers had arrived and were riding their horses around the outside of the cemetery fence, dismounting to swarm up the hill.

Captain Ross reached Jenna first, and he thought she was mortally wounded. He did not know that it was Knight Red's blood on her face, and in her hair, that it was not her blood that drenched her dress. She had an arrow embedded in the side of her right thigh, and a bolt penetrating her left shoulder. Her right forearm was gashed, bleeding. How could he touch her without causing her more pain?

Jenna felt her senses reeling, and she closed her eyes. *I must not sleep,* she told herself, *I cannot rest... I promised.* She was aware only of pain, then it ceased—she did not know she had fainted.

"Bring her up to the carriage and we'll take her to the castle," Sidney commanded, "Send word so that Doctor Thorn will be there, waiting for us."

Twenty-four

Jenna was jolted with cruel suddenness into consciousness. She gasped at the pain shooting down her leg, then up into her hip from the arrow stabbing her slender thigh. She wanted the arrow out!

Captain Ross had placed her on the carriage seat, and both he and Sidney sat opposite. The captain reached to hold her as she sat. She gasped from the pain of the arrows.

"Please, Lady Jenna, don't struggle, we're taking you to Doctor Thorn."

"Don't touch me!" she cried in distress, causing the men to sit back on their seat, away from her. Sidney had ordered the driver to drive the carriage as carefully as possible, but still it pitched a little over bumps and in potholes. "Leave me alone!"

Reaching across to the bolt in her shoulder, Jenna grasped hold of it. Being metal, it slipped against the leather of her glove. She peeled the glove from her hand, and took up a dry piece of her skirt-hem in her hand. Tugging fiercely on the bolt, she pulled it from her shoulder and dropped it on the floor. Gasping, she fell back against the leather of the carriage, closing her eyes. Blood oozed from the puncture.

"Keep away from me," she said, without opening her eyes. Neither Sidney nor the captain had moved, they both were too shocked.

Wrapping some of her skirt hem around the glove on her other hand, Jenna twisted herself so she could grasp the arrow protruding from her thigh with both hands. Drawing a deep breath, she tugged and tugged, until she felt breathless.

"Don't, Lady, don't do this to yourself..." Captain Ross began, his hand trembling as he reached across to her, wanting to stop her causing herself such pain.

"Leave me!" she cried fiercely and he dropped his hand.

Feeling the arrow move, Jenna exerted all her strength, drawing it out, gasping through her clenched teeth, unable to think of anything other than the pain. Dropping the wet, red, wooden weapon, she fell into a faint again.

Captain Ross lifted Jenna from the carriage. Mourners, congregating in the castle courtyard, watched in solemn silence as the captain, carrying the lady, rose up the steps into the castle following Sidney, who led the way to Doctor Thorn's clinic. At the doctor's direction, Captain Ross placed Jenna on a wooden bench-bed.

Jenna's senses returned to pain, bringing her to consciousness. Her eyes alighted on Sidney, and she knew she was in Mayern Castle.

"I won't stay here, take me home!" she demanded.

"We must take care of your injuries," Doctor Thorn began, then asked, "The arrows, they said she was struck by arrows... where are they?" He looked at her face and hair, covered with blood.

"She pulled them out," Sidney said lamely, backing away from the bench-bed where the captain had placed her and was now holding her arm to prevent her climbing down.

"Whereabouts, in her body, were they?" the doctor asked.

"One in her right thigh, and one in her left shoulder," the captain replied.

"I want to see the arrows, to know how deep they went," he said, "Fetch them."

Captain Ross left the room saying, "I must send word... to the king."

"Lady Jennava," Doctor Thorn spoke in a kind voice, "Allow me to tend your injuries, bandage them, then you may go home ..." to his relief she sank down on the wooden bench and closed her eyes.

"Leave us," he said to Sidney, and beckoned to his wife to bring the bowl of water to sponge the blood from her arm, to see the extent of the wound. Sometimes an arrow-wound would need stitching and sometimes it would close over and heal by being bandaged firmly.

"I want to go home," Jenna said as the doctor bandaged her forearm, then she sank into blankness again.

"I cannot rest," Jenna murmured as the doctor tended her shoulder, "I must go home... I have to seek..."

Plunging in and out of consciousness caused Jenna's temperature to rise. Beads of perspiration appeared on her brow.

Together, the doctor and his wife removed Jenna's riding habit, cutting the long black pantaloons from her legs. Sponging her with cool water, they bandaged her thigh firmly. This was the worst wound, and Doctor Thorn estimated by the blood on the arrow, that it had almost pierced her thighbone.

"She may suffer excruciating pain in the next forty-eight hours from this injury, we shall not move her anymore than necessary," he told his wife, then whispered that she prepare a strong sleeping potion.

Doctor Thorn's wife cradled Jenna's head while the doctor pressed a goblet to her lips. Jenna drank thirstily, and emptied the vessel. It left a strangely bittersweet aftertaste, but she had no idea as to its source.

"I need to go home," she said again, before sinking into such blissful rest that she was no longer conscious of pain.

~ * ~

When Captain Ross's handwritten scroll arrived, Sir Lowell read it first, before taking it to the king. As Commander of Royal Security, he had the right to receive the king's messages. Particularly so when a Captain of the Royal Guards wrote them. With the courier in tow, he quickly took the scroll to the king.

"I'm glad to know that Knight Red is dead!" Prince Edward declared, adding, "We must go to Mayern. We should take our army,

174

what if Sidra returns with her men? And she has all of Knight Red's now... how dreadful, Lady Jenna might be killed properly next time."

The king felt an overwhelming depression flood his veins. How could this lady, already unwell, sustain three arrow wounds and such loss of blood? She had fled like a fugitive to farewell her friend, only to be brought low herself. Where was Kind Heart? Should he, the king, go to her? Would this not be unseemly? It overwhelmed him and left him confused—his deep longing to see her, to be with her, to comfort her, to protect her from more harm.

"She wants to return here to Gifford, she does not want to remain at Mayern, she begs to come home," the messenger, a young soldier posted under Captain Ross, said. "My Captain, Ross, said to tell you, Sir Lowell, Lady Jennava is very distressed about having to stay there... at Mayern."

"Have Doctor Breck travel to Mayern and the moment Lady Jennava is well enough, have her brought back here. I'll send the royal carriage, and an extensive escort," the king said, decisively. "You may travel with it, Edward." He saw unveiled gladness light his brother's face and added, "Off you go then, have Bonidore pack you a trunk and take him with you, but remember, travel in the carriage, not on horseback. At the least, I will have you obey my commands."

"Oh, Cy! Thank you!" Edward cried, and rushed off to prepare for the journey.

Sir Lowell agreed with the king, "Yes, again the lady has been insubordinate."

The messenger spoke, "Sir, if I may speak, Your Majesty, never have I seen such bravery... it was due to the lady that the man, Knight Red, tumbled down the steep hill and the other, too... I saw it all... he was one of Lord Sidney's footmen, a traitor. If she had not gone to Mayern, the footman would still be an informer, and Knight Red would still be skulking about, scheming how to take another hostage. I don't think the woman, Sidra, has the spine to do anything very adventurous without Knight Red and all his men are only brutish beasts who have no brains to think for themselves."

"You saw it all? Tell us about it... the incident at the cemetery," the king requested. Sitting down, he listened to the young man's account of the attempted abduction of Lady Jennava. It seemed impossible that the criminal, Knight Red, had lost his life in such a manner but it was true.

"Lord Sidney commanded that the two bodies be hung above the gate to Mayern Castle," Stephen concluded.

The tale had been told, and Stephen answered the king's questions. The king sat, silent for a minute, then said, "You will travel in the carriage with Prince Edward and Doctor Breck, Stephen, and you will sleep with him, in his bedchamber, with Bonidore as well... we'll have a message sent ahead to prepare a guest chamber for three. Prince Edward is to go nowhere in Mayern Castle without either you or Bonidore present.

"Captain Ross will remain at Mayern until you all return with Lady Jennava. I'll have a message written for you to take to him and remind him to send news thrice daily."

~ * ~

Prince Edward arrived at Mayern Castle just before sunset. Messengers had ridden ahead, to make sure the way was clear and to announce the prince's coming. They would partake of food, check that the prince was safely ensconced in the castle, then ride back to Gifford taking news of Lady Jennava's health to the king, as well as of the prince's safe arrival.

Twenty-five

"Why is Lady Jennava in this room?" Prince Edward asked, aghast, "She should be in a guest chamber in a proper bed, not lying on that hard wooden bench."

Doctor Breck, who had followed the prince and Bonidore into the clinic, stepped closer to the bench, his eyes upon Jenna's face. "The bench is the best place for her, Prince Edward. It's best that she not be moved, or her wounds may bleed." Without turning, he asked, "Where's Doctor Thorn?"

A curtsying maid replied, "Doctor Thorn and his wife have just gone to have dinner in the great hall with Lord Sidney. They did not expect you to arrive until much later. The fore-riders, who arrived about ten minutes ago, said you would be an hour or more, yet." She saw that the doctor's attention was on the patient. Doctor Breck had his fingers pressed on her neck, counting her pulse.

"Doctor Thorn said Lady Jennava will sleep until midnight, Sir," her wide eyes were upon the prince and the golden coronet he wore.

"How... how is she... Lady Jennava?" Prince Edward asked. He could see the bandages on her left shoulder and her right arm, both with bloodstains showing through the white fabric. A crisp white linen sheet covered her body from above her breasts to below her toes. Both arms lay outside the linen cover. Her hair, stuck here and there with blood, splayed in disarray all around the back of her head and shoulders. She looked very pale, but also very beautiful.

I've seen her more times asleep than awake, the prince mused.

"Oh, she's... she's... we won't know for a few days, but I've been told that she mustn't move a muscle. Doctor Thorn said she has to be kept still."

"If you and Bonidore would like to go with Captain Ross and make yourselves known to Lord Sidney, Your Highness, I'll examine Lady Jennava for myself and I'll inform you of my findings..." his eyes were upon the bloodstained arrow, and the metal bolt, set on a piece of cloth on the wooden sideboard. Turning with his back to them, he hoped to conceal them from the young prince.

"She doesn't look very well," the prince said doubtfully, his eyes on her face. "She looks much worse than before... at Gifford."

"Doctor Thorn gave her something to make her sleep," the maid said, as if apologizing.

"We'll go and have dinner, Doctor Breck, then we'll return," the prince said. He did not want to leave her, and vowed that he would return to sit with her all night.

Jenna woke just after midnight. The ceiling she looked up at was unfamiliar and flickering candlelight did nothing to illuminate any memory of the room. A bitter taste sat in the back of her throat, and she recalled her father complaining of such a taste after being administered pain-relieving, sleep inducing drugs.

Memories—the cemetery, Knight Red, the arrows, bombarded her mind. Where was she now? She sat straight up, and the sheet fell to her waist, revealing her small rounded breasts.

Pain stabbed her shoulder, her arm and her thigh, but her eyes were upon Prince Edward, lying fast asleep on a comfortable sofa that had been carried in for him. The prince had refused to leave Lady Jennava.

Behind the sofa, Captain Ross and Stephen stood, unmoving, their eyes wide, staring at her with both shock and fascination. Bonidore sat in a chair, his eyes closed. A young woman reclined in another chair, dozing. Doctor Breck sat at a small desk, writing.

Drawing the linen cover up to hide what the men had already seen, Jenna swiveled herself to sit, wrapping the cover right around her naked body.

"Doctor Breck, I want my clothes," she hissed, sliding off the bed to stand supported by her good leg, leaning back on the bed. Captain Ross stepped sideways as if to walk around the sofa to give her support. "I want these men out of here!" she said then asked, "Are we still at Mayern?"

Doctor Breck jumped up, startled. Removing a small cloth from the top of a goblet, he stepped over to the bed, saying, "You must be thirsty, Lady Jennava, drink this, and you will feel better." He tendered the goblet, lifting it toward her face.

Jenna's eyes never left the doctor's as she took the goblet from his hand and tossed the contents over her shoulder on to the thin hard mattress of the bed. She pushed the empty goblet back into his hand.

"I feel much better, now. I did not ask to be drugged, Doctor Breck, I asked for my clothes and I want those three men to leave this room! If I'm still in Mayern, I want to go home." Her voice was stronger. Bonidore woke, and the maid sat erect in her chair.

"It's just past midnight, Lady Jennava, you need to sleep... to rest..." Doctor Breck pleaded.

"I've slept since morning, and I'm going to get dressed," she said. "Are we still in Mayern?"

"Yes, we are."

"Then I wish to have some plain water to drink, then leave here and travel back to Gifford," Jenna said firmly.

"It's impossible," Stephen muttered in Ross's ear, while the latter shook his head, hoping that the doctor would force her to take something to make her sleep.

"Dinah, go at once and find a gown, any gown, and... and fresh undergarments... for Lady Jennava and a cloak. Captain, have them prepare the horses and the carriage... make sure the rugs are still in the carriage..."

"But Sir... Doctor Breck, one company is still out searching for Sidra and the others are sleeping. We... we'll have to find everyone, and wake them up."

"Everyone?" Jenna asked, "Who is everyone?"

"Just do it," the doctor said, exasperated.

"Sir... I don't think we should..."

"Captain, I have authority from the king that when Lady Jennava is well enough to travel, that I accompany her to her home in the king's carriage... so see to it."

The captain did not reply but strode to the door, holding it open for Dinah and Stephen. He looked back to see Jennava limp to the stool Dinah had vacated, and sit on it, the linen cover now fixed firmly around her body. *What a wonder!* he marveled, *what a woman!*

"I... I have been commanded to stay with the prince," Bonidore said, cringing as the lady's eyes scorched his face.

"Then stay, but outside the door!" Jenna said.

"You're dizzy, Lady, aren't you?" Doctor Breck asked.

"Yes," Jenna replied, "but it's lessening, it'll soon pass." She lifted her arm, saying, "I'd like you to loosen this bandage, Doctor, it's too tight."

"That's because your arm has swollen, Lady, I'll redo it. I'll put more arnica on it, and some of this healing salve."

The doctor had just rebound her arm when Dinah arrived back with clothes that had belonged to Judith. Dinah helped Jenna to dress.

Prince Edward's eyes flickered open, his sleep had been disturbed. He sat up, his eyes on the empty bench-bed. His heart leapt, he imagined that his favorite lady had died.

"Where is she?" he asked fearfully.

Doctor Thorn burst into his clinic, staring at the empty bench, a flabbergasted expression on his face. "You're mad! You're not thinking, Breck," he accused, "She can't travel! Not in her condition."

"What condition?" Jenna asked, standing. "I need my riding-boots, Dinah... they must be here somewhere... and a hat, to cover my hair after we fix it up, it's dreadful."

"Lady Jenna!" Prince Edward exclaimed in wonder, his face breaking into a smile.

"She's not riding!" Doctor Thorn exclaimed, aghast.

"No, she's not riding," Jenna said lightly, "she'll travel in the king's carriage with Prince Edward. She'll likely be home in time to see her king take his breakfast!"

Jenna stepped out of the clinic with Doctor Breck supporting her on one side, and Prince Edward on the other. She was not foolish enough to refuse their assistance, especially so as she stared at the steep stone step-way in front of her. Only one person could help her walk down the narrow stairwell. Doctor Breck told Bonidore to go ahead.

Stepping down four steps, Bonidore turned as if ready to catch her when she fell. Holding the rail with one hand and the doctor's arm with the other, Jenna took one step at a time. She was breathless by the time she reached the bottom.

"You did that very well," Doctor Breck said, his voice not in the least surprised, "Wait now until you catch your breath, then we'll walk to the door."

"I'm fine," Jenna said stubbornly. Prince Edward hurried to her other side.

Captain Ross strode in through the door, having ordered the carriage and horses to be brought as close as possible. He did not believe his eyes to see Jenna, dressed in a beautiful pink dress and matching hat, already waiting.

"We... we won't be ready for a while. We've not woken all the men... and they have to dress... their horses have to be saddled... there's only one groom on duty at night, and we have had to wake others..."

"Then we shall go to Sidney's chapel, and wait there," Jenna said, "call us when everything is ready, Captain." The doctor and Prince Edward supported her as she turned. Bonidore followed, having ordered a servant to put the prince's trunk on the terrace outside the door.

To the doctor's concern, Jenna asked to be alone in the large, dim chapel. She limped to the front and painstakingly knelt before the altar. Prince Edward turned, wondering where to wait. Doctor Breck indicated a pew at the back, and they sat there. Bonidore joined them. The lady seemed a mile away, kneeling, not moving. Prince Edward yawned. It was warm, and still the middle of the night.

Jenna prayed silently, *Lord, I want to make a promise to You. I shall not cease in seeking You, I shall not eat, not a morsel of food shall pass my lips until I feel in my soul that I have found You, that I will follow Judith to life eternal... I'll seek until I find. I believe in You, Lord, but I do not know You. Please hear my prayer and help me, Lord.*

Feeling sharp pain stabbing her thigh, she leaned forward on the rail, continuing in her prayer.

Doctor Breck whispered, "Stay here, Your Highness, Bonidore, I'll go forward... she may need help to rise."

Jenna heard someone approaching. Doctor Breck knelt down close beside her, taking up the stance of one who prayed. Instead, he whispered in her ear.

"I know about Kind Heart."

"I also know about Kind Heart," she replied.

"I know what you know," he persisted.

"You think you do?"

"I know that you must be Kind Heart," he whispered, "It just came to me. I've been puzzling all night, but it fits together now... your amazing strength, your stamina—like your father had—I can't believe I didn't know it before."

"How did you come to such a conclusion?" she asked, her voice barely a whisper.

"You... you were bleeding..." he said. "I am your doctor, and I examined you in case you had been injured, internally. I discovered you to be a virgin."

Jenna bowed her head, feeling embarrassed.

"I asked myself, how could a virgin be Kind Heart's lover? It made no sense. You covered yourself very well, Lady Jennava. Making yourself seem a close friend of Kind Heart's after your father's death, you made yourself into two people—everyone believes there are two, even our king. But you cannot continue... you'll get yourself killed..."

"I've never told one lie," she said, her voice a little louder.

"No, but you have lived one," he persisted, "You allowed people to believe the worst of you. I want you to give it up."

"I... I want to give it up, too," she agreed.

He stared at her, long and hard, then said, "I believe you do."

"Then help me to think of a way. I made a vow to my father. It was written by my own hand and signed, not with ink but with my own blood. What can I do about that?"

"Just burn it... it's only paper," he said fiercely.

"I don't know where it is..." she said, "Father hid it away with other papers... I... I have not found his secret chambers beneath the castle— I've never had enough time to search thoroughly and it never seemed so important..."

"Lady Jennava... Jenna... I care for you as much as I would a child of my own, you are the daughter I never had. I've been appalled at your behavior. Myself and my wife, we felt you to be reprehensible, unredeemable, we left you to yourself, because you had Kind Heart... but it was all a lie... you *are* Kind Heart!" He swallowed and almost choked, then said, "I want to help you, dear Jenna... I must speak with Natalie, she will help me think of a way."

The definite sound of a rustle came from within the altar area. The curtains at the back swayed.

"Who's there?" Doctor Breck asked, rising and drawing Jenna to her feet. A loud click sounded out—a door had been opened. "Come out!" the doctor called, "show yourself!"

The door closed.

If Jenna had not had an injured thigh, she would have easily leapt over the rail, but due to the wound, she went around it. She hurried through the curtain, and dragged the door open. A dim passage stretched before her eyes, and at the end of it, another door opened. It was impossible to see who it was, but a dark figure rushed through the door and closed it before Jenna could get there. Jenna tried to open the heavy door, but the eavesdropper had locked it.

"Who was it?" Doctor Breck asked, "Do you think he heard?"

Turning back, to see that both Prince Edward and Bonidore were entering the passage, Jenna said, softly, "Of course he heard, that's why he fled. So many people know now... it doesn't matter any more... does it? The worst anyone can do is to tell King Cyranius and claim the reward... at least it would be over then."

"The king would not believe it," the doctor returned quickly, "I hardly believe... it. We must get back to Gifford, to safety..."

"What... who... was it?" Prince Edward asked, "Was it Kind Heart?" To his concern, both the lady and the doctor laughed as they returned to the chapel.

Twenty-six

King Cyranius waited anxiously in the courtyard of Gifford Castle. He still found it hard to believe Lady Jennava was already in Gifford District and the carriage would be here shortly. Prince Edward and Doctor Breck traveled in the royal carriage with her. It seemed unlikely, impossible even, but the fore-riders had announced it to be true. A message he had received from Doctor Breck, just before midnight, had said that the lady was seriously ill and would be unable to travel in the royal carriage for at least a week.

The king had sent Sir Lowell and his wife to the capital to assess the damage at the palace and to make arrangements to refurbish it. Sir Lowell was planning to remain there for at least a week, hopefully to recommission and strengthen the guard left on the city ruins. Anything of value left had been removed to the lower chambers, those beneath ground level. Sir Lowell would oversee the master-builders and their workers as they moved in to begin restoration.

~ * ~

For the last two hours of the journey, Jenna and Doctor Breck were able to talk in relative privacy. Both Prince Edward and Bonidore, sitting on the same seat as the doctor, were fast asleep, covered with the rugs and Jenna's discarded cloak.

The doctor, taking care not to use names, asked questions about Jenna's past and things that still puzzled him, and she answered as honestly as she could.

Less than half a mile before the horses' hooves would clatter on the cobblestone road approaching Gifford Castle, Doctor Breck reached across and squeezed Jenna's hand.

"Remember, Jenna, both Natalie and I will be there, whenever you need us, we want to give you every support."

"You have to convince your wife first, Breck," Jenna said, "How do you know she will support me?"

"Both Natalie and I live by the Holy Scriptures," Breck returned. "We are one, in God..."

"You know the Scriptures?" Jenna asked.

"My knowledge of the Holy Scriptures spans my life."

"Then I shall need to hear your knowledge," she said, and briefly outlined her most recent vow.

"I shall help you seek then and so shall Natalie."

"You... you know about eternal life?" she asked.

"Yes."

"One can be sure that God will accept one? One can know that one has eternal life?

"Yes... both Natalie and I know..."

His voice trailed, they had reached the cobblestone road and the loud clatter of the horses' hooves woke the sleeping pair.

"We're there?" Prince Edward said, sleepily, "I can't believe I slept." He had been so sure he could last out the vigil to remain awake with his wounded ladylove. "How... how are you, Lady?"

"I'm fine, Prince Edward, I'm glad to be home!"

King Cyranius, backed by many castle attendants, servants, soldiers and slaves, stood close to the carriage as a diligent footman opened the door. Doctor Breck stepped down, bowing to him, followed by Prince Edward. The pair turned and offered their hands to Lady Jennava, whom, to everyone's amazement, took their offered hands and stepped out of the carriage. She wore a beautiful pink gown and a matching hat. The king thought he had never seen anyone look so lovely. Then he saw that blood seeped through the pink silk at her shoulder, staining it red, and he swallowed, feeling anxious for her.

"Excuse me, Your Majesty, but I honestly don't think I can curtsy." Smiling so that dimples appeared in her cheeks, she inclined her head toward him. He would have liked to take her hand from the Doctor, or his brother, but before he could speak, she turned and began ascending the terrace steps to the front door of the castle. The king followed.

"I want to go straight to my room," Jenna told the doctor. Slowly, but surely, they headed that way, the king still following.

Upon reaching her bedchamber door, Jenna spoke to a maid, "Find Millie for me, Hannah."

"Oh, miss, she be gone, Captain Duff took six weeks' leave and they went away, the whole family."

Jenna sighed, feeling betrayed, but knowing that she could be jumping to a false conclusion. *Duff told Millie, of course he did. She baited me and somehow she got word to Knight Red, or Sidra, that I did leave Gifford. It may even have been Duff, hiding in the chapel...* Jenna shook her head. She felt exhausted.

"Please leave us, Prince Edward, my shoulder wound is bleeding and I think Doctor Breck will have to do something to stem it."

"Have someone bring fresh-drawn well-water, Hannah," Doctor Breck said, "And find Natalie for me, she sleeps late and may not know we've returned."

Prince Edward turned away from the closed door, to face his brother. "Come, let's find a quiet place, Cy, and I'll tell you all about it," the prince said eagerly, conscious of the many people in the castle wanting to hear the tale. "I'm hungry. Perhaps we shall eat?"

~ * ~

Both King Cyranius and Prince Edward were upset that the lady stayed in her quarters and that news of her health was hard to gain. Doctor Breck and his wife, Natalie, were the only ones permitted into the chamber on that first day. When Hannah was commissioned to sit with the lady at night, she brought back the report that the lady was not eating, or sleeping, but reading by a huge candle. She was also fasting, living only on liquids, fruit juice, cider and some herbal concoction that the doctor made from Lady Jennava's own recipe. "Doctor Breck and his wife are in there, spending all their time, discussing morbid matters from the Bible," she said.

When the king finally gained the Doctor's ear, it was to be told, "You're the king, Sire, I'm the doctor—let us take care of our duties respectively."

"You're a doctor, not a counselor," the king said, then asked, "Is Lady Jennava... dying? It's been five days since she disappeared into her bedchamber, and the last time we saw her, she complained of her bleeding shoulder."

"Lady Jennava is not dying, Sire, she has soul-matters to settle."

"Then, perhaps doctor, you should have a soul-doctor tend her."

"I believe, Sire, that I'm both a physician and a priest," the doctor said, to which the king had no answer.

"Prince Edward is eager to see Lady Jennava," the king said.

"Yes, Sire, he knocks on the door, several times a day..."

"I also would like to see her," he said.

So that's how the land lies, the doctor thought, smiling inwardly, but not outwardly.

"Perhaps I may be able to help her," the king added, then, "I do know Scripture..."

"You do?" the doctor asked, as if it was an impossibility.

"I believe in God," the king affirmed, not put off by the doctor's disbelieving tone.

"I doubt that Lady Jennava would speak with you, Sire. She... she's finding it difficult, not to believe in God, but to experience God. It's such a personal matter."

~ * ~

Sir Lowell and his wife returned, and the king was pleased to learn that work had begun, first clearing the palace of debris and cleaning the marble floors and walls. Preparations were being made to begin the interior rebuilding. Seasoned lumber was being transported from northern lumber stores. Fabric had been ordered for importation.

Sir Lowell was appalled to hear that Lady Jennava kept to her bedchamber—she had walked into her castle but had vanished to remain in her room.

"Has Kind Heart appeared?" he asked the king.

"No, not unless he's been coming secretively," the king said darkly. He told Sir Lowell of a secret chamber that had been opened inside the cave-stable. Kind Heart's gear was stored there—hats, masks, leather riding gear, various pieces of armor, shields, two arrow-proof vests, and various weapons, together with Lady Jennava's black gowns, riding habits, hats, and even some of Lady Jennava's feminine underwear had been discarded there.

"I can't understand why the man won't make himself known to us," the king said, feeling weary of the mystery. "Perhaps I should give it up."

"No. Don't give up, we'll think of something to draw him out," Sir Lowell said, but wondered what it would be.

"As far as we can ascertain, he hasn't entered the cave or his study," the king said, his voice tone still dark. "There've been no reported sightings of him since the fire in the capital."

~ * ~

Jenna had listened to all Doctor Breck and Natalie shared with her for over a week. She had listened and at nights, when they needed to sleep, she had read and prayed and read. Her senses were alert and her emotions stable—the fasting had increased her mental awareness.

It was two in the morning and Jenna was restless. Hannah had fallen asleep on the window seat, as on other nights and Jenna wanted to walk. She longed to feel cool air on her face.

I did not promise to stay in my bedchamber, my promise was to seek... until I found. I wish I were well enough to ride, perhaps another week but not yet...

Jenna dressed in one of her familiar black gowns and left her room. How much easier it was to walk now.

Stephen had been standing, with another guard, in the shadows, half on guard, half asleep. He had been commissioned by the king to watch who entered the lady's room at night. If he could not identify an authorized person, he was to inform the king.

The two guards followed her, and Stephen wondered if he should report to the king. Where was she going? She walked slowly, heading toward the small castle chapel then she changed her direction and ascended a spiral step-way to the battlements. Leaving the guard to follow and see that she came to no harm, he strode purposefully towards the guest chambers, where the king had set up apartments for himself and his brother.

Jenna reached the highest parapet and settled herself in a comfortable position in a wide crenellation. The night air was cooler here, and she was glad, it made her feel refreshed.

Perhaps all I've learned over the past week will come together in my heart, and it will make sense.

She prayed, and recalled Scriptures she had memorized.

How do I have fruit unto holiness and at the end, everlasting life? she asked herself. *Is it that I need to live a holy life, then at the end I'll have eternal life? But I'm not a bad person, I've done good. I've lived as Kind Heart... I've saved many lives.*

But, it's not of works, that's what Judith kept saying. There has to be something I must do, something that I've not yet achieved...

"Lady Jennava? Are you well?" It was the king's voice. He wondered if she had been sleepwalking.

"I'm fine, thank you," she returned, "You interrupted my meditation." For a reason unknown to herself, she felt deeply disturbed by the king's unannounced presence. If only he would go away... but he was the king and could do as he pleased.

"Forgive me, I've been wanting to speak with you, but a doctor's refusal is not to be ignored." He waited, but she did not speak.

"People have been asking about you. Lord Sidney came yesterday, bringing gifts and floral tributes for you. He wanted to thank you personally for your bravery, but Doctor Breck would not permit him to see you."

"Sidney? No doubt he wanted to thank me for being responsible for the death of Knight Red. I don't feel very brave about that. It was an accident, I meant him to tumble down the hill and to be captured, not to die…" her voice was bitter, Kind Heart had never before killed anyone.

"You mustn't blame yourself," he said, his voice kind. He wondered if this were the reason for her withdrawal. "You must come down to your great hall and see the hundreds of bouquets and gifts that have arrived for you."

"*My* great hall?" she asked, and said, "It's yours, Your Majesty, or was it to be Prince Edward's? Am I not an intruder here? Did you not command me to marry Zerka and share his castle?"

"You're too harsh, Lady," he said with sadness in his voice. "Kind Heart himself invited us to stay here and in honor of Kind Heart in whose debt I shall be all my life, I wish you to be happy here. I wish you to be happy with him and I pray that you will marry him, then it will be well for you both. Believe me, I seek only your happiness…"

Jenna bowed her head and the king continued, "Kind Heart told my commanders that we were welcome at Gifford, but you do not feel that way towards us?"

Jenna felt confused, perplexed and she suffered from guilt to hear the king refer to Kind Heart as a separate identity. She so desperately wanted him to know the truth.

King Cyranius saw that the lady still bowed her head. "Lady Jennava, I'm not your enemy, indeed, but I apologize… for my past presumptuous attitude. Please accept my humblest apologies. I wish to be your friend. If you could think of me, not only as your king, but as your friend, it would please me greatly. I'd do anything, give anything… for you to be truly, rightfully, happy."

"Anything?" she asked, her voice full of doubts.

He did not speak, he was sure she understood that he was offering all his resources—his very kingship he would place on the altar for her to be rightfully happy.

"I... I appreciate that," she said, feeling deep in her heart that he was earnest. "I... I badly need a friend. I feel I have no one..."

He did not speak, but waited.

"I have two questions," she said, "The first is the most important— how does one know for sure one will go to heaven when one dies?"

At first he did not answer, then asked, "You jest?"

"It's no jest, Your Majesty, if I do not answer this question, then I shall die, soon, without knowing..."

"You will die? How... how do you know that?" He longed to be able to understand her.

"I have sworn to God that I shall seek Him until I find Him, that I will not eat until I have the assurance of knowing eternal life. My friend, Lady Judith, knew before she died that she had eternal life. How could she know such a thing? Is it possible to gain eternal life, yet still be alive here on this earth? Or is it something that comes to you just before you die?"

He did not reply. It was such an important question, the answer of which lay deep in the soul of one who truly believed. To answer it, would be to admit that he was such a one, not always the perfect king. He would have to admit to another human being that he considered himself a sinner.

"I have less than two months," she said. "It's well known that one of my size cannot, for longer than sixty days, survive without food."

"You're earnest, aren't you? You won't eat until you know."

"No. I will not eat, and if I do not know... but how can one know? Do you know?" she asked.

"Yes... I know." He sat thinking, knowing that his next words may save her life... "You've been studying the subject of eternal life, with Doctor Breck..."

"Yes."

"You believe in God, and His Son, Jesus Christ?" he asked.

"Yes."

"You believe that God sent His Son to earth to die on the cross for sinners, for mankind?"

"Yes."

"You believe that Jesus' death on the cross was for you in particular?"

"Yes."

"You believe Jesus rose again, from the dead?"

"Yes, of course I do. He's the one who gives life, both here on earth, and life eternal." She sighed. She believed, but was bereft of peace.

"Have you said so?" he asked.

"What do you mean?"

"You have told God, have you not?"

"Told God?"

The Scriptures say, "That if you confess with your mouth the Lord Jesus, and believe in your heart that God raised him from the dead, you will be saved."

A silence settled, broken only by an owl hooting in the night shadows.

"I do believe that," she finally said.

"Then say it," he urged.

"Say what?"

"Jesus is Lord."

"Jesus is Lord?"

Turning to stand in a crenellation, he called out into the open air, "Jesus Christ is Lord! He is King of all Kings! Above all others!" He looked back at her, asking, "Can you tell the world that Jesus is Lord?"

Smiling, she said, "Yes," then called, "Jesus is Lord!"

"But do you believe it in your heart?"

"I certainly hope so."

"You should know so," he said, then asked, "And you must believe in your heart that God raised him from the dead."

"I do believe it."

"Then, call on the Name of the Lord and you will be saved."

"That's a Scripture," she said, "but how do I call on His Name?"

"'With the heart, man believes unto righteousness, and with the mouth confession is made unto salvation'," he quoted.

"You believe that?" she asked.

"Yes. One day, when I was seeking God, just as you are, Lady Jennava, I called upon him—not as a king, but as a man and he revealed himself to me through the Scriptures. I confessed my sinfulness to God; as I still do, every day..."

"Every day?" she asked, surprised.

"I kneel to pray, every morning, before I leave my room and I pray at night before I sleep. To my shame, I rarely take time to pray throughout the day, unless it's urgent. But I do make confession to God, as the Scriptures enjoin us to. 'If we confess our sins, He is faithful and just to forgive us our sins and to cleanse us from all unrighteousness.'

"The one thing we all need to do, Lady Jennava, to have peace with God, is to talk to him, to confess. Call on him and you will be saved, just do it and believe His Word. God wrote His word for us, that we believe on the Name of the Son of God, that we may know that we have eternal life, and that we may believe on the Name of the Son of God. It's a continuous belief... it goes on and on every day, all of your life, and you know that you have eternal life, and you carry on believing, never doubting, but believing."

"I do believe it... I do believe," Jenna said, her voice trembling with excitement, "But it seems too simple..."

"It is simple, Lady Jennava. I, like you, almost missed it—part of my life is being a king, the other part is still an ordinary man. Because of God's mercy and grace, He made it plain to me, and saved me, both man and king.

"Please pray. I'm going to leave you, so that you can pray and confirm your faith in God and His Son." He stepped away from her, and bowed. Turning, he left her.

Jenna knelt in the crenellation and prayed. First of all she thanked God for His Word, she thanked Him for His great plan to save mankind, then she asked God to forgive her sins and save her soul. Tears washed her cheeks until there were no more. Spiritual joy welled up within her.

He was right, she mused, after her prayer, *the king was right, it's a work of God... I believe and through His mercy and grace, He saved me... I could have missed it, it's so simple. God has been here all of the time waiting, I just had to call on him... give my will to him. 'Ask and it shall be given you, seek and you will find.' Thank you, God, for causing me to find You. Please keep me believing and keep me knowing that I have eternal life, forever and ever.*

Jenna rose cautiously to her feet, feeling weak, but also feeling a serenity she had never before known, tranquility in her soul.

She walked along to the downward steps and slowly made her way to the bottom. Stephen waited for her in the corridor.

"King Cyranius said that he'd be in the chapel. He said to remind you that you had another question for him." He followed her.

Jenna's senses raced. Her second need was to get rid of Kind Heart from her life. How could she ask this now? Would he understand? Could she break the vow she had written in front of her father and signed with her own blood? No, she could not do such a thing! But if he found out for himself... her father had made exceptions for those who discovered Kind Heart's identity—Kind Heart was commanded to enlist them as supporters. Duff had been a friend and so were Doctor Breck and his wife. What about Millie? Had Duff told Millie? Had Millie somehow contacted Sidra? Where were they now? Were Duff and Millie truly 'away on leave,' with their children?

As Jenna entered the chapel, the new sense of peace she had felt filled her with awe. At first she did not see the king, kneeling near the front. The first light of dawn was filtering through the stained glass of the chapel windows. The scene depicted in the glass was that of the Good Shepherd, a staff in one hand, a lamb cradled in his other.

King Cyranius turned and saw the light on her face. She did not need to say a word, he knew.

"Thank you, Your Majesty," she said.

"Thank God," he returned, earnestly.

They were silent for a moment, then he spoke, "I should not say this, Lady Jennava, I shall have to confess again to God, but I have to tell you then I must hold my peace forever. I wish I had met you before you met Kind Heart."

"There is nothing you could have done," she said, thinking of her father.

"When did you meet him?" he had to know, "The present Kind Heart, that is."

"I... I..." she swallowed, not wanting to mislead him again. "It's about Kind Heart that I wish to speak... that's my second question..."

His face saddened, then he asked, "Tell me..."

"You... you have stopped working on the secret tunnels," she began.

"I don't wish to learn any more of Kind Heart's secrets," he said firmly, "not until he tells me himself."

"There's a paper that my father had me sign, it's in a hidden chamber. If your men could find their way into the secret chamber, then I believe they'd find the paper."

"What do you want the paper for?" he asked.

"You could read it, Your Majesty, then you would know everything, including Kind Heart's identity... and... I wish the paper to be burned... when that happens, it would be over."

The king was deeply puzzled. He felt like he had a riddle to solve, but some of the key words were missing. "If Kind Heart does not want me to know who he is, perhaps I should not find this paper..."

"Then I can never be released from my vow," Jenna said, her eyes filling with tears. She blinked them away.

"Why doesn't Kind Heart fetch the paper for you?"

"Kind Heart doesn't know the way to this room. The room was last locked by my father and he did not show me... or Kind Heart..."

"Would Kind Heart want me to seek out this room?"

"Yes," Jenna said firmly.

"He told you this?"

"If Kind Heart writes to you, to ask you to seek this paper for me, will you do it?" she asked.

"Yes, Lady Jennava, I will." He knew that she was deadly serious about this matter. She wanted this written vow removed from her life.

"If… this paper… is burned, how will it release you, Lady Jennava?"

Jenna suddenly smiled, and said, "It doesn't need to be burned, no, it just has to be found—you just have to read it."

"Is there no other way? What if the paper is not found?"

Jenna's face darkened, then she said, "There are other ways, but they all lie within you, Your Majesty, to do all you can to find out the truth about Kind Heart. Oh, I wish I could tell you…"

"It would mean breaking your vow…"

"I can't break it or how could I ever take up another vow, one that I would want to keep all my life… how could I be trusted to keep my word?"

The king could not imagine what other vow she would wish to make. Women did not make vows, did they? Perhaps of loyalty to a king? Then it dawned on him… loyalty to a husband? Marriage? He frowned. How could a lady such as Jennava keep the vows of marriage when she had broken them before they were made? His frown deepened.

"Oh, please, Your Majesty, please find the paper. I shall pray to God that you will find it. Everything will be explained, and I won't have broken what I vowed to my father." She bowed her head, saying, "You've no idea of the burden that will be lifted from me if I can be released from Kind Heart forever."

"Is… that what will happen… if I find the paper?" he asked, now doubtful. "What will Kind Heart say?"

"Kind Heart will be so glad! I will be glad! Oh, I wish you could understand, I wish I could tell you!" she shook her head, knowing she could not explain. "Will you search for the paper?"

He was silent for a minute. "If you ask Kind Heart to write to me, I shall do as you both ask." He felt even more puzzled—Kind Heart was a mystery that perplexed him to his soul.

Prince Edward, followed by Gavin and Kevin, entered the chapel.

"Lady Jennava! How exciting you're out of your room! We've so longed to see you." The prince rushed to her as if he would have hugged her, but he stopped close to her and bowed, taking her hand, kissing the back of it. "It's good to see you so well, Lady Jenna. Will you come and breakfast with us in the great hall?"

"I believe I shall," she replied, smiling.

"You'll have a surprise," he said as he took her arm, "Flowers and gifts are everywhere, for you."

The king followed the pair from the chapel, wishing it were he, not his brother, who walked with the lady.

Twenty-seven

King Cyranius found a sealed scroll on his office desk—it was from Kind Heart. He read it, and a deep sense of sadness swamped him. Lady Jennava belonged to Kind Heart. Then he had a feeling that he could not describe, like there was something he should know, something about Kind Heart that he had missed.

Is he real? he asked himself. *Or am I dealing with an angel? No, that's not possible but something's not as it seems... Kind Heart is not the ghost of Lady Jennava's father, is he?* For a few moments, this seemed one of the most logical notions he had invented, then, the king censured himself, *I'm being ridiculous... trying to make Kind Heart a being of no substance, and I can't do that... he's part of Lady Jennava, and I'll have to suffer this for the rest of my life. I'll never be rid of him, as long as I can see her. And I do not want to stop seeing her, though she wounds me every time I look at her and know she can never be mine. When I can stand it no longer, I'll have to send her away and marry her off, or go away myself.*

He wondered if he should show the scroll to Sir Lowell? Uncharacteristically, he wavered, first one way, then the other. He decided to show Sir Lowell. He needed advice. He stood to leave the office to go to the commander then changed his mind. Sitting down again at the office desk, he read the note a fourth time.

King Cyranius, I beg you to seek and find—only by your finding will I be set free.

It was signed 'Kind Heart', and sealed with wax in which was the impression of a feather.

To seek and find? What does he want me to find? It does not speak of a paper here but suggests imprisonment 'only by your finding can I be set free'...it's a riddle... it sounds like Lady Jennava speaking, not Kind Heart.

He flattened the scroll and pushed it to the back of his desk drawer, placing other documents above it and in front of it. Locking the drawer, he wished he knew what was bothering him so deeply about that scroll and its contents.

The king commanded a large number of trusted men to enter the tunnel from the cave end, and a more thorough search be made for triggers or switches to open the secret places. He did not want to destroy the walls as before, but to have them kept intact.

"Go over and over it, inch by inch. I want you to tap it, press it, twist it and if something opens, keep it open and remember *how* it opened. Keep me informed," the king commanded.

"I'm glad you changed your mind, Your Majesty, and decided to continue the search," Sir Lowell told the king, "We'll discover all Kind Heart's secrets yet." The commander behaved like a young boy wanting to open his presents before his birthday and Prince Edward was matching company for Sir Lowell. Together with Kevin and Gavin, they were going to spend every spare minute they had down in the secret passages, hoping to learn every secret.

The days passed and Jenna took her meals in the great hall with the king, the prince, and the court. Doctor Breck and his wife remained close to her, encouraging her, spending time each day with her in reading and prayer. Otherwise, they returned to their normal duties resuming work in the castle clinic. The couple assisted the younger doctor, helping tend those who came each day with health and accident-related problems.

The king opened an unused wing of the castle and set up a throne room in a large chamber, where he met with his court each day to judge kingdom matters. People, both rich and poor trickled in, wanting royal solutions for their dilemmas.

Captain Ross, Stephen, and two young guards began to examine the newly opened wing of the castle, hoping it would yield up some long-hidden secrets.

The prince resumed his required lessons, also attending the throne room when King Cyranius sat on his improvised throne. Prince Edward was so eager to be secret hunting that he wanted to give up all else, but his brother warned him that if he were unpunctual for even one meal, he would be banned from going below. The prince solicited Gavin and Kevin's help in keeping to the king's timetable.

The two thrones in the palace, both made of wood and overlaid with gold, had been doused with oil, covered with flammable material and set on fire—the wood had burned and the gold had melted. The gold was to be retrieved and new thrones made. Sir Lowell estimated that it would be at least a year before the palace was ready to be inhabited again by the king and his court and even then, the finishing work would continue for a long while.

Jenna spent more time each day in the chapel, reading and praying. Brother Patrick, now recovered, came from his hiding place, taking up residence in Gifford Castle. Jenna discovered that though he fervently believed in God, he was unsure that a person could truly know that he had eternal life. Jenna shared what she had learned. Such sharing reinforced her faith.

Messages continued to arrive for Kind Heart—calls for help, some in code and some written plainly. Jenna decoded the ones given to her and passed them back to Sir Lowell, urging that he have the military take care of the emergencies.

"Kind Heart only accepts missions that cannot be accomplished by others," she said, hoping that such a venture would not be brought before her yet. What would she do? She had not ridden a horse since the day of Judith's funeral. In fact, she had not even visited her horses and she wondered if she would. To see Oak would be to want to ride him, she knew. She prayed that God would show her what to do.

"You must exercise your leg muscles, in particular, your thigh," Doctor Breck told her. "Your father must have had a routine of some sort that you worked through?" he asked.

"Do you think I should?" she asked.

"Yes, I do," he replied, then added, "You are who you are, Jenna, and it would be wrong to deny yourself. What you've learned is a special gift from your father to you, a talent, and you must not let it grow idle. Natalie and I will support you in every way we can. Do keep close to us, my dear."

Jenna hugged them both, blinking back tears. "You are my friends," she said, "true friends and I love you both."

Jenna ventured into the secret passage through her bedchamber, entering the room her father had set up as a gymnasium. She found it frustrating, but, using the specially constructed equipment, she began to rebuild her fitness and flexibility. *I am still Kind Heart... perhaps I shall always be Kind Heart. And who knows, perhaps I shall have to protect myself or someone else. It's not wrong to act in self-defense... or to defend others and I need to regain my concentration, my speed of movement. Doctor Breck is right.*

Each morning, half an hour before sunrise, Jenna rose, dressed in one of her usual black gowns and climbed to her favorite place on the eastern battlements, praying for the day ahead, and watching for the sun to awaken and rise.

After the second morning, King Cyranius joined her, just as the sun lifted its golden crown above the eastern hills. Jenna did not wish to admit it, but she had hoped he would come. From that morning on, he met her there every sunrise and they watched the countryside awaken with light, then walked to the chapel where Prince Edward came to escort the lady to breakfast.

Jenna treasured this unofficial meeting with the king—it was easy to pretend that there was something between them, more than simple friendship and the wonder of creation and the private knowledge that they both believed the same about God. She fantasized that he loved her, not just as a friend, and that she loved him back.

Cyranius is just like me, she told herself. *He has two missions—to care for the man who has to make confession to keep himself holy and righteous and to behave the perfect king who judges and rules and lives so far above his subjects they believe him to be infallible. I love the man and I adore the king. I also have two missions—the Kind Heart who has to be brutal to the wicked, to be severe with the cruel, and the gentle lady who loves everyone and could do no harm.*

Jenna rose earlier, with the earlier rising sun, and the king came every morning. Sometimes they just stood, watching the sunrise and sometimes he watched her and when she looked at him, he turned to watch the sun again. Words mattered not to either—they both feared that if they spoke, the magic would disappear, therefore he loved her without words, and though she did not recognize it, she loved him in return.

At night when the king prayed, he would tell himself that he would not go up on the battlements the next morning, he would sleep later. But he woke early and tossed and turned. Just to see her again. *I'm like a moth,* he told himself, *flying into the candle flame. Soon I'll get burnt.*

Jenna felt impatient; the king's men had made very little progress in the secret passages. They complained that Prince Edward and his two shadows were in their way. The king told his brother that he must not work in the same area as the commissioned team and the boys began to hammer and pry in the places that had already been covered.

Then came what Sir Lowell called 'the break-through.' Kevin remembered the 'hiding hole' in the corridor, and when the three boys investigated it, they discovered the means by which to traverse the passage to the lower dungeon. Gavin almost fell down the steep step-way, and the team soon opened the two portals within the dungeon. From there, with the help of men who had been imprisoned by Knight Red and set free by Kind Heart, they found the secret weapons-room.

The next day the team smashed the wooden panel leading into Lady Jenna's bedchamber. The king was pleased that the lady had not been there at the time.

Sir Lowell demanded that Jenna move to another bedchamber. Jenna refused at first, but then, when she was given a choice as to where she would move, she chose a suite that had its door near a secret entrance. It was just a few feet away, in the corridor. She wondered how long it would be before this one was discovered?

~ * ~

One morning, two hours after midnight, Jenna woke with a jolt, imagining someone to be in her room. *It was just a dream, she told herself, rising to light a candle. I wish I could remember what the dream was about... I never recall them. I won't get back to sleep now, perhaps I should go for a ride...*

Jenna had no idea where her horses were stabled, she wondered if she would dare walk the secret passage to the cave-stable? Was the work continuing through the night? She did not think so; it was not listed as urgent. But would there be guards in the passage at night? Neither the king nor Sir Lowell had banned her from going into the tunnels, or from riding. Jenna made up her mind. She dressed in one of her black riding habits.

Jenna entered the secret passages from the corridor by the door of her new suite. First, she went to her gymnasium and did a warm-up, followed by a vigorous work-out. If no horses were in the cave-stable, perhaps she would return here and work on restoring her ability to do somersaults. She had not scaled the heights of her routine yet.

"Who goes there?" a guard called as Jenna opened the door into the cave-stable. Every other portal had been propped open, all the way from the castle.

"Lady Jennava," she replied, "I came to see if my horses are here. I see... there are three..." Oak, Cloud and Midnight whinnied and stamped as one, to hear her voice.

"Your horses, Lady?" another guard asked. He stepped closer, and by the light of the torch, she saw that it was Stephen. "Aren't they Kind Heart's horses?"

She did not answer his question, but asked, "Does someone exercise them?"

"We've been hoping Kind Heart would come and do that," the other guard said, also stepping closer.

"I want to know if someone exercises them."

"Prince Edward comes... about twice a week he rides the white one, and a couple of men from his escort ride the others," Stephen said. "I've seen Garth riding them too, I think he takes a different one each day."

Jenna felt relieved. Garth was here or was he? "Where's Garth?" she asked.

"Since the king commissioned the guard here, he's been staying down in the village with a brother of his," Stephen said, "He comes over during the day."

Jenna gathered a bridle from the hook on the wall and took it to Oak.

"You're going for a ride?" Stephen asked, then added, "Not alone, Lady."

"I won't go alone," she agreed, thinking, *I'll take Cloud and Midnight*. She patted their necks and noses, letting them sniff and nuzzle her to become familiar with her again, to give them confidence in her presence. It had been a long time, too long.

Opening the doors to their stalls, she said, "Go... go... out to the great meadow..." The horses rushed from their stalls with such speed that Stephen and his companions had to jump out of the way.

With a deft movement, Jenna mounted Oak and, riding bareback, she urged him out of the stable.

"I think we should tell the commander about it," Stephen said, "That's why there are three of us. I'll go through the passages and tell him, while you two stand guard here. Do you think she's going to meet Kind Heart?"

The question had no answer, they could only guess that she was.

~ * ~

Reaching the great meadow Jenna urged Oak into a faster gallop, then slowing him, she steered him between the trees, under familiar branches, surprising herself to find her hat whipped off her head because she forgot to duck at a certain place. The branch almost hit her face.

Strands of her hair flew loose and she drew the pin from her chignon, shaking the auburn mass free.

Once more, she galloped Oak around the great meadow where the wind blew through her hair, making her feel exhilarated. Why had she not come riding every morning? How had she forgotten this wonderful experience?

Whistling a special whistle brought Cloud and Midnight to her side. Taking the head-piece from Oak, she put it on the white horse and, commanding Midnight to follow, she rode Cloud hard around the edge of the great meadow, across the road, through the woods and back to where Oak grazed selectively. Silver light from the descending, odd-shaped moon, lent everything a blue appearance and Jenna felt enthralled with the wonder of nature.

My Heavenly Father made all this, she told herself, then said, aloud, "Thank you God, thank you."

Remembering that the king would go to the battlements to meet her at sunrise, she whistled for Oak and Midnight to follow, and turned Cloud back towards Gifford Castle. How she longed to see him, she could not bear to miss out on watching the sun turn his tanned face to bronze as the fireball rose into the cloudless sky.

Jenna knew that the king liked to ride, but he always rode in the heat of the afternoon. When others rested, he rode his magnificent stallion for almost an hour. This was how his face and arms had become so tanned.

Moonlit hours were Jenna's favorite times to go riding.

King Cyranius, Sir Lowell, Captain Ross and a company of king's guards, waited in the woods, just outside the cave-stable, waiting and watching. When the lady did ride the white horse through the trees, they saw that although she was followed by the brown and the black horses, they were riderless.

Stephen estimated that she had been gone for two hours. Every man waiting for her believed she had rendezvoused with Kind Heart.

Sir Lowell grasped Cloud's bridle and King Cyranius gave her his hand to help her dismount. Jenna expected a censure but the king just stared at her, obviously taking in the fact that she was hatless, and her hair looked as if it had not been combed.

Not a word was spoken as Jenna was escorted back along the tunnels and through her old bedchamber. She felt that a dark cloud had descended on her life. Happiness that she did not know she had experienced until now had vanished with the unwatched sunrise.

Jenna did not go riding the next two mornings, instead she worked out in the gymnasium and though she waited until after the sun had risen, the king did not come to the battlements and he was not in the chapel either. However, Prince Edward came to the chapel as usual, and escorted Jenna to the great hall for breakfast. The king was the last to arrive, and strode in just before they sat to eat. Though Jenna found her eyes drawn to him, he did not look at her.

The king summoned Jenna to his office, and she braced herself to receive a royal reprimand.

"We have a message, Lady Jennava, for you to give to Kind Heart. We ask that you do not open it to read it before you give it to him—it's for Kind Heart's eyes alone," Sir Lowell spoke for the king.

Jenna's eyes darted to look at the king, but he stared at the floor.

"Tell Kind Heart that we require a written reply as soon as possible, written by his hand."

Jenna did not move, then the commander spoke again, "Before you go, we'd like your promise that you'll not open the scroll, nor read it."

Hesitating only slightly, Jenna said, "I promise I shall not open this scroll, nor shall my eyes read what is written." She stood waiting.

"Then go to Kind Heart," the king said. "You have our permission to go to him."

Jenna curtsied and as she rose, her eyes met his. The intensity of his stare gave her deep inner pain. Clutching the scroll to her as if it might leap out of her hand, she hurried from the room.

Doctor Breck was in the clinic with the younger doctor, tending people who had come from the villages around Gifford. In one glance, Jenna saw that the doctor's wife was not present. She found her in the doctor's apartment, on the balcony watering the herbs she had planted in long narrow, soil-filled stone troughs.

"That's a good idea," Jenna exclaimed.

"Yes, they catch the light, but are shielded from too much direct sun—I'm hoping to have a good crop of seed," Natalie agreed.

"Please leave us," Jenna said to the servant-girl, Hannah, who helped Natalie. She followed the girl to the outer door and closed it behind her.

Jenna told Natalie about the scroll then said, "I want to keep my promise not to open it, or have my eyes see it, Natalie, so please open it and hold it towards yourself and read it aloud."

Her middle-aged hands trembling slightly, the doctor's wife broke the king's seal, and unrolled the scroll.

Jenna felt her heart racing like a galloping horse. She felt sure that the king and his advisers had set a trap for Kind Heart.

Sitting down with her back to the light, Natalie read softly, "Kind Heart, As you know, in two weeks' time, on the first day of the month of June, Lady Jennava will have her twentieth birthday. We wish to honor her, on this day, with a surprise celebration, beginning one hour before sunset, followed by a banquet, to be held in the great hall of Gifford Castle. After the banquet, gifts will be presented to Lady Jennava, and we ask that you include your gift of a betrothal ring. The morning after Lady Jennava's birthday, you shall marry her in a ceremony performed by Brother Patrick in Gifford Castle chapel. We ask that the birthday celebration be kept secret from Lady Jennava, but suggest that you inform her of the wedding. Send us your affirmation, in the form of a sealed scroll, as soon as possible. Signed—Cyranius V, King of Cyran."

Jenna felt her head swim and she leaned forward on the balcony ledge to support herself.

"How can I continue with this charade?" she asked, knowing that she had no answer.

Natalie smiled, for want of knowing what else to do. "It is rather impossible, my dear, isn't it? You simply cannot marry yourself! What are you going to do?"

"I don't know, what can I do?"

"Perhaps you can go to the party, as yourself, then leave and change into Kind Heart's costume. Hopefully, the king will put you two together."

"I hoped he would do that before now," Jenna said, frustration showing in her voice. "I think Kind Heart should refuse the invitation, Natalie... Cyranius is convening the whole thing for him... to catch him out..."

"No, my dear, he thinks a lot of you."

"Cyranius? I don't believe it. He hates me."

"That's not true! Indeed no! I... hear things. It's said that he's obsessed with your happiness, and he cannot believe that you would be happy remaining unmarried for the rest of your life. Also, he thinks it's wrong..."

"Of course it's wrong, Natalie, it's horrible what people believe... it's ruined any chance I have of making a respectable marriage," Jenna said, and covered her face with her hands. "And it's my own fault... I allowed it to happen... to let people think... I did not realize..."

"Oh my dear Jenna," Natalie said, stepping over to offer comfort.

"What am I to do?" Jenna cried, allowing the large lady to smother her into her ample arms. She could not remember anyone ever holding her like this.

"I'll ask my Breck... perhaps he'll think of something," she said.

Doctor Breck believed the king would soon discover Jenna's duplicity, "Hopefully before your birthday celebration," he said. "They must be getting close to discovering the limits of the secret passages... they've several smaller teams working in different areas now."

"They'll need them," Jenna said dryly, "they have scarcely begun, the king has no idea what a labyrinth there is down there." She remembered playing in the passages with her brother, and being told then that there were areas where she was not allowed to follow him.

King Cyranius despaired of receiving Kind Heart's reply, then, one evening, it appeared on his office desk. He broke the seal and stared at the few words on the scroll.

King Cyranius V:

I shall attend on the said day, after sunset.

Signed, Kind Heart."

"He says nothing of the wedding," the king said, passing the small note to Sir Lowell.

"He had Lady Jennava write this," Sir Lowell said, "it's her hand, the same as in Kind Heart's diaries."

"Let me see it," the king demanded. He stared at the evenly scripted words. Taking his key from the small chest on the desk, he unlocked the desk drawer and drew out a sheaf of papers. Reaching to the back of the drawer, his fingers contacted the scroll. The two men compared the writing—it was the same.

Sir Lowell read the first scroll again aloud; "King Cyranius, I beg you to seek and find. Only by your finding can I be set free. Signed, Kind Heart," then he added, "it's strange, isn't it, but this plea sounds like Lady Jennava, not like that of a man."

"It's not possible that... that Lady Jenna... Jennava..." the king began, then stopped.

"Don't think I've not considered it myself," Sir Lowell said, "I wrote a list of probable people, those whom we know, who could be Kind Heart and I've included her brother—we've not heard from him, though we've written to invite him, he could reply yet and neither Polonius nor Tory have sent word of their arrival there. Although it would solve some of the mystery, I struck Lady Jennava off the list, knowing it was both fanciful and impossible. Just because we have not seen Kind Heart for ourselves... what about the distance between here and the palace... how could she have? And she would have had to ride back... to say nothing of his amazing combat skills... no, I've thought of it, indeed... but it's not possible, is it?"

"No," the king agreed, knowing also, in the depths of his heart, he longed for it to be possible. If only Kind Heart, the man, did not exist! *I'll beat this fixation yet,* he declared within himself, *she'll marry Kind Heart, and it will be over forever.*

"She promised not to read the scroll... what did she say? She would not open it, nor would her eyes look on it? She could have had someone else open it, and read it to her." Sir Lowell reasoned, his detective-mind seeking out all possibilities.

"But in the writing of these words, there's no mention as to what is being planned, her birthday or the celebration. If Lady Jennava wrote it at Kind Heart's direction, she has no idea what he refers to... 'I shall attend on the said day, after sunset' gives no inkling as to what day, or what is planned," the king reasoned. "But he is coming... we'll have Kind Heart in the great hall and we'll not allow him to leave. Perhaps... yes, we'll have the wedding performed that night."

Sir Lowell stared at his king, knowing that his determination to have Lady Jennava and Kind Heart married was troubling him like a sword to his soul.

"I'll make the arrangements," the commander agreed, "The wedding will be performed that night and Kind Heart shall not leave until it is done."

Twenty-eight

Jennava continued her chosen routine—rising between three and four o'clock to go to the gymnasium. She had regained her strength. Some mornings she rode one of her horses, but always, she went to the battlements to see the sunrise, even if it were to behold a blanket of clouds above the eastern hills instead of the blue. The king did not come.

The festive fever in her castle increased and four days before her birthday it was apparent to Jenna, but she pretended not to notice. When obvious changes were being made she would ask, "Why are you replacing that?" or "What are those lanterns for?" only to hear the trite reply: "Just needs brightening up, it does, the king lives here now you know, Lady."

~ * ~

The day before her birthday, Jenna paced along the rampart, staring at the gray mist, wondering how she would manage tomorrow. *How many people has the king invited?* she wondered. *What will I wear? I have just one blue dress, the rest are black.* Then she thought of the

212

pink dress that hung in her wardrobe, *Judith's dress. Can I wear her dress on my birthday? It was Judith's, but I don't think she would mind... perhaps I'll wear it, it's so pretty, and it is a celebration. I'll be twenty! I can scarcely believe it! I did not think I would last out to be twenty, someone could have killed Kind Heart... God must still want me to be alive...*

Captain Ross and Stephen, shadowed by two other king's guards stepped towards Jenna as she leaned forward into the crenellation, watching the rising sun shining dimly through the mist. A yellow haze covered the countryside, but Jenna felt sure that it would disperse before long and the day would be hot and summery. June would normally be hot and dry. She knew that someone was approaching her place, and dared not look. Jenna hoped it was the king. Her heart beat a little faster.

"Lady Jennava," Captain Ross said softly. He stood behind her. "We've found two scrolls that belong to you."

Jenna turned around and Captain Ross tendered a roll of parchment. It unrolled before her eyes. Jenna's heart beat faster—it was the scroll she had signed with her blood. She held her hand out to take the scroll, but he drew it back out of her reach, holding it sideways, stepping that way as well.

Stephen took the scroll from his captain, rolling it and holding it firmly in his large hand.

"Read this," the captain said, tendering the second scroll, "it's from your father."

Jenna took the scroll and unrolled it, reading:

Dearest Daughter, Jennava Charlotte Gifford:

Having entered this chamber, you now own all secrets belonging to Kind Heart. There is one thing that I must tell you, in the event that I die without giving you the key to this chamber, this being, that as from sunset on your twentieth birthday, you shall no longer be under the oath that you signed. Since it was signed to and for your father, Kind Heart, it is he who has the power to release you from it. Therefore, from that sunset on the first of June, when you have lived for twenty years, the choice is yours—to be or not to be, you are free.

Lord Frances Charles Gifford: Kind Heart.

Rolling the scroll tightly, Jenna pushed it up her sleeve.

Jenna looked into the captain's smoldering gaze, displeased with the egotism she sensed in this man. In her peripheral vision, she saw that Stephen stood close now and the other two guards had moved in—they surrounded her, staring at her as if in awe.

"You found my father's chamber," she said, then asked, "will you tell me where it is?"

"It's quite unbelievable," Captain Ross said, choosing not to answer her question, "It's also unthinkable, inconceivable, absurd, to say nothing of being insanely phenomenal! It's bizarre! You, Lady Jennava, of all people, and a woman too. I still can't fully comprehend it!" He stepped back to lean on the wall behind him, folding his arms, saying, "We would not have believed it, but then, you don't know what we found in that chamber, do you? All the documentation anyone would need to prove that *you* are Kind Heart. We've been reading amazing things, all night... it's like an absurd dream... and we found plans to the whole maze of secret passages and chambers beneath this castle... it's like a village of its own down there, amazing chambers... one could live like a mole, a king mole, in secret, under the castle..."

"You haven't told the king?" Jenna asked, knowing the answer already. "Why are you here? Why is the king not confronting me about this?" She knew that these men were out of place. Exhilarated by the astounding truth, they were as ones who had discovered an elixir of youth.

"Your father kept a diary of your progress, Lady, from when you began serious training... you were ten years old... but we need to ask... there's one place that's not marked on the maps... the gymnasium, where is it?"

"You haven't told the king," Jenna concluded, and asked, "Why have you not reported this to our king?"

"This belongs to us four, it's ours," Captain Ross said smugly, "us four and you, Lady Jennava, Kind Heart, and that's how we'll keep it, for now. You'll tell us where the gymnasium is situated, or, rather, take us there."

"No," she refused flatly. "I shall rather tell King Cyranius about your discovery," she said.

"I think not, Lady, for it will mean breaking your oath... the scroll Stephen holds says that you will keep your oath, you will protect Kind Heart's identity until your father releases you... and this scroll, written by your father's hand gives you until... let me think, but you already know about the celebration tomorrow evening, don't you? You wrote Kind Heart's reply for the king, how very convenient to be both people... but there are going to be some surprises that you don't know about yet.

"You have until tomorrow night at sunset and after that the day after your birthday, Jennava, I promise you that you'll show me the gymnasium. Won't she, men?"

To Jenna's annoyance, the four grinned at each other, obviously sharing a secret.

At the captain's signal, his men sauntered back along the high stone walk. Before Jenna realized what was happening, Captain Ross grasped her by both shoulders and kissed her fiercely on the lips. Pressing her firmly back into the crenellation, he drew the scroll from her sleeve. He released her.

"You've never been kissed before. This knowledge gives me much satisfaction and confidence," he said, smiling, "I kissed you first, and it shall not be our last."

Jenna could think of nothing to say, but longed to slap the smile from his face. She lifted her hand, but he caught it in midair. With a flick and a twist, she could have landed him on his back, instead, she slapped his arrogant face with her other hand. He would have had to release or crush the scroll to have prevented her.

"You and I shall compliment each other very well, Jennava," he promised, frowning from the sting of her hand on his cheek. Turning, he followed his men.

Jenna fumed, walking back and forth along the walk. She recalled the words her father had written on the scroll and knew that she would have to wait until tomorrow night. *Then I shall be free...* she told herself. *I shall be free. I shall be able to tell the king everything and I shall answer all his questions without worrying about protecting Kind Heart's identity.*

Jenna had missed breakfast. She descended from the battlements to enter the chapel to pray. She remained there, and her presence in the chapel was reported to the king. He wanted to go to her, there were just thirty-six hours until she would belong to Kind Heart forever, he thought. But he refused himself, and kept working on the pile of papers on the office desk. He longed for the fresh air he had missed on the battlements, but not as much as he missed seeing Lady Jennava. *I must get used to it... not seeing her... perhaps a good ride will rid me of my melancholy. I shall have an early lunch and go for a gallop on that magnificent brown creature he owns.*

~ * ~

Captain Duff rode into Gifford Castle. He was alone. He reported to Sir Lowell who delegated him to return to duty on the morrow, he would be required to organize the company of guards in the courtyard and at the front door of the castle for the duration of the celebration.

Duff found Jenna reading in the chapel and asked to speak with her privately. He followed her outside to the middle of the vegetable garden, where people could see them, but not hear their words.

"I told Millie," he confided.

She had no heart to say that she suspected this.

"It's... difficult... to keep things from ones wife," he hung his head, "I know how Samson felt."

"Samson?"

"Yes, he was betrayed by Delilah."

"Millie... has betrayed... you... Duff? Where's Millie, now?"

"In Aponia... not far away, just over the border past the king's land... she went with a group of gypsies..."

"Aponia?" Jenna was shaken. "Your children, where are the children?"

"They're over in Ferrah, with my parents. You'd remember the village, it's just over the border, but you have to go through Mayern, at the base of the hills to get to it, but you'd know that... I took them there this morning, after I told Millie that she could not take them... with her, but she didn't want to anyway... to my shame. She's always done what she wants."

"Why did she go to Aponia?"

"She went under Sidra's orders, to King Maslen's castle, to take information. I don't know all the reasons, or details, but my Millie is on the other side, Lady."

Jenna shook her head, unable to believe this news. She loved Millie, and Millie was a traitor.

"I've only found out myself, Lady. You knew that Sidra is Millie's sister, didn't you?"

"I, yes, I did know that."

"Millie wanted me to go to Aponia with her, but I... I refused..."

"You thought about it, though, Duffy, didn't you?"

He did not reply, but bowed his head.

"Thank you for coming back, that decision must have cost you dearly. But we must go to Ferrah, and bring Jennava, Aaron and David back here... Millie must have weaned David, he'll be missing her. "

"She... she's never been one to... to over-mother them, you know that, Lady. But... but... how could I know that she... she... Millie was... was..." he could not continue, his voice was choked with tears, then he gulped and shuddered and admitted, "Millie... I found out that she's been spying for Sidra... that's why she was close to you, Lady. She... Millie... heard what I said, when I discovered you were Kind Heart. She only pretended to be sleeping. She'd rather be close to you, Lady, than to her own children—there was a payment for spying, but nothing for being my wife, or mothering our children. I thought they'd be safer there... than here..." he said, now rethinking his choice.

"In that unprotected little village? Millie will have told Sidra that they're there. Do you think Sidra will spare them, if they can be used to trap Kind Heart? I don't mind Kind Heart being captured, Duffy, but I won't allow your children to become hostages in Maslen's bid to get hold of me. No, and Millie must have told them that I'm the one they need to capture... tell me, Duffy, does Sidra believe I'm Kind Heart?"

"I didn't get close enough myself to speak to Sidra, Millie will have done enough of that... I don't know if Sidra will believe Millie... I... I do know that Millie wasn't sure about it, and kept questioning me. She wanted me to talk to Sidra but as I said, I refused."

Jenna felt as if she stood on quicksand. *Should I ride to the village in Ferrah to fetch the children? Are they really there? It makes me ill to think of Millie spying... sending information to Sidra about me. And Duff... he's Millie's husband and he loves her to distraction...*

"Do you really think the children are in danger?" Duff asked, and Jenna felt very vulnerable.

She answered truthfully, "Yes, they are indeed in danger..." she knew that whichever side Duff was truly on, it did not bode well for his children.

"I'll go and fetch them," he said, determined. "You shall not come, Lady, there's danger out there. I can smell it! I don't know how many of Sidra's men are in Cyran but Millie spoke of Maslen sending gangs from Aponia. Evidently, they have a contingency standing by near our border. And... and you have more than enough in your hands here..." he frowned, wondering if he should speak of the morrow—the celebration was to be a surprise for her.

"I'm coming with you, Duffy, I'll have them pack some food from the pantry, with a skin of goat's milk for David, then we'll fetch horses from the baronial stables." She did not want to say it, but she could not allow Duff any opportunity to send word that she had done as they expected. *Whether Duff knows it or not, both Millie and Sidra know that I will not leave the children in Ferrah... the children must be rescued from such danger... I'll never forgive myself if they are harmed in any way.*

Twenty-nine

Jenna and Duff experienced a delay in gaining horses from the baronial stables. Jenna discovered that the king had filled the stables with his horses, and most of her horses had been stabled elsewhere. The king's head groom was called and he told a young groom to send a messenger to tell the king that Lady Jennava requested horses.

Feeling frustrated, Jenna waited, then, realizing that this was a 'mission' even though she was not riding as Kind Heart, she knelt there, in the stables, to pray. Her prayer was different from other times. New strength flooded her. "You'll help me, Lord, to rescue these children," she said.

The young groom returned with the messenger.

"The king went out, about an hour ago through the secret tunnel, and he went riding on one of Kind Heart's horses," the messenger said. "A large company rode with him and they had their horses in the place called 'Great Meadow' where the king's army is setting up camp."

Jenna realized that the secret tunnels were now common knowledge and the king was using the passage as an exit from the castle to go for his daily ride. How everything had changed, was still changing—she felt like a stranger in her own home.

"Perhaps we'll meet the king, on our way," Jenna said, fervently hoping that such a thing would not happen. She chose two horses and commanded that the grooms saddle them.

Jenna rode a strong young gelding named Lad—one she had not ridden before; he had been born the year before her father died, and was Oak's son.

Captain Duff rode a stallion named Marquis. He had been one of her father's favorites. He was not far off being too old for a mission such as this, but Jenna felt confident in the horse's knowledge of what was expected of him.

Having taken the road west towards Zerka, Jenna turned her horse south, heading to a small range of hills. They had not been riding for ten minutes when Jenna saw the king and his escort approaching from the west. The western lowland of Gifford district was his favorite riding place.

When Jenna did not slow down but ignored his raised hand, the king turned his horse south, in pursuit. Both Lad and Marquis gained, and Jenna knew she could easily outride him.

What if I don't return from this mission... I'll never see him again... She called to Marquis, "Slow, boy!" Jenna drew back on the reins and Lad reluctantly slowed.

Turning her horse, she waited for the king and his men to catch up to her. Soon the pair was surrounded. Jenna could not believe that the king rode with such a company, *there must be a hundred men here* she estimated.

Oak pointed his nose across to her as the king drew alongside and Jenna fondled him, while at the same time holding Lad in check—he longed to gallop free again.

The king stared at her, then at Duff.

"You should ride with an escort, Lady Jennava, we hear there are trespassers in Gifford District."

"Trespassers?" Jenna queried, "from Aponia?"

"Yes... we'll escort you back to the safety of the castle."

"Please, Your Majesty, I wish to complete... my ride. I've just begun..." Jenna disaffirmed.

"You shall have half my escort, then," the king said gruffly, turning as though to give a command.

"Excuse me, Your Majesty," Jenna spoke in a louder tone of voice, and the king looked back at her, "I must take my ride to the north of Ferrah District... more than an hour away. I shall take a shorter route, over the hills. Perhaps... if you can spare six riders, those with the younger horses, it would greatly assist our mission."

King Cyranius stared at Jenna, silent for a moment. He did not need to ask who was going on the mission with her other than Duff. It was obvious to him, he thought—*she's meeting Kind Heart... she has a message to give him and he has a rescue to action...*

As Jenna hoped, the king allowed her to continue and gave her not six men, but twelve. Before releasing them to her, he gathered the horsemen around him. As her eyes examined the faces of the chosen guards, she felt relieved that neither Ross nor Stephen was among them. *Captain Ross is planning something,* she warned herself. *I wouldn't believe it beneath him to be arranging something with Sidra...* She bit her bottom lip, remembering Ross's unwelcome kiss... it had almost bruised her lips... she felt sure that Cyranius' kiss would be tender and gentle.

Jenna pulled herself out of her musing to listen to the commands King Cyranius gave to Captain Derrick.

"While Lady Jennava is with you, ride with her, do as she says, go where she leads and when Kind Heart rendezvous with you, he's in charge. As soon as you arrive back, Captain Derrick, report to me, no matter what the hour—have me awakened, if necessary."

King Cyranius watched until Jenna and her small escort was out of sight. They rode towards the hills, and he felt puzzled. He spoke to another captain, saying, "Take three riders, Alben, don't catch them or be seen, but if you're needed, join them and give assistance. If you're able, persuade Kind Heart to ride back to Gifford with Lady Jennava."

~ * ~

The ride over the wooded hills went without incident. Turning her horse, Jenna said, "Wait here, all of you. Kind Heart will ride back to meet you and lead you to the village... Captain Duff will explain the purpose of the rescue."

She dismounted and slid a slasher from a sheath she had attached to Lad's saddle. Slashing at some heavy undergrowth she led Lad behind her, and within a few seconds, disappeared.

It had been over three years since Jenna had been to this cottage—she had not needed to come to Ferrah as Kind Heart since that last visit with her father.

The small wooden cottage was undisturbed, completely overgrown, like an ivy-covered cave. Jenna hoped that the costume she had left here would still be in its trunk and wearable. She had to slash vines from the door, and a musty smell greeted her from within the closed room of the hut.

Clothes in the trunk smelled of camphor mixed with lavender, but Jenna ignored this, and soon dressed in Kind Heart's leather costume. She shook out the silky wig, and looked for the feathered-hat in vain, then she remembered—it had been shot from her head, taken by an arrow, fired by a guard at Ferrah Castle who had mistaken her for a burglar. Memories flew back, her father had been extremely fit and well for the rescue that had been accomplished from the castle battlements. They had used the wheel on a wire to 'fly' away to safety.

Jenna left her memories, and knelt to pray—indeed, she knew she needed Divine help more than ever now. She prayed that God would forgive her this last time she dressed as a young man and that He would help her rescue the children. Taking her rolled up black dress with her, she pushed it into one of Lad's saddlebags.

Jenna had half expected Captain Derrick to follow her and when she found all the men where she had left them, she hoped her conclusion was correct—these twelve men were loyal to their king, they had obeyed his command and done as she asked.

Riding Lad directly to Captain Duff, Jenna spoke to him, saying, "Follow exactly the path of my horse and command the others to do the same—keep strictly in single-file. At the bottom of the hills, still within the woods, we'll take to a riverbed that flows from your father's village."

Jenna led the way, and the thirteen riders followed, one behind the other. This was the only way out of this wilderness, Jenna's father had told her. After passing a large rock shaped like a doorknob, Jenna's eyes searched for the huge fir-tree that was actually three trunks growing entwined together. The first Kind Heart, the one before her father, had planted land-marks all over the country, just like this. Jenna's heart lurched as she remembered that Captain Ross was the owner of the maps charting these secrets. If he knew in which direction she had ridden, he could follow her. Jenna wished that the king had found her father's secret room, then he would know all the secrets now and he would know of the routes over Lessor and Tulip Mountains. *Captain Ross is out of order, insubordinate... he's actually a traitor if he doesn't tell the king.*

Jenna chided herself as she steered Lad up out of the water, riding directly to the three entwined fir-trunks up ahead. Gaining the grassy bank, she spoke to herself severely, *I must forget the king and Ross. I must keep my mind on the task ahead and watch diligently for foes, or I'll be finished.*

Dismounting, Jenna undid one side of Lad's reins, tethering it low, to allow him to crop the nearest grass. One by one the men arrived and copied her actions, spreading their horses along the riverbank so that they would not become entangled.

"Where are we?" Duff whispered in her ear.

Jenna slid a heavy wooden weapon from a sheath at the back of Lad's saddle. She slung a small bag over her shoulder. Then she answered his question.

"We're about three hundred yards from Boen." Seeing surprise and doubt flood Duff's face, she added, "We've circled around and come in from the south—if we're expected, they'll be watching for us to arrive from the west or north, not from the south. This traverse can only be done in summer, Duffy, when the river is low enough to walk on the sand-bar along the middle. The winter rains sweep much of the sand away, but by the end of May, it has returned.

"Now, here's what we'll do..." Jenna did not change her voice-tone, but spoke softly, even though the men gathered around to listen. She outlined her plan.

"Five will remain, one to watch, four to care for the horses. Remove the saddles, rub the horses down, replace the saddles, water them then, you'll be busy. At the first sign of our return, or after an hour, redo the reins so that we may ride off immediately.

"The rest of us will walk in the river, up the edge of the riverbank to the village. Just below the miller's house is Duff's parent's cottage. While I enter the house to speak with Duff's parents and get the children, the rest of you will take up concealed positions to watch for any sign of a party lying in wait to ambush us.

"You must all wait for my signal, before we leave the river, things are often not as they seem and it will be of benefit to wait and gain insight as to what might be in store.

"Tell us, Duff, what might we expect of the village, at about half after three in the afternoon?"

"There's been a market today, La—Sir," he almost said Lady, "but they'll be about packing up. The mill will be grinding for tomorrow—the old folk'll be napping, as will the younger'uns, and there'll be a general preparing of the victuals for their evening meals, like the butcher'll still be cutting up meat... and most of the men work the fields till sundown—
"

Jenna interrupted, "So, all should be at work... this will be our clue, if the village is still, we must expect that a party is planned for us—then I shall be the one to greet it and you'll all wait to take the children if they are there. Do you hear me Duff? You will not play the brave man here—your children need a father. You'll take one child to the horses, Duff. Captain Derrick, you'll do the same, take a child, and you..." she looked at another man, "you'll take a child, that's all three—you others will watch their backs and follow... to the horses. Duff, you'll ride Lad, leave

Marquis for me—untie him and say the word, 'stay'." Jenna hoped she was wrong and that everything would be normal and no one had set a trap to catch Kind Heart when he came to collect Duff's children.

But Jenna's premonitions proved right—not a soul stirred, the mill was still and the marketplace empty, save a cart here and there, looking abandoned.

Duff stared at Jenna. He remembered how she had rescued the prince—he had waited in that tree, obediently, wondering if she could achieve her improbable goal and she had done it. Now it was his children at risk and he knew, in his heart, that he trusted her.

"God is with you," he said, tears brimming beneath his eyes.

"Pull yourself together, Duff," she said gruffly, "and pray for us, pray for us all—especially the children."

Not a person could be seen. Jenna noticed tools and equipment, abandoned in odd places. She crawled from a clump of bushes to the back of Duff's parent's cottage and peered through a window-hole. The one large room of the cottage was empty of life. Jenna felt her heart pounding; she wondered where the villagers were. Duff had left his children here, in this cottage, just this morning—surely Sidra's men did not expect Kind Heart to be here yet?

Peering around the other side of the small home, Jenna saw a thick young brigand, sitting on an upturned pail, whittling a piece of wood with his sharp dagger. A brutal spike-laden mace lay at his feet. She knew this was no experienced warrior. His clothes were tattered and his boots holed. No, this fellow had likely just joined Sidra, or he was working with Knight Red's leaderless lot. Never did a weathered warrior whittle wood with his number one weapon. This fellow had been put in an unlikely place to watch!

Jenna crept up on the man silently and with one swift movement, she scuttled him, stunning him swiftly and tightly tying his wrists to his ankles behind his back. When he opened his eyes a minute later, it was to find he could not move without pain, and Kind Heart held the point of his own dagger at his throat.

"Where are the children?" she demanded...

"Ch... children?" he stammered, blinking back tears.

"The three children who were brought to this cottage at sunrise?" She pushed the point of the blade so that it pressed his skin.

"In the mill... they're in the mill... all three... don't please don't... they said you don't kill no one... I've got a wife and mother!"

"You should be with them, not here bullying innocent people," Jenna said, then, "answer my questions, and you'll live to see them again. Tell me, where did the villagers go?"

"They took off south... t'ward the castle... we drove them... and they ran..."

"What about the old couple... the owners of this house?"

"They be in the mill too."

"How many of you are here, around and in this village?"

"Fifty meybe... a hundred... some more arrived... an' some went back t'ward Gifferd... others be on the road."

"Who do you take orders from?" Jenna asked wondering. She took the dagger away from the man's throat and stabbed it deep into the soil near the house so that only the handle showed.

"Oi joined along the way, I'm with K'nort."

"K'nort? Who's K'nort?"

"He's the brudder of the one what got killed..."

"Knight Red? Yes, K'nort is Knight Red's brother," Jennava said. She had heard of K'nort. He was reported as not being as evil as his brother, but nevertheless, like his brother, he was not one whom a person knew long as an enemy—he took delight in what he called 'warranted assassination.' 'An eye for an eye,' was K'nort's motto. When K'nort killed someone, it was usually said 'he deserved it.'

"Yeah! K'nort were right mad about Knight Red's dyin' and he says he's going to get both Kind Heart and that lady and teach them some lessons. He wants revenge for his brother's life."

The removal of the dagger had given the man confidence and loosened his tongue. "I don't reckon y' got a chance in a million on y' own... there's a couple-a-hundred men on the road north... they're waitin' for y'... how did y' get pass' them?"

"How many are in the village?" Jenna asked.

"Not many... ten or p'raps twenty... they mainly wanted to seal orf all the ways in."

"How many are in the mill with the prisoners?"

"They only have about five, or six... one for each pris'ner."

Jenna gagged the man and unbound his feet. Supporting him to stand, she pulled him towards the bushes from where she had come. Setting him down in the midst of the bushes, she whispered, "Now, whichever way you look at it, being in this village right now means that you might not live to see either your wife or your mother again! If K'nort's men don't kill you for letting me capture you, then the villagers will, or the king's men. I'd suggest you lie low until I come back and free you—then, stay in the woods until you see the way is clear to return home. Understand?" She received a nod, and tied him firmly, hand and foot, to the thickest trunk in the shrubbery.

~ * ~

Duff was angry to hear that his three children, with his parents, were prisoners in the mill. While Captain Derrick pondered on how Kind Heart had gained the information without being detected, Jenna discussed her plan to enter the mill and rescue the five hostages.

When Duff heard of the numbers of men in and around the village, with so many more out on the roads, he agreed that if they could make the rescue without making a noise, they would likely make an uninterrupted escape.

"They'll burn the village," Captain Derrick said. "We should've brought all the men, then we could have prevented it."

"We'll have to help them rebuild it," Jenna said, feeling sad. It was a pretty little village, prosperous, built by the riverside. "At least the villagers are safe... they evidently escaped to the castle."

~ * ~

Jenna climbed up behind the waterwheel, with Captain Derrick on her heels. Duff sidled around the corner of the mill house, falling into a crawl, moving towards the back door where he would wait for Jenna's signal to enter.

Climbing in a window at the top, Jenna hauled Derrick up beside her. She could hear the murmur of men's voices from below her. Silently, she moved to the protecting rail. Lying on the floor, she peered over to see that three men sat at a table, playing cards. One man watched from a window, looking toward the village and the other sat guarding the trapdoor to the cellar, where Jenna guessed the five prisoners were locked.

"Come down the steps and help tie them up," she hissed in Derrick's ear.

Placing the wooden handle of the mallet in her mouth between her teeth, Jenna rotated herself over the rail to land standing on the table-top. Snatching the mallet, she swung it, calculating each blow. One by one, the three men, fell.

"Now, Duff!" she shouted.

With a somersault, Jenna flew off the table, and the man at the window felt the ball of the mallet thump under his chin. The guard at the trapdoor stood, aghast, his eyes on Captain Derrick, descending the wooden steps, his sword extended, wearing the uniform of the king's guard.

Duff burst into the room. The man held his hands up in surrender. Pulling lengths of prepared rope and strips of strong fabric from her bag, Jenna urged that they tie the men firmly and gag them.

Jenna followed Duff down into the cellar, and it was with great relief that they found the old couple, safe and well, locked in a small cold pantry where cheeses were kept. Jenny and David, huddled in a pile of rugs, were sleeping, while Aaron was awake.

After tearful greetings and hugs, they wanted to leave the mill-house with its tied-up brigands.

Duff's parents, whom Jenna estimated as being in their fifties, were not as frail as they appeared. Duff's father elected to carry Jenny and the grandmother disallowed any person other than herself, to carry the baby, David. Aaron declared that no one was carrying him, he was big enough to go on his own. Duff stood protectively beside him.

With Derrick and Jenna to guide them in the river, they soon reached the waiting guards who expected to be called to do battle.

"Take it quietly," Jenna warned as they splashed in the water, wading along the river's edge. It was then she remembered the young man in the bushes. *I must keep my word. God would expect me to do as I promised,* she told herself. *It may be that he tells the truth, he has a wife and mother and will go back to a normal life.*

"I have to go back," she whispered, "go on, take the horses, ride single in the middle of the river on the high sand and, remember, tell Marquis 'stay'."

All the way back, Jenna expected to be attacked—she counted on it and her every nerve was prepared to defend herself. *I want to see Cyranius again, to be with him... I love him... yes, I love him... I want him to be safe... he needs to know that K'nort is vengeful... and the passage is open from the cave-stable, it would not be too difficult for men to enter there... I must warn him...*

Jenna's senses were on full alert—it was quiet, abnormally quiet. She gained the bushes, expecting to find the man gone. They would have discovered him, and a dozen men would leap on her, capture her, and drag her off to become a prisoner of King Maslen's... but the fellow was still there.

Jenna loosened the man's ropes enough for him to work his way free. "Remember what I said, you must crawl into the forest and hide until you can return to your wife and your mother... and thank God every day that you are still alive!"

Jenna's heartbeat slowed as she crawled back to the riverbank. *When I take this costume off today,* she told herself, *I never want to wear it again, not ever!*

Marquis was waiting when Jenna arrived on the grassy verge of the river. She mounted him and rode down into the water to the center. One bend in the river away from the exit place, she gained the tail of the company.

They rode up into the woods and Jenna rode Marquis to the fore of the company to lead the way through the trees.

What a rescue, the men thought, as they carried the five freed prisoners into Gifford district.

Thank You, God, Jenna prayed, *You are so gracious, Lord. I don't deserve Your compassion, yet You've protected me and shielded me from harm.*

Thirty

The sun sat above the western hills sending crimson messages to command the few clouds to change their colors when Kind Heart and company approached Gifford Castle, having ridden in from the south.

Jenna had decided not to return to the hut; it was two miles out of the way and would have taken longer. Choosing a shorter, more direct way home, Jenna was pleased she had—the toddler was now screaming in hunger and discomfort, having devoured all of the goat's milk. Jenny was sobbing softly, her leg ached and her back and head pained her. Aaron, now seated in front of a burly guard, slept. The grandparents, each riding tandem with a guard, suffered in silence—they were not saddle-seasoned.

Duff's mother hung tightly on to the pommel of the saddle, a grim picture indeed. Jenna had tried to give encouragement, but the lady just stared at her every time she said, "You're doing great, Grandmother, just great, we're only about half an hour from Gifford.

Never had the imposing outline of Gifford Castle looked so welcoming. Jenna longed to be able to cast off Kind Heart's yoke forever and rejoiced in the fact that there was only twenty-four hours before she would be free.

Unwelcome questions nagged her contemplation—it was as if her father's voice spoke in her head. *Who will care for those who are wrongfully treated, if you don't? Who has a heart that is kind enough to rescue those who are unjustly imprisoned? Who have you trained to continue the good work of Kind Heart?*

Jenna tried to conceive an answer—*Gavin and Kevin could be trained for the role; I don't think the king would allow Edward to become a Kind Heart. The prince would be eager, I know he would, then there is Duff's son, Aaron, but he's too young yet to train, and it will be years before he would be ready to go out alone.*

~ * ~

Prince Edward, with Gavin and Kevin, darted excitedly from crenellation to crenellation, atop the southern rampart, their eyes scanning the fields, the woods and the countryside beyond the castle. Ever since the king had given the news that Lady Jennava had ridden south towards Ferrah to gain Kind Heart's help on a mission, the prince had watched for her safe return.

Then, Alben and the three other riders had arrived. They had lost sight of Lady Jennava and the company, somehow they had vanished in the woods. After riding in circles and becoming lost for over an hour, the quad had managed to find their way out of the forest. Alben had decided to return to Gifford. It had been most frustrating for them.

The dinner gong sounded and the boys were just about to turn away to follow the Prince, when Gavin and Kevin called together, "Look, it looks like Kind Heart. See, he's leading the company—the horses are only walking, they must be tired. Look, there are children with them, some horses have two people on them... they must have made the rescue! But where is Lady Jennava?"

Guards, servants, attendants, slaves, all who were not needed elsewhere, hurried to the courtyard of Gifford Castle. The children and the grandparents were helped off the horses. Eyes followed Kind Heart as the slim black-clad figure with the silky wig led the late Sir Charles' horse, Marquis, into the stables.

King Cyranius, followed by Prince Edward, rushed out the castle doors. Fingers pointed towards the stables and a body of guards followed the royal pair.

Swiftly removing the bag containing her dress, Jenna handed the horse's reins into the care of a groom, and hurried to the end of the baronial stable.

"Sorry old boy," she said to a horse in the end stall, "but you'll have to make room for me." So saying, she opened the stone wall at the back of the stall, entered the cavity, and closed the wall.

"Where is he? Kind Heart? Where's he gone?" the king demanded, calling, "Fetch more torches."

But though they searched the stables from end to end, Kind Heart had disappeared.

~ * ~

Jenna moved cautiously through the secret tunnels, expecting to encounter Captain Ross and his three colleagues or others of the king's guard. To her surprise, her way was clear until she stepped into the corridor outside her quarters. Two servants, bearing trays of food, walked along the passage towards her. For a few seconds, they stood stock still, staring, until it dawned in their minds just who they faced.

Jenna stepped to her door and reached to open it.

"Ahhh!" one woman cried, "Ahhh!" Lifting her hands in shock, she released the tray into the air. Food, cutlery and crockery clattered, smashed and splashed on the floor.

The other woman trembled, but gripped her tray as if it were alive and might escape.

As Jenna disappeared, closing the door soundly behind her, the screaming woman turned and ran back the way she had come. Placing the tray on the floor, the other woman followed, knowing they had news to broadcast. Kind Heart himself was in the castle!

Stepping into her small sitting room, Jenna came face to face with two more servant-women. Together, they arranged a huge bouquet of roses, all colors, in a large silver vase.

Neither woman had seen Kind Heart before, but had often listened to ageless descriptions of him. The black leather outfit, the dark silky hair and curling moustache — but where was the purple-plumed hat?

"This... flowers... it's for Lady Jennava... it's... her birthday tomorrow..." the lady explained.

"Lady Jennava requests a bath," Jenna said, stepping to her bedchamber. The women did not move. "Fetch hot water, then!" Jenna said fiercely, waving the back of her right hand. The women bustled from her quarters. Jenna hurried into her bedchamber. She opened her clothes closet—all her black dresses were gone, only her blue dress and Judith's pink dress remained. She stared at the bag she carried; it contained a very crumpled dress, but it was all she had.

Snatching a pair of slippers from the dressing room, Jenna practically ran back through the now empty sitting room, out into the deserted corridor and into the secret passage. Taking care to close the panel behind her, she hurried along the dark tunnel and down the narrow steps. Down, down, she was pleased that no one challenged her flight. Only when she reached the gymnasium did she rest, feeling she had reached the last place of privacy left for her.

I'm more afraid of the king seeing me dressed in these men's clothes than I am of a hundred evil warriors, she chided herself. *I can't bear to imagine what he'll think of me... I can't bear it... he'll hate me forever when he knows I dress like this... I hate myself.*

What did he say? He keeps believing and he confesses his humanness every day. At least he is human, half of me is a legend, and I'm not sure what the other half is...

Jenna paced back and forth in the gymnasium, then, wanting to accelerate the time it would take for the servants to fill her bath, she dragged the wig from her hair and threw off the leather tunic, the padded arrow-proof vest, and the leather trousers. Wearing only her chemise and boots, she drove herself savagely through her workout routine until perspiration drenched her body. Beginning at the acrobatic bar again, she repeated the workout, hoping that the water in the bath would have cooled.

Lacing the front of the black dress firmly and changing her boots for the slippers, Jenna climbed the ladder and opened the portal into the tunnel. The way was clear and she soon made her way back to the panel near her quarters.

Guards standing at attention outside Jenna's door blinked—one moment the corridor had been empty, the next, the lady walked towards them. They had been commanded not to detain Lady Jennava, or Kind Heart, but to send a message to Sir Lowell if either turned up there.

Jenna found three servant-women waiting for her, one left the chamber in haste, whilst the others stayed to assist her to bathe and dress.

"King Cyranius has gone to dine, but wishes to see you as soon as you have finished your bath," a servant-woman told her. "One of the guards waiting at the door will escort you to him."

The king was still eating his evening meal when the message arrived that Lady Jennava had entered her quarters.

Jenna decided to take her time, soaking in the bath. After twenty minutes, she ordered more hot water to be brought to keep the temperature so deliciously relaxing. The pungent oils she added seemed to seep into her very being and renew her emotions.

When Natalie arrived, offering her a back massage, Jenna did not refuse, but ignored the small impatient audience to further indulge herself. Natalie used a combination of aromatic oils, finishing off with oil of lavender.

When Jenna finally opened the door to obey the king's request, the guard informed her that the king had kingdom matters to care for, and would see her in the morning.

Feeling annoyed to be disappointed when she had so enjoyed the long bath, Jenna dined alone in her sitting room, intending to retire early. Just as she completed her meal, Prince Edward was announced to her chamber. Gavin and Kevin followed him. Dressed alike, and looking extremely smart, the twins were difficult to name.

Standing, Jenna curtsied, as did the two servant-women who waited on her.

"Come, sit," the prince said, indicating the small sofa, "I wish to speak with you."

Jenna obeyed and sat beside the prince on the sofa.

"You smell nice," the prince said, adding, "I shouldn't say such things, but it's true. You look nice, too." He stood and turned to study her in the pretty blue gown. Knowing she should not remain seated while the prince stood, Jenna rose to her feet.

"No, I want you to sit," he said, "I want to look at you while you answer my questions." He waited until she sat, then asked, "What horse did you ride back from Ferrah? And how did you get into the castle? No one saw you."

Jenna smiled and said, "You'd like to know who Kind Heart is, wouldn't you?"

"Of course I would, but you won't tell me, will you?"

"If you save all your questions until tomorrow night, after sunset, then I shall tell you, Prince Edward," Jenna said.

"Do you promise?"

"I promise."

"Then, perhaps we'll talk about tomorrow. It's your birthday and my brother said that I was to confirm that you would breakfast with us... not in the great hall, but in a... a special place... it's a secret, because it's your birthday... we want to make the morning special for you," Prince Edward did not want to tell Jenna that he could not speak of the wonderful decorations with which the great hall would be adorned for the occasion of the birthday party tomorrow night, and the need to keep her out of that great chamber.

"I'll count it an honor to take breakfast with you, thank you," Jenna said, smiling. The prince's next words tore the smile from her face.

"My brother said to tell you that if you would like to invite *him* to have breakfast with us, then you may."

"Him?" Jenna asked, even though she knew the name he would voice.

"Kind Heart, of course. But I was hoping we could have you to ourselves for this last time... although I would like to meet Kind Heart and speak to him... we want to make sure," the prince faltered. Kevin and Gavin both coughed as if in warning.

"We shall see you in the morning then," Prince Edward bowed and strode from the room.

Jenna frowned now, feeling disturbed, wondering what was to be in store for her on the morrow.

Thirty-one

Other than triple the usual number of guards at either end of the battlements, Jenna stood alone, watching the sun rise on her birthday morning. She had been born at sunset, and mused that it was not until this evening that she truly had lived for twenty years. Her birth into the world had brought about her mother's death. *I don't know what it is to have a mother's love,* she thought, *Natalie is the nearest and she loves me, I know her love is real.* A movement caught her eye, and she turned, hoping that it would be the king, not Captain Ross. But it was just the guards, moving to watch horses riding towards the castle.

Jenna descended to the chapel, feeling lonely. *It's my birthday and I feel I have no one.* As she entered the sanctuary, she thought, *I have You, Lord God. You are with me. I feel Your Presence, and I thank You for that. You didn't have to make Yourself known to me but You have, and I love You for being with me.*

"Ah, there you are Lady Jennava... my... we've looked everywhere for you..."

Jenna stood, turning to see whom it was entering the chapel in such a noisy manner, interrupting her solace.

Two women hurried to her.

"Now, that simply won't do, will it... it's your birthday and you're to have breakfast with the king... we brought a special dress to your bedchamber for you to wear, and lo and behold, the bed was empty. Come along then dear, you don't want to keep the king and the prince waiting do you?"

Jenna allowed herself to be taken back to her quarters by the two fussing women who dressed her in a new delightful powder-blue day gown. Another woman arranged her hair.

Prince Edward waited in the corridor, extending his arm for her to take. To Jenna's surprise, he directed the way to the stairway upwards. Up, up, up, until they were on a topmost tower of the castle. The twins followed the pair.

King Cyranius waited at the top. All around him were colorful flags and flowers. Footmen stood to attention, waiting to serve them. In the center of the stone floor sat a small table, set with golden cutlery and vessels.

Jenna drew a deep breath, enjoying the slight breeze and the gentle morning sunshine. She stepped to the crenellation, looking at the countryside with unveiled delight. Drawing another breath, she turned to view Tulip Mountain, enjoying the spectacular view.

Both the king and the prince drew deep breaths. The lady was so very beautiful. The pale blue dress made her eyes appear all the more a shade of mysterious and the sun was trapped into small flames of gold all over her head—she looked like a princess.

Jenna turned back from looking at the view to find the king standing close behind her.

"Kind Heart did not accept our invitation?" King Cyranius asked, his eyes searching her face. He wanted the man to be here so that his heart would stop its pounding. The only way to rid himself of pain was to see them together, the king felt sure of this. Knowing about Kind Heart did not stop him desiring her, but to see them together. . . he wanted the man here! Now! "Where is he? Is he in the castle?"

Jenna did not know how to answer these questions. If she said 'no,' she lied, was Kind Heart not here? If she said 'yes,' which was the truth, he would wait for someone who could not come. She bowed her head.

"Kind Heart is not coming?" Prince Edward asked, then said, "I'm glad, we have you to ourselves..." he nearly said 'for this last time,' but stopped himself. His brother had declared that he would tell her about this evening.

Jenna lifted her chin and looked at the king, saying, "It's to be just the three of us, Your Majesty."

"Then we shall begin. Come, be seated with us." So saying, he sat at the head of the table. Prince Edward sat at the other end, and Jenna found herself guided to sit on one side. Another chair had been placed opposite her, and she blushed, knowing it was supposed to be occupied by a man, her lover. Jenna felt shattered by the farce of it all.

The breakfast meal seemed to be stilted and uncomfortable, and when it was over, Jenna felt relieved.

The king stood, and Jenna would have copied, but he told her to remain seated.

"We have a birthday gift for you, Lady Jennava," the king said, giving a slight signal to a waiting attendant. The young man brought an official-looking scroll and gave to the king. King Cyranius placed it in on the table in front of Jenna.

Jenna stared at the scroll, not wanting to open it, she felt sure it bode ill for her.

"Open it," the king urged.

Jenna did not move.

"Open it, Lady Jenna," the prince said, his voice annoyed, "it's your birthday present!"

Taking the scroll in her hand, Jenna broke the seal and unrolled it. It was the title deed to her castle; but was made out to

Kind Heart, whose identity is:

"A space has been left for his name," the prince said as if she had not read the scroll, "and your name goes under it with his, but of course, it won't be Lady Jennava Gifford anymore, will it?"

Jenna knew what was implied, but looked up at the young prince as if she did not understand.

"We planned to keep it as a secret, Lady Jennava," the king said, "but I decided, last night that we had to tell you about it... not that it should be a surprise, but then since we had it confirmed..."

Jenna frowned, feeling that his words did not make sense. "Confirmed?" she asked.

"Yes, we received a letter last night, from Kind Heart, confirming your marriage, tonight, to him," the king explained. He then asked, "Has he not told you?"

"No," she said, feeling empty, and thinking, *How could he... tell me? What are they talking about?*

"We are planning a double celebration, tonight—your birthday and your wedding," the prince said, "but it's just as well he kept away, the bridegroom should not see the bride on the day of the wedding, should he?"

"You're not pleased?" the king asked.

"I... I... perhaps you would let me see the letter?" Jenna asked in a small voice.

"Why?"

Jenna wanted to blurt out that she could not marry Kind Heart, she *was* Kind Heart! How could they have a letter saying that Kind Heart would marry her? Who would make up a story like that?

Jenna stared at the scroll. "I shall need a quill and ink at this party to write Kind Heart's name here for you, at sunset, then... this... this farce will be over forever!" Rolling the scroll, she stood, holding it close.

King Cyranius realized, once again, this lady was about to dismiss herself from him.

"I cannot allow you to leave the castle today, Lady Jennava..."

"Why not?" she countered. She longed to go for a ride.

The king and the prince stared at her. Prince Edward had been warned against speaking of Kind Heart's letter.

"What did the letter say?" she demanded. "Did it suggest that I would run away?" She saw the prince's eyes light up with delight.

"It wasn't quite like that..." Prince Edward began.

"Edward!" the king warned. How could they tell her that the letter had warned that she could be contrary about the marriage, and that it would be better not to speak of it.

"You must remain in the castle, Lady Jennava, we want you to spend the rest of the day preparing yourself for tonight— we have three hundred guests arriving to attend your birthday."

"Do... do these... guests... know about the wedding?" Jenna dared to ask.

"A few... we should tell you, Lady Jennava, your brother is arriving, this afternoon..."

"Charles? He's coming?" Jenna's eyes lit with joy.

The king was pleased; at last he'd said something to make her happy.

"Charles will be able to explain so much, Your Majesty, Prince Edward, I'm so pleased he's coming. He has no oath... he can tell you all about Kind Heart, even before sunset."

"Why do you keep mentioning sunset?" the prince asked.

"That's when I am free from my vows to Kind Heart," Jenna said.

"You... you don't want to marry him?" the prince asked

"I can never marry Kind Heart," Jenna said, looking into the king's intense stare. "I wish you'd believe that—I can never marry him!" There was stony silence.

"I shall not leave the castle, I shall prepare myself for tonight. Please have someone inform me when my brother, Charles, arrives." She curtsied, first to the king, then to the prince. "Thank you for sharing your breakfast with me, it's been most enjoyable." She walked to the opening leading to the downward step-way. Turning she smiled and said, "And thank you for giving me my castle back."

Thirty-two

Jenna descended the central stairs, her hand on the arm of Sir Lowell. Wearing the dress that she now knew the king had ordered to be made for the celebration, Jenna looked like a beautiful princess. The dress was of blue and pink silk with white and lemon flowers sewn all around it—she looked like a haze of pink and blue dawn.

On her carefully dressed curls sat the Gifford coronet, and at her throat she wore the Gifford diamonds, with a matching bracelet on her wrist. As well as the diamond ring that the king had sent with the jewels, Jenna wore Kind Heart's ruby ring. It was the first time she had worn it since Prince Edward had recognized it in the palace and she had hidden it.

Jenna waited in the foyer. She was to be presented to the king and the prince in the great hall. She hoped her brother had arrived at last. Perhaps he would also be waiting for her in the great hall.

Young Jennava stepped over to Jenna, carrying a bouquet of white roses. Jenna took them in her hands and kissed the girl. She smiled at her young namesake and decided to enjoy her birthday. *At sunset, I'll tell the king about Kind Heart,* she promised herself and began forming words in her mind, words to explain it all to him.

Music sounded out, and the great hall doors opened. Jenna stepped into the hall, ablaze with the lights of many candles and decorated so much that it was no longer recognizable as her own great hall. Flowers hung in baskets, and bouquets had been placed everywhere. Flags, the national colors, hung from every pillar and ribbons, blue, pink, and lemon, matching the colors of her dress, streamed down from the great beams.

A birthday song was played and everyone sang, "Happy birthday Lady Jennava."

Jenna smiled widely; there were so many faces she knew. How could she feel animosity when they had all come to remember her birthday like this?

The music changed, and Jenna tried hard to recall what tune was being played. Sir Lowell increased his pace, and Jenna saw that ahead of her, at the end of the great hall, Brother Emil waited. Then she remembered. Brother Emil had married Sidney and Judith. The music sounding out was a wedding march.

King Cyranius and Prince Edward, looking resplendent in new royal costumes, stood to the side, waiting and watching.

Sir Lowell, with Jenna on his arm reached the front and the music died.

"What *is* this?" Jenna whispered to Sir Lowell. The commander turned around, looking for someone. Leaving her, he stepped over to stand beside the king.

"We are gathered together today, in the presence of this congregation..." began Brother Emil.

Jenna gathered her skirt in her hand and hurried to the king. Dropping a curtsy, she stepped closer and whispered, "Your Majesty, what is happening here?"

The king looked to the double doors, still open, the guards waiting there shook their heads.

King Cyranius leaned closer to Jenna, explaining softly, "We received another letter from Kind Heart, this afternoon and he asked that we play the birthday song, then the wedding march, and when you were here, to begin the wedding ceremony and he would come."

"I cannot marry Kind Heart," she said, her face flushed, wanting his support and understanding.

Her eyes seemed to say that she would rather marry him.

"You shall torment me no more," he hissed, causing her to draw back at his fierceness.

"He's here!" Prince Edward said excitedly.

A murmur rippled through the large crowd of guests, and Jenna turned. She gasped. Stepping through the double doors at the other end of the great hall was the tall figure of a man she had never expected to see. Clad in black, wearing the costume of Kind Heart, he lifted his purple-plumed hat from his head and bowed. Memories of her father caused her to shake her head in disbelief, then as the man strode confidently on the same plush carpet strip she had walked on, she knew it was not in the least like him. His step was arrogant, her father's had been graceful but wary, like a black panther. He did not wear a leather tunic, but a heavy satin one. Jenna knew that this man's chest was so wide that none of Kind Heart's leather tunics would fit him.

One royal guard, Stephen, walked behind, followed by two more guards—Jenna recognized them.

The man dressed as Kind Heart bowed to the king with another flourish of his hat. Jenna's eyes flew to meet King Cyranius's, but it was as though he had veiled every feeling. He stared at Kind Heart with a face of stone.

Jenna looked into Kind Heart's eyes, and saw Captain Ross's arrogant hazel eyes looking back into hers. The black silky wig, the moustache, moved closer and before Jenna realized his intentions, he kissed her.

Her thoughts raced and she knew she had to stop this! *I won't marry Captain Ross, I won't! How dare he dress in Kind Heart's clothes?* As if hearing a voice from the past, Jenna suddenly calmed—it was the years of training she had rigorously received, training that warned her not to panic or she would make an irreparably wrong move.

Think, she told herself, *think...*

"Continue with the ceremony," Captain Ross commanded, gripping her hand tightly. People gasped and murmured at the sound of his deep bass voice. It had been circulated that the current Kind Heart had the soft voice of a youth.

Jenna listened to Brother Emil's monotonous voice, and she waited.

After reading about, and stressing the blessed necessity of marriage, and it's honorable state, he said, "... and if anyone present can show just cause as to why this man and this woman should not be joined, let him now speak, or forever hold his peace..."

The silence was like the eye of a storm. Jenna dared to look at the king. His head was bowed. She wished he loved her enough to speak out, *but no, he's so determined that I marry, he does not care whom it is that I marry,* she thought. Jenna felt her anger rise. The hostility she had felt for him in the past almost swamped her. How plain did it have to be? *It's inexcusable!* she told herself.

She spun around and called her brother's name, "Charles! Charles, where are you?" He was her only hope, she thought. Charles knew the truth, he knew that this man was not Kind Heart. But would Charles have the courage to stand up for her? He had always been timid.

"It's the king's command, that we marry!" Captain Ross hissed in her ear. Looking back to Brother Emil, he said, "Continue."

"No!" Jenna cried, "I cannot... I cannot... marry this man!" Looking again into Captain Ross's face, she hissed at him, "You will never be Kind Heart, a costume cannot transform you... it comes from within!" Then louder, "I will not marry this man!"

"You cannot stop this, Jenna, you are mine. Together we will be Kind Heart," he said, his deep voice thundering in her ear.

Turning, Jenna's eyes scanned some of the many faces of the guests, she wondered if Doctor Breck were there? What about Captain Duff? Was he on duty in the courtyard? If she could have them hold this ceremony until sunset, then she could reveal herself and the doctor and the captain would verify her claim. It must be less than an hour away now.

Prince Edward stepped closer to the couple. He was trying to see the color of Kind Heart's eyes. They did not look at all blue, or violet, but more green, or brown.

"Continue with the ceremony!" Captain Ross demanded.

A loud commotion rose outside and the sound of battle cries were heard, surging from the outer courtyard, moving through the foyer and to the doors of the great hall. Guests scurried to cower against the walls.

Three dozen royal guards backed into the Hall, the first one turning and hurrying forward. Bowing before the king, he said, "Forgive us, Sire, but an army of men have illegally entered the castle. We've been unable to halt all of them." Turning, he called, "Protect the king and the prince!"

Two dozen royal guards, their swords drawn, formed a semi-circle around the front of the hall where Jenna stood with Captain Ross, who gripped her arm.

"Kind Heart!" a deep voice boomed out, "I want Kind Heart. Give me Kind Heart... and his Lady, and we'll leave the rest of you in peace!"

A man who looked like Knight Red's twin stood, tall, broad and insolent. It was K'nort, Knight Red's brother. He wore knight's armor, but without a helmet.

Captain Ross, his face white, signaled for a sword from one of his men. His hand trembled as he took it.

"Don't be such a fool," Jenna said.

"I've come to avenge my brother, Knight Red!"

"Not in here!" Jenna cried, "In the courtyard!" she had fears for the safety of the king and the prince. Behind K'nort a band of evil warriors stood, holding loaded crossbows and pointing them at the king's guards.

"In the courtyard!" Jenna said to the pale-faced bridegroom, "Move out to the courtyard!" She gave Ross's large frame a push and he did as she said, his sword extended. Cries of protest from both the king and the prince were lost in screams of fear from the ladies in the large congregation.

"Stay close to me," Jenna said to Stephen and Ross's two guards. She followed closely behind the captain, and as they reached the doors, Jenna cried, "Shut the doors behind us!"

Together with the men, she shut the huge doors on the rest of the king's guards. Before anyone realized what she was doing, Jenna rushed to open a cavity in the wall. Plunging her hand within it, she called, "Stand back! Everyone, stand back!" As a portcullis slid from above the transom, stones in the floor descended to make way for the falling spikes. With a crash, the great grille effectively closed the way back into the great hall. Jenna closed the cavity and turned to find Captain Ross looking at her with a bewildered stare.

"We shall be Kind Heart together, you and I," she quoted, without a hint of humor in her voice.

"I'll do this, Jennava," he said, with warning in his voice. "It's my battle, not yours."

"At least you're not a coward," Jenna said, "I give you credit for that, but you're wrong, Ross, it's my battle!"

They stepped into the foyer. It was a grim scene, king's guards lay dead and wounded, together with many of K'nort's men.

The courtyard was lined with both king's guards and K'nort's army, all waiting for this duel to be enacted. K'nort had given a challenge and everyone expected Kind Heart to answer it in the accepted manner. All that had been voiced about Kind Heart told everyone that he would make short work of the duel with K'nort.

K'nort held a spiked mace in one hand and a sword in the other.

"Step down here, Kind Heart!" K'nort yelled spitting as if he had a bad taste in his mouth.

"Wait!" Jenna cried, but it was as if Ross did not hear her.

As the captain descended the steps, Jenna rushed to the row of armory by the front castle door, snatching a shield from one set of armor and a stave with a ball on its end from another.

Four royal guards rushed to prevent her moving outside, and found themselves suddenly swept off their feet, sprawling on the ground.

As Jenna descended the stone steps, holding the voluminous fabric of her beautiful dress in her hand behind the shield, she heard K'nort cry, "Now!" She feared that the Aponian knight would behave more like a barbarian than like a gentlemen fighting a duel.

"No!" she cried, thinking of just how unprotected she and Ross were—he would not be wearing an arrow-proof vest. Instinctively lifting the shield to protect herself, Jenna bowed her head behind the heavy metal barrier.

Some fifty arrow-bolts flew from the crossbows held by K'nort's men. A dozen clattered against her shield, falling harmlessly to the cobblestones. One tore through her dress at her feet. Spinning herself in a pirouette of satin, silk and shield, she knew she would attract any unfired bolts. She was right. A half-dozen clattered against her shield.

Throwing the oval protector aside, Jenna grasped her staff with two hands.

Captain Ross lay dead in an increasing pool of blood, over twenty arrows piercing the satin of his costume; one bolt had entered his eye.

K'nort rushed to him, plunging his sword through the chest, using both hands.

Jenna moved into an automatic mode, but remembered the encumbrance of her gown. Most of K'nort's men were involved in reloading their crossbows, a task that took at least a minute.

First, Jenna knocked down K'nort, then, moving along the line of warriors, she scuttled them, one by one. As others advanced on her, their swords drawn, Jenna twirled, pirouetted and smashed swords, maces and crossbows from their gnarled hands.

In the same second, the king's guards leapt forward, joining in the fray against the intruders. One young man pushed his sword through K'nort's massive chest.

The courtyard was a mess of fighting men, among which a beautifully gowned lady felled the greatest amount of enemies.

Leaping to a mounting block at the stables side of the courtyard, Jenna surveyed the scene. A moan caught her ear and she glanced down to see Captain Duff, an arrow-bolt through his shoulder, his face bloodstained from being hit by a mace. He gazed up at her in awe.

Jumping to land at his side, she kept the scene in her vision for a few seconds. Knowing that the king's guards now had the situation in hand, Jenna gave her attention to the captain, asking, "Where are all the king's men?"

"Sidra... she's out there, around the back, by the cave-stables with an army, at least two hundred, they're holding ours at bay. We... we did not realize that K'nort was also here..."

"What does Sidra want?" Jenna asked. She moved her face closer to Duff's, demanding, "You must tell me, Duffy!"

"No... I mustn't. No, you mustn't go out there."

"She wants me, doesn't she?"

"No... no... don't go, you must not go... the king..."

"King Cyranius finds me a torment," she said bitterly, pulling the coronet from her hair, unclipping the necklace, the bracelet and pulling off the diamond ring. She pressed them into the captain's trembling hands and said, "I want your Jenny to have these. Look after Jenny, Duffy."

She pushed Kind Heart's ring on to Duff's smallest finger, saying, "Give this to Prince Edward."

Jenna took the captain's sheathed dagger from his belt and pushed it down into her cleavage.

Running to the tethering rail, Jenna released a strong young stallion, and mounted it. Ignoring cries and shouts, she rode out of the castle gates and across the short wooden bridge that lay over the outer trench.

Rounding the castle on the cobbled road, Jenna saw ahead the reason for the absence of the king's army in the courtyard. Between her and the king's men, a couple hundred mounted horses stood and several dozen king's soldiers lay dead in the field between them. Most of Sidra's men held dreaded crossbows, whereas the king's men had swords and spears for battle at closer range. Jenna wondered why the king had not equipped all his men with shields? She could only see a few. Jenna knew the king's men were not prepared for war. The kingdom had experienced relative peace for over twenty years, and Jenna knew that they had grown indifferent. Commander Lowell was more intent on managing the grumbling barons of the kingdom than protecting the borders. Raids on innocent people happened all the time, and this was one of the reasons Jenna's grandfather had invented Kind Heart.

At the back of the enemy lines, Jenna saw a woman, wearing a red riding habit—it was Sidra. Taking care to remain out of range of crossbow fire, Jenna called, "Sidra! Sidra!"

As Jenna expected, Sidra sounded a hoarse cry for her men to capture Jenna. Turning the horse on its hind legs, Jenna hoped he had the stamina to outrun the pursuers. She had a particular spot in mind to which she would ride him. Even Kind Heart could not take on an army of over two hundred. No, she needed to use brain, not brawn here!

Around the castle she flew on the brown horse, out into the meadow, towards the woods. Within minutes, she was riding under trees, moving on to a wide path in the deeper forest. Looking back, she saw not a pursuer in sight. Slowing the horse at a certain place, Jenna halted him. Grasping the branch above, she swung herself off the animal, kicking his rump at the same time. Frightened, he ran forward. At the sound of hoofbeats, he skittered then broke into a canter. Jenna pulled herself up into the leafy green tree, out of sight. She drew the dagger from its sheath and placed the blade between her teeth, leaving the metal sheath between her breasts.

In the dozens, the men rode under and around the tree.

Sidra finally rode beneath the tree. All of her men, save five, had raced on ahead. Jenna dived down on Sidra, causing her to fall from the horse to the ground. The woman screamed and cursed.

As swift as a panther with its prey, Jenna backed to the tree-trunk, holding the dagger at Sidra's throat with one hand while the other held Sidra's arm in a deadlock. The five dismounted and advanced, pointing swords and crossbows.

"Ahhh! Ahhh!" Sidra cried, "Back off you fools! Back off! Don't! Don't! You'll break my arm!"

"Tell them to throw their weapons down!" Jenna commanded.

"Do it! Put them down! Do as she says! Ahhh! She's killing me!"

Jenna watched as the men reluctantly threw their weapons to the ground. "Back off... move back, away from your horses!" Jenna said and called to one man who would have stepped behind his horse, "Stay where I can see you!" She pressed the blade firmer against Sidra's throat.

"Do it!" Sidra cried, "Do as she says!"

The men backed away from both Sidra and their horses.

"Throw down *all* of your weapons, your daggers and your short swords!" Jenna cried.

"Don't kill me!" Sidra screamed, now feeling the sharpness of the blade on the thin skin of her throat. "I have your brother, Charles... I'll give his life for yours."

"I'll grant you your life for his!" Jenna said, feeling angry that Sidra had captured her gentle brother.

"You five! Get on your horses and lead the way to my brother!"

They hesitated, and Sidra screamed, "Do it! Do it, can't you fools see she's got the upper hand?"

The five men mounted their horses, and Jenna called, "Ride off but stay out front where I can see you." Releasing Sidra, Jenna pushed the dagger back into its sheath and reached for the reins of Sidra's horse. Sidra, her long fingernails spread like cat's claws, leapt at Jenna. With just a slight turn, Jenna swung her hand, clenching her fist as it came up under Sidra's chin. The young woman fell forward on her knees. Jenna pulled the magnificent gray mare around as Sidra gasped in pain.

"Get up!" she commanded, and gave help as Sidra obeyed. Jenna swung herself up behind the red-gowned Sidra and turned the animal around, following the five in front.

"Move! Gallop!" Jenna called as she gained the back of the fifth horse.

"Do it!" Sidra cried angrily. She clenched her teeth, grasping the mane in front with both hands. She felt dizzy from Jenna's unexpected blow.

The men took the road south. After three miles, they took a lesser lane on which they galloped for another mile. Slowing to a canter, they turned from the road and headed towards a small wood.

"Don't move a muscle," Jenna warned as she drew the horse to a halt, out of range of an arrow she could see pointing from a tree.

Longbows had a greater range than crossbows and were generally more accurate in hitting their target.

Jenna drew in the leather of the reins, pressing her elbows into Sidra's sides.

"You're hurting me!" Sidra said, then added, her voice breathless, "I wasn't going to have you killed, I wanted to capture you and take you to Maslen."

"I guessed as much," Jenna said, "for a great reward."

Sidra bowed her head and said brokenly, "Maslen said if I brought you to him, he would marry me."

Jenna's eyes widened at this news. Her mind raced—she knew a great problem that would be solved if King Maslen were to marry Sidra. Princess Anastasia could return home to her family in Rosenberg.

"He'll marry you?" she asked.

"He promised me he would and I've never known him not to keep a promise," she said, speaking like a young girl who had lost her favorite toy.

"If you allow my brother to arrive safely at Gifford Castle, I'll go to Aponia with you, to King Maslen," Jenna said, not allowing her mind to think of the final consequence of this offer.

"You... you'd do that?" Sidra asked, looking around at Jenna. "How... how do I know that you'd keep your word?"

"I'll keep it," Jenna said, "I believe you and Maslen deserve each other. Tell them to bring Charles out and let me see that he's not harmed!"

Thirty-three

King Cyranius had shouted that Jenna not follow Kind Heart. Prince Edward ran forward, only to be grasped by two guards, holding him firmly, preventing him following her. Guards hurried to form a line four men deep, in protection of their king and his brother.

Then the double-doors had slammed, followed by a new sound—the whining of chains and the slam of the portcullis falling into its place.

Sir Lowell stepped out between the guards, calling to the guests, "Don't panic, don't panic!"

"Keep Prince Edward here," the king said to the guards closest. I'm going out there!" So saying, he drew his sword and headed for the nearest side door, one leading around to the foyer.

The king, followed by Sir Lowell and a number of guards, stepped down into the courtyard to see Jenna riding off at the other end. Four of K'nort's men, all wounded, followed, riding out across the wooden bridge. They chose the opposite road to Jenna.

King Cyranius stepped to the man dressed in black, lying on his back in the middle of the courtyard. Someone had removed the black silky wig from Captain Ross's head. The king gasped as he recognized his young captain wearing a fake moustache. He drew the sword from Ross's chest and flung it to clatter on the cobblestones. It made no sense to the king, he knew it was impossible for Ross to be the legendary Kind Heart.

The battle was over and a great silence captured every heart. As the silence continued, a young guard, his eyes filled with tears, shouldered his way to his king.

Kneeling, Stephen grasped the ringed hand, pleading fervently, "Forgive me, Your Majesty, forgive me, or I shall kill myself."

"Stand up, Stephen," the king commanded, and when the young man obeyed, the king stepped closer and whispered, "Why should I forgive you, Stephen?"

"I... we found... out about her. Captain Ross... he... he wanted her... we followed our captain's orders, but..."

"What did you find out?"

"Ross found the proof, the documents... her father's personal diary in a secret room... she... she was... she is Kind Heart."

A dagger seemed to enter the king's heart, snatching his breath away. "Say no more about it, not here," the king managed, his eyes upon those closest who could hear. In that instant, he saw a clear path through the mist of the past months and knew he must protect the true Kind Heart. Many strange things she had said flew into form in his mind, making sense. Carefully drawing a breath, he commanded, "Take off my cloak." Stephen obeyed.

"Kind Heart is dead!" the king called in a loud voice and placed his cloak over his captain's body, covering Ross's face. Standing to his full height he called, "Rally the army, and chase the enemies off our lands!"

To Sir Lowell, he said, "Find a wig and have Kind Heart's body prepared to be placed on a bier in the castle foyer." Looking at the cloak he had laid on Ross, he said, "He was a brave man."

Speaking softly to Stephen he said, "Come, Stephen, come and talk... how many others know about... about Kind Heart?"

"Two, Sire... but both are... dead, like Captain Ross... K'nort's men killed them. But Sire, you should have seen her... she... she... you would have seen Kind Heart in action... here, in the courtyard... I had doubts, until I saw her."

"Come," the king said.

~ * ~

Sidra's 'trusty men' all abandoned her, declaring they would return when they had grouped with the rest of their disseminated army.

The spokesman for the five men who should have continued accompanying Sidra, exclaimed, "We're naked without our swords! You can't expect us to ride back to Gifford without them. We'll go and find them, with the rest of our men. They won't have a clue what's happening, they'll need direction. Perhaps... perhaps we should return to Aponia."

Jenna now knew that four men had been left to watch over the four prisoners who had been tied up together. Charles had only three men left alive of his escort of twelve. Jenna knew that her gentle brother would grieve deeply for those who had lost their lives.

According to Sidra's commands, Charles and the three were released and given horses to ride.

Jenna led the small band back to the castle a different way—she circumnavigated it and rode in from the west. She hoped the king's army would still be there and that she would be able to leave her brother safely in their care.

Following his sister and the lady in red on the gray mare, Charles rode horseback. He had traveled from Rosenberg in his most comfortable carriage; he hated riding in the saddle. Charles' three surviving guards rode with him, their skills on horseback superior to his.

Jenna saw the back of the king's army in the distance and reined Sidra's horse to a halt.

The army was moving away from her, marching out, following the riders ahead, to carry out their king's order to chase all the enemies off Cyraniun soil.

Riding the horse close to her brother, Jenna said, "King Cyranius will need your help, Charles. Dry your tears and show him how to put the great hall portcullis back up and take him to the gymnasium.

Answer all his questions. He needs to know all about Kind Heart, Charles. Hopefully... and with my going away, all the king's problems will be solved." She spoke lightly, yet there was a lump in her throat.

"Where are you going?" Charles said as Jenna turned the large mare.

"To a wedding in Aponia," she said as she dug her heels in, urging the horse forward. To herself she said, *probably preceded by a death... mine...*

As Jenna rode back around the castle and toward the East Forest, she saw a sky lit with a brilliant crimson. The sun had disappeared behind the distant mountains in the west. Seeing guards watching her from the battlements of her castle, Jenna waved. She knew that it would be reported to the king that she had ridden off to the east, riding tandem with a lady dressed in bright red.

~ * ~

King Cyranius and Prince Edward were absorbing the full meaning of Stephen's claims when a guard arrived claiming, "Lady Jennava is approaching the woods at the northwest side of the castle. She has Lady Sidra on her horse... with her."

The king wondered if he should go out through the tunnels to meet her. He stood.

"Your Majesty, Captain Duff has been injured. He's in the clinic and is being tended by Doctor Breck... he said to bring you these..." the man placed the coronet, the diamond jewelry and the ruby ring on the desk. "He said Lady Jennava gave them to him and specified to whom they now belong."

Before the king could say a word, another guard arrived with the news, "Sir Charles Gifford is here, Sire... he's being escorted through the cave-stables. He said Lady Jennava left him there and he requests an audience with you."

A guard who had been on the top wall-walk hurried into the chamber, saying, "Lady Jennava is riding southeast, Sire, and she has a woman riding with her... we think it's Lady Sidra."

The king had his hands full.

Thirty-four

Jenna dismounted the tired horse. She estimated it was past midnight. Sidra had moaned and whined for the last two hours, demanding that they stop to rest, but Jenna had forced the mare on and on, along the narrow forest path.

The last time she had ridden this way had been to rescue Princess Anastasia. This time, on an uninitiated horse, Jenna found the passage slower. This mare liked open spaces, not the confines of constant forest undergrowth. She had shied four times at low hanging tree vines.

Feeling through the contents of Sidra's one saddlebag, Jenna counted four flasks. At the bottom of the bag was a thick purse. Pulling it out, she found it full of pots containing lady's makeup. She drew out a small pair of scissors and a tiny, sheathed dagger.

"Where are we?" Sidra demanded, "I told you where our tents were pitched! But you've persisted in going your own way! As far as I can tell, we're not heading for Aponia." She slid from the mare. The sound of a small waterfall could be heard. "Ohh... what I would do for a hot bath! I'd give a hundred gold pieces!" Taking a flask from the saddle bag, she drank from it, declaring, "Ah... that's better."

Peering into the blackness of the forest, Sidra moved closer as Jenna tethered the horse.

"Come, there's a small cottage here... get some sleep, then we'll see what a new day brings," Jenna urged.

Sidra would have protested, but she was too tired. Jenna led her into the cottage and lit a lamp. Pulling two rugs from a wooden trunk, Jenna threw one on the narrow wooden bed and left the other on the floor. With the trunk open, the smell of musky lavender filled the room. Jenna pulled out the black riding habit she had left here last time and fetched a flask from the wooden cupboard fixed to the wall. She lifted a coil of rope from the wall.

"Ohh... I'm dead!" Sidra declared and lay on the wooden bunk bed. She was silent when Jenna left the one-roomed cottage, closing the door.

After drinking from the flask containing the herb drink she had prepared and left here last time, Jenna rubbed the horse down then led the animal to the pond. Tying rope to the reins, she allowed her the whole length so that she could graze from the lush grass at the edge of the pond and along the creek. "Just don't get tangled," Jenna warned, patting her neck. "I don't even know your name, but I know she whips you fiercely, doesn't she?" The creature trembled and timidly nudged Jenna's face.

Peeling off her clothes, Jenna entered the warm waters of the pool. She swam to the waterfall, then under it and into a dark cave. The water was deliciously warm. Moving deeper into the cave, Jenna turned over, floating on her back. The water was hotter here. High above, bright glow-worms lent light to the cave, throwing shimmering lights across the pool surface. The water, seeping from the rock, was now very hot, and Jenna moved back towards the opening, away from the thermal source.

If there is one place like heaven, this is it, Jenna told herself. *How very appropriate, to come here at the end of my life... I'm sure Maslen will kill me when Sidra presents me to him... I hope he marries her... that will be a little bit of consolation.*

Thinking about death and dying in a torturous manner was very depressing to Jenna. She wondered how she could escape from death, how she could prolong her life. *It will have been reported to Maslen that I am Kind Heart... Millie will have told her sister Sidra, and Sidra will have confirmed it to King Maslen. If any survivors from K'nort's lot make it to Aponia, it will be reported that Kind Heart is a man, and is dead...'K'nort killed Kind Heart'...I can truthfully say that Kind Heart is finished. I'm not Kind Heart. Not anymore.*

Jenna mused on her impending meeting with King Maslen. She had not seen him, but had heard enough about his evil ways to cause her to know his wrath was to be greatly feared. Those in his favor, who did his bidding, were given position and honor. How could she possibly find favor with King Maslen? Jenna knew no answer.

~ * ~

Morning light illuminated the small clearing when Sidra stepped from the cottage. Jenna had prepared a pan of fruit and fungi mush over a small open fire and had set it to cool on a stone. She dished the pink-colored goop into two dishes and gave Sidra a spoon.

"What is it?"

"Don't ask," Jenna warned then said quickly, "but it has wild strawberries in it, with honey."

"It's good," Sidra said, filling her mouth a second time. "The strawberries just need a little cream."

"It'll keep us going until we reach King Maslen's castle," Jenna said.

"I've been thinking about that," Sidra said, "and I don't think we should arrive there today. It would be better to wait until tomorrow, or the next day..."

"Why?" Jenna asked, knowing Sidra expected her to do so. This lady thought other women were all as stupid as the men she called 'fools'.

"I want to make an entrance... I want all the others to be there before us," she said, then asked, "you've done your hair differently... it looks like you've washed it... where did you get that dress? You weren't wearing that when we left the castle!"

"It was in the cottage," Jenna said, and asked, "Have you got a hundred gold pieces here, Sidra?"

"Don't be ridiculous. Why?"

"Last night, you said you would give a hundred gold pieces for a hot bath. Do you still want a hot bath?"

"You're crazy!" Sidra said, lifting her hands to her hips.

"Where do you think I washed my hair? And where did I bathe... in the most beautiful hot bath in the world!"

As much as Jenna hated sharing her treasured secret with a female like Sidra, she led her to the waterfall and told her of the thermal water source.

"You're lying!" Sidra said, backing away from the pool. "You... you're not going to kill me... drown me... or something, are you?"

Jenna laughed, "No, Sidra... if we're going to be here together for another day, you may as well share the benefits. They're yours as much as they're mine. I'll leave you to have privacy, just be careful in the pool under the waterfall that you don't go too close to the far rocks—that's where the thermal water springs from. It's boiling hot."

Sidra stared at the waterfall, then at Jenna's beautiful pink and blue gown, spread over a low branch.

Jenna untangled the horse and began to lead her away.

"Where... where are you going? You're not going to leave me here, are you?"

"No, of course not. What's the horse's name?"

"They named her Angel. I call her other names... she's a bit timid, but has plenty of stamina."

"Angel, come on, you've eaten too much, you have to take a rest from eating... get rid of your wind." The horse looked bloated.

"Don't go... stay... bathe with me..." Sidra pleaded.

Jenna tethered the horse close to a branch and pulled off the black riding habit.

Still wearing her lacy chemise, Jenna plunged into the pool and swam to the waterfall. She disappeared behind it and savored the warmth of the water. As quickly as she had disappeared, Jenna emerged, looking at Sidra who still stood on the bank, eyeing Angel. Like a jolt, Jenna knew what Sidra was thinking.

"You'll never find your way out of here, Sidra, not without me. Come on in, I won't eat you, I promise. Try pretending we're friends, just for a day!"

Jenna went back into the cave, half expecting Sidra to leave with Angel. Then she knew that Sidra would not go alone—never had she ridden alone. Sidra was not as brave as she appeared. She took courage when she had someone with her who was stronger, and who obeyed her commands. Jenna told herself, *Remember to humor her—let her be superior in some matters at least.*

Sidra joined Jenna in the cave. As much as she had moaned and whined for two hours last night, Sidra spent the next two hours praising and extolling the wonders of the thermal pool.

Jenna had long left the water, and lay dozing in the lush grass at the edge of the pool. The sun shone mercilessly down on her and she groaned lazily before rolling over into the shade under the nearest tree branches. Her legs contacted something thick and gooey and Jenna groaned louder. She had rolled into one of Angel's emissions. Rolling the other way, she slipped into the pool, pushing herself to a shady place, intending to doze on her back. This pool was luxury beyond compare.

"Oh! Oh! Oh!" Sidra cried shrilly as she stood beneath the cold waterfall. When she was shivering with cold, she plunged back into the warmth behind her, declaring, "I could stay here all day." She pushed herself out into the cooler waters.

The sound of twigs cracking came distinctly to the pair and both froze. Even Sidra was not so stupid as to call out and reveal their presence.

Jenna stared at Angel, but the horse was still. Something, or someone else was in the woods. Slowly, Jenna paddled to the waterfall. Together they moved into concealment.

"I don't want anyone else to be with me when we ride to Maslen's castle!" Sidra hissed, feeling annoyed that someone had found her whereabouts.

Jenna, having peered out from the waterfall, swam back and said, "You won't have to... it's a great stag out there, with a couple of does."

Sidra hurried from the cave, out into the open pool, laughing in glee. Jenna joined her. The does, as one, darted back the way they had come. The stag, his mouth running with water, stared at them, then turned and stalked away. They laughed together, their girlish giggles bouncing about in the warm summer air.

For the rest of the day, Sidra, now very relaxed, talked almost nonstop—first there in the pool, then at the edge while they dried in the sunshine, then lying in the cool shade, eating wild strawberries and passion fruit collected by Jenna.

Jenna learned much about Sidra, and began to understand some of the reasons how she had become this Sidra. Most of what Sidra said made little sense.

"I'm not at all religious," Sidra said, "Not like Judith or you, Jennava, I'm more of an atheist. I don't believe there's a god at all. Even humans aren't gods. See? Maslen would like to think himself a god, and heavens, is he handsome—so masculine, so powerful. I shudder every time he comes near me. But he can't even produce a live child. At least the god you believe in had a son who was alive."

In a rare pause, Jenna asked, "Why did you whip Judith so cruelly?"

Sidra's eyes grew wide. "She was unfaithful to Sidney."

"That's a lie, Sidra, and you know it! You wanted her dead, didn't you? But you wanted Sidney to be blamed. You wanted Mayern Castle for yourself."

Sidra laughed, "I'm glad I didn't get it, I wouldn't have this chance to marry Maslen."

Jenna bowed her head, unable to bear the bizarre senselessness of this woman.

"Does he believe you can have a child by him, Sidra?"

"I told him the truth about my age, and he changed his mind about me. He had thought I was thirty-four, but I'm younger than everyone thinks. How old do you think I am, Jennava?"

"When you married Sidney's father, they said you were twenty-five. That would make you four years older than Millie, you must be at least twenty-nine."

Sidra laughed, saying, "I'm just two years older than Millie. I've just turned twenty-seven. There are still plenty of child-bearing years left to me!"

"You were sixteen when you married Sidney's father? I can scarcely believe it! Sidney was eleven, and you whipped him?"

"I was not yet sixteen. And not a saucier maid would you find! I like older men," Sidra said, and laughed. "And it's true—I married for money and position, and if Sidney had not married that simpering Judith, I'd have married him when his father died."

Jenna did not speak, she wished not to listen to anymore. Then she relaxed; there was little she could do to stop Sidra's vain verbal flux.

"Maslen will be a challenge though, he's around forty, they say, but he won't confirm his exact age..." Her pink lips drew together in a pout, and she said, "He'll change my name, though, just like all the others. But if I produce a son for him, he'll proclaim me queen."

"You'll be his sixth wife," Jenna said, deciding to humor her, "I just hope you do not suffer the fate of the others."

Sidra sat up and turned to Jenna, grasping her hand fervently, saying, "Do you really mean that, Jenna?"

Sitting up slowly, Jenna stared into her eyes. Never before had she seen eyes holding such hunger for acceptance, for approval.

"Yes, I mean it," Jenna said. Who could wish a prolonged labor on any woman, ending in painful death? I've heard King Maslen breeds large babies, the best thing would be to have a midwife bring the child on a few weeks early—"

"Oh... what if I don't conceive?" Sidra asked.

"That is up to God," Jenna said.

"Oh, god, again," Sidra said, falling back into the grass.

Jenna moved closer to the pool and splashed her face. The afternoon was well advanced now, and she felt thirsty. The waterfall beckoned. Then she caught sight of her reflection. Her hair hung around her pale face in long spiral curls. She drew her curls back, holding them with her hands.

"Sidra..."

"Yes, what?" she replied sleepily.

"Come here, look at your reflection."

Together the pair stared at their joint image.

"What? What am I supposed to see?"

"Your heavy makeup has washed off, and your face is pale, like mine. Our features are the same now."

"What are you saying?"

"If we swapped hair, I could render you unconscious, put on your red dress and take you to King Maslen as a prisoner. Standing she bowed and said, "Lady Jennava Gifford, Your Majesty, and shall we marry now, Sire?"

Sidra stared at Jenna in rage.

Laughing, Jenna fell into the pool and swam underwater all the way to the waterfall. Rising up like a nymph, she cried, "I would then have to escape from him! Run for my life! Never! Never! I'll never marry! And if I do, I hope not a king. Never! It'd be bad enough marrying a man!"

Sidra saw humor in Jenna's imagination, and leapt into the pool, her pink chemise rising like a lacy frame in the water. Together they splashed each other and laughed like two small children.

After eating the salad greens and cooked root vegetables Jenna fossicked from the woods near the creek, Sidra fell silent. Jenna took Angel for a swim in the cold side of the pool, then tethered her again to graze.

Sidra sat in the doorway of the cottage, drinking from one of her flasks. She stood upon Jenna's return and tossed the empty flask to land on the grass. "I'm going to sleep, and in the morning, we'll ride over into Aponia... I hope you remember where it is and which way to go?"

Jenna did not reply, for Sidra disappeared. Allowing time for the woman to fall asleep, Jenna checked that the two daggers were where she had left them, safely up in the hole in a tree, then she returned to the cottage. Curling herself in a ball, she lay on a mat in the corner. They both knew nothing until the morning.

Again, Jenna had breakfast ready when Sidra, still wearing only the pink chemise, exited from the cottage.

"I want to bathe first," she announced thickly, moving off in the direction of the pool. She was unsteady on her feet. Jenna followed.

In the heat of the cave, Sidra said, "I always get my best ideas when I'm in hot water... I'm thinking about my entrance... it would be best to happen first thing in the morning so that they think we've ridden all night..." however, she did not share more with Jenna, so the latter left her. It was obvious that Sidra was obsessed with making the best impression before receiving her desired reward. Jenna wondered if Sidra would try too hard.

After having cantered Angel to the edge of the forest and up to the top of a ridge, Jenna walked her back to the cottage site. There was no sign of Sidra, but her portion of mush, left in the cottage by Jenna, had been eaten.

Sidra lay in the shade by the edge of the pool, an empty flask beside her, and Jenna knew that they would not enter Aponia today. Sidra slept the stupor of drunkenness.

Perhaps it's just as well, she told herself. *The longer we leave it, the grander the entrance will be. Maslen will be wondering if I've killed Sidra... he'll send spies to Gifford to find out where she is, and where I am... what a surprise to discover that Sidra captured me. I wonder if he'll believe she made me her prisoner? I wonder how astute he is? I wonder how well he can read the human mind? King Cyranius is quite perceptive, but he does not know about females. After five wives, Maslen is likely to be an expert... I dread to think of him... how can Sidra want to marry such a man? She can have him! I won't think about it... I'll just have to handle the situation as it unfolds.*

Thirty-five

Jenna, riding in front of Sidra on Angel, wore the crumpled travel-stained pink and blue gown. Her aubyn hair hung lose in spiral curls around her pale porcelain face, all the way down to her waist, making her look like a young girl, certainly not a woman of twenty years old. Jenna deliberately leaned towards Angel's neck, as if exhausted.

In contrast, Sidra, looking all of her twenty-seven years, wore her red riding habit, also travel-stained. She sat upright, her hands expertly guiding the mare across the moat bridge, beneath the raised portcullis and through the open gates. Her perfectly arranged hair, tucked neatly into a chignon at the nape of her neck, looked smart indeed even though the red hat she wore perched on her head was slightly crushed. Her face was a mask of heavy makeup and her lips as scarlet as her hat, for Sidra never went anywhere without her pots of makeup. Sidra had been determined to look as different from Jenna as possible, and she succeeded.

A groom hurried to Angel's head, grasping the bridle firmly. Two guards rushed to help Sidra dismount, but she was on the ground before they reached her, pulling her prisoner off the horse. Jenna deliberately missed her footing and fell to the stones as though exhausted.

"Get back!" Sidra said angrily, speaking to the man who would help Jenna to stand. "She's mine, and I'll present her to our king!"

Looking up, Sidra saw King Maslen watching from a balcony. It was a specially constructed balcony a few steps above the throne room. Sidra waved to him, and he disappeared. "I've done it," she said under her breath.

"Get up!" she growled at Jenna, conscious of the many guards gathering to watch the presentation.

Jenna walked behind Sidra, trying not to overdo her plight, but every now and then Sidra pulled on the rope tied to her wrists. Because she was trying to appear very much the captive, the jerking of the rope almost unbalanced her. To everyone watching, it was very convincing.

The herald at the door of King Maslen's throne room made the announcement, "Lady Sidra... and Lady Jennava Gifford... from Cyran!"

Jenna, stooping a little so as to seem a little shorter, followed her 'captor' along the purple carpet to stand before the amazing throne of King Maslen of Aponia. Before she could take in the scene, she felt the rope jerking and remembered Sidra's instructions that she was to fall prostrate on the carpet. It jerked again, and Jenna fell forward to her knees, bowing her head. Sidra moved swiftly behind her and kicked her back, making her fall on her face. Sidra curtsied to the king.

A deep throaty laugh, a laugh of utter ridicule, resounded from the man seated on the throne, and Jenna felt a chill run up her spine knowing suddenly that Sidra had no idea how to read character. This entrance had been performed in a completely wrong manner. If Sidra truly knew King Maslen, and a little about Kind Heart, she would never have made this presentation, but would have had ten men help to bring her in, using shackles and chains.

How did I allow this to happen? Jenna asked herself, *I've been dreaming! We're both in trouble now...*

"This... this... girl... she is Lady Jennava? The one that numskull woman, Millie, said is Kind Heart? She's not Kind Heart, Sidra, she can't be! And I doubt, from what I hear, that she's Lady Jennava! This is a farce!

How dare you present me with this... this... mockery! What do you think I am? This overdressed insect cannot possibly be Kind Heart!"

"But Sire..." Sidra began.

"*Be silent!*" he bellowed, as if the two words were one. Under his breath, he whispered, "I'll see them both dead in one blow!" His temper had passed its limits.

Jenna did not look up, but kept her head to the floor.

"Stand up, girl! Look at me! Let me look at you!" Without taking her eyes off Jenna, he drew a dagger from a place in the massive oak tree throne in which he sat. He held the tip of the blade between his thumb and forefinger. The moment Jenna stood and looked through her hair at the king, he threw the dagger, having aimed at the middle of her face. With a twist of her body, Jenna spun out of the way. The dagger blade swished through her flying curls to land harmlessly on the gray marble floor.

"You surprise me!" he exclaimed, his whole demeanor changing. "You're not as you appear. Why are you dressed... like that?"

Sidra could keep silent no longer, "Your Majesty,"

"*Be silent!* If you want to live, get over there with the womenfolk, Sidra!" He waited as she went, head cast downward, to stand in front of two dozen gaudily-attired women.

After scouring his eyes around the chamber as if to burn out any spies, the king gave Jenna his full attention.

"I asked a question, girl, who are you? And why do you wear that ridiculous virginal get up?"

Pushing her curls back behind her ears, Jenna said, "My name is Jennava Gifford and I wore this gown on my twentieth birthday... just a few days ago... apart from the disarray of my hair, this is how I looked, Your Majesty."

"Twenty? You're not that old yet, I'll wager." Rising from his throne, he strode to her in three large steps, walking around her, staring at her from head to foot, making her feel uncomfortable. A fearful giant of a man, she estimated him to be almost seven feet tall.

Jenna longed to pirouette and follow his eyes, but dared not. She kept her head bowed. *How could I have allowed Sidra to do this to me?* she wondered, wishing her hands were not tied.

"Look at me!" King Maslen said, standing in front of her, staring at her.

She looked into his dark brown eyes, shuttered from above by thick eyebrows meeting together in deep grooves above the bridge of his aquiline nose. His long thick mane of curling hair had not one gray glint within it, and Jenna wondered at his age. He did not look a day over thirty.

"Ah," he said, knowing that she was not afraid of him, but was observing his features.

She lowered her eyes to stare at his thick lips. His tongue moved out, moistening his lower lip and she bowed her head.

He laughed, but did not move, his boring eyes not missing a twinge of her slightly changing expressions.

"Look at me!" he commanded, and she allowed her eyes to lift and settle on his trim brown moustache. A well-trimmed beard cloaked his square chin and the king was immaculately groomed. Lifting her eyes, she looked into his, not understanding the humor she saw in their depths.

"Are you... or are you not?" he demanded.

Jenna was not sure what he asked so she was silent but could not prevent her eyes dropping down the length of his jeweled tunic, passed the gold-buckled hip belt, down the jeweled sword-sheath, all the way to the jeweled buckles on his shining black boots.

Maslen walked around her again, standing behind her.

Raising his hand, the king would have slapped her head from behind, but Jenna sighted him in her sensitive peripheral vision and spun around, ducking beneath his heavy palm. Instinctively, she lifted her bound hands as if to guard her face from a blow.

"Yes, I expected that," he said. Spinning on his large heel, he called, "Pete! Jassy! Where are you? Ah, there... come here..." King Maslen looked across to a sprightly youth, and a large young man who limped out from the thick line of onlookers. The line of guards moved apart to allow them passage to the king. The man, Jassy, used a crutch under one arm, leaning on Pete's shoulder with the other.

As they moved slowly to the king, Jenna took stock of the great oval chamber. Accurate to her first impression, the king's throne was carved into a great oak tree, a living tree. Its huge roots had ruptured the marble floor, and its branches rose right up and out of sight through the high, colored glass-covered ceiling of this exotic castle chamber. Leaves and branches of the tree hung into the chamber, secured here and there by rope nets through which they protruded. Sunlight shafts, glowing colors of the rainbow drifted down, creating a fantasy atmosphere. A soft breeze scurrying through open doors prevented the chamber becoming too hot. Jenna wondered what it would feel like at noontime.

Looking back at the king, Jenna saw that he observed her. "This... this... creature here... have you seen it before, Jassy?"

"She... she, yes, Your Majesty, she looks like the one who was in the courtyard at Gifford. She came out behind Kind Heart... then when they put the arrows in, she fairly flew, like a bird... yeah, it's her, only her hair be driff'rent, all loose like."

"She... this... she broke your leg, Jassy?"

"Yeah! She hit it with a heavy ball thing on a staff."

"Did you see her, Pete?"

"Yes, Your Majesty, it does look like her—it's her dress... only... I'm not completely sure. She looks younger close up... and she had a crown thing on her head, and diamonds everywhere."

The king was not convinced. Without speaking, he drew his sword, causing the pair to back away.

"Let's find out if this unfledged little bird has a kitten, or a tiger, within it..."

So saying, King Maslen charged at Jenna, emitting a guttural yell, pointing the weapon at her heart. The will to survive sent Jenna into automatic mode and she ducked to avoid the sword point. But he pivoted in a well-practiced manner and slashed his sword in such a way that if it had struck her, it would have severed her neck. Bringing it around and up, he could have sliced off her legs. As she leapt above the path of the slash, it caught in her dress, cutting into the fabric. The volume of the silk pulled with the sword and caught around the tip. Jenna lost her footing and fell to the floor. With a roar, the king tore his sword from her gown, pulling the voluminous skirt from the bodice as she rolled away from him.

Jenna was left with a few silk rags hanging over the skirt of her chemise. Again King Maslen stabbed down at his victim. Over and over she rolled, out of his way, wishing her hands were not tied. He followed her, stabbing at her again and again. But she rolled out of his sword's reach. Crouching like a cat on guard, Jenna waited.

Flicking the mass of silk and satin out of his way, King Maslen held his sword above his head and bowed. Everyone in the throne room applauded.

"Bring me a costume... Kind Heart's costume!" he called. "I want a complete costume, with the wig and everything!" Having said this, he commanded, "Bring this lady-bird here to me, and stand guard!"

Jenna found herself grasped and taken to him. A band of a dozen men surrounded her. He pushed his sword close to her face and Jenna closed her eyes, expecting him to injure her. She waited for pain that did not come.

It felt to her like a game of cat and mouse. She was the mouse, but he was a lion.

Sheathing his great sword, he drew out a dagger. Pushing the point into her flower covered bodice, he sliced the garment upward from the waist. With a sweep of his other hand, he tore the remainder of the dress right down the front, leaving her standing in her dainty chemise and the blue satin slippers that were so travel-stained they no longer looked blue.

Standing stock still, like a lifeless statue, Jenna kept her eyes closed, expecting any moment to feel the dagger plunged into her heart. She decided not to look at him so that she would not make any move in self-defense. She wished it to be over, finished.

"You tremble! At last, you tremble!" he exclaimed, "It took that much to make our lady-bird tremble!" He bowed and everyone applauded again.

Moving back to his prey who had not moved other than the involuntary trembles, he shouted, "Look at me! Open your eyes! Don't you realize the power I have, over you? Answer me!"

"Yes, I do realize your... power," Jenna said, opening her eyes and looking at him. She could not prevent her body from trembling. She was afraid, but unsure as to what frightened her. King Maslen was like the angel of death, she decided. He would be the one to kill her. *I'm afraid to die,* she told herself and began to quote the twenty-third Psalm in her mind, *The Lord is my Shepherd...* As her mind moved through the verses of the Psalm, she felt herself calming and forced herself to think of the lush green grass beside the crystal waters of the pool. Perhaps it would not be long before she would be there... forever...

Maslen stared at her face, then his eyes moved down, the length of her diaphanous chemise. He licked his lips, patiently watching her while her unconscious trembles diminished.

Looking around he called, "Where are they with that cursed costume?"

Turning back, he stared at her again and he wondered what she was thinking. Her meditational stare into space made him realize she was a religious person. Under his breath so that only she heard he said, "I wonder... I still don't know."

In a louder tone, he asked, "Are you, Kind Heart?"

His voice brought her back to him. "No!" she said firmly, knowing she could speak the truth. "Kind Heart is finished."

"Who taught you the skills to defend yourself like that?"

"My father," she replied, "Father taught me all he knew."

"Ah!" he said, "Your father died three years ago and now Kind Heart is dead?" he asked.

She bowed her head.

"Look at me!" he demanded and she obeyed.

"Kind Heart, your lover, is dead and you no longer wish to live... now that's one reason to give yourself into my hands... you're committing suicide with a purpose?" he stared at her, and walked around her, eyeing the length of her slim legs beneath the lace edge of her chemise.

"Why did you allow Sidra to bring you here, when you could have taken *her* to Cyranius?"

Tilting her chin, Jenna answered with the truth, "I want Sidra to gain her reward, Your Majesty. I wanted to know that you married her."

King Maslen frowned. Moving closer, he said, "I'm missing something here... explain to me what I missed."

Jenna did not answer and he moved so close she could smell sweet wine on his breath. "Explain!" he bellowed.

"Kind Heart rescued a very young princess from marriage, Your Majesty. And if you marry Lady Sidra—"

"Princess? Princess Anastasia! Yes, of course, I thought I would never forget her, but I have. I haven't thought about Anastasia since the moment I met you, Lady-bird.

"Ah... the costume," he said. Extending his dagger, he commanded, "Cut your ropes!"

Jenna lifted her wrists and sawed through the ropes on the sharp dagger he held. His eyes swallowed her every movement.

"Dress yourself, put on the wig, and everything—or would you like me to help you?" He did not wait for her reply, because he knew that she would not want any help. With a laugh, he strode to his throne and sat on it.

Hating his command, but wishing to be clothed, Jenna gave her attention to the clothes and put on the arrow-proof vest, knowing that it was not hers but one of her father's—it was too wide and too long. Creasing it, she folded it across her chest and back, for extra protection, and drew the buckles as tightly as she could. Next she pulled on the leather tunic, drew on the leather leggings, rolling them up at the bottoms and securing them with the small leather belts and buckles. She did not put the boots on because she knew she would have no balance; they were her father's and were too large. She wondered, *How did this king gain possession of these clothes?*

With deft hands, she could have braided her hair and expertly fixed it around her head before pulling on the wig, but she knew that this would have made her the person the king wanted to see. Instead, she pulled the wig over her head, then tucked her front curls up under it. An attendant tendered the moustache to her. Frowning at it, she took it, then tossed it into the air, saying, "I'm not wearing that thing!"

Folding her arms, she stepped closer to the throne, staring at the king. She bowed slightly to him.

"You're an enigma," he said. "Put the boots on."

"They're not my size, Your Majesty," Jenna said, and explained, "I won't have any balance if I wear those boots."

"Ah... at least you don't hide the fact that you have balance. And you *will* need it! And I give you a point for thinking ahead to imagine what I expect of you. So, Kind Heart—or Kind Heart's mistress? You are ready are you? I long, with frenzied fixation, to see you in action.

"Give her a staff... isn't that what she used at Gifford? Fetch one with a ball on the end!"

A guard from behind the huge tree brought a staff with a knob at one end.

"Ten of you... no twelve, three quads, form a semi-circle around her so I can see it all from here...

"That's right. Now, when I give the word..."

Placing the staff on the floor, Jenna sat and crossed her legs, pulling the wig off, bowing her head. A cry of protest sprang up all around the great chamber, and the king propelled himself off his throne. Striding around her, King Maslen stopped in front of her. The protests against her grew louder.

"*Be silent!*" he shouted.

He stared down at her, walking around her, then said, "Shall you stay seated, Lady-bird, while the king stands?"

Jenna stood.

"Ah," he said, "I see that you comprehend I tricked you before into revealing something of yourself and now you won't give us more, is that it? What if I grant you your life, to live?"

"How long? And under what duress, what twisted torture?" she asked, "A day, a week, a month? I'd rather die now."

"But what misfortune has made you feel like this, poor Lady-bird?" he taunted. "Is Kind Heart really dead? Is your poor little heart so broken that you wish to die?"

As if to answer his question, the herald announced loudly, in his monotone voice, "A message from Cyran to be presented to King Maslen!"

A messenger strode forward carrying a scroll and a black velvet bag. He bowed to the king and gave him the bag, saying, "The man who rode in with this, Sire, is out in the foyer... he said he took it from Kind Heart himself..."

The king opened the bag and pulled out a black wig. It was inside out and the inside was stained with blood, now dark crimson, almost black.

Throwing the wig down as if it were a loathsome thing, the king strode to sit on his throne, unrolled the scroll and read it silently.

"Ah," he said when he was finished. "Fetch me that small team of entertainers... the Trusty Ten they call themselves, the ones who returned from Gifford a few weeks back. I've another task for them."

Tossing the scroll to land in a cavity in the roots of the tree, he said, "Lady Jennava, the news that has arrived seems to confirm that Kind Heart is dead—his body lies instate in the foyer at Gifford Castle. He is so dead that he has over twenty arrow-holes in his body, plus the sword that K'nort put through his heart... it means he simply could not live. I did not believe it when I heard it yesterday, but this scroll has been sent from someone I trust implicitly. My Trusty team will go and pay due respects and check it out with other placements in the castle, then we'll know for sure... ah... but Lady-bird has bowed her head. Is she crying? How will we know?"

King Maslen sat thinking. Twisting around, he unlatched a curved wooden tray from the trunk and swung it around in front of himself. Reaching into a cavity in the tree trunk, he drew out a quill, an ink bottle and a roll of scroll papers. After writing on a scroll, the king rolled it up quickly. He did this three times and Jenna knew that this was something he often did. This king did not use scribes, he wrote his own letters.

Not a sound, barely a breath could be heard in the great throne room. The temperature grew warmer, and the silence continued... and the king wrote on another scroll.

Thirty-six

Half an hour passed before King Maslen's Trusty Ten entered the silent throne room. They had been called from their tent site, by the outer wall of the castle. They had been practicing a new routine to present to the king that evening.

Jenna recognized these men as the acrobats who had juggled and entertained after King Cyranius had come to Gifford. It seemed a lifetime ago now. She listened as the king dictated his orders, telling his young treasurer to give the leader a bag of gold in advance, promising more when they returned. The bag of gold was fetched from behind the great tree throne.

"Go into Gifford Castle, as mourners, and view Kind Heart's remains, mingle in the village there and concentrate on discovering his identity," the king finalized his commission to them.

Jenna felt it confirmed that Maslen had no intentions of giving her any freedom—he would never have revealed this kingdom secret if he had any intention of setting her free. As she watched the company leave, the king's eyes flew to her, then back to the Trusty Ten.

"Wait!" he called, as they turned away.

The ten stepped back to stand in line in front of the guards again. The king pointed his forefinger at Jenna.

"Look... look at this... this creature... who do you think it is? Examine it closely, see if you can find something distinctive about it, do not speak before you've all decided... you're supposed to be the world's expert ferrets. What I need is something tangible, not mere words. It may look like something you've seen before, but what, really, is it? Give me something specific!"

The ten stalked around Jenna. The jester kicked the wig on the floor, looking up at her, then back to the wig, whilst another wove in and out of the eight guards still standing around her. One young man trod on the end of the staff, snatching it up into his hand. Swinging it around close to Jenna's face, he continued circling her, pretending to buffet her, but not actually touching her.

"Is it a man? Is it a lady? Is it real?" the jester asked, but another poked him, and he was silent. The jester looked at the king, then back at Jenna. It was known that King Maslen did not like jesters or anyone who cracked jokes; the king invented his own quips and laughed loud and long at them.

Slowly, all ten returned to stand before the throne.

"Step forward, those of you who know for sure, who it is?" he asked. Six stepped forward, including the jester. Together, they lifted their forefingers to touch their left eyebrows.

"The rest of you, have you any ideas?"

"Yes Sire," three replied, whilst the other said, "I'm not sure, Sire, but my best shot is that it's the Lady from Gifford Castle, wearing Kind-Heart's weeds." He grinned, not believing his own deduction. "She had a black scarf thing round her neck when we saw her last."

The six in front, as if on a practiced queue said simultaneously, "It is Lady Jennava."

"It has her height, and her crop of auburn hair," the jester said, "a bit unruly, the hair, like she's been riding through a bush backwards, and we in front took the same note; it has one eyebrow that twitches occasionally above the other. Lady Jennava kept doing that at King Cyranius, that eve, while the meal was going... and she's doing it now, King Maslen, at you with her left eyebrow."

The king grinned at Jenna. He had noticed that one eyebrow rose now and then, but had not imagined it to be the peculiarity that would confirm her identity.

"So, Lady Jennava. We've established that you are who Sidra said you are." He turned to Sidra and nodded, saying, "Good work, my love. However you did it, we have Lady Jennava here with us." Looking back at Jenna, he said, "I never imagined you to be such a parcel of mysterious contradictions. Beauty and the beast in harmony! I'd love to discover all your secrets, Lady-bird, or shall we call you Lady-beast?" He laughed and waited, but few others wanted to pause for mirth—they were too intent on hearing the king's conclusion of this matter. It would not be the first time a female deviant had been condemned and put to death in this chamber. An expectant chill of impending bloodshed stirred through the spectators.

Staring at Jenna the king said, "I can read your eyes, Lady-bird, you never imagined King Maslen to be such a marvel, did you? You hunger to learn more about me." He chuckled as Jenna bowed her head. She could not bear to look within his eyes; they held too much intimate communication for her to begin to understand. She had no knowledge of a man like this and his lustful desires. His eyes gave her no offer of mercy or hope for future freedom.

Selecting one scroll upon which he had written, the king gave it to the leader of the Trusty Ten and dismissed them, urging, "Be diligent in the business I've commissioned."

He gave another scroll into the hands of one of his guards, then stared at Jenna, deep in thought again. Other than men leaving the chamber, no one moved or spoke. After ten tedious minutes, he stood and stepped over to Jenna.

"It's a battle of wits, you want your freedom, or death, Lady-bird, and I desire to see you perform all your stunts at once." Copying the jester's action, he flicked the staff with his foot, catching it up into his hand and said, "If you would like to run free from here, I'll give you one chance… in turn, I shall receive the rare privilege of watching you function. Put the wig on."

Something told Jenna that he was speaking the truth. He was gambling, with her life as the prize, feeling sure that in the end he would win. Twisting her hair into one knot, she gathered up the wig and fixed it firmly to her head, pushing stray curls beneath it so that they would not impede her vision.

Throwing the staff to her, the king ran to his throne and leapt to stand on it. Turning, he drew his sword, saying, "If the Lady-bird here can escape us, she shall be allowed to go free. Let's see her get out the doors there!" He pointed his sword toward the open doors of the throne room.

Jenna stared up at the king—he was too far above her for her to be able to do to him what she had done to Sidra.

"No, no, my dear, don't look to me, I'm not your freedom; it's out there, beyond my castle…"

Turning, Jenna grasped the staff with both hands. She waited, wondering if he would throw his sword at her, as he had the dagger. Scuffing the soles of her slippers on the marble to check that they did not slip, she began to walk. No one moved towards her, and she kept walking, slowly, one step, then another, until she was in the middle of the throne room. All the while, she expected something to be thrown from the king's hand. *This chamber and its king are from another world,* Jenna thought, *he has no counselors and he makes all decisions on his own.*

"The man who captures Lady Jennava, alive, shall have great reward!" the king shouted. "Cut her if you have to, but don't kill her!"

Jenna took heart at this. He said 'alive.' She would keep this in her mind until she was out of the city, she told herself, beginning to think positively of escape.

A dozen men approached Jenna, surrounding her as if closing in on a trapped animal to finish it off. Swinging the staff and pivoting, she swept them out of her way. Then, from the crowd, a tall thin man stepped out flicking a long whip. He cracked it and others fell back from him.

As the whip flashed out towards her neck, Jenna spun the staff. The leather caught around the wood, and with a flick of the staff, she caused the man to fall to the floor.

"Wonderful!" King Maslen shouted, having climbed higher now, standing on the back of his throne, up in the tree trunk. He could see it all. Never before had he been entertained like this!

One by one, Jenna scuttled those who approached her, spinning around in a breathtaking manner, causing men to lose maces, swords and staffs. Feeling cowardly, she smacked the men's legs, trying not to think of Jassy and his crutch. She had not managed to gain control over her thoughts and wondered if she could. Using the staff, she vaulted over a man pointing a crossbow. Several daggers flew, the throwers hoping to find a mark in her arm, or leg, but, turning and twisting, she avoided them all.

Jenna knew from the many misses, that those participating in this competition were mindful of the king's command, 'alive.' No one had dared deal a deathblow. Jenna had faced far more vengeful opponents. She felt as if she were partaking in a demonstration, not a real battle.

King's guards and other hopeful contestants lay in disarray all the way to the doors, and as Jenna dived through the door, she heard the king call, "Now!"

Looking up, she saw a great net, slung across the transom. As if in slow motion, she saw it descending on her. Never had Jenna moved so fast! As she somersaulted away from the impossible foe, she felt it falling on her and gave one last dive. She did a head over heels roll, flinging the staff up and backwards, to prevent the heavy metal balls at the edges of the net from landing on her head. Having lost the staff, she rolled in a tighter ball, and saw the edge of the heavy net move behind her.

A guard, carrying a mace and a spear approached. He thrust the point of the spear at her chest, and Jenna stepped back. As he lunged forward again with the spear, Jenna grasped the shaft beyond the point and pulled the man with it, wrenching the weapon from him, turning to confront others.

That man had been commanded to kill me, Jenna warned herself, now remembering the scroll the king gave to the band of guards who had left the chamber. Here they were, waiting for her with reinforcements. Jenna felt herself move into the automatic mode she had wished for, but had not been able to find in the throne room.

A dozen men rushed at her and one by one, she swept them out of her way, off their feet, making certain progress toward the far wide doorway.

"Amazing!" King Maslen cried, watching now from a landing above them. "Where did her father learn such skills?"

Down the few steps she rushed and out into the courtyard. A net was flung down from the king's balcony and she spun the spear, twisting the sections of rope on the point, flinging the whole thing away from her.

"Magnificent!" King Maslen shouted, his voice filled with ecstasy. "I can't believe it! Look at it!"

"Now!" he shouted, his deep voice reverberating across the courtyard, "Come out now, my Trusty Team!"

As Jenna gained the middle of the courtyard, six of the ten acrobats scurried in through the arches at the far end, to which she was heading. They each held different pieces of weaponry and equipment, and Jenna knew that each of them would be a match for her. She was disciplined enough to know when she could not continue and that she would not win against this joint group of six.

Turning, Jenna ran back to the net, scuttling two guards on her way. Collecting it up and swinging it as she ran, she approached the side wall, flinging the net as high as she could. It caught on the topmost battlement, and she pulled it tight. Testing that it would hold her, she then climbed quickly upward.

King Maslen's ecstasy turned to dismay. "Get her! Get her! Don't let her escape!" Under his breath, he said, "Never... never before have I seen such skill... and she has the presence of mind to take another course..."

"Fetch horses... block every exit... we must not let her leave our city!"

Having felt four arrow-bolts thud bruisingly against her back, Jenna gained the top of the wall and saw that the smooth stones ran sheer down to the road at the bottom. There were few, if any, footholds. She needed a long rope—it looked to be a drop of some sixty feet. Pulling up the net, Jenna ducked an arrow. *Alive,* ran in her mind. She dropped the net down the other side of the wall.

Climbing down as far as the net permitted, Jenna hung from it, sliding down one thin piece of rope. She felt the net being tugged from above her. She was less than half way down the wall. The net began to move up a little.

"You'll never make it!" King Maslen called. He stepped out of the way and commanded, "Draw it up!"

Jenna hesitated, he had commanded to pull her up, not to throw the net down to ensnare her and cause her to fall to her death. She knew again that he hoped to capture her alive.

Alive, she told herself and released her fingers from the rope. Digging the toes of her slippers into the wall, Jenna began to slide downward. She felt herself gather momentum. Down, down, down. In those few seconds, Jenna relaxed herself to cushion the impact at the bottom. If only she were facing the other way and could roll forward with the fall. In the split-second her toes touched the road, she allowed herself to fall limply backwards, rolling into a ball, over and over to the wall on the other side. The edge of the net, thrown by those above, landed at her feet.

Dusting herself off and glad for the protection of the leather trousers, Jenna stood. Horses' hooves clattered on cobblestones, and the animals approached the corner near the arch closest to the front gates of the castle.

"I don't believe it! She's up!" Now a little hoarse, King Maslen barked out orders as Jenna ran towards the other end of the causeway.

Sensing danger ahead, Jenna slowed. Should she leap, or duck? Fearful of something hitting her head, she ducked. The jester was waiting in the shadows and he flung a double-metal ball-whip at her lower legs. It wrapped around her calves, binding her legs together causing her to lose her footing. She dropped to her knees. As she stood, she flung the balls in two different directions, hoping to unravel the leather. Another acrobat flung a small, loosely strung net over her head, and together with two others he manipulated the thin cords, drawing them in, entrapping her. Expertly working the cords, they hoped to secure the net firmly around her to immobilize her.

Jenna felt herself ensnared. It happened so fast it almost took her breath away. In a flash, she again recalled King Maslen writing on the scrolls and she knew that he had deployed these men to be prepared for her if she were to escape from the castle. He had given them time to gain the equipment they required. His orders and urgings had driven her to them. They were his final hope of capture, if all else failed. They were experts in their profession.

In a last attempt to free herself, Jenna spun around, first one way, then the other, twisting against the net and the leather binding her legs. She kept her feet together, knowing that to try to separate them would be to lose altogether.

To the men's great frustration and amazement, Jenna freed her legs and feet. Reaching through the holes of the net, she pulled on the strong strings two men held, pulling them in towards each other. Contorting herself backwards, she caused them to bump heads and fall to the road.

Rolling on the road over and over, Jenna forced the cord from the third man's hands, but at the same time, wound herself firmly into the web.

With her arms still through the holes, she lifted the net up as she would a cumbersome dress, and continued her flight.

The jester collected the metal balls from the road and began to swing one, while holding on to the other end. As one of his companions cried, "*No*, aim lower!" he released the weapon. It met its mark, cracking against the back of Jenna's head. Dropping to her knees, she slumped forward, falling into an empty void. Blood seeped down the back of her neck and drizzled on the stones set in the road.

Horsemen arrived and four dismounted to find the acrobats staring down at their victim, their short swords extended as if expecting her to rise up yet.

"Don't touch her!" one of the king's guards warned. He looked up, but the king was no longer atop the wall. "The king will come... he'll want to see her as she is." He stared closer, asking, "Is she still alive?"

"I doubt it," one of the acrobats said dolefully, "that ball is a sure killer!" He turned on the jester, saying, "You read the scroll! It said not to spare her, but to take her alive! Now look what you've done."

The jester looked at the arch behind him as if searching for a way of escape.

"Hold him!" a guard commanded.

Foot soldiers arrived and silence settled over the onlookers. A path cleared along the road and King Maslen, seated on a black stallion, rode through the middle of his guards.

Dismounting, the king stared down at the net-covered black-clad figure lying prostrate on the road. His eyes fell on the growing pool of blood. Stepping closer, he knelt and touched his forefinger to the blood.

The trembling jester knelt, and cried, "I'm sorry... Sire."

"Yes, I saw you," the king said. "Don't be sorry, you'd all have been very sorry if it had escaped. What are you waiting for? Collect your reward from my treasurer and get on over to Gifford and bring back your report."

As one, the acrobats backed away, turned, and fled.

Leaning his ear against the middle of Jenna's back, the king perceived a slow heartbeat. He smiled a grim smile.

"It still beats," he said. "Fetch Doctor Arnold, he will know how best to convey her from here. That blow could have done damage to her neck as well as having cracked her skull. The wig might be all that holds it together."

While guards mounted their horses to do the king's bidding, others watched in amazement. Sending for a doctor meant the king wanted her to live, but to send for his own doctor meant that he valued this young woman's life. They had expected him to hang her from the wall right there as had been the fate of others.

King Maslen stared down at Jenna and while he stared at her, his close guards and royal retinue stared at him.

Thirty-seven

Unconscious and considered to be so comatose that she would die, Jenna did not open her eyes for forty-two hours after receiving the skull-crushing blow.

Jenna lay on a narrow wooden bed, in a dimmed tower-chamber with no idea where she was or who she was. Outside, dawn had not yet broken.

Her head throbbed with pain, matching her heartbeat. Turning to lie on her other side, she closed her eyes.

A middle-aged servant-woman hurried to her bedside. "Are you awake?" she asked.

Jenna opened her eyes, but did not turn her head to look at her.

"What a surprise. You're awake!" Turning she waved her hands at the guard standing inside the door. The man raised his eyebrows.

"Yes, fetch Doctor Arnold, and tell the king, quickly!" she hissed, then turned back to the patient.

"You must be thirsty," she said, taking hold of a large mug and small spoon.

Without speaking, Jenna turned and struggled as if to sit. She moaned and lay back on the thin mattress.

"No, no, dear... I'll help you..."

~ * ~

When Doctor Arnold arrived in the chamber, it was to find the large servant-woman supporting Jenna to sit, her ample arm around her, spooning the sweetened water into her mouth.

"Not too much... fetch some pillows," he ordered, moving to snatch up two himself. "Careful, I can't believe she can sit up."

The king strode into the chamber. He stared at Jenna's face, it was as pale as the bandage around her head. Her eyes were closed and Doctor Arnold was commanding her, in a loud voice, to wake.

"She came around?" the king demanded, moving closer to the bed. "Pull the curtains back... where is that blessed sun today? Light more candles so I can see her.

"Did she speak?" he asked, and listened while the servant-woman recounted the awakening of the lady.

"She has no signs of consciousness now," the doctor said, stating the obvious, "But if she continues to take in liquids, I believe she'll recover, Sire."

"Recover?" the king asked, having believed for two days that she would die. "How much will she recover?"

"That's up to the gods, Sire."

"Is it possible she could have a full recovery?"

"I don't think so, Sire," Doctor Arnold replied.

"'We can only wait and see'," the king quoted the doctor's repeated statement in a sour tone. His voice grew threatening as he said, "I'm sick of trudging up and down these narrow tower steps. I don't want to hear from you again until she speaks, or I summon you. Just do what you can and let me know the instant she speaks. I want to be able to speak to her."

~ * ~

Jenna woke, two hours later, vomiting violently. Doctor Arnold declared to the servant-woman that this was a 'good sign.' He told them to allow her to take as much liquid as she wanted, but to be prepared for more vomiting.

The sleeping, waking and vomiting continued every two or three hours, day and night for two more days. But Doctor Arnold was pleased with the quantities of liquid Jenna consumed.

Doctor Arnold himself fed Jenna some warm nourishing broth. The servant-woman on duty had felt she imparted very important news to Doctor Arnold when she had told him, "She kept the broth down and I turned the hour-glass over five times before she woke again."

Days passed and Jenna was the perfect patient, completely obedient to everything asked of her.

With Doctor Arnold on one side, and a nurse on the other, she was walked across to a comfortable chair. A rug was placed over her linen nightgown and there she slept until she woke to partake of bread soaked in broth again. The next day, Jenna ate fine-chopped venison cooked into a vegetable stew. Between eating and sleeping, they moved her from the bed to the chair, allowing her to take more of her own weight.

Still Jenna did not speak.

Doctor Arnold, summoned to stand before the impatient king, was asked about his patient's progress.

He explained, "She's making excellent progress, Sire. She feeds herself and walks on her own, though not far."

"Bah! You call that excellent! What's happened to its speech? Is it to be dumb for the rest of its existence? What are you going to do to hasten its recovery?"

"Tomorrow, we're going to bathe her and remove her head bandage. We'll let her look at herself in a mirror and we hope this will cause her to speak."

Sidra, now considered part of the king's court, listened to this news with great interest. King Maslen had made no mention of Sidra's 'reward' and Sidra, having brought it to his notice by way of the king's current mistress, had been forbidden to speak about it until Jenna was either dead or had recovered.

Sidra had informed the beautiful Meltissa, "I am going to marry the king, very soon."

In a fit of jealousy and rage, Meltissa had challenged the king.

In turn, King Maslen had summoned Sidra, commanding, "Pay your army off and dismiss them and prove to me that you have stability and fidelity. If I do not see you behaving as a subservient, chaste lady of my court, how can I ever imagine you to be a faithful wife? You'll get your reward, my love, if you're patient, but it shall be in my time. Keep yourself for that time and keep yourself for me alone."

Sidra left the king's presence deflated and blaming Jenna because he was not as ardent towards her as before. But, she believed that she would win him in the end and that he was well worth waiting for, and indeed, she would obey his commands and keep herself for him.

No one could predict the king's mood at this time. Only after Kind Heart had taken Princess Anastasia away, one day before the wedding, had he brooded in this fashion. People trod lightly and dared not provoke him.

Everyone in the castle waited for news of the lady whose name they were not permitted to mention.

Jenna stared at herself in the mirror as if she did not recognize her own image. Short curls framed her face, for Doctor Arnold had cut off all her blood-filled hair, cutting it close at the back of her head to examine and tend the injury she sustained. He had proclaimed that the back of her skull had been smashed and that if the hemorrhaging did not cease, she would die. After a whole day, the bleeding had stopped and he had bandaged her head, believing the thick bandage would help the fractures to knit if she defied his prognosis and survived. "When it mends, in a year or so," he told the king, "her head will be twice as hard as before."

When King Maslen asked Arnold how he knew about this, the doctor said that he had examined the skulls of such people, after death, and discovered that they never broke in the same place again.

King Maslen laughed at this, saying, "And I thought you were the gentle doctor, you have veins within you that are same as mine." The king and the doctor grinned at each other.

~ * ~

The Trusty Ten arrived back from Gifford. They had stayed to witness the burial of Kind Heart.

"It was done with great ceremony," Jester told the king.

"Thousands attended the funeral and they came from all over Cyran, some from other kingdoms."

"It was generally accepted that he was a son of Lord Frances Gifford, and a half-brother to Lady Jennava, and also to Sir Charles who lives in Rosenburg..." another said.

"They buried him as Kind Heart in the Gifford family plot," Jester added.

King Maslen found this hard to believe, Kind Heart, Lady Jennava's half-brother? But the more he thought of it, the more sense it made. Jennava and Kind Heart had worked together... they had supported each other in their missions of mercy and rescue. Lord Frances had trained them both.

"Sir Charles was at the funeral, Your Majesty, and it was noised about that he's planning to travel here, to Aponia, to claim his sister's remains—"

"He wants to bury her beside Kind Heart."

"Now she's reported dead, he wants her, it seems."

"You see, Sire," an eighth man interjected, "It was voiced around that Lady Jennava was killed while attempting to escape the king of Aponia's men..."

King Maslen smiled at this. Almost everything made sense, save one matter. He would speak to Arnold about that, he decided.

"I want you all to return to Gifford and discover everything you can about Lady Jennava Gifford—about her childhood, her father, her brother, her life in the castle, etcetera. Take your time, it's not a matter to hurry. Document all you find, and bring back the information to me. Consider nothing too small to report, and I will pay you according to how much you obtain that is discovered to be genuine."

~ * ~

Doctor Arnold was summoned to a private consultation with King Maslen.

"I wish to know about our patient, Arnold... you know what I am asking don't you?"

"Being your doctor, Sire, yes. I already have the answer for you. I have no doubts whatsoever, she's a virgin."

"Twenty years old and she's still a virgin?"

"Yes."

"Why did you not tell me?"

"I was not sure if, or rather, when, you'd want to know, but then, Sire, I... you... with your experience, I thought you would know."

"Of course I knew, but it didn't make sense to me then. Do you understand what this means?"

"From a doctor's point of view, Sire, and from a prospective husband's, but... I don't have your excellent mind... to consider and judge as you do... I seek only to serve you, Exalted Majesty, with all my substance, my talents, my very soul." he bowed. Doctor Arnold had never had such an intimate conversation with the king... other doctors had tended his wives and, one by one, with the deaths of his wives, they had been sent away.

"Never grovel to me again, Arnold. So far you have been more truthful, less patronizing to me than any other physician I've employed. Keep it up.

"This... this girl... she... it was either Kind Heart herself, or that corpse over in Gifford was Kind Heart... either way, Kind Heart is finished."

"That is, Sire, if she does not recover. She could never perform again as I saw her in the throne room and as I heard she did, outside. No, not for at least a year or two... she would be unable to walk down the steps right now, let alone climb a wall!"

"Keep me informed about it. Once a day, at noon, come yourself. If you deem any change in it important enough, report it to me yourself. Read it well, make sure it's not feigning this speechlessness! There'll be two guards posted at the bottom of the tower to make sure it does not climb out the window!"

Having taken the king at his word, the doctor spoke his mind, "That's ridiculous! No one could climb down that tower wall."

"You did not see it descend a more impossible wall, the tower would be child's play," the king said seriously, "I may have to incarcerate it elsewhere. As it recovers, I'd like to find a way to shape it to remain on our side or I will have to see it properly dead! I don't want to look back and wish that we had finished it, instead of bringing it back to our castle! I might sooner have brought a poisonous reptile into our midst."

A messenger reported to King Maslen, "Sir Charles Gifford has arrived in Aponia, Sire. He waits just inside our border requesting to visit you, to receive the remains of his sister. It was reported in Gifford that she died, Sire. He brings a casket to take her home for burial."

King Maslen sent an escort to bring Charles to his castle.

~ * ~

Charles climbed the steps up into the tower to visit his sister. King Maslen followed.

Jenna sat in the chair by the window, staring, not out the window, but apparently at the floor.

The brother had been warned to approach her with care and not embrace her, and that his visit must be short.

Doctor Arnold had rebandaged her head at the king's orders, and Jenna, dressed in a white linen night-dress, looked as frail as a lily.

"Jennava?" Charles asked, astounded. Was this the same sister who had rescued him? The one he had seen riding off with Lady Sidra, a little over two weeks ago?

Jenna did not look at him.

"Can she hear me?" he asked.

"She seems to... she does as we ask... with a little assistance," the doctor said. "She's come a long way... we thought she wouldn't survive... it still is not certain that she will..."

Tears filled Charles' eyes and he struggled unsuccessfully, to blink them back. "I want to take her home!" he said as firmly as he was able, his bottom lip trembling. He drew himself up to his height of five feet four inches, then shrank as the king, a foot and a half taller stepped closer.

"That's out of the question!" King Maslen said firmly.

"She wouldn't make the journey, Sir Charles," the doctor interjected, "You can see how ill she is... I'm of the opinion that she is still in an unconscious state... a trance of some kind, if you wish, caused by the trauma to her brain. She cannot walk unaided and sits only for an hour or two at a time."

Charles knelt by Jenna and moved his head about, trying to force her to focus on him. He waved his hand before her eyes, but she did not blink.

"She doesn't know me," he said the obvious, and stood. "Please, King Maslen, please, when she is recovered, please send her home. I... we will give you... anything you ask... no price is too great."

"We? Who else wants... this... this?" the king could find no word to describe his comatose prisoner.

Unaware of the conjectures his words would cause, Charles said, "Both King Cyranius and Prince Edward are most grieved at my sister... Lady Jennava's... her... accident... here in Aponia. I... we all... wish for her to be returned to Cyran, to Gifford... as soon as possible."

"You live in Rosenburg," the king said, "What is it to you that it returns to Gifford?"

"It's her home," Charles said lamely. Then he admitted, "It's not only for myself that I have come here, Your Majesty, but also on behalf of King Cyranius."

"I see..." King Maslen said, wondering if he understood this aspect at all. How close had this lady been to Cyranius? He understood that the king of Cyran was as celibate and disinterested in females as he himself was amorous and romantic.

"You'll consider it then, Your Majesty?" Charles asked, with boyish excitement in his voice. Staring at Jenna, he said, "If... if she chooses, I'd welcome her to live at my castle in Rosenburg." Turning back to the king, he said, "I have a wife and seven children, whom Jenna knows nothing about."

King Maslen raised his eyebrows. This dwarf-like, red-haired, boyish man had produced seven children? The king felt he could have been bowled over with a feather.

"We heard that your sister was not welcome..." the king said, and it dawned on him as to the reason—few men would want a woman around who could behave like Kind Heart.

"I... yes, you heard correctly Your Majesty. But, time... and circumstances work together to change people."

"Your sister has transgressed in Aponia and the charges against her are being measured. It... she... shall remain here until well enough to be judged," the king said.

After a short silence, Charles dropped to one knee beside the king, saying earnestly, "Thank you, Your Majesty, for the way you tended my sister in her great need and I beg you to continue to show kindness. If I could be kept informed of her progress, Your Majesty, I would be in your debt." He bowed his head.

"If you send a messenger to me, at the beginning of each month, Sir Charles, I shall commission one of my scribes to write to you of your sister's progress, if there be any," King Maslen promised.

"I shall leave a gift for you, Sire, in anticipation of your continued clemency to my sister."

Standing, Charles bowed. Moving to Jenna, he lifted her hand and kissed it. Closing her eyes, she smiled softly. It was the first time she had done such a thing.

"Jenna?" he called, but she did not open her eyes. "Goodbye, dear Jenna." His cheeks wet with tears, Charles stumbled from his sister's tower prison.

Thirty-eight

When it was voiced that Sir Charles Gifford was riding into Gifford Castle, both King Cyranius and Prince Edward, joined by others, hurried out to meet him. The covered coffin on the cart following his carriage spoke of an imminent funeral and burial.

Joy! The coffin was empty, Jenna was alive, and Charles had seen her and spoken to her, all this was quickly overshadowed by the news that she was ill. Charles was so depressed about his sister's condition that he wept openly.

"How... how do we know that she is not suffering some kind of torture at their hands?" he lamented. "King Maslen's a giant, dispassionate, inhuman, godless, unfeeling..."

Sir Lowell and Doctor Breck questioned Charles about the tower chamber, her attendants, the doctor, the guards, the king, the way she sat and stared and the bandage on her head. The doctor declared that he himself should go and visit her. King Cyranius did not discount this offer, but said a visit from Breck needed to be preceded by a letter to King Maslen.

"I'll tell him that Jenna is like a daughter to my wife Natalie and I," Breck said. "I want to see her and examine this head injury for myself."

Breck then went into a long discourse on head injuries and the lengths of times he had waited on various patients for signs of recovery. "Sometimes they recover and it's like a miracle and they live, others live for months, then die. Another knock to her head, though small, could prove fatal. But every day is one day more... she'll grow stronger every day."

"The incomprehensible thing is, a man like King Maslen allowing her to live and having his personal doctor caring for her," Charles said, wiping tears away.

"I shall write to Maslen, today," King Cyranius said, determined, "and ask what price he requires to secure Jennava's return... I'll ask that he put a price on her release. We'll pay whatever he asks."

Later, Sir Lowell told the king that he should commission trusted men to travel incognito to King Maslen's castle in Aponia to gain first-hand knowledge about Jenna, particularly about the 'accident' she supposedly had while attempting to escape.

"It's bad enough to have used deceit, to protect, as we did in burying Kind Heart. We have never used deceit to gain knowledge, and we shall not now," King Cyranius said. "We shall rather send visitors to Lady Jennava so that her memory may be stirred."

Secretly, King Cyranius wished he could dress as Kind Heart and ride to King Maslen's castle where, if he were not so hopeless when it came to heights, he would climb up into that tower and rescue her. Together they would ride back to Cyran. He sighed, such escapades were fantasy, impossible for him, he knew. *I cannot see a happy ending to all this,* he told himself. *I shall be forever bereft if I am unable to tell her how much I love her... to see the sunrise on her hair... to watch the iris color of her eyes change to blue... to assure her that I could never despise anything about her... I imagined she gave me torment, but that was nothing. Torment is what I feel now...*

~ * ~

A month had passed since Jenna had been imprisoned in the tower, and still she did not speak.

Doctor Arnold rolled the scroll he had written on and tied it with a ribbon. It was almost noontime, and he knew he must not be late for his appointment to report to King Maslen of his patient's progress. The king may keep him, Arnold, waiting, but he would never dare keep his king waiting.

Although Jenna had made such improvement that she helped dress herself in the morning and, with direction, sat at a table to eat, she still slept off and on all day and night. The doctor had nothing different to report to the king, other than that small progress was being made. She still had not spoken.

As the doctor moved to the door, Jenna rose and crossed to his desk, her eyes on the ink and the quill. Having noticed that she had done so, the doctor turned by the door and stood watching her. She seemed more focused.

Sitting at the desk, Jenna pulled a fresh piece of parchment in front of her and took up the quill. Dipping it in the ink, she painstakingly drew lines down the paper and smiled at the strokes.

Doctor Arnold moved back to stand behind her and when the paper was filled with lines, he placed a fresh piece in front of her, saying softly, "Draw something for me." Looking around, he said, "Draw something in this room."

Looking directly up, Jenna saw the arched window with one shutter not fully out, the curtain hanging in folds on one side, large clouds billowing in the blue sky.

To the doctor's amazement, stone by stone, Jenna drew the arched window, and set it into the curved stone wall. It was not a mere a line drawing, but, stroke by stroke, and with fine shaded lines, and dots, Jenna unfolded the perspectives of each stone with the three-dimensions of the wide sill. The folded curtain looked real. Just as she began to draw the clouds in the sky, a guard rushed into the room.

"The king is asking why you weren't there..."

Moving Jenna's hands back from the piece of paper, the doctor took the picture and hurried to show her work of art to the king.

As the doctor expected, King Maslen was pleased with the picture.

"It proves that it isn't just going to remain a limp lettuce," he said.

"I agree... the creativity part in her brain is intact," the doctor said.

"And its coordination, curse her!" the king exclaimed. "It takes coordination to look at a thing and draw it accurately. Keep me informed, Arnold," he said, then, "And... I'll come up, tomorrow morning, sometime before noon and watch it draw something."

"Sire, I've not asked you, but if she has lost the memory part in her brain, but regains her speech, and asks who she is, what shall I reply? And... you know Sire, that I'm not there all the time, it could be that she speaks to one of the servant-women, what shall we command them to say to her?"

King Maslen had pondered this eventuality. He had imagined that if she never regained her memory, he would be able to change her identity forever by telling her she was someone else. He could say he was her father, but had warned himself that this could prove to be dangerous in time. As his daughter, she could demand his throne.

He could be her brother, her uncle, any relative. The king's mind mulled over the possibilities.

"We'll speak of it tomorrow," he said, knowing he had much thinking to do on the matter. He wondered if it would not have been easier for him if she had died. *Death is so final*, he said to himself, feeling surprised. Other than his wives and stillborn sons, he had never felt sorry about anyone else dying. He remembered Charles' words; *time... and circumstances work together to change people...*

~ * ~

King Maslen very rarely asked advice of anyone. He had no advisors or counselors, but made all decisions and judgments from within his own mind, by counseling with himself. The close guards of his retinue were there to carry out his orders and bring him information. He considered himself to be the wisest man on earth. Knowing he was growing older, it was becoming an obsession to procure a male heir within the noble boundary of royal marriage. He had never before considered a female worthy of ascending his throne in her own right. But if he could father a daughter and train her as Lord Frances Gifford had trained his daughter, then that would be another matter, he now believed.

~ * ~

Jenna was sleeping when Doctor Arnold returned to the tower. The servant-woman excitedly showed him another drawing Jenna had done. It was a portrait of the servant herself.

"Amazing, she's captured you on this paper, your expression, your personality," the doctor said, staring at the deliberate ink marks on the parchment, portraying this lady's grim countenance. Not a dot or a stroke had been made but it harmonized to depict this woman.

Thin lines made the wavy hair seem real, with a few hairs escaping the severe plaited circlets around her ears—the round nose with a slight bulb on the end, thin lips turned inward, making the mouth abnormally small, which it was, the big, closely-set eyes with surprisingly long eyelashes and eyebrows of long hair hanging like fringes above the bright orbs. Finally, there was a mole on her chin with a curling hair growing from it.

"Yes! Ha! It's me, all right. Wait till me husband sees it. P'raps she'll do another, I'd like one to send to me daughter."

"The king will want it," Doctor Arnold said.

"Why?" she asked, then, knowing her question was out of place, she said quickly, "No offence... don't tell him I asked... I must keep me place. It's not for me to speak of..."

"No," said the doctor, "Don't speak of it to anyone."

Having checked that Jenna was asleep, he took the parchment to show the king. Drawing a window was one thing, but to draw a person and have the drawing resemble the subject in such an accurate manner was an extraordinary talent.

"She could accurately draw everyone she meets while she's here in my castle," King Maslen said in amazement. He knew each servant-woman, because he had personally selected those who would wait on his prisoner—they were all middle-aged, married, or widowed, and could be trusted not to enter into any intrigue with the guards or the shut-in.

The king was more amazed than the doctor at the likeness. "Imagine... someone like her could draw portraits of me and send them to people who had never seen me, and they would know what I look like! I should come up and have her draw me."

Doctor Arnold did not speak but wondered if Jenna could be forced to draw someone against her will. Such concentration would tire her.

"I'll come tomorrow, I've pressing matters to consider for the rest of today. Cyranius keeps writing letters about letters he has sent, all to which I have no intentions of replying, other than to say, no, no, no!" He did not say that he wanted to go riding and think about his dilemma of having possession of someone who was considered by the King of Cyran to be of such worth he would pay any price to have her returned. In his eyes, this girl was a criminal; in the eyes of the King of Cyran, she was a heroine. But one thing they both agreed on—she was valuable.

Would he bind her and make her his slave? No, if she recovered her senses, she would likely refuse food and water and be dead within days. He had known strong-willed prisoners to do this. *Death is so final,* he reminded himself.

Unless she recovered her memory, any punishment he meted out on her would be wasted because she would have no idea as to the reason for the punishment. It would be like punishing an innocent person. Was a person guilty of a crime they could not remember committing? He decided his prisoner was guilty.

King Maslen began conceiving a plan to shock Jenna into remembering. As soon as she could speak and reply to what was said to her, he wanted to present a 'reenactment' to her. Such a reenactment would surely return her memory.

When King Maslen entered the tower-chamber, Jenna was drawing a portrait of Doctor Arnold.

The king watched her impatiently, and before she had finished, he pulled it away from her.

"Draw me!" he commanded, pointing at himself. He stood where the doctor had been standing.

To Doctor Arnold's surprise, Jenna obeyed. The drawing took her almost an hour. She ignored the king's words, "Hurry... hurry, I don't have all day!" but she stopped obediently each time he came around to pull her hands away and view her work. The drawing was so accurate that King Maslen was not entirely happy. His eyes, even on paper, seemed to have a ruthless gleam in them and the deep dimple in his left cheek spoke not of happiness, but haughtiness as in real life. She captured the cynical downturn of the right side of his mouth, yet she also portrayed what few saw, that he had a secondary boyish gleam to his countenance. His nose was a replica of the aristocratic one he owned.

"She has revealed the boy beneath the king," Doctor Arnold said when King Maslen declared that she made him look too young and both 'childish and savage.'

They were so busy pouring over the drawing that they did not see Jenna cross the room to lie on the bed and close her eyes.

The king was fascinated that he owned such talent. "We should encourage this thing, Arnold. It would be much better for her to be occupied in creative art than in riding around interfering in matters that are no concern of hers."

Turning to the servant-woman who stood by her chair, he said, "Leave us, wait at the bottom of the steps and return when I've descended."

The king sat in the chair by the desk and looked at the doctor saying quietly, "I've counseled with less men in my life than this..." he held one hand up, with only three fingers pointing upward. "I consider you of such worth, Arnold, that I wish to hear your opinion on matters other than those of your profession." Looking across to see that Jenna slept, he asked in the quietest voice he owned, "What am I to do with her?"

"I... Sire... you honor me greatly. I... I need to know more about her to be able to give you an informed answer."

"Ask me any question you like about her... I agree... knowing about her would help you with your counsel."

"How many people... has she... and Kind Heart... killed?" the doctor asked. He knew that the man, Kind Heart had been involved in many a so-called 'rescue,' but no one called him a 'murderer.' On the contrary, even men from Aponia revered him and held him in great esteem. He was a legendary figure, one men told their boys about. He had been an example of goodness, not evil.

The king was silent for a few minutes. He could think of no one she had killed at first, then, "You knew Knight Red, one of my trusted warriors, she caused his death."

"Was he not in the process of capturing her, and he himself sacrificed many innocent people... did he not?" the doctor asked. "Did she, or Kind Heart, ever kill innocent people or destroy valuable property, as Knight Red did—the palace in Cyran?"

"Whose side are you on?" the king asked defensively, then, "Why do you question me?"

"Sire, please Sire, you know whose side I am on! I don't question *you*, Sire, but wish only to question her... this so-called criminal. Is she a murderer? Was Kind Heart a murderer? I... if she is a ruthless, cold-blooded murderer, I would not wish to tend her. It would be my counsel, Sire, that you have her put to death. I believe that no one should take life but an executioner, at the command of the king!"

Walking to the window and staring out at the clouded sky, the king did not answer. Kind Heart had, for three generations, been a thorn in the side of the kings of Aponia. That he had never killed a man was known, but that had not seemed important. Good men had been knocked down; some of their injuries had taken them out of action for several months.

"Kind Heart has never been a murderer, not in all three generations," King Maslen admitted. "This... this girl... she... I understand that the death of Knight Red was an accident, but it was caused by her. And... it's correct, he was going to kill her...

"It's no secret that Kind Heart treated all human life as equal." The king laughed and said, "Equal! He freed slaves and rescued anyone who cried out hard enough about their bonds or imprisonment. His wasted purpose for living seemed to be to save children. He took a distressed princess away from her fate of marrying me." He laughed, but it was a bitter laugh. "I have learned that Anastasia herself sent communications, soliciting Kind Heart's help. Kind Heart did not just go on a rescue, he had to be requested..."

"How old was Anastasia? Sire?"

"How old do you think she was?"

"I... I... they said she was twelve, not thirteen as her father said."

"Kind Heart wrote to me, Arnold, and said that she was only just ten years old. It made me very angry to receive that letter from Kind Heart. Anastasia looked every day of thirteen when I saw her. And her father said she was thirteen."

"You're still angry with Kind Heart, Sire?"

"I will always be angry about everything to do with Kind Heart!" he growled.

"But... was this girl, Kind Heart?" Arnold asked.

"It very well could have been!" he exclaimed.

The doctor again walked over, touching Jenna's hand, checking to see if her eyes would open. But her breathing was even and she slept. He returned to stand close to the king, waiting for His Majesty to speak.

"I've never admitted these things to anyone. I... I don't believe I've admitted these things to myself. Actually, it helps assemble ones thoughts, ones decisions, to talk ones thoughts aloud. I've always kept counsel to myself..." He cleared his throat, looking like a boy ashamed.

"All right, now. We have the facts. It... she's... not a murderer. But she and Kind Heart have been preposterous meddlers. I've heard, from reliable sources, that King Cyranius wanted to get his hands on Kind Heart, even he called him a law-breaker who committed treason against his throne. It seems Kind Heart was a law to himself."

"Like playing God?" Arnold asked.

"Like playing God," he repeated.

They were silent for a while. King Maslen stood to look out the window, checking that the guards stood to attention beneath the tower wall, while the doctor strode over to see that Jenna slept and was not lucid enough to hear their conversation.

"Perhaps you should choose a name for her, Sire," the doctor suggested, "That is, if she does not remember her own."

The king shook his head. "I still don't know whether I should send her to Cyran for a costly sum from Cyranius. For what reason should I keep her here?"

"You're greatly fascinated by her, Sire."

"Yes," he said, and shook his head.

"When you watched her run and fight for her freedom, you admired her; you did not want her to die, you wanted to own her. But you want her to choose to be with you, rather than to be forced. You want her to admire you as much as Lady Sidra does."

"How do you know this?" King Maslen asked, "Is it so obvious?"

"No, Sire. Few would perceive any of this. I see it, because I've been with you for two years now. The gods bless you with perfect health, Your Majesty, and often I stand in your throne room just to pass the time. Other than studying every book that I can obtain on medicine and doctoring, I study you and try to work-out what you are thinking."

"Why do you do that?" the king asked, now alarmed.

"As you grow older, Sire, you'll need people around you who understand you. Gaining counsel from these people will give you the balance you need to make decisions that are best for you, your kingdom and your heirs."

"Do you know, Arnold, I believe you're right, you speak truth," the king said, then asked, "Would you have felt it wrong that I married a thirteen year old?"

"No, Sire," Arnold replied, his voice indignant, "And if she was as mature as a thirteen year old, no matter her age, then it's not wrong... perhaps though..."

"What?"

"You do not want... this... girl, Jennava, here... if she does not choose you... therefore, if the princess did not choose you, Sire—"

"She was mine! I chose her, and, her stepfather chose me! That's enough," he said.

Arnold was quiet.

"She would have grown to like me," the king said, "Anastasia is the most beautiful maiden I ever laid eyes on. I desired her as I have never desired any maiden before."

"And... this... girl..."

"I did not think of her as a maiden."

"What about Lady Sidra? You promised her—"

"I know what I promised!" the king was angry. He shouted at the doctor, "I came to talk about this girl here, not about everyone else!"

They both turned to look at Jenna, who slept through their loud interchange.

Doctor Arnold softened his voice, saying, "Your Majesty, it's all connected. You yearn for an heir but you want that child to be born within wedlock, by a woman you desire, one who will be true to you. I believe all three are part of the whole in your mind now. Why did you promise Sidra marriage if she captured Lady Jennava?"

"Why do you question me?" the king said then remembered he had offered to answer Arnold's questions. "All right, I'll tell you. I wanted Kind Heart's woman, to teach Kind Heart a lesson for taking Anastasia from me. But I never dreamed that Sidra could do it. I wanted to get rid of Sidra, yet I have to admit, I'm attracted to her. When I first met her, I wished she'd never been married before, I want my wife to be a virgin. And... then, I did not know that I would react... as I did... to this... girl... even though I believed she was unchaste... yes, you're right, the three are connected."

"You do not really want to marry Sidra?"

"She would please me as a mistress, but not as a wife."

"And if she bore you a child?"

"I would want her to be my wife."

A silence ensued, and both men sat in deep thought.

The doctor broke the silence, "They are similar."

"Who?"

"Lady Jennava and Lady Sidra."

"No, you're mistaken, they're not."

"They're the same height and build, and have the same features, Sire, they could even have been sisters."

"No." He shook his head.

"Yes, Sire. Put makeup and a dark wig on this girl and see if she does not look like Sidra."

"Why do you tell me this?"

"I have no idea, Sire. It's only an observation. I believe you could build on it, if and when you needed to..."

~ * ~

Jenna was given a name that day. They would call her 'Jay.' Her golden curls were sent to be washed and made into a wig.

King Maslen announced to his mistress, Meltissa, that she was to go on vacation. She would be safely escorted to his northern castle where she could stay for a year. With a generous annual income from the king's coffers, she could then make a new life for herself, away from him.

Late that afternoon, after Meltissa had left, the king told Sidra that she would move into the bedchamber next to his. When and if she conceived a child by him, he would marry her.

Sidra was so happy, she could think of nothing else but King Maslen and her life with him. Everything paled beside the bright rainbow of this welcome development.

Thirty-nine

Doctor Arnold brought a box of different sized charcoals to Jenna, and a pile of parchment squares.

As he had expected, Jenna's pictures were completed in a much less time, using the charcoals.

She repeated the picture of the window. Doctor Arnold brought the servant-woman to Jenna, and waited while Jenna drew this woman.

Placing the previous ink-drawing of the servant-woman in front of Jenna, he said, "Draw Moyra as you did before, Jay, draw Moyra."

Halfway through her drawing, he took the ink portrait away. Jenna closed her eyes, and the doctor thought she would stop drawing. But, opening them, Jenna finished the picture.

"Draw King Maslen," he said, and when she just stared at him, he placed the king's picture on the table. As Jenna took up a piece of the charcoal, and began to draw, the doctor again took the ink drawing away. Jenna completed the portrait. It was a little different, if anything, the king looked more forbidding.

Jenna moved to her bed and slept. The doctor took the pictures to show King Maslen. He had to wait to see the king, but found him to be as intrigued as he was.

"Encourage her to draw images from her memory," the king said, having discerned the doctor's next move.

"We'll see if she has a memory there somewhere," doctor Arnold said.

"It must be there," the king said.

"Not necessarily," Arnold said, "I believe we have different time spaces in our memory. There are very old memories, and newer memories. These drawings are done from current memory, not from the past. Perhaps her past memory has gone forever."

"I'd like to shock it back!" King Maslen growled, "I might just do it too! We need some action, not these... these dormant drawings!"

Having drawn everything and everyone that the doctor placed before her, Arnold decided not to visit her the next day. She slept off and on throughout the day, not taking up a charcoal to draw.

At three o'clock the next morning, Jenna sat up suddenly. Screaming loudly, she sat trembling, and clutching her temples as if in great pain. The servant-woman sent a guard to fetch Doctor Arnold.

When the doctor entered the chamber, the servant-woman was trying to comfort Jenna who was distraught.

"She must've had a bad dream," the woman said.

Jenna's eyes were closed, and she clung to the servant as if she would never let go.

"This is the first time she's done this," the doctor said, wondering if terror would come with memories. With the knowledge he had of head injuries, he wondered if remembering and feeling pained and helpless would cause her death.

Together, they put her back to bed and Arnold left the woman sitting with her, speaking in soothing tones.

Jenna slept off and on all the next day, avoiding the desk with the charcoals.

King Maslen was impatient with Arnold's patience with Jenna, and demanded, "Make something happen, Arnold, or I will!"

"We need a picture of something from her past," the doctor suggested, "something from Cyran... perhaps even a person."

"Sidra?" King Maslen asked, then said, "and I think she still has that sister of hers with her... Millie is the name, have Sidra fetch her, but have Sidra sit for her first."

"If you want it to work, Sire, we should wait until she wants to draw again."

King Maslen would not wait, and commanded that Sidra go to the tower with Doctor Arnold.

The doctor sat Jenna at the desk and put the charcoal in her hand.

Jenna took an hour to draw Sidra. She stared at her between every stroke, and when she had finished, she lay down on her bed and slept.

Sidra had not seen Jenna since the day they had arrived here, and she was greatly shocked to see her with such short curls, so thin and sallow looking.

"If she looks like this now, she must have been dreadful a month ago," Sidra said.

"We want you to fetch your sister, Millie, here, now," the doctor said.

"Millie? But Millie's gone. I think she went home to Cyran, she left a week ago."

"Does King Maslen know this?" the doctor asked.

"No... I did not think to tell him." Sidra said.

Doctor Arnold was peeved. He asked, "Who else is here, in Cyran, from Gifford, whom Jay knew?"

"Jay... you mean? Oh, Jay..." Sidra said, and thought before answering. "There isn't anyone from Gifford here... except her, and me..."

"Yes, you're right!" the doctor said, dismissing her.

Jenna's wig had arrived that morning. When Sidra had gone, and Jenna woke, the doctor took the wig out of the box and carefully placed it on Jenna's head. Taking up a large rectangle mirror he sent for, he set it in front of Jenna at the desk.

Without hesitating, Jenna quickly drew herself. Her face was thin and gaunt, not as attractive as before, but a replica of what was in the mirror now.

"You still don't know what we want, do you?" he asked.

Placing a black cloth over the mirror, he moved around the desk and placed one hand over Jenna's eyes. Putting a piece of charcoal in her hand, he placed her fingers on the parchment. Slowly he took his hand away.

"Draw someone you love, Jay, draw a friend. Draw your best friend."

Frowning deeply, Jenna drew the portrait of a beautiful young girl. It was Judith.

"That's right," the doctor encouraged, now draw another." He placed another piece of parchment in front of her.

Moving faster than before, she drew the sweet face of a very young girl, her namesake, Jennava. With encouragement, Jenna drew her father and her brother. She would have gone to lie down, but the doctor persisted, pointing to the stone wall and saying, "Draw a castle for me, Jay, a stone castle, your home."

With fingers that trembled, Jenna drew Gifford castle. Then she slept.

~ * ~

"Who are they?" King Maslen asked, when Arnold showed him the pictures. "This looks like her brother, or a child belonging to the brother. But her brother said she had not met his wife or children." He looked at the drawing of Jenna's father, and said, "Who is this young man?"

"I believe it's her father, Sire," Arnold said. "She's remembering her childhood in this way. Perhaps that's her brother, as a boy, Sire... there's a slight family likeness, is there not?"

The king said, "Fetch Sidra, see what she can make of these portraits... she might even recognize this castle here."

Sidra recognized all of the pictures.

"Yes, I know who it is, Sire. It's Jenna's brother, when he was a boy.

"And this is Jenna's father. She's made him look about ten years younger than I remember him."

She gasped at the picture of Judith as if a ghost had come to haunt her. Her hand flew to cover her red lips.

"Who is it?" King Maslen demanded, when Sidra did not speak.

"It's... it's my step-daughter... but when she was younger... Judith and Jenna... Jay, and Judith were the closest of friends." Sidra thought of Kind Heart, and Jenna, wondering if it were Jenna who had rescued Brother Patrick from the dungeon.

"Where does Judith live now?" King Maslen asked.

"She's dead. She lived in Mayern."

"This? Where is this castle?" He placed the picture of the castle before Sidra.

"Gifford... how amazing... she's drawn it just like it is."

"This?"

"Oh! It's young Jennava."

"Jennava? She drew a picture of herself when she was a child?"

"No, it's my... my niece, Millie's daughter. Duff, Millie's husband, named their daughter after Lady Jennava Gifford."

The king commanded Doctor Arnold to continue with his project. "I want more than this, do something to stir up more than just memories!"

Having written names on all of the pictures, the doctor showed them to Jenna. But she wasn't at all interested in the words, only in staring at the drawings and touching sensitive fingers to the parchment.

For the next week in all of her drawing time, Jenna drew pictures of horses, trees, and small cottages nestled in thick woods.

On the following day, she drew the palace in Cyran.

Then she drew a picture of Prince Edward, followed by a picture of King Cyranius with a crown on his head.

When King Maslen saw them, he wondered if they were both the same person, one the boy, the other the man. That it was a king she drew was intriguing.

"She has drawn people who meant much to her, I can only think that this king is foremost in her memory, other than her brother, her father and closest friends."

Sidra confirmed the identities of the pictures.

"This is Prince Edward and that's King Cyranius... heavens, how does she do it? It's so true to life."

"Is it indeed?" King Maslen asked, staring at the portrait of the young king he had never seen. He felt resentful. The man was so incredibly handsome, every bit a man, not at all like Jenna's brother, but rock-solid.

"Enough of this pansified women's stuff," the king cried, standing to his feet. He shouted at the captain of his personal guard, saying, "Myres, set up those reenactment scenes that I planned with you and have it ready as soon as possible, then send for us, we'll be in the Jay-tower."

Arnold followed King Maslen as he strode quickly and determinedly to the Jay-tower.

They arrived to see that Jenna slept. As King Maslen strode over to the bed, Arnold could no longer keep silent.

"Sire... you could undo all we've tried to achieve."

"What are we trying to achieve?" he asked, then answered, "We want her memory returned, don't we? So far we have just had some pleasant pictures from her untainted dreams. What we need are some realities." He stared at her. Faint pink tinged her cheeks, and she looked better than he'd seen her since she had been in this tower. "All right, I'll wait until she wakes, but it had better he soon."

He strode to the window and back, then sat at the desk and wrote several communications, looking across at Jenna every few minutes.

"That's long enough," he said. Striding to the bed, he shook Jenna awake, and, pulling her to stand, dragged her across the round chamber to a chair. Sitting himself down, he released her. She stood, trembling, then turned and would have returned to the bed.

"Stand still! Fetch her, Arnold!"

The doctor obeyed his employer.

"Where is that wig? Fetch it and put it on her. And you, woman, bring the mirror... then leave us!"

The doctor was commanded to hold the mirror and Jenna was commanded to look in that mirror and tell him who she was.

When Jenna, closing her eyes, was silent, the king shouted at her, "Look at the mirror, girl! Tell us who you are! What is your name?"

Jenna blinked and bowed her head.

The king lifted his hand as if he would slap her face.

"Please don't strike her, Sire... it will set us back, not forward." Doctor Arnold stared at King Maslen, appalled. They had been working with Jenna for almost two months, and the king could end it in a second.

At that moment, Myres entered the chamber, saying, "It's all ready, Your Majesty."

King Maslen stood and said, "I'll go ahead of our prisoner, Myres, you come behind her."

"Sire..." Arnold began, his voice tone desperate.

"*Be Silent!*" Maslen bellowed, and as the doctor had heard this statement, said just like this, many times before, he knew that the king had again summoned the beast-like character within him to reach its needle-sharp claws out from the darkness of its lonely lair.

"Stay here, Arnold, and take care of it when it is returned."

"Jay, follow the king," Arnold urged softly, when Jenna did not walk down the narrow stone steps, but stood staring as if seeing nothing.

"Hurry up, hurry up!" King Maslen shouted, now waiting at the bottom.

"I don't think she will be able to walk that far," Arnold said.

"You mean... down these few steps?" Myres asked. It was he who had pointed the spear at her in the atrium. Although she had not struck him, he had suffered a twisted knee in his fall, and was only just now able to walk without limping.

"She's not left this chamber, and has no idea where she is, or who she is," Arnold explained

"I heard she was recovering..."

The doctor frowned, staring at Jenna. He waved his hand in front of her eyes and she turned to look at him. The truth of her condition dawned on him, and he said, "She is as one who sleepwalks—sees me, but the deep unconsciousness still afflicts her. That's probably why she doesn't speak. I think she's walking around in a coma... with her eyes open sometimes. She won't remember any of this..."

"What will happen if she wakes?" Myres asks.

"It depends upon where she is... if the circumstances are wrong, it could kill her!"

"She's... still... unconscious?" Myres asked.

"What's keeping you?" the king shouted, then, not waiting for a reply, said to the nearest guard, "Get up there and help Myres *carry* it down if you have to! Bring it to my throne room."

There was not room on the steps for two men to carry one person, so while the guard took Jenna's feet, Myres carried her upper body, and together they brought her down the narrow winding steps from the tower.

Jenna did not struggle one iota but nobody other than Arnold believed that she was not in the world of the conscious yet.

Jenna walked a short distance along the corridor, and when they came to another step-way downward, she had to be physically guided down the stairs. At the bottom, she kept walking and would have crashed into the wall had Myres not taken her hand and turned her to walk along the corridor. She tired, and as she had done in the tower chamber, she turned to go to her bed. Here, she would have walked into the wall. In her deep dream-state, she saw her bed over against the wall. Recent memory made the picture she required appear.

Again taking her arm and guiding her, Myres saw Jenna close her eyes as if she would sleep. "I don't like this," he said to the guard, and lifted her into his arms. As if snuggling in her father's arms like a small child, Jenna lifted her hand up around his neck and slept deeply.

"You carried her?" King Maslen asked when they stood before his throne.

"It seemed too much for her, Sire, she... I think she's faint somehow," Myres said.

King Maslen, his face more sour than lemons, rose from his throne and came to see for himself. She looked as if she slept peacefully.

"Stand her up!" he commanded, and watched as Myres placed her to stand, her arm still around his neck. The guard supported her on the other side.

"Wake up! Wake up!" King Maslen shouted, pinching the cheeks of her face together with his large thumb and forefinger. Jenna's head slumped forward when he released her. "Fetch a pitcher of cold water," he ordered, determined to make her respond. "Make it cold!"

When ice-cold water was tossed on Jenna's face, her eyes opened and, although no one knew it, there were the first signs of shock and recognition on her face. Jenna became half-conscious. Her head jerked up and her body tensed, then she stared along the line of men who all stared back.

"Ah. We have your attention now. Look at what you see here now, Lady-bird, take time to view what you have done."

Jenna's mouth dropped open, and she felt she relived a recent nightmare. This was King Maslen's throne room, was it not? She swayed on her feet. Was she still here? Had she not stood here earlier today? But this was different.

"Don't fall over, Lady-bird," King Maslen said in a taunting tone, then he spoke to Myres and the guard, "guide her along the line here... slowly..."

Jenna's eyes moved along the men as she was walked in front of the line. An assortment of thirty guards stood, some with their heads bandaged, some their legs and arms, and some of the bandages had been stained with red. Jassy was there with a new bandage on his now-healed leg, leaning on his crutch. Then, at the end of the line a boy of about six stood with an ill-fitting bandage around his head, and his arm in a sling.

The child had decided to join in the 'game.'

Sure that she was in the middle of a dream, Jenna frowned in disbelief. King Maslen had told her that this is what she had done, and Jenna knew that there was little reality here—never would she have harmed a child. Her head pounded in an alarming manner and she would have fallen had not the two men held her firmly, one on each side of her.

Angry that a child stood with the men, King Maslen indicated to Myres to take Jenna out into the atrium.

A group of twelve men stood as they had before, all armed and staring at the criminal. On the floor lay a pile of clothes and a wig.

Jenna wanted to close her eyes and blot this scene from her view and she did. But she still felt the men holding her on either side—she was half-conscious, not asleep.

"Open your eyes! Put the clothes on, Lady-bird, and the wig..." a deep voice thundered in her ears.

When Jenna did not respond, King Maslen tossed more ice-cold water from the pitcher in her face. She gasped, and opened her eyes.

"Let her stand alone," King Maslen commanded, and the men, releasing her, stepped away from her.

Jenna stared at the clothes on the floor. Had she not just put them on? She looked wildly around this chamber, and felt her head throbbing in great pain. Throwing it back, she looked up above her. A net hung from the beams, and she felt sure it was going to fall on her. She tried to move, but not a muscle or a nerve would obey the dictates of her mind; it was as if she had been paralyzed.

King Maslen repeated his dictate, and again Jenna tried to step forward to where the wig lay.

Like a leaf falling from the tree with no help from any downward breeze, Jenna folded and slumped to the floor.

King Maslen threw the remaining water in her face, but she did not move.

Sidra rushed from behind the king and knelt beside Jenna. She used the skirt of her dress to wipe the water from Jenna's face. "I don't think she is breathing! No, she's not breathing..." Tears gushed down her face, as she muttered, "You can be such a bully, Maslen."

Pushing Sidra out of the way, the king leaned his ear on her heart. He could not hear it beating. Deep in his mind, he heard a phrase convicting him, *Death is so final...* Lifting her into a sitting position with one arm around her, he slapped her face, saying, "Come, come. Wake up!"

With a gasp as if she had risen from the depths of a deep lake, Jenna drew in a deep breath, and her body stiffened as if suffering a spasm. Then, as quickly as the spasm had come, she relaxed, again unconscious.

"Myres, take her back to Arnold," the king said, his voice deeply disappointed. He had wanted to see her try to fight his men, to be humiliated, to cry to him for mercy. Now it was he who felt humbled, the eyes of his men suggested he was showing cruelty to one who could do nothing to help herself. "Take her... take her!" he shouted impatiently, passing her into Myres hands as if she had stung him.

Forty

Jenna wavered between semi consciousness and unconsciousness for a week. She refused all solid food, but drank copious amounts of honeyed water, cider, fruit juice, broth and thin vegetable soup.

~ * ~

The Trusty Ten arrived back in Aponia with a sheaf of information about 'Lady Jennava Gifford.' In an uncharacteristic manner, King Maslen shut himself away from everyone to read through the information brought him. Usually, he read communications and reports while sitting on his throne with everyone watching and wondering what he was reading, then again wondering while he wrote. Sometimes he informed his court, other times, he kept matters to himself.

At the same time, another communication arrived from King Cyranius, requesting that King Maslen accept a visit from Doctor Breck and wife, who were both greatly distressed as to the health of their elected daughter, Lady Jennava.

King Maslen was considering allowing Doctor Breck to visit and tend his prisoner when Jenna regained her speech and awareness.

Doctor Arnold had grown despondent, having given up hope of Jenna making further recovery.

The continuing nightmare haunted Jenna's mind and she relived the original demonstration engineered by King Maslen. But included in the nightmarish reenactment were the bandaged men, and a dozen young boys, all clones of the original, with the accusation in their staring eyes that this was what she had done. Just as she relaxed to sleep and gain rest from the nightmare, it began again.

When Jenna regained true consciousness, she thought at first she was in one of the cottages, and that she had been suffering a horrendous dream. Climbing out of her bed, she staggered and would have fallen if the servant-woman had not been close enough to jump up and support her.

Staring around at the chamber, which seemed foreign to her, Jenna said, "Where am I?" She allowed the woman to draw her back to sit on the side of the bed.

"Where do you think you are?" the woman asked, wondering if her charge would speak again. It was just after dawn, and this woman had only been in the tower for five minutes.

"I... I don't know..." Memories surged, and Jenna's head pulsated and pounded. "Oh, my head. What did they hit me with?" She closed her eyes, remembering the jester with the bolos and the net over her head."Oh, my head," she repeated, "It's pounding like a hammer."

"Lie down, Jay," the woman said.

Jenna allowed the woman to press her backward on to the thin mattress and place the cover over her, but she groaned in pain and misery. Never before had she suffered such a headache. "What did they hit me with?" she repeated.

"Stay there, Jay, and I'll have them fetch the doctor."

The moment Jenna closed her eyes, she felt herself sliding down the wall. *I must roll backwards,* she told herself, but she kept falling and falling and falling...

She sat up slowly, pushing her feet over the side of the bed. Standing, she swayed then staggered to the source of light.

The servant-woman hurried to her side, saying, "Let me help you back to bed. You must lie down... Doctor Arnold is being fetched."

"I feel better upright and I need to see where I am," Jenna said, and pushed the shutters outward. Her arms and shoulders, unwilling to obey her dictates, felt as if they belonged to someone else.

Shivering from an intake of cool morning air, Jenna stared out at the city beneath her. A mass of deeply shadowed stone walls and buildings greeted her eyes. Being in the north tower of the castle, the dawn light was rising from her right. Yellow shafts splintered upwards, illuminating distant clouds, but no countryside was visible; all that Jenna beheld belonged to the capital city of Aponia.

"I'm in Aponia," she said, stating the obvious. Looking downward, she felt queasy in her stomach. Yellow plumes of the feathers in the guards' helmets were small dots to Jenna. The men stood side by side in the stone balcony at the base of the tower.

Turning away, Jenna looked for a bowl, "I feel sick," she said, allowing the servant-woman to give her support. The floor rose up to meet her and she sank into a faint. The feeling that she was falling again engulfed her. She was falling, falling, falling, and there was nothing beneath her.

Doctor Arnold entered the chamber.

"She fainted," the servant-woman said. Together they lifted her and carried her to the bed. The servant recounted Jenna's words.

"Fetch a goblet of cold water," the doctor commanded, then spoke to his patient, "Jay, are you awake?"

Jenna's long eyelashes lifted and her violet eyes stared at the doctor. "Who are you?" she asked.

"You don't remember me?" he asked.

"I've never seen you before."

"I'm Doctor Arnold, and I've been commissioned by King Maslen to take care of you."

"How... how long have I been here?"

"How long does it feel?"

Jenna did not answer immediately, then, "It... it feels like it's been a long night. It was yesterday that I came to Aponia. Yesterday morning..."

"You look troubled, tell me about it."

"I've had this terrible nightmare... it's been going on and on, it feels like several days have passed and I keep feeling as though I am falling, it feels as if I've been falling forever. I was brought here yesterday, wasn't I?"

"It's been a little longer than that, Jay," he said.

"Why do you call me Jay?"

"Your name begins with 'J', does it not? Your voice is croaky. Are you thirsty? Would you like to sit up and drink some water? There's also orange juice on the shelf over there... in the painted jug."

"I'd like to get up, Doctor Arnold," she said, and turning the cover back, she sat around on the side of the bed.

Doctor Arnold gave her the goblet, and Jenna drank deeply, then she said, "I feel sick in my stomach. I felt it this morning when I looked out of the tower, all my strength seems to have drained away, I feel so weak..."

"Perhaps you should see if you could sleep."

"No, I don't want to... I keep having the same bad dream... it's horrible."

"A little sleep will help you, but we'll prop you up, that will help your head." So saying, he placed several pillows where her head should go, and gently pushed her to lean back on them. He watched her eyes close. She slept for over an hour, until the feeling of falling brought her back into sudden wakefulness.

The servant-woman hurried to her side with a breakfast tray. Drawing a small table to the bed, she set the tray down on it. As usual, a bowl of porridge, a slab of cheese, and a goblet of milk had been set on the tray. Sitting on the side of the bed, Jenna ate the cheese and drank the milk.

"You're not going to eat your porridge?" Doctor Arnold asked.

"I never eat that," Jenna said, "I like fruit." Her eyes scanned the room, but there was no bowl of fruit anywhere. Other than the bedside table, the desk, the king's armchair, and two wooden chairs, there was only a partition by the far wall, and the bed against this part of the round wall. The shelves on the wall at the head of the bed held an assortment of goblets and covered jugs. Two windows, one smaller than the other, lent light to the stone chamber.

Jenna's eyes flew back to the doctor's. He was observing her. "You're much better this morning, Jay," he said. "How is your head now?"

"It aches fearfully," she said, then, "I'd like to dress, I hope there is something I can wear?" She remembered her torn dress and Kind Heart's costume.

The servant-woman, having received a nod from Doctor Arnold, drew Jenna around the partition to where the two dresses Jenna had been wearing hung. One was dark green, the other dark blue, otherwise, they were very plain and ordinary as commanded by the king. The servant-woman helped her take off the white linen nightgown.

A bowl of lukewarm water sat waiting and Jenna would have washed her own face, but felt strangely spent. She allowed the servant-woman to care for her, and to dress her in the unfamiliar clothes. To the woman, there was little change in Jenna from other mornings, other than the fact that she spoke and seemed to be much brighter-eyed, alert. Taking up a wide-toothed comb, the woman began to comb Jenna's hair.

"My hair! Who cut my hair!" Jenna cried, staring at herself in the small looking glass that had been built into the back of the wooden partition.

"The doctor did!" Fleida growled, and added, "Just be thankful you've got such a head of hair. I'd do anything to have curls like yours. Be still, let me finish combing it!"

Emerging from behind the partition, Jenna moved to the desk, and sat in the king's comfortable armchair.

Doctor Arnold had been waiting for her. In front of him was the pile of drawings Jenna had done. Having placed them in the order that Jenna had drawn them, other than the two of King Maslen, which he placed at the bottom, Doctor Arnold showed her the first one, with its title folded back so that she could not read it.

"How quaint. You've drawn the window here… it's quite good, you have good perspective… the shading is excellent."

He showed her the drawing of Moyra, the servant-woman, and Jenna said, "That's very realistic. She looks formidable. Who is she?"

"What's going on here?" the servant-woman asked, frowning. Not comprehending Jenna's state, she thought the girl to be jesting.

"Fleida, keep quiet! Sit down, over there, by the small window," Doctor Arnold said. Taking up a small piece of parchment, the doctor placed an open book upright so that Jenna could not see what he wrote. Dipping a quill it in the ink, he wrote:

Your Majesty, Our patient is at last fully conscious, and talkative. She believes she has only been unconscious for one, or two days at the most, and remembers nothing of the ten weeks in this tower. Although she says she has no strength, I do not wish to leave her. She is almost as coherent and alert as she was when I saw her first in your throne room.

He signed the note, 'Arnold,' rolled and tied it with ribbon.

"Fleida, I'd like you to go yourself, and tell the king's messenger to give His Majesty this scroll. When King Maslen comes here, you must wait downstairs. Take your knitting with you, if you wish."

"I'm not supposed to leave here, am I?" Jenna asked, having watched the doctor's movements, and the servant-woman leave.

"No," Arnold agreed. "King Maslen will want to speak with you now that you are fully awake."

"I've been unconscious since yesterday morning," Jenna said, adding, "it seems like a long time."

"It's been a long time, indeed," the doctor said, then, "tell me about it, Jay, tell me what you remember, after you left the throne room… I didn't see you in the atrium… tell me about it…"

Jenna did not speak for a minute, then, "I remember escaping from a net that fell from above. I had thought, as I stepped into the atrium, that I only had to get out of the castle. King Maslen had said that I could go free if I escaped. He said, 'Let's see her get out the doors there.'

"Six acrobats waited in the courtyard, and I knew that they could fell me and capture me, so I... I took up the net... and ran for the wall."

"You climbed down a sixty-foot wall?" he asked.

"I had the net, then I did not climb—it was too smooth, I slid the rest of the way..."

"It is a wonder you did not break your legs."

Jenna smiled wanly, saying, "I wondered myself. It was an extreme effort to force myself to relax and to curl over backwards when I hit the road. It's that fall that I keep dreaming about. It's a wonder I don't have bruises and pains everywhere. Although I managed to make a wave, the road was very hard."

"A wave?"

"It's a term my father used. He took me for a vacation to the ocean so that I would understand exactly what he meant. Father told me to make myself into a wave in the ocean and to imagine myself as flexible as water. The rock cannot harm the wave.

"It can smash it into droplets, that all," the doctor mused, trying to comprehend how one could pretend to be a wave of water.

The door was flung open, and footsteps rose up the stone steps. As King Maslen stepped into the chamber, Jenna stood and curtsied.

"So! Our Jay-bird is awake and chirping!" he exclaimed, striding towards her. Jenna backed away, and he laughed. In all ten weeks, she had never curtsied to him, nor backed away. Her stare of blankness had disappeared.

Sitting in his armchair, the king commanded, "Close the shutters on that north window, Arnold, the wind is chill today." Turning to Jenna, he said, "Tell me about it all."

King Maslen listened as Jenna told him how she had awakened that morning and had realized where she was and what had happened to her the previous day. She repeated all she had told the doctor, and answered the king's questions regarding her attempted escape 'yesterday morning.'

Whenever King Maslen laughed, or chuckled, Jenna thought it was because she had failed to escape. Never did it dawn on her that he laughed because she kept referring to that unhappy morning as if it were yesterday.

Taking up the sheaf of drawings in his hands, the king showed them to her, one by one, folding back the name, as Arnold had.

Jenna's color rose as she recalled her loved ones—she felt sure that this king collected such pictures of people to taunt prisoners like her.

Then, when she saw the drawing of the cottage the other side of Tulip Mountain, Jenna's heart raced.

"Where is it?" the king demanded.

"Where... where did you get... such a drawing?" she asked.

"I'm asking the questions here," he said.

Jenna swayed on her feet. How could she tell the king where this place was? It was a secret! Then she wondered, *Do I have any secrets left... any that I need to keep?* She decided to tell him as little as possible.

"It... it is a cottage, deep in the forest—"

"On the northern side of Tulip Mountain, is it not?" he asked, holding up another, asking, "Where is this one?"

"Who... who drew these?" Jenna asked, her mind trying to think who it could have been. Other than herself and her father... then she remembered she had taken Captain Duff to the cottage on Tulip Mountain and near this one, in the woods near Ferrah District. But she had not shown him the others, and the king was holding up yet a third.

"Who owned these huts, and what were they used for?"

"It... they belong to Kind Heart," Jenna said lamely. "They were... like resting places, if you please."

King Maslen stared at Jenna for a few seconds before showing her the drawing of Prince Edward. He did not wait for her to name the prince, but placed the one of King Cyranius at the front. Jenna's eyes lit up a little, but she was quick in seeking to conceal her delight in seeing his handsome face. But King Maslen did not miss a thing.

Doctor Arnold stood, and said, "Perhaps Jay needs a drink of water, Your Majesty, then she should sit down and you should tell her about her long day here." The doctor believed his patient should be told the truth.

"Why should we do that, Arnold?" the king asked, his eyes not leaving Jenna's. He too perceived her weak physical state and wondered if she would faint on him.

"Jay needs to know that you have spared her life, not just for one night, but multiples of that."

King Maslen smiled and agreed, "Yes, fetch a drink, little bird, and be seated. We shall indeed make you feel indebted to us, you have much to thank us for."

While Jenna moved to the shelves at her bed-head, choosing to drink orange juice instead of water, King Maslen perused the pictures again, his mind mulling over Jenna's past.

"You can tell her anything you please about the past ten weeks, Sire," the doctor said softly in his ear.

"Yes, I can, can't I?" he agreed.

Arnold fetched the chair belonging to the duty-servant, and moved it close to the desk. Jenna stepped to it, and sat down as if she was unsure of herself.

She shivered, and said, "Would you mind if I fetched a shawl? I saw one when I dressed..." she did not wait for a reply, but moved to the partition.

King Maslen, in a sudden fit, stood and turned, his hand upon the hilt of his sword, as if he expected her to emerge from the partition carrying a weapon.

Perceiving the king's alarm, Arnold hissed, "No, Sire... no, you misread her..."

Jenna returned, pulling the shawl around her shoulders. She frowned.

King Maslen spun around, and plunked himself back in his armchair.

"You're thinking it's cold for this time of year, aren't you Jay?" Doctor Arnold suggested.

"Yes," she said, then, "yes... it's very cold, but we're quite a lot further north, aren't we? Aponia is much colder than Cyran." She sat and looked at King Maslen expectantly.

"What would you say, little Jay-bird, if I told you that you had been here much longer than one day and one night?" he asked.

"I could believe it," she said, after a short pause, "I feel as if it has been a long time."

King Maslen said, "You *were* unconscious for a long time... Doctor Arnold here, believes you were in a coma, but because you were able to take in sustenance, you have survived. You've been here just over ten weeks."

Jenna closed her eyes and shook her head slightly. This news was a great shock to her.

"It's not just that Aponia is north of Cyran, but it's fall. Harvest is almost done. We're heading toward the month of September..." he paused to allow time for Jenna to absorb this truth. He sensed her vulnerability, and drew his finest instruments of blackmail.

"Your brother, Charles, visited you while you were... unconscious... he told us everything about you, Jay..." King Maslen's voice was soft, and his eyes roved her face as he spoke. He knew his words were striking deep.

"Ev- everything?" she asked, "What do you mean... everything?"

"Everything is everything," he said, then added, "We know all about your role as Kind Heart. That's why Charles did not want you, why he still does not want you, because of Kind Heart. King Cyranius did not want Kind Heart, did he? He still does not want Kind Heart."

Jenna did not speak, she felt shattered. Her head spun in an alarming manner. She found it hard to breathe.

"King Cyranius has been corresponding regularly with me," King Maslen said truthfully, then lied, "He has given you into our hands, quite gladly. He does not want you to return to Cyran... he wrote, said clearly, and you knew it. Kind Heart committed treason."

Jenna's mind almost did a flip. It was one thing to believe and accept that she had been here for ten weeks, but to believe that King Cyranius did not want her back? Then she remembered his disdain, his command that she marry Zerka. His recent command that she marry Kind Heart.

"Is it hard for you to believe that Cyranius will not receive you back into Cyran?" he asked.

"I... I... I, no it's not difficult," she said, then, "I believe it." Then she added, as if to herself, "It was despicable, I hated it too—"

"You hated what?" he demanded.

"Kind Heart. I once told King Cyranius how I hated Kind Heart!" Jenna bowed her head, not wanting King Maslen to see that tears sequined her eyes. *It's too late,* she told herself. *I'll never be able to go home.*

"You did not see this picture, did you Jay?" he asked, holding up the ink drawing of himself. "Look at it," he said, and waited as she dashed away the tears with her fingers.

"You drew this picture, yourself, Jay, with your own hand but using my ink, my quill, my parchment. See the king you drew? You belong to this king, little Jay-bird." He drew a deep breath and continued, "But what shall I do with you? I have no answer, yet. Until I decide, I want you to stay here in this tower. You'll receive no harm if you remain here, do you understand?"

"Yes, I understand," she said sadly.

King Maslen stood, and Jenna followed, keeping her head bowed. The king grinned at the doctor, who also stood.

"I'll come again, in a few days. In the meantime, Doctor, keep me informed as before—noon, each day, and if necessary, anytime."

Forty-one

King Maslen did not visit Jenna again for three days. Although he thought of her often during the day and listened to the doctor's reports with great interest, he deliberately kept away. How could he, the king, show any particular interest in such a scrawny prisoner?

But it was obvious to the court that their King was distracted. He performed his duties, wrote his correspondence and judged his subjects as if his mind were not fully on what he was saying and doing. He wrote himself notes all day long, and at the end of the day, took them with him to his bedchamber.

It did not take much conjecture to decide just whom it was the king considered at this time—enough news of the prisoner in the jay-tower filtered back from guards and servants for the court to know that their king was contemplating the jay-bird's future.

Sidra was resentful to hear from the court that her Maslen thought so much of Jenna and she decided to challenge him about it one night.

King Maslen answered her with a question. "If I offered you either a chest full of gold or an army of two hundred Kind Hearts, which would you choose?"

"The army," she replied, "I could conquer the world."

"And if it were five hundred chests of gold and one hundred Kind Hearts?" he asked.

She thought a little this time, then answered, "Five Kind Hearts would be worth more than much gold."

"Yes," he said. "That's why I have to consider what I do next with her."

"I just want you to spare some thoughts for me, Maslen," she said, in her pouting fashion.

"You have me all night, every night," he said, then added, "Keep thinking of me, Sidra, all day, every day. You please me. But you would please me more if you did not question me. My days belong to the kingdom and I'm considering the kingdom when I think of Jay. You don't have to be jealous of her. I have no desire for her now. Think not of her, think of me."

~ * ~

Jenna had asked both Doctor Arnold and the servant-woman that she be permitted to have a Bible to read, or at least, a volume of the Bible. Doctor Arnold took her request to the king and he said that any number of books could be taken to her from the extensive castle library.

The librarian, a quaint little man of over fifty years old, quickly fetched a volume for the doctor, saying that he thought it was the only one they had. When she had read it, he would look for another.

Jenna was delighted, it was the book of Ecclesiastes, a book she had never read.

She spent all the day, between meals, reading the volume, seated on a pillow on the floor by the window where she could gain the best amount of light upon the handwritten words. She began to make her own notes from the words she read.

This is where King Maslen found her when he came to offer his proposition.

She stood quickly when she realized that the king had entered, and she curtsied.

"You're looking much better," he said, sitting in his chair.

"I'm feeling better, Your Majesty," she agreed.

"Sit down, Jay," he commanded, then said, "I've given you much consideration. With the help of my Trusty Ten, I've set up a gymnasium. I want you to train yourself back into top form and, with the same pay as I give my captains, I'll employ you to teach chosen men the skills your father taught you."

Jenna stared at the king as if she could not believe his words. She stood, and backed away.

The king held up his hands and looked at each palm as if wondering what he had done. "What? What is it?"

"You... you mean? To... to do combat?" She shook her head, and said, "No, Sire, Your Majesty, I could never do that—"

"What? Why not?" He frowned deeply and swallowed. Anger rose in him and he forced it down deep. His face changed color. "Why not? Answer me!"

"I... I... ask anything else of me but not that! Please, Your Majesty! I don't want to... not ever... ever... behave... like that again... it's time for me to lay it aside..."

"That... that book you have been reading?"

"Yes, Sire, God and common sense both tell me that as a woman, I cannot continue to be what I was never designed to be—"

"Not even for the purpose... of training others?"

King Maslen stood and Jenna backed a few steps further away.

"You will be what I design you to be! God has nothing to do with it at all! I made you a good offer! It was not for refusal! Who do you think you are? Your life is not worth a spit!" Clenching his fists, he fought to regain his self-control. "I must consider, but be prepared, Jay-bird, you shall yet do as I ask!" He saw that she opened her mouth as if to speak, and he commanded, "You'll not say it! You'll make no more refusals!"

Jenna bit back the words she would have said, but thought them, *I'd rather die, I'd rather die.*

King Maslen stomped out, fuming. Cursing people along the way, he went out for a long ride and to ponder his next move.

"He could have asked anything of me but not that!" Jenna lamented, trying not to think of what the king would demand next. What was it that she needed to be prepared for?

~ * ~

Early the next morning, King Maslen visited Jenna again. He placed an oblong box on the table in front of Doctor Arnold and sat in his chair.

Recognizing the box, Doctor Arnold's mouth dropped open. Then, when the king spoke, Arnold stared at him as if he did not know him.

"Sit, Jay-bird. I wish to give you a choice, today. Do you know what happens when a man, or a woman, any person, for that matter, loses both thumbs, and both his largest toes?"

Jenna swallowed, but did not answer.

"The choice is yours, Jay-bird. In that box, there are the instruments Doctor Arnold needs to do such an operation on you. After that, you shall be designated to sit under my table and eat the crumbs I throw to you. You will never walk properly again, let alone ride a horse... that is, if you survive!"

Jenna, feeling horror rise in her throat, did not answer. She bowed her head.

"What? Would you rather be a crippled slave than be strong and powerful to be admired and modeled?" He stood and stared at her bowed head.

As the king stepped to the table, Doctor Arnold whispered, "If you give me one week, Sire, I shall persuade her..." He did not want to tell the king, but one, or two days would be enough, he believed.

"Three days, Arnold, three days. She's yours for three days, then we'll finish it. I've wasted more than enough time here." He tapped his forefinger on the box, and said, "You'll uphold my words, and my method, Arnold!" The king stomped from the tower-chamber. He hated to be thwarted, but now wished he had conferred with Arnold before he had decided. He had not believed within himself, that his Jay-bird would rather be crippled, or worse, than to become active again.

"Bah!" he growled as he passed guards on duty standing to attention, "Bah!"

~ * ~

Doctor Arnold had previously ordered fresh fruit and vegetables to be brought for Jenna, also jugs of fresh fruit juice and cider had been brought each day.

After King Maslen left, the doctor told the servant-woman to remove every particle of food, every drop of liquid. He also sent for Captain Myres and told him of his plan to have Jenna visit the gymnasium later. The captain said that he would come with an escort, he did not want to miss out on this!

By mid-afternoon, Jenna was both hungry and thirsty.

"I want you to come downstairs for your drink of orange juice," Doctor Arnold told her. He put the box under his arm.

Not suspecting what was in store, Jenna obediently followed him. Guards fell into step behind them, but the doctor knew that Jenna had no strength to attempt to escape. It was enough to descend the steps, walk along the corridor, descend more steps and move outside, down a terrace and into the large gymnasium. Spacious arched sides gave the chamber fresh air, and a well-trussed roof kept off the rain. Smells of straw and horses suggested the stables were not far away.

Jenna felt exhausted from the long walk. However, she looked around the chamber with interest.

Three of the Trusty Ten were there, working one of their routines on the equipment. Ropes hung from the beams beneath the roof and the men slithered up and down, swinging from one rope to the next. Ropes with rings attached to the ends were used like trapezes.

Jenna saw Myres arrive.

"You'll stay here, guarded by Captain Myres and his men, until you agree to do one hour's workout in this chamber. Then you may drink orange juice, do the workout and return to the tower. The alternative, Jay, is in this box and neither you nor I want that, do we?" He stared at her, and Jenna bowed her head.

Tears sprang to her eyes. She knew she did not want to teach others, but to do an hour's workout and build up her strength; she was no longer sure if this would be so wrong. To stay alive, this is what she wanted—that was not a difficult choice.

I could gain my strength and escape... she told herself, thinking of the cottage in the forest, and the beautiful waterfall, the thermal pool. What would she give now, to drink the crystal water from the waterfall? But could she give away the training her father had given her? Would she not rather lose her life than divulge their secrets?

"I'll stay with you, if you wish," Doctor Arnold said, having seen the despair on her face. He had no other pressing work.

"Is... is there a... a holy man... with whom I may counsel?" Jenna asked.

"You mean a Christian?" he asked, then answered, "Not in Aponia, none I know of."

"I have no one," she said, her eyes sequined with tears.

"Tell me about it, talk to me," Doctor Arnold offered.

"You wouldn't understand," she said.

"Try me," he persisted.

Jenna told the doctor about her childhood; the thrill she gained from working out in her father's gymnasium, the self-worth that had flooded her when her father commended her. "I used to feel so good about myself. My brother Charles was short and flat-footed. He was a failure in my father's eyes. But I? I made my father feel proud.

"As I grew older and Charles did not return, but was received as a nobleman in Rosenburg, I felt guilt and remorse from having been the reason my brother left. It was not until I was older that I realized he had gone for the inheritance."

She explained about the castle, in Rosenburg, how Jenna's mother's brother had nominated Charles as his heir.

"Then my father made me sign an oath with my own blood and it was then that I wished I had never learned the special skills. But it was a vow that could not be broken, I knew I had to keep it. Perhaps because I signed the oath, the thrill of rescue missions lost their glow. It became to me, not a challenge at all, but something routine, mundane. The only joy was to know that we saved lives, to save someone was the reason for

Kind Heart in the first place. If we achieved this, we were satisfied. Most of all, I liked to rescue a child..." she thought of the young princess, Anastasia, and grew quiet.

"Tell me more," the doctor urged.

"After Father died... everything I did was like walking uphill without support. Then, Judith, my friend Judith, died and I knew there was more to living and dying than Kind Heart. I felt it was time for me to be what God designed me to be, then I learned that there was a way out. On June first, at sunset, when I turned twenty, the day I left Cyran. It was over at last, I believed.

"Why should I go back? Why?"

"It's not back, Jay, but forward. Where else can you go? You belong in Aponia now, to King Maslen. He's your master, and you must obey him. It was very generous for him to offer to pay you a captain's salary."

"Will... will King Maslen use his men to make war on Cyran?" Jenna asked.

"Is that what you are worried about, Jay? I think you have less to worry about than that. Just think about today, think about taking in one small goblet of juice at a time."

"You're all sick!" Jenna cried, "You're as sick as he is. You want me to train others for warfare. I can well imagine that with a large number of men like Kind Heart, they would do away with me, King Maslen will keep his pay, and somehow seek to conquer the world."

Doctor Arnold frowned at her.

Sitting down, Jenna pondered her dilemma. Her eyes kept straying to the box. It was bizarre. They threatened to cut off her thumbs and her big toes. She did not want to admit it, not even to herself, but she knew that she would give in before she allowed that to happen. She would train all day long if it meant keeping herself intact!

I'm just a bluff, she told herself miserably. Closing her eyes, she wished she could sleep, but her thirst had now grown to overwhelming dimensions. *If I'm going to give in, I should not do it too soon, or it will seem I'm easily persuaded.*

"Jay, open your eyes," Doctor Arnold said. He stood close to her, holding the goblet within her reach.

Jenna did not take the goblet but folded her arms.

"You believe in the one they call God, Jay, I know you do. Is it not, in your God's eyes, as wrong to deprive yourself of fluid as it would be not to give it to someone else? To harm your own body is as great a sin as harming someone else's."

"I wish you would not reason like that," Jenna said, feeling crushed. "If you don't believe in God, then don't use him to reason against me."

"If you believe in some kind of life eternal, Jay, then it's an easy option for you to choose to die," he taunted.

"No it's not!" she declared, "You should think about it sometime."

"I do, often," Arnold said, "And I choose life. Do you not choose life?" He paused. "Of course you choose life. Why do you think you tried to escape? Did not the word 'alive' ring in your mind, and spur you on? I believe that you survived the injury to your head, Jay, because you wanted to live. Choosing to live is to choose what is right."

"Of course living is right!" she said fiercely, her voice a little hoarse because her mouth and throat were so dry, "It is the quality of living in this place that's so suspect!"

Doctor Arnold smiled grimly and stepped back from her, placing the goblet on the stone floor. "Why don't you drink it, and live? Live just one goblet, one morning, one afternoon, one day at a time."

Jenna watched as three more of the Trusty Ten joined the others. They were enjoying their workout, and it made Jenna feel all the more contrary.

She tried to imagine how she could evade teaching combat methods.

"My training was not for combat," Jenna said, "It was... calculated defense, not aggressive attack..."

"Just one day at a time, Jay. You know you won't be teaching anyone until you are at peak condition... I expect that to be well into the winter."

Jenna wondered if he realized that at peak condition, she might attempt to escape again. Her eyes lifted to the beams above her. Once she was up there, she could climb anywhere she wished. It would not be hard to escape, if she had her strength back. But it would mean she would be practicing deceit.

"One day at a time," he said, adding, "I'll have to go soon, and you won't see me again until sunset, then I must go to dine with the king. You'll be ill with thirst soon."

"If... if I decide to workout," Jenna said, "I don't want an audience... I'm out of condition, you know that, Arnold. I... I would just look like a... clown."

"There have to be at least two guards here, Jay, and I will have to stay." He did not believe she would be able to do an hour's workout.

"I want a pair of cloth trousers... like those that jester is wearing and a short tunic, like his," she said, then added, determinedly, "I'll not wear those leather things of Kind Hearts!"

"I'll have the jester find some more trousers like his."

"I need more than one goblet of juice."

"If you do the workout, I'll have another brought."

"All right."

"You agree?"

In answer, she reached for the tumbler. Knowing she should not drink it too fast, she sipped it, savoring each swallow, wishing it were a goblet full of her father's herb drink.

Forty-two

King Maslen could scarcely believe the news, brought to him by his Captain, Myres. It was almost sunset.

"The jay-bird has completed an hour's workout," Myres said, then at the king's obvious incredulity, he said, "Mind, she had to do it in three parts, with a rest in between, and she was almost dead after the last bout. And it wasn't like anything I've seen before in a gym." He laughed. "Like you'd expect from a girl! She mostly did stretching exercises. When she did a few press-ups she nearly passed out."

"Press-ups? She did press-ups?"

"Sort of. And she attempted to climb the ropes, but her arms didn't hold her properly. She slid and fell off at the bottom. She was crying and complaining about cramp in her arms." Myres grinned, and said, "Doctor Arnold didn't let her know, but he was worried when she went on the beam—he thought she was going to fall off, she was so shaky."

"Which beam?"

"Oh, it wasn't one of the high ones, just one of the lower beams. She walked across it, but lost her balance... then she tried to roll instead of just fall off. She landed a bit awkward, winded herself, got a bruise or two, I'd say. No, it'll take her a while before she can workout up top."

"She can take as long as she likes," King Maslen said, "I wouldn't expect her to be in form before spring, even if she works out every day. Where are they now?"

"I escorted them back to the tower. The doctor sent for something to eat. She's had nothing all day."

King Maslen grinned. He would wait a few days and visit the jaybird while she was exercising in his gymnasium.

Jenna gained strength each day. Walking the distance to the gymnasium was tiring enough, but working out made her feel exhausted. Some days after the hour's exercise, Jenna did not have the energy to walk back to the tower; she had to rest first. Doctor Arnold complained loudly, saying he did not have time to sit watching her catch her breath.

The doctor set up a desk at the gymnasium and took a pile of books there to read while she exercised.

On the fifth day, King Maslen came to watch her. She did not know he was there until she did a jump-turn on the low beam. When she saw him, she lost her balance, fell off and stumbled to her knees.

Determined not to stop, because to stop meant she would have to get started again, Jenna rose quickly and strode across to the poles, set vertically into the ground, the first just two feet tall. Up she climbed, higher and higher. With slow and deliberate movements, she moved from pole to pole, practicing stretching exercises ten feet above the clay floor. Keeping her eyes upon the next round flat surface where she would place her bare foot, she refused her nagging impulse to look down past the top of the poles. If she did so, she knew she would lose concentration and balance. Never before had heights bothered her. Perspiration rose on her brow, and she felt every nerve in her body screaming in protest.

While King Maslen watched in amusement, the doctor stared at her with bated breath. He knew she was working beyond her capabilities.

"She's pushing herself," he said the obvious.

"Good," the king said. "Tell her that from tomorrow, she'll workout for two hours in the morning, and an hour in the afternoon. Next week, we shall double that."

"Sire, it would be better for her to take a day of rest tomorrow. Her muscles need time to repair—"

"Bah!" the king said, then, "You've pleased me, Arnold, you succeeded where I failed. She can have tomorrow off but after that, it'll be twice a day. I expect to see some action from her in a few weeks."

"You might have to confine her elsewhere," Arnold said.

"I've thought of that," the king agreed, "but I'm hoping she'll accept that she has a position here, with a salary."

"I don't think she'll accept anything from us, Sire."

"Bah!" the king said, turning and walking away.

~ * ~

Jenna was glad to be able to rest the following day. Although it had only been an hour a day in the gymnasium, she felt pains where she had never before had pain. She wished she could rest for a week.

Secretly, Jenna began to enjoy the workouts. She would have preferred exercising in the evening, but Arnold insisted that she do two hours midmorning and another hour late afternoon.

"Next week, you shall do three hours in the mornings and two hours in the afternoon," Arnold told her, adding, "King's orders!"

So far, Jenna had not attempted anything higher than the poles, but she had built up her confidence, and had worked on the lower beams until she knew she could work on the higher ones and combine her workout with the ropes. Little by little, she added more challenges to her expanding drill.

Almost three weeks after having begun exercising, Jenna returned to the tower feeling, for the first time, that she was gaining back some of her familiar equilibrium.

As before, she wished to bathe, but accepted that her lot, after a workout, was a large bowl of warm water. After washing and changing, she ate a hearty meal and settled down to read by the window in the diminishing daylight.

~ * ~

King Maslen was waiting for Jenna in the gymnasium one morning. A group of six men, including the king's captain, Myres, and the jester, stood around him. "I want you to teach these men how to use their peripheral vision," the king told Jenna. When she frowned, he said, "Don't look as if you don't know what I'm talking about. In the throne room, I lifted my hand to slap you, and you avoided me and my sword. You anticipated where it would fall. Show them how to avoid getting struck!"

"I... we need some equipment, if I'm to show what my father taught me."

The king grinned. He had imagined that she would refuse, but here she was, agreeing. "Tell Sarates here what you want, and he'll have his slaves build it for you."

"Firstly, Your Majesty, they must know how to fall without harming themselves."

"Bah! That's second nature to these men. Why do you think I chose them? Just get on with setting up the equipment."

Jenna gave instructions to Sarates, whom she knew to be the steward of the gymnasium. With the slaves under him, he kept all the equipment in safe working order.

In two days' time, the new equipment was ready to try. King Maslen came to watch.

A set of smooth horizontal poles ten feet off the ground, six parallel one way and six parallel the other, had been erected. Not far enough apart to avoid hitting one's head, if one fell between them, but far enough that it was not possible to merely step from pole to pole—smaller men would have to leap, a tall man could stride. Above hung sacks of grain, weighing about ten pounds each.

"We'll begin with half-sacks of grain, but you should be able to do this with full sacks," Jenna said when Myres stared in disbelief at the swinging sacks. Sarates and the slaves, with one guard, were giving a demonstration, swinging the bags across the poles.

341

"The training is for awareness of flying weapons, and avoidance of such," Jenna said, adding, "We have only four swinging sacks, but we need to be able to deal with twelve at once. The sacks swing at different heights—one will hit your head, one your chest, one your middle and the other is aimed at your legs. You have to move from pole to pole avoiding the sacks swinging back and forth. The operators at the sides can hold a sack and send it at the same time as another so that two arrive together, or they can have them all swinging at once. If they tangle, they swing around and it's more difficult to avoid them."

"It's impossible!" Doctor Arnold exclaimed, "No one could do that, not if they are unable to time their release. You may duck one, but the other will hit you before you can turn around!"

"That's the way it is with weapons," Jenna said.

"It's a long way to fall, too far."

"I don't intend to fall," Jenna said, adding, "Shall I show you how it's done?" She longed to add that she had mastered this same drill when she was only ten years old, but knew that she would be seen as boasting. No, she would save it and tell them later if necessary.

"I'll go first," Myres said, determined. He longed to gain more approval from the king by learning the 'Kind Heart skills'.

The king, the doctor, the would-be contestants, and a few other spectators climbed specially erected scaffolding to watch the exercise.

Myres stared at the poles, and scratched his head. "How do I get up there?" he asked.

"I'll show you," Jenna said. Taking up a staff, she ran and vaulted, letting go the staff and grasping the pole. With a deft movement, she swung herself to stand on the pole. She wavered a little, then dropped to swing by both hands, releasing herself to land at Myres' feet.

"There's a ladder over there if you'd rather," she said, causing him to glower at her and yet shout for one of his band to bring the ladder.

"I can see we need some pole-vaulting exercises," King Maslen said. "She must have been practicing with that staff to do that so well."

"Yes, she has... she put in an hour with the staff yesterday, and spent three hours on the high beams," Arnold said. "I couldn't watch her, it made me feel ill. I think we should have a safety net, Sire. If someone fell, and hit the upright poles—"

"Bah! If they take the time to build up their strength and confidence as she has done, then there's no need for nets. Do you think there are going to be nets when the real thing is being enacted... when enemies are climbing our walls?"

Myres took their attention up on the poles but from their viewpoint, they looked down on him. One sack was released and he avoided it, then a second and he teetered as he took a large stride onto another pole, but when the third came at him just as the first returned, he was knocked off the pole falling so awkwardly on the clay beneath that all the wind was knocked out of him.

Jenna knew better than to give any help or comfort. Even when she was a child and her father had banged her on the back and tried to soothe her hidden tears when she had fallen, she had hated it. How much more would a warrior.

"Show us how it's done, Jester," the king called.

The jester copied Jenna and vaulted to the poles. It was obvious he was very confident.

Over-confident, Jenna thought, warning herself. *Never be over-confident, it always brings defeat but be prepared for the unexpected.*

The jester faced the slave with the lowest bag, and as this was released, the slave at the opposite side released his. The first bag was avoided, but the second made a strike. Everyone gasped as the jester was hit in the head. He fell across the poles, again whacking his head with a thud, sliding through them and falling to the ground.

He knows how to fall, Jenna told herself, *but not Myres...* she wondered if she should repeat her warning for them to have training on how to fall. Before any one attempted this high pole evasion training, one needed to know how to land if one was hit!

"Show us what you can do, Jay," the king commanded.

Vaulting up to the poles, Jenna waited as the lower bag swung passed, then she stood, one foot on one pole and the other on the one crossing it. She swiveled out of the way of the lower bag as it returned, watching the slave catch it, and knowing he would send it back to her within seconds. Twisting and turning, Jenna kept the four swinging bags in her vision. She had practiced on the beams yesterday and was now able to combine agility with avoidance. Although she had to focus her concentration and movements, Jenna found this an easy exercise.

Try as they may, the controllers of the bags could not make a strike. To everyone's amazement, Jenna did not move very far across the beams, but remained in one place. By twisting and turning her body, she avoided the 'missiles'. Though many flew accurately toward her, she turned in time to have them swing past, some within an inch of her slim frame.

One slave grew frustrated with her ability to dodge his bag, and he grasped hold of it, waiting for the right moment. He released it as the other three swung toward the victim. Jenna ducked the one that would hit her head, curved her waist to avoid the middle one, doubled over to avoid the one aimed at her chest, then side-stepped the one that would have hit her legs. When she perceived that they would swing back and twist, becoming a combined flying tangle of dead weights, she dropped through the poles, swinging around one, back up around another, until she was at the last pole, from which she dropped to land down on the clay floor.

Jenna received applause from the king and the spectators on the scaffolding. King Maslen commanded his men, "Practice this exercise until you can do it as well as Jay-bird. When you're working up to eight bags of grain at twenty pounds per bag, I'll come to view you.

"By the middle of winter," he commanded, "you will all be able to do it with twelve bags."

While Jenna wondered at his confidence, Captain Myres and the chosen students groaned inwardly. They could not believe they had so gladly agreed to be trainees for this impossible assignment.

Forty-three

King Maslen, followed by Doctor Arnold, preceded Jenna back to the tower room one day. The usual escort of guards followed.

Once in the tower, the king dismissed the servant-woman who waited for Jenna's return. At the king's command, Myres stepped up into the chamber.

The king addressed his prisoner, "I want two things, Jay, and the first is that you agree to receive payment for the instruction you are giving my men. The second is to give me a pledge that you will not attempt to escape from this castle. The alternative being that you will continue to go to the gymnasium, but will be confined at other times, to a prison cell."

When Jenna did not speak, he expanded on his offer, "In becoming a paid employee and giving your pledge, you'll be permitted to reside in this tower. There'll be no guards, other than those normally posted in and about the castle. The women, however, will continue to change duties throughout the day and before nightfall to tend your needs—food, water, clothes and whatever. You'll be confined here on trust, Jay, and I'll consider it a most serious breach if you do not keep to your schedule between this tower and the gymnasium. You must be in either place, or moving between. However, if you prove true to your pledge, I'll consider granting you more freedom within the castle."

Jenna averted her eyes from the king; she had no alternative other than to agree, she knew this.

Doctor Arnold spoke up, "Your being in Aponia, Jay, is of your own doing, you must accept it now. To continue to fight against it will be to degrade your quality of life."

"I am not so ignorant, Doctor, that I do not see this myself," Jenna snapped. Tilting her chin and looking King Maslen square in the eye, she said, "I give you my pledge, King Maslen, for one year, that I shall not attempt to escape from this castle if you allow me to live in this tower and pay me for working in your gymnasium."

"And after one year?" he asked.

"I shall not leave here without reviewing the matter with you, Your Majesty."

The king's mouth skewed into a sneer. Somehow his prisoner had managed to twist his offer so that she was in control, not he. She still did not accept that she was his captive, not a free person.

"Repeat your pledge, Jay, and leave out the one year—it's not for you to place a time on it. Perchance I shall want you to leave here, in one month, or six months, or six years..."

"Therefore, Your Majesty, I give you my pledge, until you release me, that I shall not attempt to escape from this castle if you allow me to live in this tower and pay me for working in your gymnasium."

King Maslen turned to the doctor and his captain, saying, "You are witnesses of this pledge and shall be also when Jay is released from it."

The king smiled suddenly, and Jenna was struck by the normality of his smile. No longer did he seem cynical and sarcastic. Like the king he was, he had mandated his own way and was now happy.

"I don't want you as an enemy, Jay, I'd prefer you to be on my side." So saying, the king swiveled on his heel and strode from the tower.

Feeling that she had betrayed herself and God and feeling so very alone, Jenna wept.

~ * ~

No longer did the king go to the Jay-tower. He visited the gymnasium if he wished to see how his paid prisoner was progressing. Jenna spent most of the day in the gym now, but was permitted one day off each week. On the day off, she read and browsed through books sent to her from the library. The volume of Ecclesiastes remained with her, and Jenna worked at memorizing it, a small portion, three or four sentences each day.

It was a memorable day when the librarian accompanied a trunk full of books to the Jay-tower. The books were various volumes of the Holy Scriptures. Jenna counted twenty-eight volumes in all.

"They were sent from the king's southern-most castle. I wrote letters to six places hoping they would have more of the volumes."

"Thank you," Jenna said, meaning it with all her heart.

At the librarian's command, she chose two volumes to keep for reading first; words of the Apostle Paul to the Romans and the Gospel of John. Jenna was told that when she had finished with these, she could order two more. Jenna pleaded that she be allowed to retain the Book of Ecclesiastes, because she was memorizing it. The rest of the books were returned to the library.

The words of the books gave her strength, while at the same time encouraging her and admonishing her.

That day, she memorized a verse from the book of Romans, feeling it had been written for her, *For the good that I would, I do not; but the evil which I would not, that I do.*

~ * ~

The mornings grew cooler, and Jenna welcomed her workout times. The six trainees each were now able to balance on the poles, avoiding the four swinging bags.

King Maslen commanded that the weight of the bags be increased, and two bags added.

"They're not ready, Sire," Jenna protested, "they need time to work on their landing skills, to fall without injury; only Jester here can land on his feet, or with a somersault. Someone will end up with broken bones, especially if the weight is increased. The impact of a twenty pound bag will cause the fall to be more awkward."

Jenna felt frustrated. The men had been told not to listen to her instruction, but to the king's. All of them still had far too much pride and self-confidence, Jenna realized.

"It's an attitude of mind, Your Majesty," Jenna said. "My father always said that one must be as nothing to be able to become something."

"Bah!" the king said, ignoring her words of wisdom, "they have had so many falls, that surely they have the strength to continue. They'll continue to learn how to fall while they are learning evasion. The heavier weight won't make much difference." He saw the disagreement on her face and said, "If you can do it, Jay-bird, they can."

"But Sire," Jenna began.

"*Be silent!*" the king shouted and Jenna obeyed.

"Show us how it's done, Jay-bird," the king commanded, when the bags were all in place.

Jenna vaulted to the poles and moved to the middle of the crisscross pattern. At the king's signal, four men released their bags. Not fully prepared, Jenna dropped through the poles, grasping on to the one at her feet, yet keeping her upper feet linked to it. With a graceful motion, she swung herself back upward to stand again on the pole. As the bags returned towards her, she twisted herself in a circle, moving from pole to pole, avoiding the four heavy sacks of grain. King Maslen signaled and the two new men released their bags. Jenna expertly evaded them.

"Stop, stop, stop!" the king shouted.

One by one, the slaves grasped hold of their respective bags.

"How is it, Jay-bird, that we have a half-dozen men here to swing, catch, and return these bags?"

Jenna stared up at the king, seated on the scaffolding. Not understanding his question, she was silent.

"If your father taught you, and it was such a secret thing, who then flung the bags when you learned this exercise?"

"My father had a double set of pulleys arranged from the beams above, and it worked its way around and around as he turned the handles. One set of bags went around one way, and other went the other way. It could be sped up at will."

"I want it built! Just as you say."

"It... Sire... it's much more difficult to work with."

"Have it done, start now! These are men here, not children."

The new contraption, a great priority, was begun that moment and by the end of the week, it was fixed to hang from the beams. At the king's command, eight bags of ten pounds each hung from chains attached to the pulleys.

"Now we won't have tangles," he said, "this is what we should have been using all the time."

The next morning, Jenna was commanded to demonstrate how to work with the new equipment.

With Sarates already turning the handles to cause the bags to rotate, all of them at differing heights, four moving one way and four in the opposite direction, Jenna vaulted to the poles. She remained in a crouched position to avoid the first bag, then stood, turning and dodging as she worked her way to the middle of the set of poles. Her eyes did not look down, she knew the poles would not move—it was the bags that required her full concentration.

Across the poles, to one end, she moved, then back to the middle, all the time avoiding the heavy sacks.

"It looks too easy," the king shouted.

"Swing the sacks as they pass, Sarates," Jenna called.

No longer did it appear to be easy. As the sacks swung passed Sarates, he gave them a push, causing them to swing back and forth, making their path more unpredictable. Jenna, however, continued as always, evading their touch, though by a hairsbreadth. Those watching, expected her to be unbalanced at any moment.

Two sacks, swinging crazily, crashed into each other before swaying haphazardly. Jenna crouched to avoid them both hitting her, then another swung around the bag on the longest rope. If she did not move quickly, it would knock her off her perch. Diving under the poles to swing from her hands, Jenna hauled herself up on another pole, staying low to avoid a sack. Standing, she moved across the poles, obviously in control.

King Maslen became bored and called for someone else to take Jenna's place.

Myres climbed the ladder as Jenna jumped to the ground, landing in a somersault.

"Come and sit here, Jay-bird," the king commanded. It was the first time he had invited her to watch from the scaffolding. She climbed the heavy ladder and sat on a wooden plank, as far away from the king as was possible.

Myres lasted one minute under the new contraption. One sack hit him in the head, and, copying Jenna's tactic, he grasped hold of the pole as he fell and began to haul himself back upwards. Standing, he dodged a sack and strode to another pole to avoid another. Sarates pushed the sacks as they rotated passed him and Myres was caught off guard. One struck his chest, and another impacted his legs. Over he went. Jenna wanted to close her eyes, but forced herself to watch.

One leg stayed up on the pole momentarily, the other falling beneath him. Myres went down, crumpling on the hard clay beneath with a loud roar of agony.

He lay, unmoving, but moaning and groaning, then swearing, yelling that he could not move his leg to get up from the floor.

"Take him away and have the army doctor look at him," the king said, then commanded, "Jester, get up there! Show us how it's done."

While Myres bellowed death threats at those who carried him away, the jester vaulted to the poles. He lasted three minutes but when knocked off, he landed quite tidily.

Another trainee was ordered to climb to the place of the runaround. Sarates, perspiring profusely, ordered a strong slave to take a turn with the handles.

The trainee, a young soldier, lasted less than a minute. A sack hit him in the back and he fell, cracking his forehead on a pole, falling unconscious to the ground.

"What is it here?" the king asked when the man did not move. "Are you all to be whipped by a mere slip of a girl?" He commanded that another recruit take the stage. After a brief discussion by the four trainees remaining, a young man climbed to the poles.

This man did not last ten seconds. He avoided only one bag, the highest one, but then one knocked him on one side, then another on the other side and he pitched off the pole, lifting his arm to save his head. A loud snap caused everyone to gasp. The injured man howled in pain, and again the king commanded that he be removed to the army clinic. It was obvious, by the way his arm hung limp as he was helped to his feet, he had broken his arm.

"Sire, please," Doctor Arnold began.

"*Be silent*! Don't you think I know when enough is enough!" the king bellowed. "Three left! Three out of six! And one of them is my captain!" He stood and turned, his eyes fixed upon Jay. "Get yourself to your tower, Jay-bird and stay there! I'll consider where we go next!"

Jay rose, and instead of climbing down the ladder, she leapt from the plank, landing neatly on the clay of the gymnasium. Moving quickly, she snatched up the woolen blanket she used as a shawl and threw it around her shoulders. Before the king could blink, she had gone.

"Bah!" the king said as he moved to the ladder to descend, "if I could not so vividly recall her pleadings, I'd say that Jay-bird planned this to get my best warriors off my stage!" He spat and added, "I hope my captain's bones were too strong to be broken!"

At the base of the steps, the king stared up at the crisscross poles and said, "Why did it need to be ten feet off the ground? Why poles? I say we remove all the poles and lower the gizmo that turns the bags. Let's do it on the ground next time!"

"It shall be done, Sire," Sarates said, eager to please his angry king.

~ * ~

That afternoon, the sky grew dark early and storm clouds gathered. Jenna was alone in the tower, save for Moyra, the servant-woman, who sat by the light of a large candle, knitting furiously. Winter would soon come and she wanted to complete the tunic for her grandchild. Looking up, she saw that Jenna stood by the window, staring out at the black thunderclouds. Cold air gushed in the window, blowing on Jenna's face and further chilling the air in the tower.

"You'll catch cold if you stay there!" the woman called. "Close the shutters, light the large candles and read some."

"I like the fresh air and I'm not in the mood to read," Jenna said. Her mind was upon the three men who had been injured. She wished she had news.

"Then do some drawing. Doctor Arnold brought you some paints, as well as that charcoal, and you have the ink and quill as well."

"You know I don't believe I did those drawings, so why do you persist saying that I did?"

"Because I saw you, Jay. I watched you with my own two eyes. Anyways, why would we lie to you about such a matter? What's in it for me?"

Jenna shrugged her shoulders, then jumped as lightening forked down from the sky. For a split-second, every little stone house, its roof, the walls, the very lanes in the city, were illuminated. Jenna's heart pounded loudly in her breast. She hated thunder and lightening! It had always terrified her, ever since she could remember.

Crash! Rumble, rumble! The thunder seemed to make the very stones in the tower walls quake. Lightening lit the sky again, and just as quickly, the thunder sounded; it was close. Jenna leapt back from the window feeling unnerved and out of control. Snatching the shutter-handles, she closed them and fixed the catches to secure them. With trembling hands, she pulled the thick drapes across the portal, as if to block out the world.

Lighting the large candles at the desk, Jenna sat, trying not to imagine when or where the next lightening bolt would strike.

Closing her eyes, she pictured the scene she had viewed out of the tower window. Every little crevasse, and there were thousands of them, had been visible in the brilliant light of the fork lightening.

Taking up a spear of charcoal, and placing a large piece of parchment before her, Jenna began to draw. By closing and opening her eyes and picturing the outside world, she painstakingly drew the city. The thunderstorm raged outside, but Jenna ignored it, concentrating on the drawing.

Moyra came to stand behind her, watching now as Jenna shaded the picture, giving it dimensions and perspective. Across the top edge Jenna drew the top stones of the window, at the bottom the window ledge in its three-dimensions as she had seen on her first drawing. Taking the brush, she wet the block of red water-paint and worked it to a dark paste. With careful strokes, she framed the sides with the dark red of the curtains.

"There you are, I said you could do it," Moyra said, watching as Jenna dipped the quill in the ink. "What are you writing?"

"Jay's tower-home," Jenna said, adding, "or should it be house?—or, nest?—It's hardly a home."

"It's all you've got," Moyra said then watched as she wrote the word 'home'. "It's more than many in this city have got. Why, I've seen several groups of small children sleeping out on the streets... a couple in our little street."

"In this weather?" Jenna asked as she pegged the picture on the other side of the clothes partition to dry.

"In all weathers."

"Where are their parents?"

"Haven't got none. Or they've ran away from them. So, anyway, you should be grateful, a paid living and in the king's castle. From all they say, he thinks highly of you, too."

A gust of wind rattled the shutters and the candle flame beside Moyra snuffed out from the breeze.

The servant drew her heavy shawl closer around her shoulders, saying, "It's near dark. I hope Joan comes earlier than sunset seein' it's such a bad night. She knows I want to go to my daughter's house in the city tonight."

"Do... would you go down, now, Moyra, and find out how the men... the ones I told you about, the three hurt in the gymnasium... find out for me how they fared?"

"You've been fretting about them since you got here, haven't you? Right. I'll go and ask about them."

Moyra was gone less than fifteen minutes. When she did return, she told Jenna, "Captain Myres has broke his leg; a bad break, they say—it'll take some three months before he'll be right again. And Carl broke his skull, at the front; he's still out of it. Wilhelm only has one broken arm. Doctor Arnold is with them, and has to do a report for the king." She collected her knitting and pushed it in the bag she always carried. "I wish Joan would hurry! Could be an hour before she gets here if she don't come early. She's a widow, too, with no children at all... I don't know why she can't come early tonight."

"Why don't you go now, Moyra? I've promised the king that I'll stay here, so I will. Just go. I'm not needing you. Joan can fetch my meal."

Moyra did not speak, but Jenna saw that her eyes lightened at the thought. Without another word the servant turned and left the tower.

Jenna sat at the desk again, wondering what she would draw. She thought of the drawing she had done of Gifford Castle, and wondered if she could draw the great hall. Her mind then strayed to King Maslen's throne room and how awesome it was, and how strange, to have the oak tree in the middle. She decided to draw King Maslen's throne room. Having made the outline with charcoals, she decided to paint the huge domed glass roof, using colors for the glass. Then, using greens and browns, she colored the tree.

Having pegged the finished picture with the other, to dry, Jenna wondered how long Joan would be in coming.

The door swung open at that moment, and Joan entered, followed by another woman, wearing a thick cloak. To Jenna's surprise, Sidra's face was revealed when the hood was pushed back.

"Where's Moyra?" Joan asked.

"She wanted to get into the city before dark. There was no reason for her to stay so I dismissed her."

"That's even better!" Sidra said, pleased, then sat in the king's chair. "Oh... what a walk! All those steps up here! I'd never endure it." She closed her eyes for a minute, then, sitting forward, she stared up at

Jenna. "You have to leave here, Jennava. I've come to help you escape..." she paused, obviously awaiting Jenna's reaction.

Jenna opened her mouth, then closed it—she knew there was much more to this offer.

"Show her, Joan."

Joan opened her large hessian bag. Pulling out a wig, a dress, a cloak and shoes, she placed them on the desk.

"You're to dress as me, Jennava, and when you walk out of here, no one will stop you. The dress and cloak have one hundred gold pieces sewn into the hems and seams. I owe you." She laughed, adding, "Remember?"

"And if I refuse?" Jenna asked.

"There's to be no refusal," Sidra said, "or I swear I'll have you killed. If others fail, I'll do it myself!"

"Why?" Jenna asked, feeling unnerved at her fervor.

"Joan... check that no one is outside the door," Sidra commanded, and waited for the servant to open the door, look out, then close it.

"I... I... I'm pregnant. I'm having Maslen's child."

Jenna's eyebrows raised and she smiled, saying, "That's wonderful! He'll marry you now, won't he? Isn't it what you wanted? Have you told him yet?"

"I've not told him! I'm not sure if I'm going to keep it... I've been feeling just dreadful!"

"Then why did you climb all those stairs just now?"

Sidra's voice rose several decibels as she replied, "Because getting rid of you, Jennava, is more important to me than keeping this child! Don't you see? Having you here is ruining it all! I simply can't cope any longer with, 'Jay this, Jay that and Jay the other'! I won't have any peace of mind while you're here. I'm not even sleeping. And I'm not going through another night like last night. I kept waking up, thinking of you and I threw up this morning, too."

Jenna frowned and looked across at Joan who rolled her eyes back into her head.

Jenna stepped close to Sidra, saying, "Women often throw up in the early stages of pregnancy—"

"Not me! It's not the pregnancy! It's you!"

Jenna frowned. Surely Sidra was showing signs of being unbalanced. She wondered if she should not humor her then speak to the king about it.

"Well? Are you going to do as I ask?"

"And if I get caught?"

"You won't get caught. I've made arrangements for them to release a horse for Lady Sidra tonight from the stables. After you ride out of the castle, it'll be up to you. I suggest that you ride to Rosenburg... to your brother Charles. He wants you—"

"Charles wants me?" Jenna asked, doubting.

"So does Cyranius. He has written, many times, to Maslen, asking him to name his price. Cyranius is prepared to pay anything to have you back."

"What... what does King Cyranius want of me?"

"How would I know? What does any man want of a woman? But you? I suppose he wants what Maslen is getting... your wonderful, marvelous expertise in the gymnasium. That's all anyone talks about! How Jay is doing this on the poles... and that... and how that she doesn't fall off while everyone else does!" She stood and glared at Jenna, saying, "I can't stand it, I tell you! And, when I'm dead and gone, and... and our baby is either dead too, or not, then Maslen will marry you as he always wanted and I shall be forgotten." She dropped back into the chair and buried her face in her hands and wept.

Kneeling by the chair, Jenna waited. Sidra cried for a long time, real tears.

"You're distraught, Sidra, it's not as you say. I shall never marry Maslen, never."

It was as though Sidra had not heard. A minute passed. Then, Sidra dashed the tears from her eyes, making the eye makeup stain her cheeks.

"Please, please, Jenna. Please go. Please leave, or I swear I'll go insane!"

Standing, Sidra moved across to Joan's bag and drew out a large flask. To Jenna's astonishment, she stepped to the bed and poured half the contents on the top cover.

"I am going to throw a candle on this bed, Jennava, and it will ignite. As yourself, or as me, you'll have to leave this chamber, so make your choice."

Jenna turned to Joan who said, "Let me help you dress in the clothes, Jay, and I'll make your face up to look like Sidra's."

In an instant, Jenna decided to obey. *At least I'll gain time to think and plan, if I can walk about the castle looking like Sidra... I hope people see her when they look at me.*

Within a few minutes, she was transformed from looking like herself, into a Sidra-look-alike. The dark wig and red lipstick made the impression complete.

"Perhaps you'll need a change of clothes?" Sidra asked, her voice sweet, "and perhaps you have some things... from here... that you would wish to take with you... put them in Joan's bag..." she pressed the bag into Jenna's hands.

Moving behind the screen, Jenna collected the clothes she wore in the gym. Looking up, she saw the two pictures she had just drawn, and unpegging them, rolled them together and placed them in the bag with the clothes.

An alarming sound, such as Jenna had heard before, erupted in the tower-room. It was the same noise that had repeated within the palace at Cyran when it was on fire.

Jenna stepped from behind the screen. The bed was on fire, as were the curtains. The door was wide open.

Snatching up the three precious volumes of Scriptures and pushing them in the bag, Jenna hurried out the door, slamming it behind her. She raced down the steps, three at a time. Half expecting there to be a dozen armed men waiting for her, she felt surprised and pleased that the corridor was empty. She slowed her step, deciding that she must at least walk like the person she depicted, that was, until she found somewhere safe to consider this new turn of events.

Forty-four

Guards inclined their heads towards Jenna as she walked passed; she headed on a familiar route, to the gymnasium. The stables were beyond the gym and she hoped they believed she was headed for the stables. That she was alone could have seemed odd to the guards.

Flares spaced along the way lent flickering light to the passage, making the 'escape' seem peculiar to the fugitive.

No guards stood by the gymnasium door, and Jenna entered the wind-blown chamber, feeling cold and numb, both inside and out. She had no idea what she would do next. Where would the king be right now, she wondered? Should she escape? What about her pledge? How could she make her promise mean nothing? She knew that she could not. *A pledge, though without blood, is still a pledge. Words are not meaningless gabble, my words can't be retracted. I'm bound to this castle until King Maslen releases me.*

I can't stay here, not dressed as Sidra... she told herself, then wondered where she could go.

Lightning lit the chamber and Jenna thought for a moment that bodies hung from the beams. It was the sacks of grain. She shivered, wavering between freedom and bondage. She wondered how far she would get if she took a horse from the stables. It was only two hours ride at a fast rate to the cottage just over the border where she could soak in the thermal pool.

I made a pledge to King Maslen, she reminded herself, *and Sidra will remember the whereabouts of the pool...*

"Please God," Jenna whispered, "Please tell me what to do. Light my path. Guide my footsteps. You know I hate being here. I hate this gymnasium, I hate violence, fighting and combat. I hate it, God. Do You hate me for having to be here, God? You are the Prince of Peace, the one who said we must love others. What do I do? Where shall I go? Please, God, guide each step I take from here..."

It's not God's fault that Father taught me defense skills... we have to live with the choices our parents make, choices I have made, too... "Please God," she whispered, "Use my mistakes for good, if you can."

Jenna left the gymnasium. She wondered which way she should go, and again decided that she did not want to be dressed in Sidra's clothes. *It's deception,* she told herself, dreading that Maslen would find her like this.

A bell began to toll in the castle, the sound shattering the air. Guards ran passed her, and Jenna decided to go in the opposite direction. *They've discovered that my tower is on fire,* she supposed, as the bell continued to toll.

As men hurried passed, Jenna continued in the opposite direction. She found herself stepping up into the atrium. A group of six guards at the throne room door were discussing whether or not to leave their posts. Deciding that they might be needed, that they must discover the meaning of the bell-toll, they all hurried off along the dim corridor.

Jenna entered the empty throne room. Wind scurried in here, and the oak tree groaned and creaked against the surround through which it grew.

Moving to the back of the throne, Jenna changed into her gym clothes, pushing the wig and Sidra's clothes into the bag. Wondering where she could hide the bag, she knew she needed to tell the king that she had not attempted to escape, but had left her tower-chamber because she had no choice; it had caught fire.

King Maslen is not that stupid, he'll guess that others were involved. How can I tell him that it was Sidra? I can't. But he'll not harm her when he knows she carries his child, will he? Jenna felt sure that the king would want to protect Sidra. *She's become unbalanced. She has been thinking only of me and making me into something I'm not. People can do that if they harp on and on about something. They invent a catastrophe in their minds and make it happen if they can. She was like that with Judith, she wanted her out of her life, just as she does me...*

Well, I'm going to keep my pledge! I didn't give it lightly, and I'm not going to break it. God help me, please help me. I want to do what's right. But, perhaps, in this place, nothing is right...

Jenna wondered where she could go to wait for King Maslen. If he was dining, and was called to view the tower-fire, he may not come to his throne room until tomorrow morning. He always attended his throne room in the mornings. She may have to wait all night.

Taking the bag with her, Jenna climbed the tree. Up. Up. Up. The net above was made of strong rope. It held back hundreds of leaves that had fallen off the branches of the old oak tree. Close to the trunk, there was a gap of about ten inches. Jenna pushed the bag up through the gap to rest on the net. With careful maneuvering, she wriggled up through the gap herself. Grasping the bag, she climbed higher and higher.

The trunk splayed out into many branches, and Jenna found what she had been searching for, a place to hide from eyes below her. *If only I had a drink or something to eat, I did not have my evening meal, and I'm hungry. Still, I've gone without before...*

With the bag as a pillow and the cloak as her cover, Jenna fell asleep in this unlikely haven, feeling safe from the conspiracies of the night.

~ * ~

Midnight had not long hatched when footsteps woke Jenna. Whispers, murmured replies, more whispers and Jenna perceived that someone, perhaps more than one, climbed into the oak tree. She froze. She did not want to be discovered now. It was the king she wished to give herself to, not a bunch of his guards. *How can they have discovered that I'm here?* she wondered.

Whispers continued, sounds of people in the tree were obvious—creaking branches, scuffling sounds of climbing, the soft drop of feet on the marble of the throne room floor and instructions uttered in low voices. Jenna had no idea what was happening. Some men were doing something to the king's oak tree.

"Are you sure it will work?" a deep voice rumbled its tones to Jenna's ears.

"Absolutely," the reply came, "It's foolproof. Just two ropes to release, and poof, the king is snared."

Jenna lowered her head beyond the branch, straining to listen. That last voice had the same tones as the jester's.

"I still think we should bring crossbows."

"No need," Jester said, "They're too cumbersome to carry and they take too long to load. We'll use swords."

"Right then. We'll all be ready to enter right after the king, then we'll take care of any guards, and when we let down the net, we'll have him!"

"I'll take care of him!" the voice belonging to the jester said, "But we need him trapped in the net. Don't try anything before he's firmly wound up. He's an expert with his sword. We have to get him entangled on the floor first."

"It's expedient that they're all out looking for the jay-bird," the deep voice rumbled happily, "the king has his focus on her capture... he's at the stables, now, waiting while they search the place again... seems no horses are missing, but we need to be ready, perchance he should come here before breakfast. We must let down the net before he looks up and sees that there are two."

"He'll not perceive it," the jester said, his voice full of confidence, "It's such a good match to the other, he won't notice it. We'll make a diversion to get him off the throne, such that he won't even consider the net. We'll see if we can get ourselves that prize hostage we talked about, when the time arrives..."

"Let's get out of here, before he decides to come... he's been known to come here just to think... he does his planning and scheming in here..."

Sounds of footsteps faded and the great doors opened and closed. Jenna wondered what the men intended to do to King Maslen? The jester had said, 'I'll take care of him.' Were they intending to kill him? What could she do?

Suddenly, Jenna knew. She must rescue the king from these conspirators. *This is no 'set-up' she told herself. No one knows I'm here. King Maslen has men out in the city looking for me, they are not looking in the castle. He believes I escaped. He believes I broke my pledge. The best way to assure him of my subordination is to foil this dastardly plot against him.*

Jenna wondered if she should climb down and examine the net, perhaps to release it so that it was already on the floor when the king came. She moved downward a few feet.

The doors flew open, and Jenna slid close to the trunk. Some five dozen guards, all carrying flares, entered the throne room, lining up, lighting the way for the king to walk to his throne. The chamber sprang alive with light.

Jenna saw King Maslen stride through the center of the two lines, then he disappeared from her view.

When the king sat on his throne, the guards placed the flares in holders all around the chamber. Jenna peered down, viewing the men through small holes in the blanket of leaves. She could not see the king, but could see some of the many guards as they spaced themselves out around the chamber.

One by one, captains entered, giving their reports on the night's search for the escaped jay-bird.

Jenna listened, fascinated, feeling sure that if she had been out in the city, they would have found her.

"Every sector of the city has been searched, but she has not been found?" the king queried.

"No Sire."

"And no one reports any sightings of her?"

"No Sire."

"She had no horse, she must be sulking in some corner somewhere, dressed as some beggar child. I wish we knew what she was wearing!"

"We searched every street-camp and every place where the children sleep, Sire, they saw no strangers tonight."

"What of the woman, Moyra?"

"We gained the address where she has gone, Sire, and she will be brought here."

"And the widow, Joan?"

"She's still not been located, Sire."

"Bah."

Silence ensued.

Jenna knew that Jester and his men would not attempt an assassination with so many guards present in the throne room. But she needed to be alert, Jenna felt sure they were waiting. She wondered, should she climb down now and reveal herself to the king?

Something within her again urged her to wait. *He will not believe me,* she realized. *If I don't give Jester time to reveal himself, King Maslen's life will be at risk another time, and perhaps I shall be in a prison chamber by then. Jester would not want me around! No. But with God's help, I shall be!*

The doors opened, and Moyra entered. A young man stood with her.

"The servant, Moyra, and her son-in-law, John."

The couple was escorted along the carpet to stand before the king's throne.

Jenna listened as the king bellowed his questions and Moyra answered him truthfully, telling him that Jenna had dismissed her early.

"Bah! I should have known it! She was always in control, that one!" the king stormed. "Go home, John and Moyra, go home; it's her I want, not you!

"I want everyone out there! Surround the city and keep the gates closed. Action a street-by-street, house-to-house search, beginning from the city walls and work inwards, all the way to the castle! Go! All of you, go!"

One by one the guards bowed and began to take their flares to leave the chamber.

"Leave one or two lights and leave me here, I need to speculate."

When the throne room was quiet, other than the groaning of the wind in the tree far above, the king said softly, "How does a jay-bird think? Where is she now?

"She gave me her word, her pledge..."

Jenna jumped as the king shouted, "Guards! Guards!"

Four men hurried in through the doors.

"Have them search the castle again, every inch. And go and light the gymnasium; climb up on the scaffolding, search up on the top beams. I have a notion that she may not have left my castle, but that she's hiding somewhere here. Go!"

When the throne room was silent, he said aloud, but softly, "No one saw her leave. Someone would have seen her. No, she must be still here, waiting until we stop looking. Well, I'll not stop looking."

The throne room doors swung open, and Jenna's heart leapt. The jester and a group of six guards entered. The moment had arrived. Jenna instinctively flexed her fingers and shrugged her shoulders back.

King Maslen was silent as the group approached the throne. Moving to form a semi-circle, they kept some twenty feet from the throne. The two men, at opposite ends of the semi-circle, stood close to the pillars around which the ropes of the net had been fixed.

Jenna estimated that their distance would be the circumference of the net above; the two at the pillars were waiting to release the thin ropes securing the net.

"How convenient," the jester taunted. "We find the king alone, and the jay-bird missing. Perhaps the jay-bird will be blamed for the king's demise. We hope so."

The king stood and the sound of his sword being unsheathed came to Jenna. "Guards! Guards!" the king shouted.

Jenna began to slither down the tree, keeping her descent slow and silent. *I cannot fail, I must not be blamed for King Maslen's death... he must not die in this way...*

"How sad. You sent your guards to look for the jay-bird. Now there are only our men out there."

"What... what... how?" King Maslen's eyes circled his throne room, and for the first time he wished he had commissioned personal bodyguards as Myres had often urged. "How much... do you want?" the king asked, his voice unsure.

"You wish to pay us?" the jester questioned, then said, "Wish on, small majesty! We want it all, Maslen, we want your throne and we want you dead!"

The king stood up on his throne, pointing his sword.

Jenna had reached the net. Turning herself to lie along a branch, she peered through the gap She could see the king's head beneath her.

"Tell you what, Maslen, come down here, and it will be just one on one; winner takes all. I quite like one on one."

"You forget, Jester, I no longer believe in taking people at their word. No, come and get me."

"Bring in our hostage!" the jester called.

The throne room doors opened and two guards entered, holding Sidra, who wore a red satin nightdress.

"Trent! King's guards are coming! Help us! Out here!" a guard at the door shouted, his voice very convincing.

Together, the guards holding Sidra released her and returned to the doors. Four of the six ran to the doors. There were just two guards with the jester.

Pulling off a cloth gag, Sidra hurried toward the throne. Her voice hysterical, she cried, "They came and took me from my bed, Maslen, I was so afraid. What's happening? I'm cold..."

King Maslen, having seen the exiting guards, stepped down from his throne, pointing his sword towards the jester, his eyes fixed upon this dangerous foe. The sound of clashing swords beyond the throne room doors spoke of a battle in the atrium. Believing that help was at hand, the king stepped closer to Sidra.

"Go to my throne, Sidra, you'll be safe there."

As the two men's hands reached to release the net, King Maslen's eyes flew to them, then to the great web above, falling on him. He backed up and would have turned, but it was too late. The trick had worked! Together, the rope snare covered the king and Sidra.

"Release the rest of it! Loosen it up!" shouted the jester. He stepped over the web as the king and Sidra struggled against it. Sidra dropped to her hands and knees, crying and screaming.

King Maslen plunged his sword through an opening in the net, waving it at the approaching jester.

Reaching down, the jester dragged the net towards him, using both hands. The king was unbalanced and fell to his knees. The net tangled around his hands. Flicking the net again and again around the king's wrist, the jester pulled it tight, causing the king to release his sword.

"On your knees, Sire? The king kneeling to the jester? This is your dying image, little majesty. Remember me well. Death is so final, isn't it?" Drawing a long thin dagger, the jester stepped closer. "Bow your head, majesty, or I shall stab your face, one eye at a time! If you bow your head, I shall stab your back; it will go right to your heart, and it'll be quicker for you!

"No! No!" screamed Sidra, horrified, staring through the net, watching the metal of the blade glint orange light from the flares. "No! Don't! Please don't kill him! No! Help us! Someone! Help! Oh, God, help us!"

The king did not bow his head, but stared up at the jester and the knife, his face showing complete disbelief at what was about to happen to him.

Jenna slithered down to stand on the king's throne. Jumping to the net-covered floor, she dived at the jester, her hands outstretched to prevent the dagger from descending into the king's eye. Pulling the jester's arm to impact her raised knee, she heard the dagger clatter as it fell, point first to the floor. The jester yelled in pain, feeling that his arm had been broken.

Twisting, Jenna flung the jester around, telling herself not to be too confident—this was the jester who was a match for her own skills. Lifting her other knee, she caught him in his stomach, hitting his back with her clenched fist, winding him with such force that he dropped to his knees.

Jenna's peripheral vision showed that others approached, with drawn swords. The false fracas outside the doors was over, and the guards hurried back to watch the murder of the king.

Grasping the king's sword with both hands, Jenna swung it in warning to those approaching. One man pushed his sword back in its sheath and bent to collect the net in both hands. Holding the sword in one hand now, Jenna bent herself and jerked the net with her other hand, causing the man to sprawl forward on the marble.

"Jay-bird! Join us!" a deep voice called. It was the man called Trent, the one who had planned the assassination with the jester.

"Never! I'll never join murderers!" Jenna shouted.

"We'll give you half Maslen's kingdom!" Jester offered.

"If you gave me all of Aponia, or all the world, it would not be enough to buy my soul!" Jenna shouted, then twisted around to avoid a spear hurled at her by Trent's hand.

The king shouted, "Behind you, Jay!" Jenna pirouetted. The dagger, thrown by the jester, flew swiftly past her, finding another human mark, an approaching guard. It entered his chest, and with a grunt, he fell backwards, dropping his sword. After a frenetic spasm, he lay still on the marble.

Jenna approached the jester, holding the sword towards him. Leaping to his feet, he backed away. She stepped closer, keeping the other guards in view. Swinging the sword in a threatening manner, she pirouetted, causing the steel to slice the air with an ominous swish. As one, the rebel guards stepped backward; save the man called Trent.

The jester ran to his cohorts, crying, "Give me a sword and we'll fight her! Give me a sword you cowards!"

Moving closer to the king, Jenna slashed and sliced at the net.

"Behind you, Jay!" the king cried, his voice hoarse. He was so tangled in the net he could hardly move. A haunted look came from his eyes; he now depended upon his jay-bird prisoner for his life. *Death will be so final,* he knew.

Pivoting, Jenna engaged swords with Trent. King Maslen's sword was unfamiliar and heavy and Jenna used both hands. Within a minute, she had flicked Trent's sword from his hand but at the same time the long blade tip of hers pushed right through his wrist. Jenna, feeling mortified, pulled back on the sword, drawing it out, causing blood to gush from both sides of the crippling wound.

"Finish it! Kill me! Kill me!" Trent cried, falling to his knees, his eyes large, ogling the dreadful wound.

"Get back, get away from your king!" Jenna said, waving the sword close to Trent's face. She wanted him off the net. Turning, he crawled away supporting himself with one hand, the other useless. All bravery gone, he only wanted to quit the chamber and to get away from the one who had spoiled their 'foolproof plot'.

From the corner of her eye, Jenna saw the sword coming like a spear, aimed by the hand of the jester, it's target the king.

Lifting her sword, Jenna again pirouetted flinging the weapon upward, catching the flying sword in flight. Everyone in the throne room stared in awe as sparks showered from the clash of the two swords. The sword aimed at King Maslen rose in the air then fell harmlessly to the floor.

Trent collapsed before reaching the doors. The jester ran to him while other guards backed away from Jenna, turning to run like frightened rabbits.

Laying the sword down, Jenna gathered up the net. She lifted it off Sidra, untangling her hands. Sobbing and crying, Sidra retched and threw up on the floor. She gasped, spitting out tardy vomit.

"Oh... I'm faint, so faint..." she cried, unable to rise.

Still the jester sat with Trent, seeking to hinder the hemorrhaging. Jenna kept him in her peripheral vision.

"Where are your guards?" Jenna asked, but already knowing the answer.

"They went looking for you," King Maslen said, then added, "Watch that jester, Jay, he's got Trent's dagger."

"I know it, Sire, but I want to free you."

Jenna sliced and slashed at the rope, but the king was well and truly tangled. She needed to be able to cut the ropes close to his limbs. "I'll get his dagger," she said, "then I can cut you loose."

Jenna stepped towards the jester and as she had hoped, he stood, aiming the dagger at her.

"Get out of my way, Jay, or this dagger will be for you. Get out of my way, and let me complete my purpose here! I will not die without knowing he is dead! *Get out of my way!*

Jenna realized her mistake—if she moved aside, he would throw the dagger at the king, if she did not then she would have to take it. She focused her full concentration on the dagger, while at the same time swiftly rotating the sword in front of her.

"That will not stop me! The dagger will get past your blade. I shall aim for your heart, Jay-bird."

He stepped closer and closer, and Jenna, still rotating the sword, stepped backwards with short careful steps.

"You're still in front of the king!" he shouted. "I'll kill you, I will!" so saying, he released the dagger. As Jenna had planned, the dagger struck the blade of the sword and with a loud ping flew harmlessly to slide across the floor.

"Out! Out!" Jenna cried, moving closer to the jester. He stepped back. "Move faster! I want you out of here!" The jester turned and walked toward the doors, stopping to stare down at Trent, lying still in an expanding pool of blood.

Jenna turned intending to fetch the dagger and the jester spun around also. He threw a small knife, one he had concealed within a pouch inside his belt.

Within her mind, Jenna knew what he had done, but she also thought of the king and turned back, knowing that the knife would impact her somewhere but she was not sure where. How much could be imagined in a split-second—then came the searing pain, in her upper arm.

Still holding the sword with both hands, it was as if Jenna hardly flinched. The jester's eyes darted everywhere as he searched for another weapon. Jenna stepped towards him, every nerve in her body screaming at her to drop the sword and do something about the excruciating pain.

The jester fled from the throne room.

Jenna staggered back to King Maslen. Kneeling in front of him she cried, "Pull it out, pull it out!" Lifting his hand, he grasped the knife handle, but it would not budge.

"Hold it tight," she said, and pushed herself sideways, away from him. The knife came free. Taking it from him, she cut the rope from around him, freeing his other hand from the tight coils. He continued pulling the net off himself.

Jenna felt faint from the pain of the wound in her upper arm. The knife had pierced into the bone, and she felt the warmth of her blood soaking her tunic sleeve.

King Maslen staggered to sit on his throne while still dragging net rope off his arms and shoulders. He trembled in shock, remembering the jester's taunts. How very close to him the presence of death had descended. Neither Sidra, gasping on the floor, nor Jenna's voice, brought him back to the reality of all his prisoner had done to save his life.

"I need to make sure they've all gone and that they don't regroup," Jenna said, standing and walking towards the doors. She felt spent, faint. "Your guards should be returning." She hoped that the jester would not come back. How could she protect the king or Sidra now?

"I hope some of the king's loyal men are out there."

The doors flew open and king's guards rushed into the room. The sight in front of their eyes was of grave concern. Bodies and blood seemed to be everywhere. Sidra lay weeping on the floor and rope was mingled with blood. The king languished on his throne as if suffering a heart attack and, right here, in front of them, was the prisoner they had been searching for all night. While her left hand dripped blood, she clutched a small dagger in the other hand.

Captain Paulas, commissioned to stand in for Captain Myres, stared at Jenna and shouted, "Put the dagger down! Put it on the floor!"

Jenna stared at the pack of guards surging into the throne room. Knowing that these were some of the king's men who had entered with him earlier, she knew she must submit to them. Crouching, she placed the dagger on the marble.

"Kick it here, to me!" he cried. Having seen Jenna at work, he did not want to get too close before the weapon was away from her. With a push, she sent the weapon sliding to the captain.

"Secure her!" he called, and a quad of men rushed to obey him.

They forced her to kneel on the floor, twisting her arms viciously behind her back. Jenna cried out in pain as her injured arm was wrenched in a vice-like grip.

"Fetch chains!" the captain demanded, and two men behind him hurried to do his bidding.

Striding to the prisoner, the captain kicked her in the back. The shoulder above her wound screamed in pain, and Jenna entered a void—she fainted.

"Sire... are you injured?" Captain Paulas's voice broke into the king's lassitude.

The king started and he looked around his throne room, reliving the battle that had taken place here. Lifting his hands, he stared at them, one after the other. He stood, and the captain stepped back, waiting.

King Maslen shook his head, wondering how he had avoided being wounded, or killed but he was not marked at all, not one scratch.

Sidra's sobs came to his ears and he watched as she crawled closer to him.

"Where's Jay?" he asked.

"The jay-prisoner is in our hands, Sire... we're having chains fetched for her."

"Chains?" he asked, his mind racing over all he had seen her do. "No, not chains." He remembered the small dagger. "She's injured. Bring her here to me."

The guards dragged Jenna to fall prostrate before King Maslen's throne.

"Fetch Doctor Arnold," the king commanded.

"But Sire... the jester said she tried to kill you—"

"What! He dared to stop to lie to you? It wasn't her! She covered me—saved my life. It's the jester who's responsible for all this derangement! I'd... I'd be dead now if he'd had his way! A dagger in my brain, that's what he wanted! Find him for me! He had a dozen cohorts, about eight left! I want them all. Bring me the jester, kill him if you have to! I want to see him dead. Get word out to our men in the city to change the manhunt. Tell them that the jay-bird is in captivity and we seek the jester and any king's guards who cower when questioned. Take crossbows and shoot anyone who will not halt."

As the captain turned on his heel, the king called, "Leave me a dozen men, Captain, with drawn swords. Let them stand at the back of this chamber. You do not know how closely death has stalked me here in this chamber. This jay-prisoner, as you call her, she saved my life, not once, but many times."

So saying, King Maslen knelt beside Jenna. Her sleeve was red with blood. "Tell Arnold to hurry!"

Sitting on the floor, the king tore the fabric away from Jenna's wound. Taking a piece of rope and looping it, he secured it above the gash, pulling it as tight as he could. Then, lifting her to sit in his large lap, he cradled her upright in his arms.

Jenna opened her eyes to look up at King Maslen.

"Why did you do it, Jay? Why did you save my life? Am I not your hated enemy?"

Jenna felt as if the king faded away, and she closed her eyes.

"Don't leave me, little jay-bird. Tell me why you stood in the way and why you took my dagger? I saw you. You could have avoided each one of them, just as you evaded those wheat-bags but you deliberately remained in the path."

Sidra, shivering, pulled herself up to sit on one of the larger roots at the base of the throne. She listened as Jenna answered.

"I... my father... it was something I learned from him. We believe that the greatest... most noble... thing we could do was to follow the Lord Christ's example... to give our life... for another..." her eyes fell closed again.

~ * ~

Doctor Arnold arrived and examined Jenna's arm while guards held their torches, staring solemnly, in a circle around the king and the doctor. "It needs pressure applied, or I shall have to pack it with ice to stem the bleeding. She must not lie down—you're right in propping her up. When the bleeding ceases, I'll have to stitch it."

He turned and looked at Sidra, who was sobbing quietly, rocking herself back and forth. "Lady Sidra?"

"Shock, Arnold. Me, too, I'm feeling peculiar... I've never felt like this in my life before. It has shaken me... to the very core... of my being..."

"I'll mix you a compound to revive you, Sire," Arnold promised, "and one for Lady Sidra."

Jenna's eyes opened and she said, "Sidra? Is Lady Sidra all right?" Looking into King Maslen's eyes, Jenna asked, "Did she tell you? Did Lady Sidra tell you? She must tell you."

"Tell me what?" the king asked, his voice almost back to normal.

"The child..."

Turning to Sidra he asked, "What... child?"

"I was going to tell you, Maslen, but, I wanted to be sure..."

"Sure?"

"Your child... I think I bear your child..."

"You think?" he bellowed.

"Oh, don't!" she cried, "I didn't know it would feel like this. I thought it was a time when one was happy and well, but it's been terrible... I can't think properly, I throw up and I don't sleep... and it's just beginning."

King Maslen blinked. He had known Sidra was not herself, but had put it down to a plunge in her cantankerous nature, not to a pregnancy. How blind he had been.

"How long... how long have you known?" he asked.

"About two months... but I'm not sure... I keep thinking I'm going to lose it."

"What? Miscarry my son? Never!" he turned to the doctor, commanding, "Send for a sedan-chair and have Lady Sidra taken to her bed. She shouldn't have been here in the first place!" Turning back to her, he scolded, "What do you think you were doing, coming to my throne room in the middle of the night?"

While Sidra burst into tears, the king remembered that she had had no choice in the matter. He shook his head, telling himself to regain control.

"Where... where shall I have Jay taken to tend to her... the tower being burned, shall I have her taken to the clinic?"

"What? No. Not the clinic. Take her to a guest chamber and commission a couple of upper servant-women to care for her... then tend Sidra and report to me here. I shall stay here, but bring me that compound yourself... I'll not be poisoned after all this!"

Shaking his head, the doctor began to give commands, while at the same time thinking, *One moment I have nothing to do but watch a prisoner working out and the next, I'm overcome!*

The king called a guard to him, saying, "Myton! Have my throne room cleared of the rope and the bodies. Have the blood mopped up, every last drop!"

Forty-five

The king sat on his throne, staring at nothing in particular, seemingly oblivious to the activity he had commanded to take place. But his mind buzzed with the unbelievable nature of the night's activities.

Death is so final, he told himself, *I could be dead—blinded, a decapitated corpse. Trent would have put my head on a stake and hung my body on the wall.*

Who would have taken my throne? Jester? Ha! But why do I make mirth of it? Trent did not have the loftiness to last as king.

If Jay had accepted their offer... they could have crowned her queen. She'd have kept them all in order. I've never known such a strong-minded woman—never a person, man or woman, with such courage; but such a selfless spirit.

It dawned on him that she had always been unselfish; she had been schooled to consider others as worthy of risking all to save.

But... me? She saved me. I who oppressed and tormented her... I've treated her as a law-breaking peon.

He searched his memory to recall every word she had uttered in his throne room during the confrontation.

"Bring a candelabra!" he shouted, and scavenged for a quill, ink and paper. Taking his time, he wrote down all Jenna's words. Then he recorded all the words that the jester and Trent had said. Beads of perspiration crowded his brow as he considered the jester's self-appointed quest to kill him.

"If you gave me all of Aponia, or all the world, it would not be enough to buy my soul!" she had said.

I do not have your soul, Jay-bird; but I have your loyalty, your trust and I have your person.

I can never let her go. No. I can never let her go now. I must find a way to commit her to me forever.

King Maslen knew that the plot would not have failed had it not been for Jenna, who somehow had been hiding in his oak tree. He looked up into the darkness of the net and the branches above him.

An insecure feeling flooded King Maslen and he ordered guards to climb the tree to search it. "Someone could be hiding there still!"

The bag Jenna had taken into the great oak was brought to King Maslen, and he examined each of the items with interest. Two volumes of the Holy Scriptures. *Obviously of value to her,* he pondered, *she saved these from a tower that perhaps was already on fire?* A dark wig, clothes the same as Sidra's, then, in the bottom of the bag, two painted pictures Jenna had created—one of the city out of the tower window, marked 'Jay's tower-home' and the other of his throne room. He pondered on the pictures and knew within himself that it had not been her idea to set the tower on fire and escape.

She did not leave my castle but kept her pledge, he told himself, feeling deeply satisfied. *Not only that, she risked her own life to save mine. I have someone in this castle whom I believe I can trust for the rest of my life... it's a rare privilege indeed. It's something infinitely valuable, and I need to protect it... it's more valuable than any other thing in this wretched kingdom of mine.*

Remembering Jenna's red lips, he thought of Sidra. Did Sidra put red lip color on Jenna? Who else knew that they looked alike if they exchanged hair color? What part did Sidra play in pressing for Jenna's escape, the king wondered? Jenna had known Sidra's secret. He decided to visit the pair and learn the truth.

Doctor Arnold was with Jenna when the king entered the bedchamber without knocking or being announced. The doctor had forced a cold compress into the wound and was binding it firmly. Jenna protested as loudly as she was able. Seated in a chair by a candelabra, her arm was propped up on a small table and secured firmly at the wrist by a man-servant.

"It's aching... I want to put it down," Jenna said, gritting her teeth against the pain.

"You want to bleed to death do you?" the doctor snapped. Having tied the bandage tightly, he stood, turned, and almost walked into the king.

"Your Majesty!" he said, bowing before striding to the sideboard. The king followed. "She needs to be sleeping when I stitch it. It will bleed forever if she does not remain still." He sprinkled a little powder into a goblet and half-filled it with fruit juice.

Understanding that Arnold was going to drug Jenna, the king strode to her side. He crouched down so that his head was level with hers.

"Jay," he said softly. She opened her eyes and looked at him. "Who set fire to your tower-home?"

Jenna's lips parted, but she did not answer.

"Who gave you Sidra's clothes and the wig? Tell me their names, all of them!"

Jenna knew he would find out eventually, so she replied, "Lady Sidra and... the servant-woman, Joan."

King Maslen frowned, but did not speak. He rose and left the chamber. Before he reached his mistress's bedchamber, Doctor Arnold joined him.

Together they entered the room to discover that Sidra now slept. If it had not been for Arnold's warning, King Maslen would have shaken her awake, but he agreed, if indeed Sidra was with child, she needed time to rest and forget the terror of this past night.

To the king's satisfaction, the servant-woman, Joan, was located sleeping in the servants' quarters. Hauled from her sleeping-mat, she answered all the king's questions truthfully and affirmed Sidra's part in Jenna's escape.

King Maslen could forgive Sidra for failing to tell him of her condition, but he was not sure he could forgive her for committing the treacherous act of forcing Jenna from the tower and urging her to escape.

"She were, like, a bit out of her mind at the time," Joan told the king, "even Miss Jay knew that. She kept looking at me, Miss Jay, as if she were wondering why Lady Sidra were acting so strange. I'm glad Miss Jay decided to go along with her... I'd hate to think what would have happened... I think Lady Sidra might have tried to set *her* on fire!"

"There's enough to deal with without imagining more," the king said, adding, "you'll stay with Lady Sidra and serve her. You'll report to me if you're concerned with anything she talks about. You're not to leave the castle without my express permission. Do you understand?"

"Yes, Sire. And thank you, Sire," Joan dropped a curtsy, smiling. She held Lady Sidra in great awe. To be commanded to stay with the lady was a great promotion for Joan.

Doctor Arnold confirmed that Lady Sidra was indeed with child, "Perhaps even three months along the way," he told the king. The doctor was most happy; he now was involved in the very venture for which he had been engaged—to bring into the world an heir for the king.

King Maslen knew that he would not be able to contain the news of Sidra's pregnancy for long—every tongue would be passing it on quickly. Something had to be done, and soon. He would have to marry Sidra, and crown her as Queen of Aponia so that their child would legally own the title of prince. If Sidra bore a son, he would be heir to his throne.

The king sighed, thinking, *If only Sidra were Jay. I have to keep them both now, the treacherous one, and the trustworthy one, but how? Force will work with Sidra; but I shall lose Jay if I cannot combine love with constraint. But Jay does not love me, not as a lover; how then does she love me?* He felt confused. Jay had risked all, yet would not give him all; he knew she would not agree to marriage. *I'm growing soft. Or is it bitter experience? A woman forced into marriage is like trying to swim the stormy sea with a millstone around ones neck.*

How then does Jay love me? What manner of love is it that these Christians manifest? If I could understand what binds her to her God, perhaps I could learn how to bind her to me... but where, in all of Aponia, will I find a Christian to talk to him, to understand her?

He sent for the librarian and asked the man to engage knowledgeable helpers to search out passages from the Holy Scriptures on the sacrifice of Christ and about the way Christians loved one another. The passages were to be written out so that he, the king, could put them together without having to carry heavy volumes about the castle.

"Do it today!" the king commanded, not realizing how demanding this mandate was.

The next day, King Maslen discovered that Christians had 'brotherly and sisterly love' for one another. This love was the way that others knew they were Christians. "Greater love has no man than this," the Christ had said, "that a man lay down his life for his friends."

At least I've established that I'm her friend, the king mused, feeling pleased.

"Let love be without dissimulation. Abhor that which is evil; cleave to that which is good. Be kindly affectioned one to another with brotherly love, in honor preferring one another," he read.

The librarian explained the meaning of 'agape' to King Maslen. "It is love that is an action; different from 'Eros' which is intimate love between man and woman. Agape love enfolds all mankind—men and women, children too and there are no class, race, or age barriers. The love that Christians are enjoined to exhibit is love that cares, understands, comforts and protects. Others are to be treated as being worth as much as oneself. To 'do unto others as you would have them do unto you' is a Christian ideal."

"Even if it means giving one's life. Or perhaps taking on suffering for someone else," the king suggested, thinking of Jenna's stand to protect him against Trent and Jester.

"Yes, that's it, Sire," the librarian said, then turned to a young slave, commanding, "Tell King Maslen what you know, Daniel."

"The Holy Scriptures say in the book of Romans, 'God commended his love towards men, that while we were yet sinners, Christ died for us'…the Bible, from cover to cover, Your Majesty, is telling out the message that men can be reconciled to God through Christ's sacrificial death on the cross at the place called Calvary. It also says in the Biblical letter of Paul to the Philippian Christians, that we need to have the same mind that Christ Jesus had, who, being in the form of God, was also equal with God; but then, he made himself of no reputation and took upon himself the form of a servant, made in the likeness of men. As a man, he humbled himself and became obedient unto death, even the death of the cross. The message for Christians, is that we're to behave as Christ behaved, and to love others as he did. While we were enemies towards God, the Scriptures say, Christ died for us."

"Where did you get your name?" the king asked.

"I was given the name Daniel when I came into the king's service here in Aponia."

"Daniel, that's a Biblical name, is it not?"

"Yes, Sire. It was given to me as a jest, but I like it, Sire."

"You're a Christian?"

"Yes, Sire."

"A Christian who can read and you're a slave, a eunuch," the king said, smiling, "you'll serve me well. I will hear counsel from you. I also have a task for you."

Turning sharply to the librarian, the king said, "From where did you get Daniel?"

"He was brought here with children who were taken as slaves from the kingdoms to the north, Sire," the librarian said. "They were selected because they had been taught to read and knew several languages."

"How many more are there?"

"Three, Sire. The others serve in the Winter Palace."

"We shall meet them when we make our journey south."

Three days passed, and Jenna's arm began to heal. She disliked the thick meaty broth that Doctor Arnold commanded her to consume three times a day.

"It will enrich your blood supply, as well as giving you strength," he told his reluctant patient. When Jenna declared that she wanted to get up and walk about, he told her that if she remained resting for another day and swallowed all the broth he ordered for her, he would permit her to rise.

In the meantime, Daniel, the slave, arrived in Jenna's bedchamber, carefully carrying a box containing volumes from the Bible. After introducing himself, he offered to read any volume Jenna chose. She was delighted, as she had been bored resting, dozing and sitting wide awake, propped up in the large, four-poster bed.

When she had asked why she had not been confined to a place like the tower again, she had been told that the king had commanded that she be treated as an honored guest, and installed in a guest-chamber.

"You have been sent to read to me?" Jenna asked, her voice doubtful.

"Yes, Miss, King Maslen wants you to hear words of comfort and encouragement. "That's why I chose the Psalms, and I also have Ruth, Esther, Matthew and James," Daniel told her.

Jenna listened to Daniel's soft voice reading from the Psalms. To her later dismay, she fell asleep and when she awoke, Daniel was gone. But, summoned by those who watched, he returned and again read to her until she again fell asleep.

Jenna was disappointed that she had slept but Doctor Arnold was very pleased.

A number of beautiful dresses were brought and Jenna was given an option as to which ones she wished to keep to wear.

"Who sent them?" she asked, but already knew. King Maslen was treating her with kindness. He was grateful for what she had done in saving his life. Inwardly, Jenna felt averse to accepting the dresses from the king.

"King Maslen ordered them to be sent for you," the gushing servant told her.

Jenna stared at the servant-women. These women were different from those who had attended her in the tower. The other women were older, coarser and much less elaborately dressed. Joyce and Vicky, arrayed as ladies, were obviously upper-servants. Jenna knew enough about castle protocol to know that there were large gaps between classes of servants. Vicky and Joyce would never fraternize with servants of such low station as Moyra or Joan.

When the servant-women dressed her and helped her to stand, Jenna could not believe how weak she felt. She needed their support to walk from the bedchamber to the sitting room just through the arch.

"You lost quite a quantity of your lifeblood," Doctor Arnold said, as if scolding her. "You will have to exercise patience until your strength returns."

Jenna stared around the sitting room. Now she realized the source of the aroma drifting into the bedchamber, a soothing fragrance, the scent of roses. The room was filled with vases of roses, every color one could think of—white, scarlet, pink, yellow, orange, crimson and many with two-toned petals. The roses had been carefully set into lovely arrangements with gypsophilla to enhance them.

"What beautiful roses!" Jenna exclaimed.

"The king sent them for you, all of them," Joyce said. "He's coming, this afternoon, to visit you."

"I should have the roses taken to my bedroom," Jenna said, sitting forward in the chair and reaching out her uninjured arm to draw one from the nearest vase. She breathed in its sweet perfume.

"Doctor Arnold won't permit flowers in the bedchambers of his patients," Vicky explained.

Jenna smiled, knowing now that this very matter had been the subject of the argument she had heard a day ago, between the king and the doctor, wafting from the sitting room.

She was being kindly treated, and Jenna wondered if the king would reward her. Perhaps he would allow her to return home? But did she want to return to Cyran? Did King Cyranius really want to see her again?

Forty-six

King Maslen was furious! Although three of the traitorous guards had been captured and three others killed, Jester had not been sighted. The gypsy camp was abandoned, and the king had sent riders out to locate the jester's friends. When the travelers were found, the jester was not there, and they claimed they had no knowledge of his whereabouts. They were heading south, to go to Rosenburg where they would spend the winter. In a fit of rage, King Maslen ordered that they all be slain.

~ * ~

The king entered Jenna's sitting room. Standing, she dropped him a curtsy and he told her to sit.

To Jenna's surprise, Sidra came into the chamber, seating herself in a chair the king pointed toward. Daniel and Doctor Arnold entered, followed by Captain Paulas and, finally, Captain Myres helped by a guard on either side of him entered the chamber. At the king's signal, Joyce and Vicky left the room followed by the guards.

"Jennava Charlotte Gifford," King Maslen said in a serious tone, "You shall no longer forever be known by that name, but according to your choice to rescue me, to save me from certain death, you shall hereafter forever be known as the sister of King Maslen of Aponia, Princess Charlotte." He placed a title deed in front of her and said, "Half the kingdom of Aponia belongs to Princess Charlotte, this is the title deed. According to right, you shall choose one castle in which to reside and a palace shall be built for you in the place of your choice, to be used at your will. You shall, of right, own and command half the royal army. Believing that you will do what is right for the throne and the kingdom, you shall own half the kingdom's treasures and control half of the funds in the royal treasury."

Jenna's eyes widened in amazement—never was she prepared for such a reward! Words fled from her, and she could not imagine how to answer.

King Maslen placed another scroll in front of her and unrolled it, saying, "This is the deed you must sign to agree to receive the name change; it states that your twentieth birthday is tomorrow, the tenth of October... the only other condition being that ownership of half the kingdom may be forfeited if for any reason you choose to live elsewhere than in Aponia. In that case, your half shall revert to me. If you do not want to accept half my kingdom, you are free to leave, to return to Cyran or to any other place you choose... but still, I should like to have it known in Aponia and to the world, that you are Princess Charlotte, my sister... and you shall be given reward enough to purchase a castle in any kingdom, with enough funds to maintain it for the rest of your life..." his eyes were upon Jenna's pale face as he added, "perhaps you need an hour or two to consider."

Silence took over the rose-filled chamber. Sidra's eyes narrowed— she wished Jenna to refuse. Then she remembered Maslen's reminder that she owed her life to this girl.

Jenna found her voice and said, "I'm deeply honored, Your Majesty... it is indeed a great honor... and, you are very kind to grant me my freedom... to give me the right to choose... I know it can't have been easy for you to decide to allow me to leave..." she faltered and everyone in the chamber believed she would reject King Maslen's offer.

It was as if Jenna's whole life flashed before her... her childhood, her teen years, Kind Heart, Gifford Castle... King Cyranius and his declared torment... Here she was now, with this incredible opportunity to be a princess, never to have to dress in men's leather clothes and to be protected rather than having to protect.

"I accept half your kingdom, Your Majesty, and I shall do all in my power to live up to your expectations as a princess of your realm. As for your army, I should like you to command it all. If, or when I need to use any of the military, I shall discuss it with you first." Taking up the quill, she signed the document. A wide smile broke out on the king's face.

"My sister," he said, "You are my chosen sister." Very seriously, he kissed her on each cheek. Turning to those in the chamber, he reminded them, "As stated before you entered this chamber, you are all sworn to secrecy in this matter. The deed recording Princess Charlotte's previous identity shall be kept locked in the royal vault with other confidential kingdom documents.

The next day, a great celebration took place in the Royal Castle. Princess Charlotte, King Maslen's one and only sister was twenty years old. This was her presentation banquet. It was reported that, because of her wealth and beauty, the princess had been kept out of the public eye. Now it was time for her to rule in Aponia in her own right. News of her existence spread quickly and the speculation was that she was the last of three princesses born to Maslen's mother, all reported to having died soon after birth.

Jenna decided not to think about her first twentieth birthday celebration—it had ended in such disaster. But now, she was Princess Charlotte of Aponia, and half of this kingdom belonged to her. She decided to forget her past and enjoy the glory that was hers now.

Tomorrow, King Maslen would marry Sidra who would be renamed 'Masla' and she would be crowned queen of Aponia after the wedding. Her title was in name only, Queen Masla would not rule. Although the ceremony would be private, the coronation celebration would last a week.

Then the royals would travel to the Winter Palace where they would reside for four months. Because King Maslen wanted his child to be born in the Capital, they would travel back two months before the birth.

When the celebrations were over, the king's cavalcade accompanied King Maslen, Queen Masla, Princess Charlotte and the court to the south of the country to the glory and warmth of the Winter Palace. All along the way, having been forewarned, villagers, farmers and gentry lined the way to cheer and throw flowers. Princess Charlotte herself threw the smallest denomination of coins—mites to the poor, the peasants and the children. Never had this been done before in Aponia; many children who received the mites had never before owned one. They stared in awe at the small coin with the image of King Maslen impressed on one side, then shouted their thanks and praises to the beautiful princess and to their king.

Back in Cyran it was reported to King Cyranius that King Maslen had married Lady Jennava. Witnesses had seen the pale-faced lady wearing a headdress that covered her hair; then, after the marriage, she had been crowned as 'Queen Masla' of Aponia. Prince Edward wept declaring that his heart was broken forever, but King Cyranius did not speak, it was as if this news meant nothing to him but that the matter was finished forever. She would never return to Cyran, they would never see her again, everyone believed.

Jenna loved the Winter Palace so much that she decided to have a similar palace built for herself; perhaps a little smaller, but to the south-west, instead of the south-east of the country. She would reside there in winter and when the weather was fine, she could ride to the king's palace to visit. To Jenna's surprise, King Maslen supported everything she wanted to do and he offered unlimited manpower and funds. He commanded that preparations be made for the building of Princess Charlotte's palace.

"You really do not understand what half my kingdom is worth," he said, smiling at her, "if you lived to be five hundred years old, you could not use up half my kingdom!"

Wishing not to take over a castle in which someone else already resided, Jenna studied the positions of three castles reported to be uninhabited. To her surprise, one seemed located near the place where Sidra and she had enjoyed the thermal pool.

"How is it that I did not see this castle when I rode through the woods there, Maslen?" she asked. Together they examined a map of the area.

"That castle has been uninhabited for over fifty years. The owner was condemned and executed by my father for insurrection against the throne. Because of the crime and the fact that there were no heirs, the castle was vacated and left empty. It'll be overgrown. But I'd like to see this thermal pool you speak of... perhaps it's just over the ridge that's marked here." He pointed his forefinger to a spot on the map.

"Let's go there, before the snows come," Jenna said enthusiastically; "And if it's inhabitable enough, I'll stay there for the winter."

"All right!" the king agreed, "We'll go tomorrow... that is, if you think you can ride... with your arm..."

"Of course... I could ride with both arms tied behind my back," she said with a lilt in her voice. She wanted more than anything else to ride free, to enter the woods and smell the familiar odors of nature.

To the queen's chagrin, the pair rose before sunrise the next morning. Together the king and his new sister rode to inspect the abandoned castle. The day following her husband's departure, Queen Masla ordered a carriage and commissioned an escort to ride with her. She was not going to miss out on a soak in that wonderful hot pool. The thought of her husband and his new sister being together was vexatious. Doctor Arnold said that he would accompany her, knowing that the king would expect this.

~ * ~

The castle was, at first, difficult to find, then laborious to enter. Having predetermined that this would be the case, Maslen had commanded soldiers to bring tools, slashers, axes, saws and spades, to clear the way. It took two days to lay open the path to the castle doors and to unblock them for entry into the huge courtyard. By this time, the queen had joined them and was full of complaints.

King Maslen sent men back for more supplies, food, bedding, furniture and furnishings.

However, the interior of the castle was in good repair—strong covers had been placed over furniture. Rugs and mats had been rolled up and stored safely in an enclosed room.

The king sent for more servants and slaves; he was determined to help his new sister in her venture to make an identity of her own. Maslen knew that his wife would not abide Jenna in the same place; the queen needed the king to herself.

Dispatches arrived for the king and he sent captains out with orders to take care of the kingdom needs.

While the castle was swept, scoured, scrubbed and refurbished, King Maslen walked with Jenna, the doctor, and chosen members of the court to visit the thermal pool. Masla rode in the sedan chair that Doctor Arnold had commanded to be brought.

To everyone's surprise, the pool was only four hundred yards from the castle, after descending a small ridge. The king commanded that a path be cut through the forest, over the ridge and down to the pool.

"Come in and bathe with us," the king called to Doctor Arnold as he sat among the dry seeded grass at the edge of the pool, soaking his naked feet, watching enviously. Peeling off his outer clothing, the doctor obeyed the king without hesitation. The air was chill and all in the group stayed in the water for two hours. Guards, lining the small clearing, looked on with great envy.

The cottage was used as a dressing room and King Maslen declared, "This is choice, we should extend this hut—or shall we tear it down and build a pavilion?"

"We should commission it right away," Masla agreed.

Jenna nodded her approval, saying, "Let's have a pavilion, with a pantry and a comfortable sitting room with a fireplace for the winter time."

"We'll begin tomorrow," the king said. He sent to the capital for slabs of white marble and other materials. The king had trees felled and together with Jenna, they arranged tree branches on the ground, marking gardens to be planted around the pavilion and the pool.

In a fit of great pleasure, the king spoke to the guards, saying, "After you've escorted us back to Princess Charlotte's castle, you may return and bathe here... mind, just this once... we won't have you slacking at your watch."

That night Jenna slept in her own bedchamber in her own castle, and she felt she lived in a fairy-tale dream. *This is my castle,* she told herself. *The king and queen of Aponia are sleeping in my guest chambers.*

Suddenly, she remembered a past prayer; she had asked that God use her mistakes for good.

Thank You God for reminding me. Help me to use this wonderful castle and resources, my position, for others... and as she lay there, an idea sprang into her fertile, Kind Heart mind.

Forty-seven

Jenna delighted herself in decorating her castle with the most colorful furnishings available. She explored the massive building with great fervor, tapping and banging the walls to discover any secrets. Not a foreign sound came to her ears and she would have abandoned it, but her determination and diligence kept her working until every wall had been examined. She then began on the floor. Her patience was rewarded.

In the great hall, behind a dais where once may have sat a judgment seat, one large marble slab in the floor sounded different from the others.

"It's hollow, there's a space beneath," she told her helpers. "Let's see if we can find a trigger somewhere."

When no secret release was discovered, Jenna commanded that the stone be pried and lifted. Under the square was a steep step-well.

"Fetch torches and we'll go down there."

A guard carried a torch down to light the way for Jenna to follow. Several workers stepped down into the chamber behind Jenna, all carrying torches. Soon the steps were filled with guards—no one wanted to miss out on this great discovery.

Exclamations sounded out, they had found the castle treasury. Opening a chest, Jenna saw gold coins glinting in the light of the torches. Another chest held scrolls and Jenna guessed that these would show plans of the castle.

"There's another opening over here, Princess," a servant called.

"We'll have a look in a moment," Jenna said. Looking up at the captain of her guards perched on the steps, she saw his eyes glittering with wonder. "My brother will want to know of this, Captain Sebastian, send a messenger and bring back an escort. These treasures must be conveyed to the Royal Treasury in the Capital."

She turned and, taking a torch, she stepped under the low arch into a well-paved tunnel. The camber sloped downwards and, after just a few feet, there was a steep step down, just one. A few more feet and there was another, so it continued. The tunnel ended at a dead-end.

After banging and tapping and nothing being revealed, Jenna said, "We'll return to the chamber and examine the scrolls."

By the time King Maslen arrived, Jenna had found the trigger to open the wall. To her express joy she found it entered a small assembly of caves, one of which led into the hot pool under the waterfall. The king was delighted with Jenna's discoveries.

"Not only have you added to our treasures, but you've found a wonder in our kingdom which can't be replaced."

Jenna's eyes darkened.

"What then?" Maslen asked.

"The top of the ridge is our border with Cyran, Maslen."

"What? Are you saying that Cyranius owns the hot pool?"

"My father built the hut on the Cyraniun side of the border; yes, if the ridge is the border, the pool does not belong to us."

The king stared at Jenna long and hard. He strove not to show his thoughts on his face. She had said 'us,' and Maslen knew in that moment, he had won. Princess Charlotte belonged to him, to Aponia, forever.

"We'll buy it off him, if we have to," Maslen growled.

"Not until we have to," Jenna enjoined. "Let's wait until he discovers it... he's never shown any interest in this area before... it's really quite overgrown from the Cyraniun side... anyway, Maslen, I want to move on from here. I want to open the other two uninhabited castles before the snows are too heavy; I want them to be winter homes for homeless children... a place where they can learn useful skills."

"What about *this* castle?" he asked.

"When the others are ready, I'll return here for the rest of the winter..." she said, and noting the glint in his eyes, she asked, "or, did you wish to reside here... with Masla?" she knew the answer even as she spoke and said quickly, "Do it, Maslen; it would be great to walk through the tunnel, out of the grasp of the cold, and bathe every day. Masla can go in the sedan-chair."

He grinned and nodded, knowing that she had learned very quickly to read his mood. "Masla would like that," he said. But everyone in the chamber knew that it was he who would like it. This place was a winter paradise.

"What have you named your castle?" he asked.

"I haven't thought of a name," she said, wondering what may suit such a place.

"Therefore," the king said, "We shall call it 'Charlotte.' It shall be registered, 'Charlotte Castle'."

Over the next two weeks, Jenna, with an extensive escort commissioned by Maslen, visited the other two castles, beginning at the one furthest to the north. This one was surrounded by a moat and was in a state of much disrepair. Three small lakes could be viewed from the castle windows and balconies. There was no part of the castle that did not have a view of a lake.

"It will take at least a year to rebuild and refurbish it," her adviser told her.

"See it started then, right away and have it enclosed from the weather before the heavy snows," she commanded.

"That's only about six or seven weeks away," he said, "And there'll likely be much rain and hail before then."

"Then treble the workers," Jenna said, "I want it enclosed before winter... I want double shutters fixed at every window, so that the heat from the fireplaces will stay within the walls... then the work on the interior can be done. I want it inhabitable before next winter." The treasury of this castle was unlocked and empty. Plans and charts of the castle revealed no hidden passageways.

~ * ~

The other castle was a little south of the capital, and again, hidden in a huge forest. Like Charlotte Castle, it was well preserved and had a treasury with a hoard of treasures. Jenna again informed the king and had the treasures sent to the Capital. Charts and plans showed a labyrinth of passages beneath the castle. All led to extended escape routes in the case of invasion.

More troops arrived, commissioned by King Maslen, and Jenna wondered why he felt the need to have so many around her. That they came and went at their commander's bidding did not bother her, but that the king wanted twice-daily reports as to her whereabouts and well-being, seemed to Jenna, to be unnecessary. She wondered if Maslen did not fully trust her.

Realizing that she would not be entirely welcome at her own castle, Jenna tried to think of some part of the decorating that she could do that would take up her time. After entering each of the castle chambers, she returned to the capital and purchased paint, plaster and embellishing materials. Two covered carts were commissioned to transport the materials to the castle. She had discovered this one had a name—it was Greenwood Castle. Because she liked the name, she decided to keep it. The other one in the north she had called Lakelands.

King Maslen sent a message urging her to return to Charlotte Castle, but Jenna replied that she was too busy.

Having commanded the ceilings to be plastered, Jenna herself helped build the platforms for the task. After the plaster had set, she commissioned the ceiling to be painted. The one in the great hall was done with the help of her own hand, in a shade of grass green. Then, because this had taken only a day, Jenna decided to make the ceiling attractive to children. Servants stood by to send the color she required up on pulleys, to clean and change the brushes she used and to make sure she had fluid to drink.

Although Jenna was very tired, she viewed her day's work with great satisfaction. The ceiling in the great hall at Greenwood Castle was like a forest of trees. The servants and guards applauded her. They thought she had finished.

Jenna worked on the forest ceiling for a week more. She painted larger than life sized deer in the woods, squirrels, rabbits, owls and birds of every breed and color. The ceiling came alive. Neglecting their duties, men and women came to watch, returning again and again to see the magic appear above the princess's brush.

At the end of each day, Jenna's arms, shoulders and back ached; she felt exhausted. Rising to the topmost battlement, she stayed until the taste of paint had gone from her throat, yet the next day at sunrise, she was back up on the topmost scaffolding ready to add to the amazing mural.

Having received word from Lakelands Castle that the great hall ceiling had been plastered and painted in blue, as she had commanded, Jenna rode north to create a masterpiece there. The ride was a profitable time imagining what she would paint on the ceiling.

King Maslen, having heard of Jenna's painting at Greenwood, rode there to view it for himself. He could not believe that his chosen sister had done this all with her own hand. Although the air was icy and snow lay on the roads, he rode north to Lakelands to watch her at work.

Jenna painted land on the blue background; she then painted a large barge-like boat in the middle of the ceiling. It was Noah's Ark. On the land around the ark, she painted animals and birds, two of each kind—zebras, elephants, tigers, lions, sheep, giraffes, cattle, pigs, small and large animals, horses, and birds of the air in the blue around the edges of the chamber. When there were no spaces left on the ceiling, Jenna had the walls plastered and painted birds then lower down, more animals all the way down the walls.

King Maslen watched in wonder as Jenna painted an eagle in flight on the wall. She painted it in a flash, having loaded the brush with more than one color, she made the feathers of the open wings in one sweeping movement.

Jenna had not noticed the king's entrance, so intent was she on her work. The animals had appeared from the tip of her brush like magic, and because she had commanded three servants to hold the brushes ready for her with the paint also at the ready, she was able to move with great speed.

The king did not speak until she had finished for the day; it was dark outside and she had been working by the light of several torches held in the hands of willing servants.

"Maslen!" Jenna exclaimed, brushing a rebel strand of curling hair back from her forehead with the back of her hand. "How long have you been here?" She stepped to him, and lifted her face for him to kiss her cheeks.

"I've been watching... for a while," he said, not wanting to tell her he'd been there over half an hour. "It's good to greet you in such good health. I see you're almost finished here... you must come down to Charlotte and do some art work there."

"Do you think so?" she asked, wishing now that she could bathe in the hot pool. "But Masla..."

"Masla just said to me, the other day, she misses you."

"Really?" Jenna asked, then, looking up at the eagle, she questioned, "What do you think of it?" her voice was eager, seeking his approval.

"I... I... it's... beyond words..." he began, lifting his head to sweep his eyes across the panorama.

"You don't like it," she said sadly.

"What? How can you think that? You must know it's amazing. It's such a wonder, a marvel, that words can't describe it, Charlotte! Your touch, the reality of it... it's beyond words, beyond price, almost beyond belief!"

Jenna's face broke into a wide smile.

"You'll come to Charlotte and paint a mural in our great hall?" he asked, his voice eager.

"Yes, I'll be finished tomorrow, then I'll come and do one at Charlotte."

The king again kissed her cheeks, saying, "We missed you, it'll be good to have you back there."

~ * ~

Jenna gave more time to planning and painting the combined mural in the large great hall at Charlotte. She divided the ceiling into four and painted four different scenes, all extending down the walls to floor level. One depicted the green pastures of Psalm twenty-three, with the still waters, the sheep, and the shepherd. In the background trees, lurked wolves with greedy amber eyes. Another picture, merging from the forest of the first, showed David approaching Goliath with armies from each side watching. The third was a mural of Jesus' birth, with shepherds, angels and the open manger itself with the mother, baby, father and animals, all larger than life, so that from the floor they appeared to be life-sized.

The fourth was a creation scene, again with birds and animals, and because she had painted them before, around the ark, this was completed in the fastest time. Using the folk-art method of painting that Jenna had seen villagers use, she painted large flowers all around the base of the mural. Every kind of foliage and flower was depicted and people 'oohed' and aahed' as they watched.

The pavilion was now enclosed and Jenna painted the ceiling in the large dining-chamber with an enlargement of the creation scene in the great hall of Charlotte Castle. She took her time with it, wanting to keep out of the queen's way. Especially enjoying painting flowers, Jenna created new colors with unusual combinations.

Masla had been congenial toward Jenna, and seemingly enjoyed her company, but Jenna remembered a saying her father had taught her, 'Familiarity breeds contempt', so she shortened the time she spent in the queen's presence, seeking to busy herself with other tasks.

Arranging and engaging tutors for skills to be taught to the kingdom's homeless children took much of Jenna's time. Young men flocked to Charlotte Castle in the hope of finding employment in one of the princess's castles.

To Jenna's disconcert, Maslen took an interest in the newcomers and demanded that he have them screened before they be allowed an audience with her. A great argument ensued.

"You don't believe that I have the intelligence to engage the right tutors for the children, do you!" she demanded heatedly.

"You may have the final say," he said, "but I'm not budging on this—why, any creep could walk in here, and—"

"What? Since when did you determine that I couldn't look after myself?"

"Since you were... revealed... as Princess Charlotte, that's when. This is one matter in which I'm sitting on my throne about!"

"Well then, you may as well complete the recruitment for me. Engage whom you want, and I will get on with other important matters."

Maslen smirked at this and Jenna knew he was pleased to have won. Whatever the battle was about, Jenna had no idea. It did occur to her that there was some ulterior reason for the king's scrutiny. But she shrugged it off; she was too busy to dwell on it.

Every evening, Jenna, wearing a swimming outfit she herself designed after the style of her gym costume, swam in the thermal pool with the increasing group of young ladies who attended her. King Maslen had commissioned daughters of the nobility, selected from all over Aponia, to be ladies-in-waiting for both his wife and his sister. Masla chose the more sophisticated young ladies and Jenna was content with those not chosen by the queen.

A ring of guards stood at the pool edge, their faces and spears pointing away from the water. They had been warned upon the threat of death not to look on the ladies as they bathed. Jenna wondered at the great security, but as she had never been a princess before, she accepted it as being normal.

King Maslen set up a throne on the dais in the great hall and he judged the kingdom matters from there. Due to the increasing blizzard-like weather outside, few folk came before him for adjudication. Only the more important matters that could not wait were presented for his verdict.

That military that came and went in large numbers did not cause Jenna any disconcert. Guards were everywhere.

Jenna watched Masla's size increasing with satisfaction; the queen seemed to be keeping excellent health now, and her whining and complaining only reinforced to everyone that she was maintaining her known disposition. That King Maslen would have a child in the spring seemed more certain than ever.

As the weather declined after mid-winter, Jenna spent her mornings swimming outside in the warm but snow-drenched pool, while Masla, who enjoyed the heat of the water inside the cave, soaked there. At other times Jenna could be found in the library, reading one of the many books that King Maslen had ordered to be brought from the Winter Palace. Everyone agreed that both Charlotte Castle and its adjoining thermal pond were a winter dreamland.

One very cold day, the womenfolk were denied their trip to the pool. Jenna thought it was because it was so very cold. She retired to the library.

A guard burst into the small chamber. "Princess Charlotte, the king requires you in the great hall."

From his urgent tone, Jenna wondered if something had happened to Masla. Then she remembered it was the throne room she was required to attend... what could be wrong? The king had never before summoned her there.

Announced, "Princess Charlotte, sister of the King of Aponia," Jenna walked along the purple carpet. She mused as she walked, *I wish it was green carpet, it would complement my mural—this purple looks out of place.*

A group of four men stood before King Maslen. They parted and stood, two on either side of the carpet, as Jenna approached. Her heart jumped as she recognized all four as they raised their heads to stare at her, after bowing. Three stared in unveiled astonishment, while the eldest looked on without a hint of his crushing bewilderment.

Jenna wore her now longer than shoulder-length auburn hair loose and it framed her lovely face like a surround of sunrise cloud, making her porcelain-like skin seem as translucent as the snow outside on the ground. She was almost a year older, but to the men had only changed to be more beautiful. The elegant purple dress she wore made her look very regal and very much a princess. Two young ladies followed her.

"Sister dear, I would like you to meet Sir Lowell, Commander of Kingdom Security in Cyran, Major Frayne, Captain Derrick and Captain Philippe. They have a battalion of soldiers from Cyran, just over the ridge, right outside our pavilion."

"Oh," Jenna replied, unable to focus on the king's words. It was like being doused with icy water, to see these men again. She felt she viewed ghosts from a distant past life.

Collecting his thoughts more rapidly than the others, Sir Lowell turned back to the king, repeating his previous words, "The top of the ridge is the border between our two kingdoms, Your Majesty, and therefore we claim the pavilion and the land around it to the top of the ridge as belonging to Cyran. You trespassed on our property when you built the pavilion."

"Oh," Jenna said, her eyes taking in the lighter color of his hair. The golden-blond had turned white, and he looked much older than she remembered.

"Perhaps, Sister, we should offer to lease the pavilion and the land around it." King Maslen felt his heart sink; it dawned on him that these men recognized his chosen sister. He had not imagined this scenario or he would not have summoned her to stand before them. He wondered how many of them knew her and calculated that all three captains did; he was unsure about Sir Lowell.

Jenna gained her self-control, and answered, "It would be better if we could purchase it from Cyran, Brother." Turning to Sir Lowell, she said, "We would be prepared to pay whatever your king asks... the pavilion and the land around it are important to us... perhaps, perhaps you could return to Cyran and ask your king to put a price on it."

"How much land would you require... to go along with the pavilion?" Sir Lowell asked, his eyes drinking in her whole being, her disposition, her voice, those things he remembered and recognized. *Being a princess suits her,* he decided, then he felt guilt at his approval of her in this enemy kingdom.

Jenna replied, "There's a strip of land within the Cyran border that is named 'The Bad Lands'. It's the forest area at the eastern edge of what you call, 'The King's Land.' We'd like the purchase to include this strip, with its forests—"

"That would give Aponia a border advantage."

"Not if the border were taken to a valley, rather than a ridge," Jenna offered, "Perhaps the valley could even be deemed as 'no man's land'. That way, there'd be an advantage for both kingdoms, with a high ridge each. We'll pay you well for the land deemed 'no man's'."

"I'd have to view the terrain on a map, but you, Princess, seem to know the area... very well."

"I've pondered the matter with a map in front of me," Jenna said, knowing she had to avoid the trap he was setting, to get her to admit she had ridden through the area. "I already have a map on which I drew a line, to mark where I felt the border would best be resituated."

Sir Lowell looked back to the king, asking, "Are you favorable to resetting your boundary, Sire... at a worthwhile price?" His raised eyebrows told everyone that the price would be very high.

The king waved his hand as he answered, "It's Princess Charlotte's decision, she'll pay Cyran for the land if she wants it and it will belong to her."

"Your sister?" Captain Philippe could keep quiet no longer. "But where will she find such a payment?"

King Maslen gave the four most important men of the kingdom of Cyran, save the king and the prince, the most amazing news they had ever heard, "Princess Charlotte owns half of Aponia; therefore it's entirely her decision as to what she buys or what she builds."

"Half... half your kingdom?" Sir Lowell's mouth dropped open. He lost control of his thoughts for a few seconds as his mind sought to consider all possibilities. *Did Lady Jennava lose her memory; does she know who she was? Or is the title 'sister' just a farce? Is she... his mistress, or his wife? What's going on here? How can a citizen of Cyran own half the kingdom of Aponia?*

"Half the lands, half the castles, half the treasures and half the treasury..." King Maslen said with a slight grin on his face, "and half of my army is hers to command if she chooses," he added. Had he really given this girl all that? Would he be the laughing stock of all Europe? Could it become rumored that his sister was in fact, Lady Jennava? He hoped not. Then he wondered if it mattered if everyone knew? *It does not matter,* he told himself.

"You... Your Highness, Princess Charlotte, you reign... with... your brother?" Captain Derrick asked, his voice filled with wonder.

"No," she answered, smiling, "My brother is so very good at that so there's no need for me to sit on a throne; I have much more relaxing things to do with my time..." she realized they had moved far from the subject of the land. "Perhaps... as you are already here, perhaps you would like to dine with us, in our great hall... and, yes, we'll send food down to the pavilion for your men." Turning to the king, she asked sweetly, "You said there were troops at the pavilion, didn't you, Brother?"

"Yes... yes. We'll send food and they can bunk down in the pavilion for the night... bathe in our pool... their pool." King Maslen stroked his beard, his mind moving too fast for him to keep up with it. An agreement with Cyran? Could such a thing be possible? Yes, an alliance may solve his most agonizing problems.

"If... if we could have your marked-out map, Princess Charlotte, we shall return to Cyran at first light, and we'll take your request to our king."

The troops in the pavilion had a luxurious soak, a great feast, and all eyes looked upon the mural on the ceiling and walls with great wonder. Those with young children wished they could bring them here to behold the marvel of it.

The four men dined at the king's table with the king and queen of Aponia and the beautiful princess, Charlotte. They recognized Queen

Masla as the outlaw, Sidra, who was wanted in Cyran for a number of crimes.

That Lady Jennava, once Kind Heart, had somehow worked a miracle in this kingdom would be something to ponder and discuss on the way back to Gifford. What would their king surmise of this amazing turn of events?

Forty-eight

King Cyranius and Prince Edward had to hear the amazing story several times before they could begin to grasp the fact that Lady Jennava was alive and was not the one who had married King Maslen. That she was the king of Aponia's sister and owned half the kingdom seemed impossible.

"There's a certain likeness about the new queen's facial features and those of Lady Jennava... or, as they have named her, Princess Charlotte. It's possible that with less makeup on her face, that Sidra, or Masla, as they call her, could be taken for Charlotte... Jennava," Sir Lowell said.

Both Prince Edward and King Cyranius stared at the commander. Never had they seen him so troubled, so confused.

"I'm considering kingdom security of course, Sire," the commander explained, "just imagine... she was Kind Heart... she knows the lay of our lands, our forests, all of our kingdom—it's stamped on her memory, she knows it as well as Prince Edward knows the rooms and corridors in the palace."

"But that doesn't mean she'd betray us," Prince Edward said. His heart felt huge and he longed to see her again. His joy showed on his face; he was excited beyond his self-control.

The king's face, however, was unreadable—he did not allow the turmoil in his mind and heart to surface.

"King Maslen was not what I expected, at all," Captain Philippe said, "It was reported that he was vicious, perverse, pig-headed and he was not like that at all."

"He's changed," Sir Lowell said, "He's greatly changed. Perhaps it is that Princess Charlotte brought about the change... to give her half his kingdom, she must have done great deeds to have earned it."

"Perhaps the rumor was true then," Prince Edward began, then clamped his hand over his mouth.

"Rumor? What... rumor?" the king asked. He then remembered he had commanded his brother to 'voice no more rumors.' "Tell me... this... rumor," he ordered.

"It... it was voiced that... that King Maslen had been the target of assassins... that a... a woman in his royal castle foiled the plot and saved his life," Prince Edward said.

"Who else heard such a rumor?" the king asked, his eyes roving the circle of men. He realized that all were guilty. His eyes remained on his commander.

"It's my duty as Chief Commander of Kingdom Security, to examine all news from other kingdoms, Sire. However, I did not take much notice of that particular rumor, although I heard it from more than one source. The said encounter was reported to have happened before King Maslen married Queen Masla, whom at that stage was rumored to be Lady Jennava."

"Tell us what you heard about this... that encounter," the king urged.

"It was reported that guards were out scouring the capital city for a female prisoner who had escaped from the castle. Then, when the king entered his throne room in the early hours of the morning, an execution had been planned and a group of assassins awaited him. It appears that the certain prisoner they were all looking for saved the king from the assassins."

"How many assassins?" Prince Edward asked excitedly. He had no doubts that the rescuer of King Maslen was his favorite lady.

Sir Lowell shook his head and did not answer.

"How many?" King Cyranius asked, his voice eager. If it were one or two, then any warrior could have foiled them, but more? Only one such as Kind Heart could have won.

"I heard three different accounts of it, Sire, they ranged from eight men up to twenty."

"It had to be Kind Heart!" Prince Edward exclaimed, "It had to be Kind Heart!" He stared at his brother, now brooding, then looked at the other men, silent, staring at the king.

"Princess Charlotte must be Kind Heart!" Prince Edward fell silent then, thinking, and scheming.

"What shall we do about the offer to purchase the land?" Captain Derrick asked, breaking the silence. "Princess Charlotte told us to request you to set your price. She awaits our reply."

"I have to consider it... how we will reply," King Cyranius answered, adding, "We need time to consider."

Prince Edward did not need time to consider. As soon as he could, he sought Gavin and Kevin, and told them about Princess Charlotte. The boys agreed that they needed to see her themselves. That night, three of Kind Heart's horses, ridden by three boys, left Gifford Castle and headed north east through the forest, toward Aponia.

King Cyranius was just rising the next morning when Bonidore, followed by a guard, hurried to give him a small piece of parchment written upon by the prince. It read,

Brother Cy; I have to see her. Kevin and Gavin are going with me. Don't worry about us because I believe she could never harm us. And we have her horses, they'll know the way.

Your loving brother, Edward.

King Cyranius had no doubts as to where his brother had gone. "When did they leave?" he asked.

"We are having it checked, Sire," the guard answered.

"We'll go to the stables and find out," the king said grimly as he shrugged into warmer outer clothes.

That Prince Edward and the boys had ridden out before midnight was of grave concern to King Cyranius. It would be icy in the woods, freezing cold, and in the area named 'The Bad Lands' there were patches of deep swamp and quicksand.

Sir Lowell was mortified to hear of the Prince's venture. He barked out orders for a contingency to prepare to leave right away to follow the prince; then, in the possibility that the prince be lost in the forest, he commanded several more companies to ride out with them, prepared to spread out if the prince's trail was unable to be followed.

"I shall ride to this... this so-called Castle of Charlotte," the king said, his voice showing his disquiet.

"Charlotte Castle, Sire," Sir Lowell said, then, "it would be just as well."

"Why?" the king asked, having no idea what his commander was thinking.

"You shall confront the lady yourself, Sire. She was a landowner in Cyran, one who swore loyalty to this throne, to you here. How can she accept allegiance in the name of being a sister to another king?"

"She has Freedom of the Realm, Lowell, as both Kind Heart and as Lord Frances Gifford's heir, she owned the bequest, Freedom of the Realm. No one can tell her what to do or what not to do, any more than one may seek to command myself... or for that matter, Maslen.

"We shall go, Lowell, but we'll hold no animosity toward her. I believe we tread on quicksand if we show ourselves at all hostile. We've no reason to suspect any devious motive for her wanting the land, other than to enjoy these so-called thermal waters, have we?"

The question was unanswered and preparations were quickly made for their soon departure.

~ * ~

Prince Edward and his two cohorts arrived at the pavilion midmorning. Winter sun filtered through leafless branches, spilling light onto the white marble building ahead. It glowed like crystal in a matching setting, several inches of icy snow making the ground crunchy underfoot.

While they held their horses in check, viewing the goal ahead, a voice rang out through the crisp morning air.

"Halt! Who goes there?"

Within seconds Aponian guards, all pointing spears at them, surrounded the prince and his small escort. The numbers of spears left the three boys breathless.

"Dismount, now, nice and slow," the captain commanded.

"I am Prince Edward of Cyran, and I've come to visit Princess Charlotte."

Jenna was swimming vigorously, exercising in the outer pool, and heard the encounter. The prince's young voice echoed across the steaming waters and, even above the sound of the waterfall, she heard his claim. Swimming swiftly to the pool's edge, she called to the servant-women to bring her ample fur coat. She stepped from the pool into the coat and pulled the cover off her hair. Semi-damp curls fell all around her shoulders.

"Prince Edward?" she called. But the reply came in a volley of glad whinnies; three horses attempted uselessly to break away from the guards who held them.

"Bring the boys to me," she commanded when she realized that six guards had grasped the three, an arm each. "Release the prince."

"Which is the prince?" one guard asked unnecessarily. It was obvious; Gavin and Kevin had sandy-brown hair, clearly twins. The prince was younger but taller, dark-haired, a child of nobility and wearing the clothes to prove it.

"Prince Edward," she said with a glad note in her voice, "What a surprise."

"Princess Charlotte?" he asked, his eyes telling him that this was Lady Jennava, looking more beautiful than he remembered. The guards released him and stood, waiting for instructions from the princess.

"Perhaps we should go into the pavilion?" Jenna suggested, "near the fire. There's a pantry too, with food and drink... while you refresh yourselves, I shall dress." she turned to the captain, saying, "Perhaps you should inform King Maslen that we have the Crown Prince of Cyran here as our guest."

When King Maslen strode into the warmth of the dining-hall in the pavilion, it was to find his princess-sister laughing and chatting with Prince Edward as if he were an intimate friend. He recognized Edward by the drawing Jenna had done of him and it unnerved him to realize that this royal from her past could be so familiar with her now.

Jenna introduced the two, then, turning to Gavin and Kevin, said, "I hope these two boys weren't your only escort, Prince Edward?" She saw the answer upon their faces and said, "Your brother will send his army after you... did you tell him where you were going?"

"I... we left a note..." Prince Edward said, his face turning red.

"We wanted to see you," Gavin offered.

"We had to come," chimed Kevin.

"It was a bit thoughtless..." Edward said meekly.

"Are you telling us that... that... you... you boys... just rode over here?" King Maslen asked, shocked. He viewed Edward with kind eyes, wishing he had a son like him. Jenna did not miss one glimmer of his dark eyes.

Turning to the captain of her guard, Jenna commanded, "Have a quad leave now for Cyran. When you meet Cyraniun soldiers, inform them that Prince Edward has arrived safely at Charlotte Castle."

King Cyranius and his large escort met the four from Aponia just after noon. Sending over half the men back to Gifford, the king continued with the rest. They did not stop at the pavilion, but rode up and over the ridge right to Charlotte Castle. It was near sunset.

Jenna had almost completed taking Prince Edward on a tour of her castle when a herald announced that King Cyranius had arrived at the gate.

"Your brother came himself," Jenna said, feeling surprised, and looking forward to seeing him again with an intensity she could not understand. *It's been such a long time,* she told herself.

"Oh no," the prince said, "it'll be like facing a dragon."

"What do you mean?" Jenna asked, shocked at his tone and description.

"Ever since you left Cyran, my brother has been different. He... he's been getting worse, too..."

"So grumpy," Gavin offered.

"Worse than grumpy," Kevin said, "much worse... it gives everyone a bellyache, just to be around him."

"I'm sure that's not true," Jenna said lightly, "We'll go down and greet him."

King Cyranius's inner eyes lit up to behold Jenna and they lingered briefly, then as they fell on Prince Edward, they ignited with censure.

King Maslen stepped into the foyer, feeling the silence as if it were a solid thing.

"King Maslen, King of Aponia," the herald announced.

The two kings faced each other, each summing up the other. As if cued to do so, they inclined their heads towards each other in mock bows, more like excessive nods of the head.

"Perhaps, Cyranius of Cyran; we should converse!" It was not a question, but rather a statement. "We'll retire to my sanctum, just Cyranius and I."

Whenever King Maslen spoke of just himself, that is what was meant, but never before had Sir Lowell been excluded from his king's presence. However, as the king of Cyran moved to follow the king of Aponia, he waved his commander aside. The two kings went into the sanctum alone and the door was shut.

"I want to see the quadruple mural in your great hall again, Princess Charlotte," Edward said, his voice relieved. He turned in the direction of the great hall. Jenna obliged by following but wondered what the two kings would find to talk about that would be of interest to both.

Forty-nine

King Cyranius jumped within himself to feel King Maslen's arm fall across his back, grasping his shoulder in a brotherly touch.

"Your visit here is a provision of the Almighty," Maslen said, and indicated a seat. "I'd like to speak as friend to friend or brother to brother," he said, adding, "I know you may find my suggestion somewhat hard to understand, but hear me out."

~ * ~

The two kings remained in the sanctum past the usual time for dinner on these winter evenings.

Masla, in a fit of rage that her husband had abandoned their usual routine, commanded that food be brought to her quarters where she would dine with her ladies-in-waiting.

When, finally, the kings emerged, it was as if they had been friends forever. King Maslen escorted King Cyranius to sit beside him in the place Jenna usually occupied. The queen's place remained empty.

Prince Edward sat beside his brother and Jenna sat beside the young prince.

Jenna at first felt relieved that King Cyranius could not look at her from his position. Then, she felt sorry for she could not look at him.

Prince Edward was unusually quiet; he was pondering the fact that he had not been able to bring up the subject of Kind Heart to the princess. He longed to discuss the past with her, but every time he hinted to it, she talked of other things.

Music, as usual, was presented after the meal, followed by a few dramatic presentations—singing, and a mock sword-fight.

Everything seemed as normal but Jenna knew that it was very different. Besides Sir Lowell and Bonidore, captains from the Cyraniun army sat amongst the court for dinner. Eyes constantly darted to Jenna—eyes filled with wonder and admiration.

King Cyranius, Prince Edward, Sir Lowell, captains and chosen guards were escorted to guest quarters.

As Jenna fell asleep that night, she found it difficult to believe that King Cyranius was truly in her castle. Secretly, she looked forward to seeing Cyranius again at breakfast. What she did not know was that King Maslen and King Cyranius continued their parley well into the early hours.

The next morning, Jenna entered the great hall to discover that King Maslen had invited the two Cyraniun royals to take breakfast with him. She wondered if Masla were there and if it would be rude to intrude. She decided against it and later learned that Masla had taken her breakfast in her own quarters.

Cyraniun soldiers seemed to be at every turn in the castle—they congregated to the great hall, where they waited for their king, drinking Aponian ale and making friendly conversation with their Aponian peers. It was a strange day, an unplanned, unannounced union.

Jenna retired to her sitting chamber, knowing that to go for a swim would be out of the question. She occupied herself in designing future murals. Her ladies talked quietly while doing embroidery.

Late in the afternoon, Jenna decided, *Enough is enough; if I'm Maslen's sister and own half of his kingdom, I should be allowed to be with them.*

Jenna was admitted into the chamber by the captain Maslen had delegated to her, Sebastian. She felt surprised to see him there, then glad; she should be welcome here if he was. This was the chamber she would have chosen as an office, but Maslen had claimed as his sanctum. Around a table sat Maslen, Cyranius and Edward with the Cyraniun captains standing behind them. Myres and Paulas stood behind their king and Frayne and Lowell were seated together. Sebastian returned to stand guard inside the closed door.

All eyes turned to look at Jenna and those seated stood as one. The silence and serious stares greeting Jenna made her feel out of place. There was no place for Jenna to sit, and none of those at the table moved aside.

"Sister, but what can I do for you?" Maslen asked.

"I thought I may join you, Brother," Jenna replied, and at the perplexed stare that followed, she asked, "Or perhaps you are not discussing anything I need to hear?" Her eyes dropped to the table top where a sheaf of maps, scrolls and parchment pieces lay beside an open volume of the Bible.

"Well, then," she said as the awkward silence continued, "I'll leave it to the capable menfolk." As Jenna turned she expected them to prevent her leaving and was surprised to exit through the door held open by Sebastian, who had the audacity to grin at her.

I feel humiliated, they're talking about me... I know they're discussing me! I hate it! Maslen hasn't given me half his kingdom; the title's not worth the paper it's written on. I should be in there, how dare they discuss me while I'm absent. Men! They think women are there to grovel when required and be disposed of at ones whim! I wish I could live somewhere else... perhaps I will... perhaps I'll go to Greenwood. As she walked she calmed a little, realizing that she would, eventually, learn what this meeting was about... she hoped that Cyranius would sell her the land.

She found her feet taking her to the queen's quarters. Masla could shed no light upon the discussions taking place in the king's sanctum.

"It's about you, Charlotte, no doubt. They all know who you are... you still look the same person you were in Cyran," she clamped her hand over her mouth, remembering that she had sworn an oath not to discuss or reveal her sister-in-law's previous identity. To cover her error in front of her ladies, she expressed sympathy for Jenna, saying, "Don't worry about the menfolk, we'll hear about it. It always comes out in due time and you can be sure Maslen is only thinking of your good, Charlotte. He has high regard for you. Actually, I'm glad you're his sister... I need to keep telling myself that you're not a rival, not at all. But Maslen cares a lot about you... and... and I admire you too."

Jenna could scarcely believe her ears.

"I'll not forget my first swim in the pool down there, Charlotte. You said we would be friends, and we are, aren't we?"

Before she could reply, Doctor Arnold was announced to the chamber. Jenna would have left, but Masla urged, "Stay, Charlotte, please stay."

Jenna did stay, and watched as the doctor felt for the baby across the large barrel of Masla's stomach.

"He's huge, isn't he?" Masla asked.

"Not that large, but he's doing fine," Arnold said, adding with a grin, "It's you who are huge, Your Majesty..." He stepped back as if avoiding her slapping him. To his surprise, she smiled at him.

Masla declared she would eat the evening meal in her private dining chamber and that her sister-in-law was invited to join her. Jenna agreed. Still feeling contrary towards Maslen, Jenna believed it would be better to be away from his presence. A pang of disappointment swirled in her heart as she realized she would not see Cyranius this evening. She wondered how long he would stay and hoped she would see him tomorrow.

After dinner, Masla urged, "Come, the babe is kicking like fury, come and feel his feet."

Jenna gingerly placed her hand in Masla's and found it guided to the top of her stomach. Her eyes widened in wonder. To feel a baby's kick, before it was born!

"It's the kick of the next king of Aponia," Masla said and no one dared argue with her. "Maslen has a name for him, Charlotte. See if you can guess."

"Maslen the second, I'm sure," Jenna replied, smiling.

"No, try again."

Jenna closed her eyes, trying to imagine what Maslen would call his son, if it weren't his own name. "He'll want his son to have a name of his own, and it will be very grand, unusual... princely and kingly."

"Oh, don't!" Masla said, "You'll guess!"

"No, I'll never guess," Jenna said, and laughed. She took a large dried fig and bit half of it, chewing on it, thinking, *this is fun. Masla's behaving just like a sister*. She said, "I have to give in, I'll never guess. Do tell me,"

"It's to be Horatius, Prince Horatius."

"Horatius. It's a mouthful!" She pushed the rest of the fig into her mouth and puffed out her cheeks.

They all laughed.

"I'll probably call him Harry," Masla said, smiling widely.

Then Jenna asked, "And if it's a girl? What shall her name be?"

Masla's face clouded, and she cried, "It's not a girl! It can't be a girl! Maslen will be furious if it's a girl."

"I shall pray it's a boy," Jenna said seriously, "I should have been a boy."

Masla shook her head, saying, "That's about the most stupid thing you have ever uttered, Charlotte! Just imagine! If you'd been a boy, none of us would be here. Charlotte Castle wouldn't even exist. Oh, I'll get a headache if I even consider it! Arnold won't let me have even a small drink! I think too many serious thoughts when I can't have my wine! I'm tired, can't we end the evening with a highlight, not a regret?"

Jenna smiled. Masla, indeed, was more rational without her wine! And her ladies had given her a pleasant evening, one she was sure she would never forget. Other than Judith, Jenna had never been close to another female. Rising, she kissed Masla, and said, "I love you, and I love your baby already. I shall pray, every day, for God's blessings to be upon you both."

Gripping Jenna's hands as if she would never let go, Masla said, "Thank you for that, Charlotte. I need all the prayer I can get. In spite of what Arnold claims, this child is large already, and I'm afraid of it. Promise me that you'll come when he's born, that you'll stay with me..."

"Will Maslen allow me to do that—to be with you?"

"He won't make that decision... I'll ask Arnold, rather, I'll tell Arnold that you have to be there!"

"I'll be there, if I'm allowed," Jenna promised.

~ * ~

Jenna slept badly; she dreamed of Cyranius all night. His eyes had been everywhere in her dream, eyes that accused her, eyes that spoke words of censure. She could not remember exactly what his eyes had said, but she felt she could only do wrong in his eyes... his reproachful, condemning eyes.

She descended to the great hall to learn that Maslen was taking his breakfast with his wife. She supposed that as neither Cyranius nor Edward were there, they slept late.

But just after sunrise, the Cyraniun king with his brother, commander, captains and guards, had taken their leave of the Aponian king and had left to ride back to Gifford.

Jenna ate breakfast with the waiting court. She would have descended to the tunnel to enjoy a morning swim, but guards standing by the dais barred her way.

"King Maslen commanded that no one be permitted to leave the castle," a guard told her.

In frustration, Jenna decided to go to the library—she remembered that Cyraniun soldiers would have slept in the pavilion, and assumed that was why Maslen had not allowed her to go to the pool to bathe.

She had not been in the library long before Maslen joined her. He entered alone and waved the women out, closing the door himself. They were alone.

"You knew that Cyranius and his brother returned to Cyran, before first light?" he asked.

"No; I assumed they were still here." Then she remembered, there had been no Cyraniun guards in the great hall for breakfast.

Remembering King Cyranius and his disconcertingly intense eyes, Jenna said, "It's just as well," then thought, *he unnerves me... I can't think clearly when he's near... I'm not thinking clearly today because I dreamed of his eyes...*

King Maslen said, "We have a deep concern... one that I shared with Cyranius... and one in which he is willing to give assistance... I did not tell you before, Charlotte, because I believed the problem would've been solved before now."

Jenna wondered, *what problem could possibly belong to the two kingdoms?*

"The Jester has been sending ridiculous threats... the first was a demand for a duel, just you and him. Then, when we thwarted his promised vengeance, he dictated that you be placed in his hands, given to him, or he would burn down the royal castle. He's had some fires started, but we set a curfew in the capital city and with extra troops have thwarted his resolve. I believe we drove him from the city in our extensive efforts to find him..."

Maslen digested Jenna's look of utter shock at this news and said, "Oh but there's more, much more, my dear... it's been my turn to protect you. Jester named our Winter Palace next and managed to kill four guards there... you didn't realize, but we moved here so that we could have the most number of guards around us both. We don't believe that Jester knew, not at first, that Kind Heart, Princess Charlotte and Jay were one and the same, but we feel from his last communication that he's discovered the truth." The king placed a scroll in front of Jenna.

She read:

Maslen, Masla, and Charlotte,

You still have not granted me the required duel I demanded! Your lives are all in danger at all times! I shall win in the end! How many children will have to die at Greenwood, or Lakelands, before you give me Kind Heart? Surely one so-called princess's life cannot be worth a king's, a queen's and countless children as well? Have the so-called Princess ride out from Charlotte, before sundown, Wednesday, or you shall not live long to regret it.

Jester

"He's insane!" Jenna exclaimed.

"I'm glad you recognize that, my dear. Of course he's insane. But being both deranged and a murderous mercenary, it is a dangerous combination. I should know, I hired him myself once. He's the best assassin left—"

"What support does he have?" Jenna asked.

"He's collected a small band of Knight Red's and K'nort's leftover hopefuls and it seems he's very selective and that makes him all the more formidable."

"Where would he get funds? Who would give him resources—weapons, horses?"

"There are always barons who believe they'd profit from one king less and, to my shame, rumors that you once were Kind Heart have not been quelled... therefore, some would wish to know that Kind Heart was gone forever... we suspect a couple of barons here, and one named Zerka, from Cyran, support the Jester, and, perhaps, there's some support from Rosenburg."

"And... Greenwood—the children?"

"We've recalled military from several provinces, and have sent them to both Greenwood and Lakelands... but we do not wish to deplete our protection here... it will be here that he'll be watching... he seeks blood... yours, and mine."

"You know I won't allow anything to happen to innocent children! Tomorrow? He'll be waiting to see if I leave here."

"I'd like you to go, my dear, first thing tomorrow morning—"

"To Greenwood?"

"Oh no! Not Greenwood. This is where Cyranius comes on the stage... you see, we want to make it look quite legitimate, as well as taking care of that land you wish to purchase... and Cyranius's guards can help with the routing of the Jester. You'll be so far away, Jester will be confused at first, then he'll follow."

Jenna frowned. Maslen was not making sense. He also had a gleam in his eye that she had never seen before now. She knew he was many steps ahead of her, and to think that Cyranius was involved as well, her frown deepened.

"Don't scowl so, my dear, it does not become you. Here, read this..." Maslen placed a scroll in front of her, saying, "One thousand acres will be yours... ours... if you do as Cyranius asks..."

Jenna read:

For legal title to the pocket of land, five miles by one mile, as marked upon the map, Princess Charlotte shall travel to Gifford Castle and shall paint two murals; one on the ceiling of the great hall, and another in a chosen chamber; after which she shall travel to the Royal Palace in the Capital City, where she shall paint a mural on the ceilings of three chosen chambers, including the chapel.

"I won't do it!" Jenna exclaimed.

"Why not?"

"I... I..." Jenna had no idea why she felt so contrary.

"Take your time, but tell me... why don't you want to return to Cyran?"

"You... you want me to go?"

"Answer my question, Charlotte, then I shall answer yours. Why don't you want to go back to Gifford?"

"Gifford is all right... but... it's him!"

"Him? Who?"

"Cyranius."

If Jenna had not been so intense with her thoughts of King Cyranius, she would have seen satisfaction cross Maslen's face. However, before she could recognize that she had given the answer he expected, he asked, "What has Cyranius done to you?"

"He's a woman-hater."

Maslen's eyebrows lifted and he smiled, saying, "If the idea bothers you that much, forget it; Cyranius quite liked it. You may not know, but he's been troubled over the years, by the jester who had his origins in Cyran." The king rose and began to walk away from her.

"He did?" She tried to remember if she'd heard of the jester and his exploits before coming to Aponia.

Turning back, Maslen said, "It was Jester who stole children to be slaves... and he masterminded Prince Edward's kidnapping... I had nothing to do with that. But I did employ him to discover where you'd hidden Anastasia, and he was very upset that he could not find her for me. He missed out on a large reward, so that's another reason for him to be angry with you. We'll just have to forget about owning the pool; I'll see if we can negotiate some kind of joint ownership..." he turned the door handle.

"Maslen! Come back, let's talk about it," Jenna called.

"What's there to talk about? You've decided not to go, haven't you?"

"I... well... tell me again... how many murals does he want?"

"Five, altogether," Maslen said. He stepped back.

"When... when would I have to go?"

"Jester will be watching... he'll want to see you gone tomorrow..."

"How can Jester be watching?"

"Not watching with his own eyes but he must have a spy or two here, in your castle. And... our men have reported strangers in the forest, some came right up behind the pavilion. Each time they sought to apprehend them, at least one guard was killed; and these are what were attached to the arrow or the dagger-handle."

Maslen unrolled a thick roll. A dozen small pieces of parchment were marked with a jester's face, with a twisted smile on it.

"I want no one to know, other than the two of us, that you'll ride to Cyran tomorrow... I told Cyranius that I believed you'd agree and he's having his men set traps everywhere for the jester. We'll have troops escort you and follow you... between myself and Cyranius, we'll catch him! Cyranius is going to have signs posted all over Cyran, as we did here in Aponia, with a large reward for the jester's head."

Jenna bowed her head, unable to imagine Maslen and Cyranius considering her existence of such importance. *I've been wrong about Maslen, he has been protecting me, not spying on me...*

"What? What displeases you?"

Looking up through misty eyes, Jenna replied, "I'm not displeased... but it's all so much trouble. Why don't you do as Jester asks?"

"Would you win?" he asked, throwing her off-balance.

"Perhaps... not... now," she replied, then remembered that her strength was building up from all the vigorous swimming she had been doing.

"I don't want to lose you," he said gruffly, asking, "You'll travel to Cyran?"

Jenna looked at his face and saw a boyish eagerness on it. Maslen was not planning something bizarre, he was genuinely seeking to rid the kingdom of this menace and she knew he wanted the land. His own life, and Masla's had been threatened.

"How much... how long... did you talk... about me?" Jenna queried, knowing she had to ask.

Maslen smiled his widest smile, saying, "It was *all* about you."

Jenna bowed her head again, feeling exposed.

"You'll go to Cyran?" he asked again.

Thinking of Gifford and its gymnasium, Jenna wondered if she trained for a week or two, could she face the jester? With her death, Jester would have what he wanted. Perhaps he would leave Maslen and Masla alone after that.

"Don't even think of it!" Maslen growled, having seen the indecision, the telltale twinges of her face.

"What?" Jenna asked, startled, realizing she had been silent too long.

"You know what you were thinking! You're not going to duel with him. Don't think I haven't considered it. We could have arranged the duel and had him killed before he got to you, but if it went wrong, he could use a poisoned dagger-tip and I'd never forgive myself. Jester is known for his grotesque presentations. You will not be his victim, not while I have breath!"

Jenna stared at him, surprised at his fervor.

"I'll not lose you, Charlotte, I'll never lose you!" He spoke with such force that Jenna started.

Then, he changed tone, and said, "I trust Cyranius to protect you. He has a long list of debts to repay Kind Heart."

Jenna swallowed, trying to imagine Cyranius thinking of her as a creditor. Before she knew what was happening, Maslen kissed her cheeks and said, "Make your packing discreet; take gowns as befits your princess state, not just your painting clothes. I'll have half a dozen saddlebags sent to your room. The team you used here to paint with shall follow you. Cyranius wants a welcome party, or something of that sort there first, to inform Jester that you are there and to draw him out. Then, when you're ready, he'll have scaffolding set up to suit and he'll make sure there are a variety of paint colors. You'll be ready to leave at sunrise?"

Jenna nodded, feeling a little numbed—it was happening too fast. Maslen was far ahead of her, and they both knew it.

"Cyranius will have a carriage waiting for you when you exit the forest. You'll be hailed as Princess Charlotte of Aponia and they'll announce you as First Princess of our Realm."

Fifty

The King and Queen of Aponia kissed Princess Charlotte farewell and watched as she rode out of the gate of her castle followed by an escort led by Captain Sebastian. She wore a blue velvet riding habit with a matching hooded double-lined cloak in case the weather turned inclement. The morning was crisp and clear. Icicles glistened in the rising sunlight, making the forest a winter wonderland. Soon, the thaw would come, and winter would morph into spring.

Jenna had chosen two of her ladies, Sara and Jane, who declared they were good riders to accompany her, and they were very excited at the great adventure, traveling into a foreign country.

Just as Maslen had stated, a carriage awaited Jenna on the road at the forest edge. She felt both relieved and disappointed that neither Cyranius nor Edward was there to meet her. Three captains she recognized waited for her and rode in front of the carriage. The Cyraniun escort rode behind, led by Derrick, Frayne and Sebastian.

The road wound through four villages, all of which had been alerted that Princess Charlotte of Aponia was traveling through them this day. People waited to hear from the watch that had been set up that the princess was approaching. Because there were no flowers to throw in the path of the carriage, people waved scarves, shawls, ribbons and shouted their cheers and notes of welcome. Jenna felt shy of the publicity but, with the curtain pulled back, she waved from the window.

"I saw her, Mommy; I saw her," a little girl cried in delight.

"She's wearing blue," another said in awe.

"She's real pretty!" a young boy exclaimed.

"She should be, she's a princess."

No one in Cyran could remember seeing a princess. For over a century, only boys had been born to the royal family.

~ * ~

Prince Edward paced from the great hall to the courtyard, then back again, impatient. King Cyranius remained in the office, busying himself with signing and sealing official documents. Fore riders had arrived with the news that Princess Charlotte was now traveling safely in the carriage and would not be long in arriving at Gifford. No sign had been seen of the jester, and those who knew about him felt thankful.

When Jenna stepped from the carriage in the courtyard, memories bombarded her—a deluge of pain and pleasure in a medley of both sorrow and joy. The grief of her past swept her, winning the battle over fluttering happiness, and tears threatened to flood her eyes. Gritting her teeth, she blinked a few times, commanding the tears to retreat. How could she cry now? Guards, soldiers and castle staff lined the area, watching and waiting. Sir Lowell and his wife gave her obeisance then, one on either side, they turned to escort her to their king.

Cyranius and Edward stood at the top of the steps, and as she moved across the courtyard towards them, they descended.

They bowed, she curtsied. King Cyranius then grasped her two hands and kissed her cheeks as Maslen had done. But Jenna had not been left breathless by Maslen. As color mounted in her cheeks, the king extended his arm to her. Placing her hand upon it, she allowed him to escort her up the steps and inside Gifford Castle. Prince Edward followed.

To her relief, the king escorted her to the guest quarters where, with her ladies, they could refresh themselves and change. However, he warned her, "A banquet is prepared for you, Princess, and invited guests are waiting as we speak."

Jenna did not keep them waiting long.

"King Cyranius, King of Cyran and Princess Charlotte, First Princess of Aponia," the herald announced as they entered the great hall.

King Cyranius drew Princess Charlotte along a reception line, introducing each person himself.

"Captain Duff."

The captain bowed and when Jenna extended her hand to him, he kissed it.

"Jennava, Aaron and David," the king continued.

The children stared at her in awe, and Jenna knew they had been told who she once was and cautioned not to speak. Seriously, she kissed each one, but did not trust herself to say a word. She wondered if Millie was in the castle.

"Doctor Breck."

There were tears on the doctor's cheeks as he kissed her hand.

"Doctor Breck's wife, Natalie."

The 'introductions' with their many memories went on and on, and Jenna felt strange when she arrived at her place at the heavily laden table. King Cyranius sat one side of her and Prince Edward the other. This was the welcoming banquet. Jenna felt it was supposed to be a 'welcoming home.' Instead of feeling happy, she felt torn. Though she was hungry, she found it difficult to concentrate on the food.

Charlotte Castle is more home to me than here... I truly like it there, more than any other place on earth. This place holds too many painful memories...

"Cy said that I may tell you there's to be a ball in your honor tonight. You... you missed... the other... your birthday..." Edward whispered while the desserts were being presented.

"A ball? Jenna paled. She was a princess who had never been to a ball; she did not know how to dance! She wanted to say that she had come here to paint, not to party. A ball meant that there would be invited guests.

"Guests will be arriving soon, on account of it being so cold... they are staying the night here at Gifford."

"It's not good weather for a ball," Jenna said lamely. This chamber was a little smoky from the huge fire, and Jenna knew it would be too warm in here to dance.

"We've a surprise for you," Edward whispered, then drew back as his brother caught his eye.

There was little time to spare after the meal—time only to bathe and change.

"I... I haven't brought a ballgown," Jenna said when she stepped back in the guest chamber.

"There's one here for you. King Maslen had it sent all the way from Aponia," one of the Cyraniun maids said, "and your bath is ready, Princess."

Jenna did not want to admit to her ladies that she could not dance. *I don't want to dance, either,* she told herself. *Men hold women too close for no purpose other than to seduce them...* She wished Cyranius would cancel the ball. Taking a small piece of parchment from the drawer of the small ornate table, she wrote a note to the king, using Kind Heart's code.

Deciphered, it read: 'Kind Heart never attended a ball, and was not taught to dance.' Jenna felt sure he would have learned the code, or he would have Duff decipher it for him. A maid took the parchment to a messenger for delivery to the king.

While Jenna relaxed in the heavily perfumed water in the bathtub, a reply arrived. It read, 'I shall come early to escort you to the ballroom,' and it was signed, 'Cyranius.' To the surprise of the ladies in the room, Jenna scrunched the note in her hand and threw it in the fire. The flames devoured it in their orange tongues, disgorging it as ash.

He still demanded the ball! Jenna felt contrary and wished she had never left Charlotte. She thought of the warm pool and smiled, thinking that it would soon be hers. *The sooner I do that painting, the better; I want to go home.*

Jenna dressed in the gorgeous powder-blue ballgown, shimmering with sequins of a deeper sky-blue and mauve. The ladies exclaimed their wonder at the beauty of the ballgown, but Jenna felt transported to another time—over a year ago. Cyranius had provided a gown then, it had been intended as a wedding dress. She shook off her feelings of moroseness, but wondered how she could endure this ball?

While Jenna's ladies dressed her hair, a knock came to the door and it was announced that King Cyranius and Prince Edward waited to have a short audience with Princess Charlotte before the ball.

Jenna hurriedly chose jewelry from the small selection in a leather case. Maslen had sent the case with an official courier who had followed. *He forgot nothing,* Jenna mused, *except that I can't dance and he didn't know about that.* The ladies placed the amethyst and diamond tiara on Jenna's head. It had matching necklace, earrings, and bracelet.

"You look like a queen!" Jane declared.

"No queen could ever be so beautiful!" Sara contended.

"You girls had better get ready, quickly," Jenna said as she moved to the door. She wondered what Cyranius would arrange with her not being able to dance? Perhaps she could sit and watch?

King Cyranius, having raised his forefinger twice to quiet his brother's fervent exclamations as to Princess Charlotte's breathtaking beauty and radiance, escorted her to a wide corridor in the castle. It was brightly lit with extra torches and large candles. He ordered the guards at one end to close the door and the others to wait around the corner. There were just the three of them in the corridor.

"If you watch us for a few moments, Princess Charlotte, I feel sure that you'll learn quickly."

The king and prince began to dance together, Edward taking the role of the lady. Jenna could not help herself: she laughed aloud, the sound of it echoing along the corridor.

King Cyranius dropped his hands to his sides and strode to her, saying, "Perhaps you have another suggestion, Princess. How were we to know that your father had neglected to educate you as a lady!"

Jenna stepped back as though stung, and the king regretted his words.

"I'd much rather have been forewarned. I could have taken lessons, or we could have planned some other event, not a *ball*." Jenna refused to look at him, and there was an awkward silence.

Turning to Edward, Jenna said, "Show me those steps, Prince Edward but do it slowly... no, I won't do it with you, just pretend you have a lady."

Edward danced along the corridor and as he returned, she stepped in line with him, following his path.

"What about other patterns?" she asked, still moving with the prince, "the ones where men and women form lines and somehow interact with each other..."

"They're easier to learn, one just follows what the others do," Edward volunteered, "I'll move into those and we sometimes take hands, like this..." and he took her hand and they moved in a full circle. "Then I bow, you curtsy, and we move back to our original place."

Jenna followed the prince, keeping almost in time with him. King Cyranius watched, now believing that Jenna had lied when she said she could not dance.

The young prince showed Jenna several other movements and interchanges, including heel-toe tapping movements.

"The one-on-one is most difficult," Edward said, "we should practice it again, but together. I took six months, once a week at dancing lessons, to learn to do it properly before I was allowed to attend a ball, but you're doing so well... let's dance together."

As Jenna stepped toward Edward, she found her hand taken and Cyranius drew her around to face him. Entwining his hand in hers, he captured her slim waist with his other hand, and began to dance. She followed his lead, blushing at the feel of his hand on her waist, but her past training and nimble feet did not permit her to stumble. Soon she kept perfect time with him. Her body relaxed and she dared to look up into his eyes. The anger she beheld caused her to stiffen.

"You've done this before, haven't you?" he questioned, accusing her.

Reading his tone, but deciding to ignore it, she replied, "No... it's easy; I had not realized it would be so easy."

He stopped abruptly and dropped his hands to his sides. Jenna retorted, "Just because you found it difficult, why should I? Anyway, I don't wish to dance. I came here to paint, not to be paraded at a ball. I shall return to my room and I shall not attend your ball!"

With a swish of her skirts, Jenna hurried along the corridor and around the corner.

"Guards!" Cyranius called, wanting them to stand in her way, to stop her leaving.

Two muffled cries came to his ears, two thuds, another thud and a deep curse.

When Cyranius and Edward rounded the corner, the three guards were collecting themselves up off the floor, and Princess Charlotte had disappeared.

"I... I... tripped," one sought to explain.

"One moment we stood in front of her and we did not touch her, and, she... she spun out of our way, but then, she... but... we tripped and fell," another stammered.

"She's gone."

While the king scowled in perplexity, the prince's eyes were filled with wonder and delight. *If only I could have seen her,* he thought.

~ * ~

Jenna swept into her chamber, not surprised to see that both Sara and Jane were dressed for the ball. She sat heavily on the chaise longue, her dress billowing out, covering the seat. Her anger with Cyranius was replaced by anger with herself. *How could I have been so undisciplined?* she asked, feeling both embarrassed and annoyed. *For years, I've been able to control my feelings and concentrate on the task at hand... but when he's there... he makes it impossible. And he'll come after me, or send a guard...*

"Is there something distressing you, Princess?" Sara asked, knowing there was.

"Is the king going to come for you... again?" Jane queried, knowing that something untoward had happened.

Jenna did not reply, but watched the door, waiting, wondering how she would react when it opened.

The door did open and Prince Edward was announced to the chamber. He stepped over to Jenna, who stood, and he placed a roll of parchment in her hands. His eyes twinkled. The parchment was sealed with the king's seal.

She read:

I apologize. Please forgive me. Not just for tonight, but also for other times I doubted you. I was wrong, I have been wrong, and I know that tonight I was wrong. For all the times I misinterpreted you, forgive me. For all the times I misunderstood you, forgive me. For the times I disbelieved you, forgive me. I shall never doubt you again.

And it was signed, simply, 'Cy.'

Jenna stepped to the fire and threw the paper into it. How long she stood, staring at the orange flames, she had no idea. No remembrance of any past apology from a man could she recollect. *It's very difficult to apologize... to admit you're wrong. It takes courage.*

"Princess, will you come to the ball?" Edward asked.

Turning, Jenna stepped to place her hand on his arm and together they walked out of the room to where the king waited. She could not meet his eyes, feeling that if she did, she would not be able to keep back the tears that threatened to come. *I can't understand myself,* she mused. *One moment I was happy when I danced with him, then I was angry, now I'm sad... close to tears... I hate this moodiness, I can't tolerate myself anymore...* She concentrated on the walk. Their way was lined with royal guards, all resplendent in their Cyraniun uniforms.

To Jenna's surprise and wonderment, King Cyranius and Prince Edward escorted her into a brightly lit tunnel, opening from the great hall. They descended steps, glowing from the radiance of hundreds of colored lanterns strung above them. Then, they looked down a wide marble stairway into a huge, sunken ballroom.

We discovered this... after you left..." Cyranius said, watching her eyes, "this is the first time we've used it."

Fifty-one

The glass-like floor of the ballroom dispersed a magnificent rainbow of colorful reflections. Around the large chamber guests waited.

Trumpets sounded out and all eyes turned to watch as King Cyranius, Princess Charlotte and Prince Edward descended the stairs with Sara and Jane following.

Jenna's eyes circled the many and diverse people as she was announced. She wondered if she would have to endure introductions all the way around the ballroom.

Her eyes recognized many assembled there. Zerka was one, standing to the side as lop-sided as ever, leaning toward a pretty young lady, his earring almost dangling in her eye as he bowed. Sidney stood alone. Baron Ferrah stood with his wife. Jenna calculated that barons from most districts had come with chosen members of the king's court and upper-staff present.

The musical instruments drowned murmurs and exclamations, wonder and questions about the princess, then the music quieted. When the king's feet touched the floor, he said softly, "We shall open the ball."

Before Jenna could reply, they were swirling together across the floor, and into the middle of the brilliantly lit ballroom. Everyone watched, spellbound. Minutes passed before others joined. The ballroom came alive. Prince Edward danced with Sara; she was the same height.

"You do forgive me, then?" Cyranius asked.

Jenna did not answer; the pressure of his hand holding her waist, drawing her closer to him disconcerted her. It was enough for her to concentrate on his steps.

"You do forgive me?"

"It is written, seventy times seven," she replied, adding, "but do I not also need forgiveness?"

"One hundred times," he said, looking down at her, "and I've forgiven every one of them. She was not much shorter and now she looked into his eyes, just briefly. He knew she was concentrating on the dance.

"Do you find me so formidable?" he asked.

"Very," she replied.

"I'm sorry."

"Are you?" she dared to query, then said quickly, "Kings need to be formidable." He gave no reply.

After a moment, he resumed the conversation, asking, "King Maslen has not held a ball for you?"

"We've had celebrations, banquets and such, but no. Maslen rather seems to favor combat demonstrations."

The dance ended and King Cyranius escorted Jenna to sit on the middle of three chairs, on the royal dais. Edward, escorting Sara, sat on the third chair. Sara, joined by Jane, moved to stand behind Jenna's chair.

Conversations sprang up and Jenna asked, "Tell me, Your Majesty, why did you... convene... this ball?"

"To present you to our people here in Cyran..." the king answered, "and—"

Prince Edward interrupted, saying, "We wanted the ball over before Jester heard about it. We believe that the news of it will get to the jester and when he comes we shall capture him."

Jenna allowed a sour expression to scour her face. *I'm the bait,* she thought, *but who else shall be harmed? Jester will do the unexpected...*

"What is it?" the king asked.

"I'd rather face him myself and end it. It's a dangerous game to play, Your Majesty! He'll know *now* that I'm here."

"I hope he comes!" Edward said excitedly, looking around at the guests, who all looked back to them, waiting for the next item on the program. He saw his brother lift his forefinger ever so slightly and sat back in his chair.

"No, we don't want him here!" Jenna said firmly, thinking of the prince and the king, their safety.

The king signaled the conductor.

"Shall we?" he asked, standing and bowing to Jenna, waiting.

"Perhaps... but should I not dance with Edward?"

"The next one is mine," Edward said, remembering his brother's promise.

The couples lined up in two long lines, the length of the ballroom. The king drew Jenna to the front.

Jenna found the second dance challenging; it was very diversified, and required more skill and concentration.

As Cyranius watched her, he knew without a doubt that she had not been taught this well-known folk-type dance. Twice she turned the wrong way and three times almost grasped the hand of the wrong partner. One man she turned to was Baron Zerka and the king knew, that if she could have, she would have definitely turned the right way, to her correct partner.

Zerka was cordial to Jenna. As part of the dance, he bowed, and taking notice of the other ladies, she curtsied.

"I'm married, you know," he managed to impart, before they changed partners.

Sidney's face was unreadable. He asked, "Have you seen Sidra? I heard she was married and is living somewhere in Aponia."

"Sidra? Who... is... Sidra?" Jenna asked seriously, glad to turn away from him.

Edward took Jenna's hand for the third dance, and Jenna saw that the king did not move from his seat.

The couples formed circles, the men in the outer circle, and the ladies in the inner one. Partners changed until Jenna was back with Prince Edward.

Escorted back to the dais, Jenna saw that the king was missing from his place. The prince smirked; now he would have the beautiful princess to himself.

After several more dances, all taken with Edward, a herald called, "Ladies, take your partners for the next dance, the Ladies' Choice."

"What is this dance?" Jenna asked.

"It's like the first one, one doesn't change partners," Sara told her. Stifling a giggle, she hurried to curtsy to Prince Edward who shot a disappointed stare at Jenna, then stood to bow and accept the invitation.

The music began and the prince and the lady-in-waiting began the dance.

Jane hurried off to curtsy to a handsome young royal guard, and Jenna supposed that he would be neglecting his post if he accepted, which he did.

Jenna stared around the chamber; Sir Lowell was dancing with his wife as was Zerka, and other barons and a buxom young lady had chosen Sidney. Jenna sat back in the chair, watching.

King Cyranius strode from a side door, one Jenna had not noticed before, and mounted the three steps to sit in his chair on the dais.

"This is the Ladies' Choice," he said, then asked, "You did not see someone you desired to dance with?"

"There's no one here with whom I want to dance," she said firmly.

His eyebrows raised, and he had to ask, "Not even me?"

"You weren't here."

"And if I had have been?"

"A dozen young ladies would have swarmed up here to snatch you away," she replied with a light smile on her face. Jenna saw the signal, a guard stepping inside the open door placed one hand across his chest, and the king stood, bowing, excusing himself.

"I'll try to return as quickly as possible. Promise me that you'll dance while I am away?"

"No, I can't promise that, I don't wish to dance."

He stepped to her chair and she stood, knowing she angered him. Cyranius was not used to anyone saying 'no' to him.

"Perhaps you could explain to me... why you find it so... so odious?"

"Please, Your Majesty, I don't wish for other men to hold me as you have done... I don't wish their arms about me, or their... their hands on my waist."

King Cyranius saw her eyes glittering with the threat of tears. Then he saw that she discerned his close observation and her effort to blink back the tears. She bowed her head, then raised it with a weak smile, saying, "I'd much rather throw them on the floor."

At that, he laughed lightly and said, "I'll return as quickly as I can." Sir Lowell followed the king.

After the next dance, tables were carried into the ballroom and set alongside the marble walls, all groaning from an amazing assortment of finger foods. Trays of assorted liquids were carried in and set on the tables in front of the food.

People mingled as they ate and drank. Prince Edward remained by Jenna's side, for which she felt grateful.

Sidney slid to her other side and asked, "I'm curious to know, Princess; they say that you own half of Aponia?"

Jenna saw many people catch the baron's question and they also caught their breaths and heads turned her way.

"You heard correctly." Jenna replied. Turning away, she saw Zerka sidling up to the prince. As he made conversation with Edward, Jenna saw a gloved hand glide out toward the table. Someone, standing behind Zerka, dropped a minute amount of powder into the prince's goblet. The powder sank down through the fruit juice, dissolving.

Pushing past Sidney, then Zerka, Jenna grasped the wrist of the small man who wore the black gloves. He gasped and pulled away only to find himself sprawling on the floor.

The prince reached for his goblet. With a quick step, and using both hands, Jenna snatched it from his fingers. She spun to confront the culprit.

Collecting himself up off the floor, the man took a step backwards.

"I do not know you, Sir?" Jenna said, stepping nearer.

"My name is Isard... Sir Isard."

"Whom do you represent?"

"District thirty-five; Baron Nashon could not attend so I came in his place." He looked around seeking a way of escape, but the guests, now quiet, were drawing closer, curious at this odd confrontation.

Prince Edward stepped to Jenna's side, his eyes wide.

"I believe this is your goblet, Sir Isard. Perhaps you'd like to drink it?"

"I... I... no. It's not mine." Turning, he would have pushed his way through the crowd.

"It's my drink, Princess," the prince said.

"Guards! Where are my guards?" Jenna called, knowing she must not let him escape nor could she let the contents of the goblet spill. She wondered, *is it just a drug... or is it poison?*

Two quads of Aponian guards began to clear a path to the princess, one from behind her, one from behind Sir Isard. Cyraniun guards shouldered their way through the crowd.

The man leaned toward the floor and drew a thin dagger from a sheath inside the top of his boot. Holding the handle, he raised it slightly as in warning.

Screams, cries and gasps sounded out and people, as one, moved away from the red-faced assassin.

Jenna pushed the goblet into Edward's hands, warning, "Don't spill it and don't drink it!" She pivoted to stand in front of the prince, shielding him.

Sir Isard stepped closer to her. Lifting her voluminous skirts to grant her freedom of movement, Jenna bent backwards and, as he ran at her, she side-kicked the man's knees, one after the other. He toppled backwards, then fell forward. Before he reached the floor, she grasped his arm, smacked it on her knee and pulled the dagger from his slackened grip. Bellowing in pain, he fell forward on his face.

When the first Cyraniun guard arrived, Jenna was holding the dagger between two fingers, by its blade. Captain Derrick shouldered his way to her. Two guards held Isard.

"What? What happened here?" Derrick asked, confused, taking the dagger. Sir Isard was a trusted district official, a master-servant of a respected baron.

"Release me! How dare you," Sir Isard fought to shake the guards from his arms.

"Hold him," Jenna said, stepping closer to the captain, saying softly, "I saw him put powder in this drink, Captain Derrick." She took the goblet from the prince.

"Is it your drink, Princess?" the captain asked.

"No, it's mine," Edward said, stepping closer.

"I shall drink it then, and end the mystery," Captain Derrick said, smiling cynically, reaching for the goblet.

"No... only one person should drink it," Jenna said. Looking at Isard, stepping closer to him, she asked, softly, "Perhaps you'd rather face the king's executioner?"

While the Cyraniun guards looked baffled, Isard blanched. "All right, give it to me; I'll drink it. What is it? Fruit juice?"

"Hold him," Derrick commanded as the guards slackened their hold. "Give me the goblet," he said to Jenna, reaching for it. Towering over Isard, he pressed it to the man's lips and demanded him to drink it all.

"Nothing to it," Isard said, leaning his head backwards and swallowing the contents as the goblet was tilted by the captain. Isard licked his lips, shaking the guards away. They unhanded him, and he lurched toward Jenna, saying softly; "It will just make me sleep... a potion to gain some time I was told." He belched violently, and clutched his stomach.

"Why the prince's drink?" Derrick asked.

"Orders..." Isard staggered, "I'll not say... whose... and p'raps... you won't... find... out..." he grasped his chest, buckling over on his knees. With a strangled gurgle, he fell forward on his face.

"Make way here!" Sir Lowell's voice rang out loudly. The king and the commander had been summoned.

Jenna's eyes were on the prince, who was watching Isard, a look of horror on his young face.

The man convulsed, his body jerking uncontrollably.

A path was cleared for King Cyranius and he arrived to see the man eject blood from his mouth and nose. Then Isard lay, contorted in body and his eyes open, dead, on the ballroom floor. The king stiffened as one frozen.

"We must clear the room... close the ball!" Captain Derrick exclaimed, wondering how many other goblets held the powder delivering this sudden, violent death. How could he tell the king this was intended for his brother?

Edward rushed to the table and vomited into a half-empty crystal punch bowl. As he retched and vomited again, Jenna rubbed his back. Similar reactions came to others who had been watching. Four ladies fainted.

Jenna, who once had been sickened by the sight of blood, felt strangely aloof. It was the first time she had kept a clear head when seeing that crimson red. *Isard deserved that,* she told herself, feeling callous. *He was a human soul... how sad to have been so corrupted because of the greed for position or money.* She took Edward into her arms and he sought to repress his sobs against her shoulder.

Guards, called together by Sir Lowell, began to clear the ballroom telling the guests to make their way to their quarters.

"The ball is over!" cried Sir Lowell, "The ball is over."

Fifty-two

Invited to meet in the king's sanctum, Jenna was not surprised to find Prince Edward absent.

The young prince had been unable to stop himself retching and the king was concerned for him, that he had ingested something contaminated and had been poisoned. The royal doctor was summoned.

Jenna felt sure it was the horror of Isard's death, the intimidation that it was intended for him, which gave the prince his queasy stomach. A lad his age would likely suffer deep shock from the close encounter.

Two captains, five advisers and two scribes waited with Jenna in the king's sanctum.

King Cyranius was still with his brother and the Doctor.

Silence stretched out in the chamber as everyone waited for the king and fears crawled in most minds that Edward had absorbed some poison.

When the king finally arrived, accompanied by Sir Lowell and Captain Philippe, he had eyes for one person only. "Princess Charlotte," he said, "you averted a personal tragedy and we are... I am... profoundly thankful. My brother is now sleeping, and Doctor Parry assures me that there's no present danger."

"The tragedy is still out there, Your Majesty," she said, her voice ringing clear in the silent chamber. "What are you going to do about it?" Her eyes included them all.

When no answer was given, Jenna asked, "Was there some kind of... diversion tonight?"

"Why do you ask?" Sir Lowell queried.

"King Cyranius and you, Sir Lowell, left the ballroom. It was in your absence that Isard dropped the poison into the prince's goblet. What was the diversion?" She was greeted with silence, so asked, "What did Jester threaten?"

"How do you know it was the jester?" the king asked. He was still recoiling from the prospect of almost losing his brother.

"We must stop playing games, gentlemen. It's obvious to me that there have been several distractions tonight. One horror planned was the prince's death. While we were all grief-stricken by his anguish-filled demise, someone here in the castle would have delivered a message. Will you tell me what other tragedy struck to summon you so suddenly from the ball?

The king answered, "We received two messages from the jester threatening to burn two villages. We are yet to discover if that were just a... a... diversion as you suggest... or if the attacks actually happened... how the messages got in here, we don't know. We sent messengers out and have servants and guards watching to see if we can discover the couriers."

"I feel sure we can expect another..." Jenna began. Everyone turned as a knock came to the door and she said, "this will likely be our next instructions."

Sir Lowell stepped to the door, and a scroll was placed in his hands. "It was attached to an arrow and fired from the forest," the messenger explained.

Sir Lowell would have broken the unmarked wax-seal to read it, but Jenna stood beside him, asking, "Is it addressed to you, Sir Lowell? If it's addressed to Princess Charlotte, then do you not think I should open it?"

Sir Lowell placed the scroll in her hands. On the outside, it was addressed, 'Princess Charlotte.'

I suppose the others were for me, too she mused. Having read it, she took it to Cyranius and said, "I must go to him. If I don't, I'm causing innocent people to be hurt…"

"Isard was not innocent," Lowell said, stepping closer, wanting to read the scroll.

The king, however, read it aloud, "It's you I want, Jay. How many more will have to die before you come to me?" A picture, a jester's face with comical hat on the head, followed. "It's from the jester," he added, his voice not angry, but burdened.

Sir Lowell took the note and read it over twice. Then he said, "He wants you alive, Princess."

"You're right, Sir Lowell."

"To duel with you… to the death?" King Cyranius asked.

"No, perhaps that is what he wanted last week," Sir Lowell said, "but now, there must be something else. If I remember correctly, most other notes threatened Princess Charlotte with imminent death. This is the first communication from the jester not cursing her to die."

"He could have ended it before now, or sought to," Jenna agreed. "The poison was in the prince's drink, not mine… no one suspected Sir Isard, you all trusted him. The thought of poison did not enter my mind when I drank from my goblet. It was filled twice with fruit juice, and like the prince, I left my goblet on the table." She would not allow her mind to dwell on Isard's death and how easily it could have been hers. A ball was a friendly, peaceful occasion, the king's presence the safest of places.

King Cyranius's captains had monitored all the guests and no strangers had been allowed to enter the castle, and certainly not the ballroom.

"Someone here in this castle is waiting for your reply," Sir Lowell said, "If the prince had died, then would you not have done as jester asked?"

"Yes… but even from this averted tragedy, we have valuable knowledge; we know now about Isard, and we can rightfully suspect his

Baron, Nashon. And you're right again, Sir Lowell, someone is waiting here in the castle for our answer... to take it to the jester," Jenna said, then asked, "Perhaps you should call everyone who is still awake, and I suspect most shall be, call them to the great hall, and we shall voice a proposal... we need the messenger before we send a message; it would be a verbal message..." she paused, wondering, *who in this castle would know enough to take messages to one of the jester's men... or perhaps even to Jester himself? It has to be someone we all know... someone who knows the jester... who would support him with their life. Who could be that close to him?*

King Cyranius did not want to do as Jenna asked, but after five minutes debating the alternatives, he agreed.

Jenna then suggested, "Once the word is out, you must have as many trusted men as you can spare out in the woods, watching every exit—the walls, the and someone is going to have to leave to take the word to the place of contact, the next in line to the jester..." she paused, knowing that this would be what Jester would expect.

Sir Lowell agreed with this strategy and together with the captains, they laid plans.

"We should sound the gong, then," Sir Lowell said, looking at the king.

"Wait," Jenna said, "I believe Jester will be far ahead of us and our plans; he will know already what we are saying here... this will be how he expects us to act."

Silence pervaded the chamber; no one had any other suggestion.

"I have what you may label as a hunch, in the guise of a traitor," Jenna said, then asked, "Where is Captain Duff's wife, Millie? Is she in the castle, here?"

While the men looked at each other, Captain Philippe answered, "Yes, she's here."

"I'd like you to fetch her. I have a feeling she may throw some light upon our discussions."

The captain left the chamber and returned with Millie.

Jenna decided to waste no time, and asked, "Where is the jester, Millie?"

No one in the chamber, other than Jenna, believed Millie would have an answer. But Millie, looking into the king's serious face, then Sir Lowell's glowering countenance and the other men of the military she believed someone had informed on her. She had been waiting and watching, and when a quad of guards and a captain had come and snatched her to take her to the sanctum she had been caught unaware.

"Who was going to take your next message to the jester, Millie?" Jenna persisted.

Sir Lowell perceived Millie's face showed signs of guilt. She stepped backwards, looking around the room, not at the men, but for a way out of there.

"Do you realize, woman, that you can be charged as an accessory to an attempt at murdering Prince Edward?" the commander bellowed, stepping close to her.

Millie hid her face in her hands, losing her composure for a few seconds, then looked up, crying. "I did not know they were going to poison the prince!"

Jenna knew they had to keep the pressure on her to gain the information they needed. "You carried the messages... to someone outside the castle, Millie. You must tell us where he waits, and you must tell us now."

Millie turned to Jenna, and everyone expected her to give the answer they wanted. Instead she gave the strangest response, "Have you ever broken a promise? Well, I'm going to! I promised my mother I'd never ever tell anyone, I swore on my own soul! But I'm going to tell you. Sidra is your half-sister, Jenna." She stared around at the men in the room, all staring back at her. No one knew of this twist, but they all considered the possibility of it being true. Perhaps Kind Heart, Jenna's father, once had a secret mistress, Sidra's mother?

Jenna frowned, feeling disoriented. Millie had used her old name and it was her name, her favorite name for herself. Jenna glanced fleetingly around the chamber, realizing that these men already knew all there was to know about her—most of these men had also been at

Charlotte, shut in Maslen's sanctum, *discussing me, all day, and half the night previous,* she reminded herself, feeling crushed.

"My... sister?" Jenna asked, unable to think of the jester in the light of this revelation. "How can Sidra... be my sister?"

"Half-sister. You shared the same mother, and you both have her facial features. Your mother got sick of her Kind Heart husband always being away and she formed a liaison with my father. But your father made her give up Sidra... only she wasn't called Sidra, Sidney's father named her that; her birth name was Marina. Your father paid my mother to raise Sidra. My father went along with the secret—money can buy anything, he said.

"I'm Sidra's half-sister... so what does that make you to me? Nothing, we have no relationship and Sidra had all the education, all the money from the rich baron, with secret visits to the baroness. Not even Kind Heart knew about them... then, seven years later, your mother bore you—no doubt that Kind Heart was your father; my father was dead, then your mother died.

"But me, I didn't fit anywhere and you and Sidra were like day and night; she was evil and you such a goody-good. I wish to see you and Sidra *both dead!* Why do you think I went along with Jester's plans? I want you dead, that's why! Now he says he wants you alive! Not me!" Millie raised her hands like claws and would have flung herself at Jenna, but Sir Lowell grasped her arms and held her tightly. The woman leaned forward, bowed her head, cursing, then wailing in anger.

Jenna collected her thoughts, telling herself to keep to the concerns of the night. Stepping closer to Millie, she said, "Millie, stop crying! I don't wish you dead, I never wish anyone dead, but if you want to live," she waited, and Millie quieted, "if you want to live, Millie, you must tell us how to find jester."

"Jester will kill me if I tell you," Millie said. Sir Lowell released her, and she dashed away her tears.

"You will die if you don't tell us," the commander growled. He had lost patience with this treacherous woman. None of them had suspected this second betrayal. When Millie had returned, she had been the repentant, humble, subservient wife. Duff had accepted her back. The children had been overjoyed to have their mother home again.

"I'll die; one way or another, I'll die. I'll not tell you."

"Then take a message for him, Millie. Tell him I'll do what he asks if he ceases his path of destruction."

Protests broke out in the chamber, and the king spoke, "We won't allow you to do that, Princess."

"Regardless of what you think you will allow, Your Majesty, and what you will not allow, I believe that one small life is of little consequence when one considers how many lives this man has taken already. He's bizarre and I'll not stand by and watch it any longer!"

The men in the chamber stared at her. Although she had taken off the jewelry, she still wore the amazing ball gown. No one believed that Princess Charlotte was 'one small life'.

Sir Lowell, however, thought he knew her tactics, in the light of Millie's treachery. He believed Jenna was seeking to gain time. "You would face Jester, Princess?"

"First, we must send Jester a message of compliance so that he stops the mindless killing of innocent people. I told my brother, Maslen, that I was willing to face the jester," Jenna said.

"Brother?" Millie cried, "Brother? He's no more your brother than I'm your sister."

"Brotherhood, or sisterhood, is not just having the same parenthood," Jenna replied quietly, "but we are not here to discuss King Maslen's choice of a sister, but to ask that you take a message to the jester."

"I'd much rather take you to him... *Princess*," Millie said, emphasizing the last word with contempt in her voice.

"I shall go with you... perhaps we shall leave now?"

Protests again circled the chamber. When they subsided, Jenna asked, "What other suggestion is there? My brother, Maslen, at last count had seen more than fifteen loyal guards killed by jester and his cohorts. Twelve were married men. There are mothers, fathers, wives, sisters and children in Aponia who have been bereaved of loved husbands, fathers, sons and brothers." Her eyes circled the sanctum and she read surprise. "You may not think of soldiers in such terms and it grieves me that sometimes men are thought of as simply guards, or shields, or bows and arrows. If there had been a war, you would expect to lose lives but this is not a war; deaths such as these, in peacetime, are unacceptable. Jester is threatening more lives. There's an obvious way to put a halt to it, and that is, to do as he asks. You here, and King Maslen, in Aponia, have your armies out there, searching for him, setting traps for him. It was one thing to have Jester in Aponia, but to bring him here to Cyran, I cannot understand the strategy... why did we not keep him in Aponia? If I cannot meet him here, in Cyran, I shall return, tonight, to Aponia. He will follow me there, where I shall likely encounter him before I reach my brother." The chamber was silent. King Cyranius' eyes bored into hers and she could not continue to look at him.

"We agree with King Maslen," he said, "we cannot lose you, Princess..."

"You cannot afford to lose your brother, Your Majesty! If I had stayed in Aponia..." Jenna paused, and it dawned on her. Her eyes again met with Cyranius' but she could not read him. *There's a purpose, other than painting, or even the jester, in my being here... they all know, but not me. Why do they want me here? Why do they keep it from me?*

"We won't allow you to go to the jester," Cyranius said firmly.

"He no longer intends to kill the princess," Sir Lowell repeated his previous opinion.

"There's someone else who has offered a reward for me. Millie, who is it? Jester has changed, hasn't he? Who offered him a prize?"

Millie shook her head, and Jenna persisted, "Someone... important... gave Jester an offer, Millie. Am I right, or wrong?"

Millie's eyes circled the chamber. She was calculating the risk—could she tell the truth and still keep her hands on her part in the jester's reward? If only she could get Jenna to go with her. Jester would be forever in her debt! She remembered how Jenna had once gone with Sidra, to Aponia. If, perhaps, she acted somewhat friendly... gave them some significant disclosures... Animosity fell from her face like autumn leaves and congeniality replaced it.

"You're right, Princess," Millie said, her voice changed as well. "At first, Jester wanted to duel with you, to kill you, but then he got an important message... he... was offered an amazing amount, and... and refuge and a castle to live in—"

"Who... who could offer that, Millie?" Sir Lowell asked.

"He wouldn't tell me... he just said he'd take me with him if I would... I would..." she faltered with the word, knowing that the sentence for treason was death, "in-inform for him, and convey... messages."

Then she blurted, "You don't know what it's like; having to fight for your bread as a young girl, and to fend off the men who came to visit your mother... and... and then... my sister... a discarded mistress."

"Sidra, you mean Sidra?" Jenna asked, her voice soft, then she told Millie, "Oh no. Sidra... our shared half-sister... she's married to King Maslen... he gave her a crown. She is Queen Masla, and is carrying his child."

"What? I didn't know!" Millie cried, her eyes wide with this news. She shook her head, wondering if she had heard rightly. "I heard it was you—"

"You did not stay in King Maslen's castle, or you'd have known," Jenna said.

"I... Sidra... she wanted to marry him... but... she did? He calls her Masla? It is she who is married to the king?"

"You went off with Jester," Jenna said softly, then asked, "were you not with Jester when he attempted to kill King Maslen?"

"I left the castle some time before the attempt," Millie admitted, her tongue now loosened, "I rented a small house in the capital, a place for Jester to come when he needed to hide. It was a small house in the city wall. We... we lived there for about two months... then, after the... the attempt... Maslen had all Jester's friends killed. Jester was overcome with revenge, and... he sent me to... to set myself up... back here at Gifford. I didn't want to leave, I felt nobody would want me here. Jester believed Maslen would reward you by sending you home, and he wanted to come here to take revenge but it all changed. He thought you had disappeared, then, not long ago, he found out that Maslen had made you a princess... he was very angry at that... but, I don't think even he knows that Sidra is Masla... we thought it was you, then, that Meltissa had returned and it was she who married the king and became queen.

"Did he really give you half of his kingdom?"

"He did," Jenna replied.

"It made Jester all the more mad!" Millie said, "he was hard to live with. 'Half the kingdom for what she did to me!' he would say, over and over. I was afraid, all the time... when he was in a wild mood, I thought he would kill me just for practice.'"

The room was silent; everyone knew that Millie was battling within herself. All minds were filled with aversion toward her, but they also knew that she held the key to the whereabouts of the jester. That she was off-balance made her all the more malevolent—she could pretend to agree, and betray them in an instant.

Turning to the king, she asked, "You don't pay for information, do you, Your Majesty?"

"No," the king replied quickly, before anyone else could interject.

"I thought not. But what if I told you that someone... someone who was in that sanctum chamber at... at that castle, they call Charlotte... they told Jester what went on there; what would that be worth, then?" She looked from Cyranius to Jenna then back again.

"Are you suggesting that someone... one of my trusted officials or King Maslen's closest... one of these... you are saying they are a traitor?" King Cyranius asked, disbelieving it.

"One of them." She looked at Jenna, and asked, "Have you not told the lady... what was said... proposed... there? Jester knows. He told me."

King Cyranius lost his composure for a few seconds; his mouth dropped open, and his eyes widened, glistening.

"When... when did you see the jester last?" Sir Lowell asked, feeling shattered. The meeting in King Maslen's sanctum was little more than two days ago. How had Millie seen Jester... unless Jester was very close to Gifford?

"I didn't say I'd seen him..." Millie said, realizing her slip, then she admitted, "But, oh, he's close all right... closer'n you'd ever realize."

"Who is it... the one who is close to the Jester?" Lowell asked.

"There is only one person... one man it can be," Jenna said, with certainty in her voice.

Fifty-three

Jenna sighed; the room was close and she felt drained. *I'd like some fresh air; perspiration is not my favorite fragrance.* The men perspired, not from physical exertion, but from anxiety. Jester was not far from Gifford and there was a certain captain, from Aponia, within this very castle, who was in close contact with the jester. How could they contain the secrets held in this small chamber?

Jenna pondered the new information. Millie slumped to sit on the floor and no one prevented her, though she was in the king's presence. She behaved as if tired; hugging her knees beneath her long olive-green skirt, she hid her head in her arms. Jenna knew, from the past, that Millie was wide awake and listening to everything.

It had dawned on Millie that perhaps she would never be allowed to leave Gifford and would never to see Jester again. She felt defeated, the adventures were over, but deep within, she experienced relief. As she hid her face and closed her eyes, she sought to piece together the fact that Sidra, her kin-sister, the one who shared the same father with her, was a queen! Why should this make such a difference? What was the difference? Would she feel badly if Jester accomplished his worst goal, to kill the king, the queen... and the princess? King Maslen would have what he deserved... but what about Sidra... Masla? What about her child? A boy would be next king of Aponia. What an honor! *But what a disgrace I am... Lowell won't let me get out of this one... and Duff—I can't face him...*

She reached her hand into her sleeve, feeling a small pocket there, fingering the vial containing a small measure of liquid. The jester had sent it to her, asking her to put it in food or liquid for Princess Charlotte, tonight if possible. She wondered if she had the courage to take it herself... *What's left... for me? Better this way, than the hangman's noose...* With quivering fingers, she drew out the stopper, and, slowly turning her head to the side, she swallowed the contents, feeling surprised to find that the liquid had no bad taste at all...

"If you'll excuse me, Your Majesty, Sir Lowell, Captains and Gentlemen; I'm tired, I'll take my leave," Jenna said. "I'm sure you'll be taking Captain Sebastian into safe-keeping, Sir Lowell. Or perhaps he's already left and gone to tell Jester that we're questioning Millie?"

"Captain Philippe, go and locate Sebastian, now," Sir Lowell said, "take him to a cell, one of the small ones, downstairs."

The captain bowed himself from the room.

"Captain Sebastian! Of course! Who else? It has to be Sebastian!" the king exclaimed, then frowned, knowing others had determined this some time earlier. "I'd like to see you, Princess Charlotte, privately."

"Tonight?" she asked.

"It's morning," he replied, but kindly. "Yes; as soon as I've completed all we can... here," his eyes were on Lowell, and he knew his commander wished to speak with him.

"I was planning to go to the chapel before I did retire, I'd like to pray. I need guidance, it's so difficult to know what the best course would be."

"Nothing is best—it's all downhill!" growled Lowell, his eyes on Millie who did not move. He wanted to ask more questions of this double-crossing woman.

"I'll find you in the chapel, then, Princess," the king said.

Jenna realized he expected her to wait in the chapel for him. She felt sure he was going to prevent her from leaving the castle. *I don't know whether I will go, I'm not sure about anything right now… I'm tired, and should leave making a decision until tomorrow. By then, they should know the names of any other traitors in this castle… they'll question Millie…*

To Jenna's surprise, Sara and Jane waited in the corridor, just along from the sanctum door. She remembered, with a small amount of concern, that she still wore the ballgown. It seemed days had passed since the ball…

Guards lined the corridors and halls, all along the way from the sanctum to Jenna's quarters.

With the ladies' help, Jenna changed, then urged the pair, "You're both very tired; I want you to sleep."

"Where… where are you going, Princess?" Jane asked.

"To the castle chapel to pray."

"We'll come with you," Sara said. "We'll change from our ballgowns, and come—"

"No, you both must get some sleep. We've no idea what the morrow will bring. Stay." So saying, Jenna left her ladies in the room.

Jenna entered the chapel timidly. So many memories hovered in Gifford Castle; but this particular chamber was crowded with them. Aponian guards followed her into the chapel itself, filing along the back to stand guard. *They're either keeping me in, or keeping someone else out. I guess it's both.*

It was difficult for Jenna to concentrate on praying.

I'd really like to go home… to Charlotte but I feel torn. I'm sure King Cyranius is able to take care of himself. She shuddered, wondering how she would have felt if King Cyranius had received the poison. Such an idea caused her mind to cloud with unfamiliar blankness. *I would not wish to live if he had died like that, tonight,* she told herself. *Dear God, please take care of us all. What a thin line we tread. A person can be here one day, and gone the next… like Judith, and Father, just memories…*

King Cyranius entered the chapel to see the princess, still kneeling near the front.

She heard his footfalls, although soft, on the carpet and stood. He wore his warmest cloak, made of ermine and lined with lambs wool. She felt he was so handsome that she could not keep herself from staring at him.

"Perhaps we could walk," he suggested, adding, "up top. I sent for your cloak." he waited while an attendant helped her don the heavy, blue garment.

Jenna knew he meant the battlements, and moved with him.

As they rose up the last steps to the top of the highest battlement, he said, "In the light of all that has transpired, I feel I owe you an explanation."

"It would be helpful..." she agreed, but could not tell him the truth of what she really wanted to know. *Why does he want me here, in Cyran? I must find the courage to ask him.*

He waited until they were outside on the stone walk. Guards, having followed, kept an unobtrusive distance.

It was chill, almost freezing, and not even yet was the sky lightening to greet the dawn. The many orange flares glowing both within and without the castle walls minimally irradiated the inky star-studded canopy.

He was silent, not sure where to begin.

Jenna decided to ask the question that she longed to have answered, "For what common purpose did you and my brother, Maslen, agree to my coming to Cyran?"

"I... perhaps I should begin from when first we met."

"When you met Maslen?"

"No... when I met you."

Jenna remembered the time, and place. *The palace, his palace...* She frowned, wondering what he was going to tell her.

"Then," he said, "perhaps I should start where we left off... on the battlements, here. Do you remember what I said?"

"We talked about many things," she replied.

"I once told you, Princess, I sought only your happiness. Do you remember?"

"Yes," Jenna replied, "It was when happiness seemed further from me than ever."

He turned to her, asking, "What would make you happiest of all?"

Jenna frowned, the dialogue was moving in an incomprehensible direction. Silence stretched out, and for long minutes neither spoke. The king waited patiently.

"The answer to such a question is not accessible to me," she finally said. Silence prevailed again.

"Perhaps, Princess, it is that you do not think of your own happiness at all?" He left the question hanging and waited, but she did not speak. Drawing a deep breath, he plunged into his thoughts, seeking to explain his deepest emotions to her.

"I once believed I had obtained complete happiness," he said, "I had settled my soul-matters with God, I successfully ruled a kingdom, safeguarding it from both external and internal battles, I had an heir in Edward to continue my father's line and God granted me continuing good health, with a sound mind."

Jenna turned to him, and saw that he looked at her, seeking to find her eyes.

"It all changed when I met a certain landowner in my kingdom, a lady. Believing I disliked everything about her, I found myself unable to remove her from my mind. The more I learned about her and the more I saw her, the more I longed to be with her, until I was being consumed by her."

King Cyranius' voice had taken on an intensity that was foreign to him, and Jenna stepped back a little. She tried hard to concentrate on his words; there was something happening between them, and she felt the cool air enveloping her, drawing her to him, as if it were a solid thing.

"Then... when Kind Heart... you, Princess, when you rescued Edward from Knight Red, yet I did not know it was you, then..." he swallowed, remembering his gratitude and respect, then continued, "it was then that I became engrossed with wanting Lady Jennava Gifford to be happy and for Kind Heart to have happiness, yet it was my own happiness I really wanted; with you. I felt that if you and Kind Heart would marry and be happy, I would no longer feel the torment that plagued me day and night... torment to want you, yet believing you could never, ever, be mine."

Jenna drew a deep breath, remembering his words at the planned 'wedding;' *You shall torment me no more...* how could she forget?

King Cyranius bowed his head, leaning his hands against the top of the crenellation.

"You... you wanted me... all that time?" Jenna asked, feeling shocked. Then, like a stab to her heart, she remembered Maslen's claim that Cyranius did not want Kind Heart. "Maslen... he said that you gladly gave me into his hands and that you did not want me to return to Cyran because Kind Heart committed treason."

"Maslen lied. Kind Heart could not commit treason in Cyran, you owned Freedom of the Realm so you could do nothing wrong.

"There was never a day went by, after you left Gifford here, that I did not wish you back. I almost went crazy when I was alone at night, thinking of all the times I should have known, should have guessed the truth; hating myself for behaving so cold and aloof to you. I despised the king in me, the king who made me so distrustful. Maslen told you that lie before you saved his life." The king stood to his full height and looked at her again, saying, "There was nothing about Lady Jennava Gifford that the man in me did not desire, there was nothing about Kind Heart that this king did not wholly admire, and there is nothing about Princess Charlotte that I do not love."

Jenna took another step back from him. It was too much to take in. She remembered his visit to Charlotte, and asked, "You... you talked about this... with Maslen?"

"Yes."

"Why did you not talk about it... with me?"

"Maslen did not feel it was wise. He said we needed time together, to become better acquainted... to understand each other more... in the light of past misunderstandings... he refused me when I requested that I approach you there at Charlotte."

"It was his idea for me to come to Gifford?"

"Yes. He suggested that I commission the paintings... he seeks your utmost happiness..."

Jenna gulped. Maslen had changed more than she could conceive. It had always hovered in the back of her mind that if Sidra died, Maslen would want to marry her.

As if reading her thoughts, Cyranius said, "Your unselfish heart is what changed Maslen, or perhaps I should say, God used your unselfishness to change him. He told me that he had never experienced such selfless giving, such sacrifice. The more time he spent with you in the role of a brother, the more he wanted your happiness. He said that if you found happiness with me, then he would give his blessing... he gave me reason to hope."

Jenna could not discern her feelings; she felt numb.

Silence ruled again on the topmost battlements. Then the king spoke again, "I once shared with you, Princess, that I am two persons within one; the king and the man. Is it possible, Princess, that you hold even the smallest spark of love for either?"

"I... I never think of you... as two," Jenna replied, "to me you are one; king and man combined. And, yes, I care deeply... about you." Jenna tried to fathom the depths of her feelings for him, and found herself unable to do so.

Before she realized what was happening, King Cyranius dropped to his knees and, taking her hand in his, smothered it with kisses. His intensity startled her and she would have pulled away if she had not discerned his gravity and the unparalleled state of his humility.

"Marry me, Princess Charlotte; please tell me you will be my wife." He looked up into her startled eyes, and said, "I vow before God I will love you, honor you, protect you and provide for you in every way I can, all the days of our lives. I... I love you beyond... words... beyond reason." He kissed her hand again, bowing his head, waiting for her to reply.

Jenna's heart pounded within her breast and she felt that she fought a great battle. The past had caught up with the present, and she could think of nothing but this man, this king, his love! Tears welled up from her eyes, washing down her cheeks blinding her, and her whole frame shuddered.

Feeling the trembles in her hand, he released it, and his shoulders drooped. She loved him but not enough to marry him, he thought, keeping his head bowed, trying to regain some vestige of dignity. But it was more than a blow to his pride; it was as if a death blow had been dealt to his heart.

Jenna moved to the crenellation, and leaned both arms down on it for support, sobbing uncontrollably, unable to control her breath in the intensity of her emotions.

King Cyranius heard her sobs, and gathered himself together to stand. The lady was weeping; he remembered another occasion she had wept, but it was not like this. She wept now as if all was lost, forever. He waited, unsure, then she turned, and he knew that the tears were not against his love but, inconceivably, she was weeping, because of it.

Suddenly, they found themselves in each other's arms and he surrounded her, holding her tight, close to him. She leaned on him and wept and as the sky began to brighten, she still wept.

Finally, Jenna said, "I wish I had known, I just wish I had known. How much time we have wasted."

He kissed her forehead, and she lifted her face to his. He kissed her eyes, tasting her salty tears. He kissed her cheeks, then her lips.

When finally they moved apart, she said, "If I had known, I'd never have left your side."

"Oh, Jenna, my sweet Jenna." Then he kissed her again, and it was a long kiss.

"You will marry me?" he asked as shafts of sunlight beamed up into the sky above the snow-clad mountains.

"You... you really... wish to marry?" she asked, then felt embarrassment from asking such a question.

"Only you, dear Jenna, only you."

"Yes," she replied, "I'll marry you, Cyranius, only you."

He kissed her again, this time with more passion. When they drew apart, she felt breathless.

"When?" she asked, feeling that she floated.

"As soon as would be appropriate," he replied, then added, "as soon as we get rid of the jester."

Jenna felt her feet land back on the stone walk. Jester. Why did they have someone in their lives like the jester? Recalling her new life in Aponia, she said, "Soon after Maslen's son is born, in the Spring."

"We'll keep it a secret, until the jester is captured," the king concluded, "then we'll make our plans."

They turned to look at the ascending sun, knowing that this was the most glorious sunrise of their lives so far.

Fifty-four

Prince Edward, with Gavin and Kevin following, walked along the battlement walk.

"We won't tell Edward, yet," the king whispered, then called, "You're up early, Brother, you must be feeling better."

"It's not early, Cy, and I'm hungry—breakfast is waiting, everyone's waiting! Many of our guests have made plans to leave right after they've eaten." Edward spoke with censure in his voice. His brother was neglecting breakfast to spend time with Edward's own favorite person.

"We'll come down right away."

Edward scowled, then stepped between Jenna and the king.

"Did you hear about Duff's wife, Millie?" Edward asked, his eyes on her red nose. "You look cold, Princess Charlotte."

"Millie?" Jenna asked, thinking he was going to tell her that she was locked in a cell, awaiting trial.

"Millie killed herself, Duff and the children are going to bury her tomorrow morning, over in Zerka District."

Shocked with this news, Jenna looked up at the king, who said, "She poisoned herself, perhaps just before you left the sanctum last night. Sir

Lowell could not wake her... she was cold, clammy. Doctor Breck said it was some kind of poison that made her fall into a deep sleep, and she did not wake... not like that other poison... Millie went without a struggle, peacefully."

"I shall attend the burial with the children and Duff... it will be hard for them," Jenna said, then asked, "You found Sebastian, I hope."

"He could not be found..."

"Sebastian? Why were you looking for Sebastian?" Edward asked.

"Sebastian is a traitor; in league with the jester," the king explained.

A morbid atmosphere reigned at breakfast. Calamity had deemed the ball a fiasco, and now there were rumors of traitors, with another person being poisoned.

Guests' minds were upon travel arrangements, soliciting extra guards for escorts so that the likelihood of meeting mishaps along the way was diminished. If possible, guests would leave together and travel in convoy to effect extra security.

With so many people moving out of the castle and carriages being prepared, horses and men coming and going, it was not difficult for Jester to slip alongside a waiting servant, disguised as a castle footman, and enter Gifford Castle.

Jenna had thoughts and eyes for none other than King Cyranius. His eyes toward her were tender and, after breakfast, he asked that she stand with him to bid farewell to those leaving. After this, he offered that she come to the sanctum to discuss developments as they came to hand.

In the sanctum, a letter was dictated for King Maslen, informing him of the recent incidents.

"Maslen will be most grieved about Sebastian," Jenna said. "He trusted him with his life."

"Every person," Sir Lowell said, then corrected himself, "that is, most people, have a price."

"The jester does," Edward said, "I heard that he wants a castle before he wants a duel with you, Princess Charlotte." Then he asked, "Where would he take you, if he did manage to capture you?"

"To Rosenburg, I believe," Jenna replied.

"To King Fredrick?" Cyranius asked.

"No, it will be the king's brother-in law, Count Roxaud, Anastasia's step-father, who wants me. The Count will never forgive Kind Heart for thwarting him in marrying Princess Anastasia to King Maslen. Also, Anastasia is second-in-line to the throne, after King Fredrick's son, Prince Nikolaus."

"Prince Nikolaus is deceased," Sir Lowell said, "he died a few months ago... early in August, it was..."

"Klaus is dead? I did not know." Jenna said, then remembered that she herself had been recovering at that time. "I did not hear about it. What happened to him?"

"He fell off his horse," Edward said, "the report we received said he broke his back and died a day later."

Jenna paled. Prince Nikolaus' death changed everything. Princess Anastasia was heiress to the throne of Rosenburg. When King Fredrick died, she would be queen. "King Fredrick will want Anastasia to return home to him," she said.

"Yes," Cyranius agreed, "He does. We receive petitions every month, requesting that if we know where the princess is, we must send her sent home."

"Count Roxaud will want her —if he can find her and keep her until the king dies, he could become regent. If she were safely returned to King Fredrick, he would appoint someone else to be her guardian," Sir Lowell said.

"Yes, it's always been known that there's no kinship between Count Roxaud and the king," Jenna said, then added, "the Count treated Princess Anastasia abominably; I believe if he could have gotten his hands on her, after I rescued her, he would have killed her. As it is, she has permanent scars on her back from having been whipped by him."

"That's horrible!" Edward said, unable to imagine what it would be liked to be whipped.

"You know where the princess is?" King Cyranius asked, then answered for her, "of course you do."

"But what would have happened... if you had... if you hadn't been able to return to her, to tell her when it is safe for her to go home?" Edward asked.

"I made arrangements," Jenna said, knowing that there was much interest in this room regarding the princess and her whereabouts. "If I had died or never returned, Princess Anastasia would have gone home at the right time; this time being when King Maslen married, and his wife survived the birth of a child. I did plan for it, Prince Edward. Kind Heart's life was such that it was never certain a mission would not end in death."

Jenna's mind reeled. She paled, and stood.

"What is it?" Cyranius asked.

"I... I... it... it is not important," she replied, then sat.

"Something has upset you."

Squaring her shoulders, Jenna revealed her thoughts, saying, "My brother, Maslen, would have known about Klaus's death... Prince Nikolaus. He must know, he would not now be permitted to marry Anastasia, as heiress to the throne. It made his decision to marry Sidra much easier for him. King Fredrick only allowed the betrothal because he believed Klaus would marry, and bear an heir."

"If King Maslen had married Princess Anastasia, he would have owned two kingdoms." Edward said, speaking the thought on everyone's mind.

"I'm glad these matters are in wiser hands than ours," Jenna said, remembering these same words once said by her father. "But I do need to go to Anastasia and take her back to her home... to the king."

"We shall go with you," Cyranius said.

"We shall?" Edward asked, excitedly, adding, "Yes; we shall take a large escort and Jester won't have a chance to get to any princess!"

All eyes turned to look at Jenna, who smiled and said, "That would work very well—a grand procession of both Cyraniun and Aponian military to escort Princess Anastasia home. A Rosenburg escort would soon join us."

"It would be very grand!" Edward exclaimed, his eyes shining.

"When?" Sir Lowell asked, knowing that he would have to organize the Cyraniun troops. "And we'll need to know which way to head."

"Not tomorrow," Jenna said, thinking of Millie's burial. "The morning after. This will give time for me to write to Maslen and request cavalry to meet us at the south border the morning after tomorrow. We'll ride south, to Rosenburg."

"Princess Anastasia is in Rosenburg?" Edward asked.

"I must not yet say where she is," Jenna replied, "But soon you will know where she has been, all this time."

The day was filled with making arrangements, sending messages and discussing options.

Late in the afternoon, Jenna sought out Duff and his children. They were with Duff's parents, whom, Jenna discovered, now resided permanently in Gifford Castle.

The chamber they sat in was a large composite sitting-dining room, one set apart for those captains and families who lived in the castle. A fire burned warmly in the center. Children and adults, not needed elsewhere, shared the warmth and relaxation of the room. A huge cauldron of stew simmered on the fire.

Jenna commanded that she not be announced, and felt chagrined that everyone in the room gave her obeisance.

Jenny and the grandparents greeted her with apprehension. They had all been crying.

Duff, dressed in common clothes, sat apart from the family and others thumbing through a sheaf of maps, obviously not able to concentrate on what he was trying to read. When he saw Jenna, he jerked himself to his feet, bowing.

Jenna stepped across to him, offering condolences. He did not thank her, nor speak, but bowed his head, shaking it in shame. Jenny took Jenna's hand, and the latter moved across the room to sit on a bench with the girl.

"I didn't go to see my mother," Jenny said, "Dadda said I could go with him, but I didn't. They are going to nail the coffin shut at dawn, and we have to bury her after that. Granma and Grandad won't go to Zerka—they're staying with Aaron and David.

"I should have gone to see my Mommie for the last time, but Dadda won't go again."

"Do you want me to go with you to see her?" Jenna asked, adding, "We could go now, if you want."

Young Jenny thought about this, then shook her head slowly, saying, "I want to remember her for the good things she did... I don't want to think about anything else..."

Jenna looked across at Duff, who did not look up from the scroll he was holding. It was all so very morbid and depressing. *What hope can I offer? What does Jenny have to look forward to? She thought of Duff...*

"Your Dadda is a very brave man," Jenna whispered, adding, "You need to remember how brave he is, and you must help your brothers to grow up to be brave like him."

Jenny gave a wistful smile.

"If you change your mind and want to visit your Mommie for the last time, then send for me, and I'll go with you," Jenna promised, adding, "I'll ride with you, tomorrow morning, to Sweetwoods."

"You will?" Jenny asked, brightening.

"Yes, I will," Jenna said, kissing her cheeks and taking her leave.

Jenna felt very tired and, remembering that she had not slept the night previous, decided to retire early. *I'll go to bed right after dinner... I can't miss seeing Cyranius at dinner; I long to be with him again...*

Fifty-five

The king escorted Jenna to the door of her chambers, and to the surprise of the two ladies, Sara and Jane, he kissed her on the lips; a gentle 'good night' kiss. Jenna wished it had lasted longer.

Jenna was quick into bed, knowing that she would need a good night's sleep to cope with the demands of the days ahead.

"Your milk and honey, Princess," Jane offered.

"No, I don't feel like it tonight; I'll sleep well without it," Jenna said, "but I'd like to read a verse or two, so bring me the lamp and set it on the table beside my bed."

Jenna continued her reading in Jeremiah, and concluded by reading two verses aloud, "For I know the thoughts that I think towards you, saith the LORD, thoughts of peace, and not of evil, to give you an expected end. Then shall ye call upon me, and ye shall go and pray unto me, and I will harken unto you."

The last thing Jenna heard was Sara's whisper, "I'll drink it then, rather than tip it out."

Midnight had not long passed when a small hand caressing her forehead, woke Jenna with a start. It was young Jenny.

"I couldn't sleep, and Charles said he would bring me to you so we could go and see Mommie. Please come; please... I... I do want a little look..." Jenny whispered. The girl hugged a heavy woolen shawl around her long thick nightgown.

"Charles? Who is Charles?" Jenna replied, sitting up, stretching, swinging her legs over the side of the bed, shivering in the cold air.

"He's a friend of Dadda's... and the king's friend, too," Jenny said. "I was crying, and Granma complained that I should be sleeping because the boys were waking because of me, then she told me to go and sit by the fire for a while in the sitting room, and Charles was there. He said he would bring me to you... and he did bring me, to your door."

Jenna collected her warm blue cloak and would have wrapped it around her nightgown, but thought better of it. This castle was no longer her home; and there were still guests staying within its walls, to say nothing of the many royal guards. She moved behind the partition and dressed in her warm blue day gown, placing the thick velvet cloak around her shoulders.

Sara and Jane, sleeping in the same bedchamber, did not stir.

Taking Jenny's hand, Jenna kept her steps small, and together they moved down through the dimly lit castle. Jenna was well aware that eyes watched her descent, but felt comforted that the castle was under such alert guard even in the small dead hours.

"She's... she's been put in a cell, downstairs," Jenny said, her voice trembling, adding, "I hope we can find it."

When they reached the lower level, Jenna recognized the passage ahead, stretching out, with doors all along it. Not one was open. Guards at either end of the passageway stood to attention.

"Dadda didn't say which one." Jenny's voice was filled with dismay.

Turning back to the guards at the bottom of the steps, Jenna asked, "In which cell did they place Millie? Her daughter wishes to see her."

"I'll take you there, Princess," a man replied, and moved ahead to open the second door.

The cell contained, not one coffin, but three, two on wooden benches, and one on the floor. Jenna wondered if one coffin held the body of Sir Isard.

"This one," the guard said, lifting the lid off, revealing Millie. Moving across to the cresset on the wall, he took the thick candle out, and lit its twin, causing extra light to illuminate the dim cell. Backing away, he left them.

Collecting Jenny in her arms, Jenna lifted her to view the still form lying in the coffin.

"She... she looks just as if she is sleeping," Jenny said. She stared at her mother's face for a minute, then, turning, she hugged Jenna, saying, "Thank you for bringing me. She doesn't look bad at all, does she?"

"No," Jenna said, hugging the girl close, knowing that Jenny had heard talk about her mother.

Jenny laid her head on Jenna's shoulder, saying, "I'll go back to bed now; I'll be all right to sleep now."

Jenna, however, stiffened. Her eyes were upon Millie's face, the color in her cheeks. She did not look as if she were dead, but sleeping, as if she would wake any moment. As if in answer to Jenna's thoughts, a nerve in Millie's cheek twitched, twice. Jenna felt her heart jump, and imagined Millie's eyes opening. They remained shut.

Turning away from the coffin, Jenna set Jenny on her feet by the door. She would have stepped back to the coffin, but the door opened.

"Charles!" Jenny said, her voice glad. "Mommie just looks like she's asleep."

"Ah, now you'll be able to sleep... I'll take you back to the chamber... or our friend, Benny, here, will; if Princess Charlotte agrees."

"All right, thank you," Jenna confirmed, wanting to return to Millie. She frowned; somehow Charles' voice was overly patronizing. She wondered if he always spoke to children in such a tone.

The young guard, Benny, lifted the girl into his arms, cradling her against him, turning to stride out of the cell.

"Thank you Princess... good night," Jenny called.

Charles stepped aside, as if waiting for Jenna to follow.

"Just a moment, Charles, I'd like to speak with you," Jenna said. Stepping across to the coffin, she stared at Millie's face before brushing the backs of her fingers on Millie's cheek. Although Millie's skin was cold, it was not hard; it had the texture and feeling of one who lived.

"Is it possible that Millie is not dead?" Jenna asked. A voice Jenna dreaded to remember, replied. The voice, though disguised, had a soft rasp beneath its camouflage.

"Anything is possible."

Pivoting to view the newcomer, Jenna knew that underneath the masquerade, was the jester. Dressed as a royal Cyraniun guard, the same as Charles, the pair stood in front of the open door. Folding his arms, Jester gave a backward kick to close the door.

How can I have fallen into such a trap? Jenna asked herself, feeling greatly alarmed. She wondered how she would fare, taking on these two, in such a small space with no weapon. She turned back to the coffin, but kept them both in her peripheral vision.

"How did you do that, Jester?" she asked, her tone casual.

"Do what?" Jester returned, his voice surprised; he was wondering how she could have seen through his fastidious disguise.

"Poison Millie, yet she still lives."

"She took your drug."

"My drug?" Jenna asked, shocked.

"I gave it to her, for you; but, I suspect, she decided to take it to prevent herself being interrogated."

"She will wake?" Jenna asked.

"She will wake, in about ten hours; but it will be another day before she feels like herself again."

"So, then; I'm supposed to be sleeping, like Millie?

"Yes. And you were also scheduled to take the drug in the last drink you partook of... the milk and honey you often take before retiring... but tonight Sara drank it instead."

Jenna's heart lurched again. Sara. This meant only one thing; Jane was in Jester's pay. She looked more keenly at Charles, remembering; he was the young guard that Jane had danced with at the ball. *Oh how friendship can be used to turn minds and hearts and gain control,* she mused.

"If... if I had taken the drug, what would then have happened?"

"That's where we need to catch up a little," Jester said, still not moving his stance. "But it's all up to you, Jay. How many people in this castle die before you do as I ask; that's for you to decide."

Jenna did not answer, but stared at him. His disguise was amazing. Over his shock of blond hair, he wore a dark brown wig, immaculately styled. His facial skin had been darkened and his eyebrows and moustache colored to match his hair.

Jenna's thoughts raced; she wondered how many men were in Jester's pay.

"How many do you want to die, Jay? Young Jenny? And Duff? Aaron; and David; the grandparents; perhaps the prince; and the king?"

"You know that I want no one to die," Jenna said, feeling ill.

"Ah, yes, but of course I know that; all too well. It does not matter to you how many of *my* friends Maslen killed; or—"

"It does matter!" Jenna cried, interrupting him, adding, "Every life matters; I'm shamed and sorry that people die untimely deaths."

There was a silence, and Jenna turned back to look at Millie. The door opened and Sebastian stepped into the cell.

"What do you want of me?" Jenna asked, turning back to face the three.

"Just that you take the drug that was intended for you," Jester said, "then we'll continue with our plan."

"You'll leave the castle here, and harm no one?" Jenna asked, hoping that this would be the case.

"We knew that you would want that," began Sebastian.

"We'll tell you this much," Jester said, "We want to leave with as little fuss as we can, as soon as we can... not a squeak, see, or we'll have to deal with the guards outside here... and we know you wouldn't want that. Once the alarm is raised, we'll be killing people all the way out of here."

Jenna could see that the jester's eyes had an excited glint in them. One way or another, he tasted victory.

"I'd rather have preferred to ride."

"We can't have that!" Jester snapped, "I don't want to begin counting heads here, but I will. If you keep throwing in your own ideas, then I'll start naming names of those who'll die in Gifford before we leave."

Jenna felt trapped. She bowed her head, remembering how he had planned to kill King Maslen. *He's bizarre,* she reminded herself.

"We have thirty partners in Gifford," Sebastian said proudly, knowing that the voicing of a number would hasten her decision.

"Yes, and with a minimum of two each, we could take sixty, or more, out," Jester said, "they're all awaiting my word."

Jenna wondered; if she could get to the jester and immobilize him, perhaps his whole 'plan' would collapse. He was the inventor, the commander of this dreadful conspiracy.

As if sensing her thoughts in her hesitation, Jester said, "I'm warning you, Jay, I have my mind set on my castle in Rosenburg, and I'll stop at nothing to get you there so that I can have it." Turning to Sebastian, he said, "Show her your little keepsake, Seb."

With great pride, Sebastian stepped over to Jenna, holding a thick curling lock of hair between his fingers. "This came from the king's head, tonight. His own valet, Oren, gave it to me. You see, Oren wishes to leave Gifford tonight, with us; or, perhaps he shall use his dagger for something other than the king's hair?"

Dread surged through Jenna's veins; she could not even swallow, or blink. *My love; my new-found love... and I can do nothing to save him if they do not leave without murder.* She wondered if Oren would have enough evil within him to murder his king. *'Every person, faced with the wrong set of circumstances, is capable of every evil,'* her father had once told her. *'Trust no one completely, other than those who have proved their loyalty to you in some form of personal sacrifice.'*

"I have no choice," she whispered, thinking of her deep love for Cyranius.

"I was hoping you'd say that," Jester said. "Here, Seb, give her the drug."

Sebastian brought a small flask to Jenna, saying, "You have to drink it all. He drew the stopper out, and said, "Take off your cloak, careful now, then sit down on it and drink it all."

Jenna slipped the thick cloak off her shoulders, allowing it to fall to the stone floor. She asked, "How am I to travel, then? In Millie's coffin?

Had you not rather take her out, then I shall climb in and save you the effort of having to lift me..." *I cannot bear them touching me,* she told herself. Feeling so powerless was such a devastating experience that Jenna wondered if she would faint.

"No; you travel in that one," Sebastian said, pointing to the coffin on the floor. Turning, he asked, "Shall I get her to climb up in the coffin first?"

"As long as you're not going to try anything, Jay," Jester said, adding quickly, "No, Seb, stay where you are. Jay can lift the lid off herself, she's well capable of doing that. When you're lying down in the coffin, Jay, Seb will bring you the drug."

Jenna moved to the coffin, feeling detached from herself. *This cannot be real, please don't let it be real, but a nightmare,* she wished. As she pushed the heavy lid from the coffin, she half expected to see Isard lying in it. This coffin was much larger than the one in which Millie lay. But the coffin was empty. It was double-lined, another coffin inside the outer, padded with thick lambs wool. *This coffin has been designed for the living, not the dead,* Jenna told herself, feeling somewhat comforted. *I have no choice,* she reminded herself as she prepared to step in and lie down in the coffin. *But to take such a strong sleeping potion... I'll spill it, I'll not drink it; I'll travel with my wits intact.*

The cell door flew open, banging Charles in his back. Jester swung about on nimble feet, his sword extended in a position ready to defend.

"Frank?!" Both Jester and Charles exclaimed together.

"What are you doing here, Frank?" Jester asked. He waited impatiently as the man to regained his breath, at the same time searching the inside of his thick cloak for a message.

Jester took the message and stepped closer to a candle. He cursed, softly; then repeated the curse, louder. "Bring me that flask!" he called to Sebastian, adding, "plug it."

Jenna hoped that the message held a reprieve for her. At least they were not going to use the drug.

"What is it?" Sebastian asked.

Jester did not reply, but stepped over to Millie and stared down at her. "It's a pity," he said, but with no emotion. Turning back to Sebastian and Charles, he told them, "Doctor Thorn was heard gloating that he had cheated us and sent death, not sleep. Of course, he would be thinking we had used the drug last eve. Millie will die, as would Jay if she drinks of it; Thorn wanted to cheat us; no, she can't take it, we need her alive so that she can answer Rexaud's questions. After that, he promised I can have my duel with her, then I'll get my castle."

Another guard, this time, dressed in the Gifford uniform, entered the cell. "The escort from District thirty-five has arrived. They're going to have the horses changed and return right away." His eyes flew across to Jenna, and he said, "they'll be coming for Isard's coffin; you'd better get it closed quickly."

Sebastian and Charles stepped closer to Jenna. The feeling of helplessness grew overpowering...

"Climb in then," Sebastian growled; "and not a squeak; not a cough, not even a yawn!"

Fifty-six

King Cyranius sat up with a jolt. His bedchamber was in darkness, but he felt alarmed. What had awakened him with such urgency? He could not remember having been dreaming, he rarely dreamed.

Someone had called him. A cry seemed to echo in the shadows of his mind and he thought of his brother's voice tone. Perhaps Edward had called? Throwing back the bedcovers, he snatched his all-encompassing night cloak and threw it around his shoulders, covering the black silk of his embroidered royal nightshirt.

"What is it, Sire?" a guard asked as the king, now carrying a cresset, strode the short distance along the corridor to his brother's bedchamber.

The king did not answer, but pointed at the door, which the guard hastened to open.

Extending the light to illuminate his brother's face, Cyranius saw that the lad slept soundly.

Bonidore, who reposed in the same chamber, sat up, climbed out of bed, bowing and shivering, asking, "Sire, but is something amiss?"

Kevin and Gavin stirred, the former sitting up, then poking his brother, whispering, "It's the king! Wake up!"

Cyranius would have turned away, but a peculiarity caught his eye—his brother's hair seemed to have a gap at the front. Moving the light back, he reached out and touched the spare place. A wide lock of Edward's hair was missing.

"Did someone come here tonight?" the king asked, recalling his last sight of his brother. *No hair was missing when we parted to retire,* he thought, frowning deeply.

"No, Sire," Kevin answered.

"Oren came in, Sire," Bonidore corrected, "the boys did not wake."

"Oren?" Cyranius asked, puzzled. "What did he come for?"

"The same as you, I presume Sire, he looked closely at the prince. I thought he had come on your behalf to check."

"Go back to sleep," the king commanded, not wanting to wake his brother and frighten him.

Out in the corridor, he commanded, "Find my valet, Oren... he should be in the servants' quarters. Tell him to attend me."

It was yet two hours until sunrise, and Oren should still be sleeping. The king's valet would arise before the king and would have His Majesty's clothes waiting when the king awoke.

When Oren could not be located, King Cyranius summoned Sir Lowell, who in turn, sent for the two captains who were on duty that evening—one in the castle and the other on the gate.

At first, other than Oren not being found, nothing seemed amiss.

"The escort arrived from District thirty-five for Sir Isard's coffin, Sir Lowell," Captain Derrick said, "and it left within the hour; other than a few other departures, there have been no unusual circumstances."

"What exactly are you looking for, Sire?" Sir Lowell asked.

King Cyranius was not sure why he felt so unsettled. He drew his commander aside and asked, "Why would Oren, my valet, visit Prince Edward in the night; and why would the prince be missing a section of his hair?"

"Did you wake him?" the commander asked.

"No, but we shall," the king said, knowing that Sir Lowell was thinking of the strange poison that Millie had taken—the sleeping death.

~ * ~

To their relief, Prince Edward woke the first time his brother shook him gently, calling his name.

Sir Lowell frowned at the prince, looking at the short stump at the top of the lad's forehead. He could not imagine why a section of hair would be missing from the prince's thick crop of dark brown curls. On questioning Bonidore and the boys, no answer was apparent. Edward could think of no reason why a lock of his hair should have been cut.

King Cyranius had been thinking of Jenna, but could not substantiate his rationale for checking on her. Guards had been posted to attend the corridor outside her quarters, and there was no reason to fear anything was amiss. Yet something nagged at him and it was like a lump beneath his lungs—something was wrong.

"I want to check on the princess," he said, his tone such that denied argument. "Captain Derrick, fetch the doctor's wife. Tell her to enter the princess's bedchamber and bring us back the report that the princess is sleeping."

"I'll dress," Edward said eagerly.

"No," Cyranius said, "rest a little longer, and I'll send word that all is well." His eyes crossed with Sir Lowell's and he knew his commander's thoughts. *Such unnecessary fuss, Sire. Oren will be here soon, setting your clothes ready and we all could have had an extra hour or two's sleep.*

It's quite all right, Sir Lowell, but I cannot sleep until I know that all is well with those I love most... the king's eyes replied, to which Sir Lowell just sniffed and raised his eyebrows as they awaited the arrival of the Doctor's wife.

No guards stood in the corridor of the guest chambers. This was unusual. When Natalie entered the bedchamber, carrying a lamp, she went first to the princess's bed. Golden curls fanned across the pillow, and to Natalie, they were counterpart to Jenna's own. She would have turned away, but took the lamp across the room to the two beds, set in an L-shape in the corner. The covers were folded back as if both beds had been slept in, but both were now empty. Natalie stepped through the large archway, into the small sitting chamber; it was empty.

Returning to the corridor, she said, "Princess Charlotte is sleeping, but the two ladies are not in their beds.

"We'll take a look," the king said, feeling relieved, yet still in a small amount of turmoil.

Sir Lowell and Natalie followed him into the bedchamber. They all stared at the empty beds.

"We must find the ladies," Sir Lowell said, adding, "perhaps one of them is with Oren."

The king frowned at Sir Lowell's suggestion. He looked across at the form in the bed, trying to imagine if he could see Jenna breathing. The shape was not moving, but the king was not surprised. It was difficult to ascertain such in the dimness. It dawned on him that Jenna would be a light sleeper and that if twice people had entered her bedchamber, she should have awakened. He had to know if she was all right. Fear swamped him, it was an undeniable yearning that could not be stilled.

"Wake her," he commanded, looking at Natalie.

"Sire... w-wake her? But, we all know the princess was very tired, exhausted—"

"Wake her."

Natalie placed her lamp on the bedside table next to the Bible volume and bent to touch the shoulder, pressing it, shaking it gently.

"Princess; Princess Charlotte; wake up!"

There was no response, and Natalie shook harder, calling louder. The king stepped closer, alarmed, but expecting Jenna to wake and all to be well.

Taking his cresset to the other side of the bed, Sir Lowell held it closer to the head on the pillow. Then, sure that the hair was of a different texture, straighter, a more blond shade than Jenna's, he swept back the bedcovers.

"Lady Sara?" the king's voice flowed with disbelief.

"Where's the princess?" Sir Lowell spun around as if expecting to be attacked. "Captain!" he called, summoning Derrick from the corridor.

Natalie gasped at the sight of Sara's white face. Reaching over, she felt her neck for a pulse. It was barely discernible, very slow. Then she sought to lift Sara's eyelid, finding it unwilling to move. "She's been poisoned, like Millie." The doctor's wife wrung her hands together, saying, "But where is the princess... where's our Jenna?"

"Captain, have them ring the bell—we must check the castle and find the princess, or discover where she's gone," Sir Lowell said. "What caused your alarm, Sire?"

Cyranius shook his head, then replied, "I woke, having imagined someone cry out. At first, I thought of Edward; but it was more like Jenna's voice, calling to me. She needs me to help her. But where is she? We must find her!"

~ * ~

Jenna was warm inside the coffin. Holes had been drilled, spaced under the lid so that she received fresh air. The lamb's wool was warm and Jenna again felt glad that she had not been forced to take any drug.

The coffin had been secured on a narrow cart, commissioned specifically for the purpose, and although it pitched about with the fast passage, behind its two horses Jenna experienced quite a comfortable journey.

At first, she had prayed and entreated God to wake Cyranius and alert him to the danger she faced. Then, she wept, again praying, petitioning protection for both the king and the prince.

She called out, "Cyranius! Cyranius!" It was a call of anguish, of hopelessness. Her cry was lost among the many hoofbeats.

She remembered the verses she had read, and now she quoted them, "For I know the thoughts that I think towards you, saith the LORD, thoughts of peace, and not of evil, to give you an expected end. Then shall ye call upon me, and ye shall go and pray unto me, and I will hearken unto you."

Again Jenna prayed, then she slept.

The cavalcade, having taken a shortcut through District twenty-seven, changed horses in District thirty-three. Keeping the pace fast, the jester threatened to divide the riders into two if those less saddle-seasoned kept falling behind them. When they reached the north plain of Lotharingia it was almost noon, and they stopped to water the horses and rest a while.

"We'd like to take the pace a little slower, Jes," Charles said, having made his lady-love, Lady Jane, comfortable to take a nap in the sun by the riverbank. Not a patch of snow lay anywhere, and the day was unusually warm.

"I'm a valet, not a horseman!" Oren complained. He felt that his whole body was bruised. "We shall go ahead then," Jester said, mounting his horse. "You'll rendezvous with us at Roxaud."

Sebastian stepped to the jester, saying, "She's thirsty and wants a drink," he flicked his head sideways to the cart containing the coffin.

"Well, she can't have one," Jester said unreasonably, "we have to keep going."

"Cyranius won't catch us now," Sebastian said.

"He has Kind Heart's maps," Jester said, "until we are across the plain, he could still run ahead of us, if he guesses our path and if he left Gifford before sunrise. We've a cart and he will have only horses."

"He couldn't have left before sunrise," Sebastian maintained. "The earliest they would have found Sara would be breakfast time

"I'm not taking any chances," Jester said. "We're leaving now."

"We're going to rest a little longer and do as you suggested," Charles said, "we'll rendezvous with you at Roxaud."

Jester continued riding the rest of the way across the Northern Lotharingian plain, heading southward, now only ten men escorting the coffin.

~ * ~

King Cyranius, with a cavalry of three hundred, intercepted the riders led by Charles before the latter reached the Northern mountains between Lotharingia and Rosenburg. The king's horses out rode those of the absconders and soon Charles and his cohorts were surrounded. A battle ensued, and those who did not wish to die a hasty death, surrendered.

Within minutes, King Cyranius with the majority of the company, were galloping towards the mountains, having left the prisoners with a company to take them back to Cyran to be tried.

Sir Lowell, riding at the front of the cavalcade with King Cyranius, saw the cart containing the coffin, with its small escort, as it rose up the narrow mountain track, drawn behind the two horses.

But Jester had seen the Cyran uniforms, and he recognized both the king and the commander. He urged the horses on faster, but the distance between them shortened.

When Jester reached the top of the pass, he called at Sebastian to hurry. "Use your whip, man! The way down will go much better! They're gaining! I'll not have them stop us now! Not when we have our own castle in view!"

Halfway down the mountain, the unthinkable happened—a wheel on the cart broke loose.

Jenna felt the jolt as the coffin slipped to land with a thud on the rocky path. She felt herself slide in the coffin, her feet pressing against the end.

Cursing and swearing, Jester dismounted to examine the damage. The horses shied and whinnied, frightened.

"The cart's finished," Sebastian stated the obvious. Men from behind dismounted, calling, "Cyranius and Lowell with a huge company are behind us just around the bend."

The cart and horses blocked the path. Jester quickly took stock of the situation, and commanded, "Release the horses. Lift the coffin off the cart."

"What are you going to do?" Sebastian asked.

"We're going to push her over the edge," Jester said, "If we can't take her, then we are not going to leave her for him!"

"No. You said you were going to keep her alive," Sebastian argued. He had joined this venture for riches, not to murder the princess. He drew his sword.

Jenna closed her eyes in fear at the jester's words—she was trapped in this wooden box and he wanted to push it off this mountain! *I'll die,* she told herself, *I will die.* Then a divine calm came over her, as she remembered, *But I'm ready; by faith, I'm trusting Jesus will take my soul to Heaven...* then, in a flash, Jenna felt great sorrow. *I won't ever know what it would be like to be his wife... oh, God, You can save me, if You will; Your thoughts are of peace, and not of evil; therefore I call upon You, and pray to You; hear me, oh Lord.* She wept.

Drawing his sword, and giving a signal, the jester engaged in battle with Sebastian. The men behind the cart joined the fray, and soon Sebastian lay dead on the path. The jester had sustained a stab in his upper arm.

"Push the coffin over the edge!" Jester shouted urgently, holding his arm, "then we'll escape."

The remaining men obeyed their leader. Dragging the coffin off the broken cart, they sent it sliding down the escarpment, to plunge over the bluff. A splintering noise came to their ears as they drew their horses ahead of the cart.

Sir Lowell saw the malevolent deed as he descended the mountain path. Although there was room for two horses, the Cyraniun cavalcade rode single file. The commander cried out as he saw the coffin disappearing over the bluff. He spurred his horse on faster, and dismounted when he reached the abandoned cart.

The king joined him, asking, "Where is the coffin? Have they taken it on foot?"

Sir Lowell could not speak, tears rose in his eyes and he felt choked.

"Where is it?" Cyranius asked, horror flooding his being. His eyes followed Sir Lowell as the commander stepped over the escarpment and on to the rocky downslope.

"No-o-o-o!" cried Cyranius as he followed the commander. His cry bounced off the mountain walls, echoing like a lost child.

~ * ~

Jenna had heard the battle and hoped Sebastian would win. But when she heard Jester's repeated command, she felt deep dread. The coffin lifted, and she wished she could somehow brace herself, but it was impossible. She must relax, she told herself; they were going to push the coffin off a mountain cliff! At best, she would die quickly, but at worst... she did not want to imagine it.

She felt and heard the coffin sliding slowly on gravel and her feet were hard against the bottom, then she knew it was airborne. Closing her eyes, she forced her body to let go its rigidity, then the impact came, and she knew she had not fallen very far.

The coffin cracked on a rocky ledge, jarring her feet, her legs and her stomach, causing her to feel winded, stunned.

The double-lined box splintered into pieces and Jenna fell forward on her knees. A section of the lid smashed up on her forehead, and she fell on it, feeling that she had dissolved into a bright sunlit hole.

King Cyranius slithered his way downward behind Sir Lowell who had slowly slid himself down to the top edge of the precipice. They could see Jenna, wearing her blue dress, lying on what looked like a plank teetering on a narrow rocky ledge, like a doll lying on a small seesaw. Pieces of wood splayed in all directions. Some pieces had fallen hundreds of feet, down to the chasm floor.

"She's not moving," Cyranius said the obvious.

"We need rope," Sir Lowell said, "we must get to her before she regains consciousness." He looked into Cyranius' shocked eyes and knew they thought the same; *if she regains consciousness...*

While lengths of rope were collected from various riders and securely tied together, Sir Lowell commanded that fifty riders follow the Jester and capture him, bringing him back, dead or alive; "Preferably dead," Lowell said grimly.

When the commander returned to the top edge of the bluff, he could not believe his eyes.

King Cyranius, tied to the end of the rope, was being lowered down the sheer cliff face.

"Why did you let him do that?" Lowell demanded.

"He's the king, we could not stop him," Captain Derrick replied, "besides, he loves her more than his life and I think it's fitting."

"He hates heights," Lowell said, turning to see that the rope was being kept well secured.

"He isn't considering the height at all," Derrick said, "he'll be all right, Sir; there's angels watching her, that I believe; look at that plank she's on. What's holding it there? It's going to go any second now..."

The commander stared, finding himself agreeing with Derrick—angels were protecting her.

Cyranius carefully stood on the edge of the plank against the cliff-side, knowing that his weight would keep it down and it would cease vacillating. He crouched, placing his hands on Jenna's ankles. She was missing a slipper and a thin spear of wood had pierced her foot, causing it to bleed. The red of the blood in the brilliance of the early afternoon sun seemed out of place.

Pieces crumbled off the edge of the ledge and, reaching out, the king grasped Jenna's arms, lifting her away from the most ominous danger where her head had been lying on the plank with nothing but air beneath it.

Cradling Jenna in his arms, he spoke as to a child, "Jenna, Jenna, wake up and tell me you're all right." His heart thudded loudly in his chest. "Jenna." She did not respond, and he could not tell if she breathed. She was limp, too limp it seemed. Her head lolled backwards and he supported it with his hand. Looking down at her pale face, he saw a growing bruise in the middle of her forehead.

Lifting his eyes toward the bright sun, he cried, "Please God, please let her live! How can it end like this?" he gently touched his lips to her forehead.

Jenna opened her eyes and his handsome face, full of concern and love for her, filled her vision. She smiled a weak smile.

"Jenna, you're all right!"

"I... feel... so weak," she murmured, then closed her eyes.

"Don't leave me, Jenna, don't leave me," he said.

"No," she replied, her eyes flickering closed, then open, "I'll never leave you."

"I'll never, ever let you leave me, Jenna darling," he vowed. "I can't live without you; you're my one love, now and forever."

"You are my only love, for always," she agreed, "I want always to be at your side."

"Oh, my darling; we shall never be apart again," he vowed.

Fifty-seven

Prince Edward waited eagerly for the arrival of his favorite person. News had preceded the returning cavalry, and the castle buzzed with the recounting of the awful events on the mountainside.

"The jester's body, as well as Sebastian's, are being sent to King Maslen and he'll be told of the princess's amazing escape from death," the fore-rider told the breathless audience. He turned to the prince, saying, "Your brother was very courageous, if he weren't the king, he'd be receiving a medal! He climbed down over a bluff to rescue the princess."

~ * ~

The journey back to Gifford was slow for both Cyranius and Jenna. At first, Cyranius had wanted Jenna to rest, but she would not hear of it. "We need to be at home to make the arrangements for Princess Anastasia's escort to take her home."

The army doctor had pulled the splinter from her foot and had bandaged it. Other than patting salve on her bruised forehead, he pronounced her to be well enough to ride. "The princess was stunned for a few minutes, that's all," he assured the king.

Having left in such haste, the cavalcade had not brought tents or food, and it seemed wise to return home.

~ * ~

Princess Anastasia was returned to King Fredrick under an escort representing three kingdoms. Leading the escort of Cyraniun, Aponian and Rosenburg military, were King Maslen and Princess Charlotte, with King Cyranius and Prince Edward.

Count Roxaud had been sent into exile, and the king of Rosenburg had pronounced himself guardian of his niece, Princess Anastasia.

Until Prince Edward met the beautiful Princess, Anastasia, who at the time of their meeting was dressed like a village girl, the prince had fancied himself to be in love with Jenna. In the secret place of his emotions, he believed he would always love her and his heart would be broken forever because Jenna loved his brother.

But, at the first sight of Princess Anastasia, Prince Edward promptly forgot his first love. Never before had his heart leapt in his chest like this! Then, as Anastasia's blue eyes locked with his, he knew that his love was returned. Yet this was just the beginning; love was just in its conception.

Great celebrations resounded in the kingdom of Rosenburg—the princess had come home! King Maslen did not stay for the celebrations; he wanted to be in Aponia with his wife who would be traveling to the capital as soon as he arrived back. He sought a private moment with his sister and Cyranius.

"You must come to our capital for your wedding," he said, adding a warning, "I shall not take it lightly if you elope!"

"Then we shall be following you in a day or two," Cyranius said.

"What? You plan to be married that soon?" Maslen asked.

"Walk with us," Jenna whispered, wanting to leave the many attendants behind them.

They moved into the palace garden and Jenna said, "We were married before we left Gifford, Maslen, the night we arrived back from the mountain..."

"What?" he cried, turning to Cyranius, "you promised to have the wedding in Aponia."

"So we shall, Maslen," Jenna said, adding, "and I thank you for that. But Cyranius and I promised each other we would never be apart, and how could we do that, without being married?" She looked from one man to the other, and said, "You had it all worked out, didn't you? Cyranius has not told me all the details, Maslen, but you planned it all, that day at Charlotte; you wanted me to marry Cyranius. And I shall lose my half of Aponia." She tried to make her voice sound sad.

"No, Charlotte, you won't," Maslen said seriously. "I knew that you would not place possessions before happiness. My main concern was that I could not prevent the truth being circulated about who you really were. I thought it could be contained, but no. The best protection you can have for life is to be married to a king. And I had a hunch which king you would choose. No, Charlotte, you still own half of the Kingdom of Aponia."

Jenna's eyes widened; she had not expected this.

"But it's all with one exception," Maslen said.

"An... exception?"

We, that is, Queen Masla and I, we shall have a son, and when you have a daughter, we will have them betrothed. When they're of age, they shall rule over the joint Kingdom, which shall be Cyran and Aponia combined. Perhaps we shall name it, 'Cyronia?'" He bowed his head, then raised it with a coy expression on his face, saying, "If God blesses us... both, with joint grandchildren, then we shall be blessed indeed. I could ask for nothing more".

~ * ~

Princess Charlotte and King Cyranius were ceremonially married in the capital city of Aponia, that week.

King Maslen gave the beautiful bride away, and both Princess Anastasia and young Jenny attended the bride as bridesmaids.

Prince Edward stood with his brother at the ceremony, and his eyes were not on the bride, but on the younger princess.

King Fredrick attended the wedding, as did Jenna's brother, Charles.

~ * ~

Queen Masla's confinement was long and she grew very impatient, believing she would die before being delivered of a child. The doctors could not agree as to the position of the baby—some said it was breech, others said it was huge, a monster with two heads, and she would never survive the birth.

Doctor Arnold, who had been very puzzled for some time, woke one night, realizing the state of his patient, the queen. He hurried to the king's bedchamber to wait impatiently for the king to wake.

"She's having twins, Sire, I'm sure of it, now. One is behind the other, the front one is breech, and the back babe has its head in the right position. As the back babe is born, the front one will turn of its own accord."

~ * ~

Doctor Arnold's diagnosis proved correct. Queen Masla was delivered of a large healthy boy, Prince Horatius Maslen Charles.

Jenna and Cyranius were there in the Aponian royal castle for the birth, and it was Jenna's privilege to carry prince Horatius to his father. The baby looked like a miniature of King Maslen, who broke down and sobbed when he took his small son in his arms.

Cyranius stepped closer to look at the newly born baby, and to kiss his queen.

Half an hour later a daughter was born, a female version of the tiny prince. The king was overcome. A son and a daughter on the same day.

The queen was pronounced to be well, and this was cause for great celebration. The curse was broken, the queen had survived.

~ * ~

Two years later, Queen Charlotte of Cyran, who had never left her husband's side, bore a daughter to King Cyranius. A week after the birth, a betrothal paper arrived.

King Maslen demanded that his son, Prince Horatius, be betrothed to the new little princess.

This would be a new generation of royals.

Meet

Carolyn Ann Aish

Carolyn Ann Aish was born Carolyn Ann Gundesen, in the town of Waitara, Taranaki, New Zealand, in 1948. She grew up New Plymouth, and now resides in Inglewood beneath the spectacular Taranaki Mountain.

Carolyn earned a place in the 1996 Guinness Book of Records (music section, page 144) for the longest hymn published, "Sing God's Song." This is also listed in the 2003 Guinness World Records book.

Carolyn's series, "The Frencolian Chronicles," enjoys rave reviews, creating an on going following for Carolyn's work. Carolyn currently has over 40 books published.

Among the many series Carolyn has written for children is "The Nine Lives of Rastus," based on the lives of Max Corkill and his beloved cat, Rastus. KIND HEART is Carolyn's first published book for adults.

Works From the Pen of Carolyn Ann Aish

Kind Heart - King Cyranius is a woman-hater, and Lady Jennava hates most men. This does not prevent them from secretly falling in love. But a phantom-like masked man towering between them crushes loves petals before they bloom...

Royalty, romance, mystery, escapism—this book has it all. Just remember to breathe.

Stepping Stones - Forced to leave her sister in a dungeon, Michela goes with her guardian's to take part in the 'King's Test.' Does the king really believe she can spin straw into gold?

Michela denounces the 'King's Test' as a charade. Will she find death, or will she find love?

Letter to Our Readers

Enjoy this book?

You can make a difference.

As an independent publisher, Wings ePress, Inc. does not have the financial clout of the large New York publishers. We can't afford large magazine spreads or subway posters to tell people about our quality books.

But we do have something much more effective and powerful than ads. We have a large base of loyal readers.

Honest reviews help bring the attention of new readers to our books.

If you enjoyed this book, we would appreciate it if you would spend a few minutes posting a review on the site where you purchased this book or on the Wings ePress, Inc. webpages at:

https://wingsepress.com

Thank You

www.ingramcontent.com/pod-product-compliance
Lightning Source LLC
Chambersburg PA
CBHW071958110726
47910CB00005B/1577